Vampire Bride
The Bitten Bride Series
Book One

By

K.L. Novitzke

Vampire Bride
Copyright 2015 © K.L. Novitzke

Cover by JRA Stevens

Vampires are a myth, but for Charlie Preston vampires are real.

With the mysterious appearance of a man by the name of Maxwell Barnett, Charlie's life changes in a matter of minutes. Unfortunately, not for the better.

Every vampire is assigned a bloodline and Charlie is about to learn that she's Maxwell's property. There's no easy way of accepting that you were born to nourish a vampire. No easy way of accepting that he wants you to be his vampire bride.

From seduction to murder, Charlie and Maxwell face many obstacles together and against each other, but what Charlie doesn't know is that death is the only way to survive what's coming.

Krystal Novitzke

Acknowledgements

After years of writing and rewriting, of having these characters in my head dying to get out, there are more than a handful of people who helped me make it all possible. And I'm sure I will forget some of them.

The most important would be my very tolerant husband who was my makeshift proofreader in the very beginning of writing this story and child-wrangler. If it wasn't for him keeping our two very rowdy boys occupied, it would have taken me twice as long to complete this story. Of course, I can't leave out those two rowdy boys, Owen and Evan, who didn't understand why I was sitting in front of a computer screen nonstop and made writing one simple chapter take days.

To my family that has showed genuine interest in my writing endeavors even though they knew nothing about it until it was well on its way to publication. And I can't leave out all my fellow coworkers, who have showed nothing but support and who happen to be eagerly waiting for a signed copy.

Next would be the wonderful Wattpad community where I first started posting Vampire Bride. To think I was extremely nervous about writing a vampire story on there, but after getting over four million reads I tried my hardest to give them a story to die for. Those awesome readers have shown such positive support for a story that was nothing short of a diamond in the rough. They stuck by through my second-guessing and switching things up. I hold their loyalty close to my heart.

It was there as well that I met some pretty awesome authors in a book club. Ever since I've been greatly indebted to them as they have helped me create eye-catching graphics and spread the word about my stories.

The journey continues for these characters that came from my heart and constantly have conversations in my head, keeping me up all night. I hope they keep you up all night too, so anyone who sticks around for the ride deserves a sincere thank you!

Prologue

Maxwell

My thoughts have been occupied with one object for many years now. Nothing can hinder the daydreams, and nothing can stop the nightmares that plague me on a daily basis. It feels as if I'm in the deepest depths of Hell, enduring indescribable agony, but I'll endure whatever Hell brings my way to get what I want—what I need.

It's been over a year that I finally found what I was searching for. Over a year since I began watching Charlie Preston. After all this time, I still can't confront her. As if her rejection is an option. Her acceptance of who I am…what I am, determines my survival in this world, and what I am isn't easy to digest.

Just the sound of her name makes my bloodless heart beat, and tricks my dead lungs into breathing. She's all I can think about, and my willpower is fading fast. Even the thought of her soft, tan skin causes my hands to shake with the overwhelming need to touch her.

Tonight is like any other night; I crouch in the shadows that gather around her house, becoming invisible. The only light that threatens to give away my presence comes from the street lights lining the nearby road. I shield myself behind trees and bushes from prying eyes.

It's almost midnight and she sits on her couch, with a bowl of ice cream in her lap as she watches TV. Her dark brown hair is pulled back into a ponytail and her small, curvy body curls up in the corner of the couch.

Occasionally her hair flips from side to side as her head jolts at the ridiculous scene playing out on the screen. She even waves her spoon in the air yelling obscene words, adding to her dramatics.

Prolonging the inevitable is all I can do to keep her world from crashing down, because once I tell her what she was born for, everything will change. She's meant to live in the vampire world, she's meant to nourish me. Each vampire is given a bloodline to feed from, and the words I keep repeating to myself explain it perfectly. "She's mine," I mutter between tense lips once more.

Chapter One

Charlie

Nothing appealing catches my attention to keep me alert. I've been here since seven this morning and the slow ticking clock finally says it's after eleven at night. The more I glance at those stupid numbers, the slower the hands tick by.

Knowing that I'm forty-five minutes late and counting for my night out, no doubt my good friend Juliet will have a lecture waiting for me when I finally do arrive. Juliet may be happy-go-lucky at times but an enforcer nonetheless. Keen attributes every junior high teacher has on their résumé, I imagine. My head thumps against the desktop in defeat as I contemplate staying in this dank office or facing a disappointed Juliet. A groan of protest rumbles in my chest, which loudly sounds throughout the room. An echo almost taunts me.

A voice sounds from down the hall. "Charlie?" The footsteps get louder and louder until they stop outside the open doorway. "Are you ready?" Morgan, my faithful assistant asks, trying to hide a yawn with her purse slung over her shoulder and keys in hand. The jingle of the metal expresses her anxiousness better than any words can.

"I was ready hours ago, but unfortunately there's work that has to be done. So much work that has to be done." I don't make eye contact with her for the very reason of knowing what I'll see: an exhausted and irritable Morgan.

Wanting more than anything to stay and finish every last detail, I decide against it. After placing all the scattered papers into organized piles, I follow Morgan to the front of the building. A quick glance at the front reception area is the last thing in view before a flip of the light switch makes the room go black.

"It's Friday, it's Friday," Morgan chants as she shimmies her way to her car. Stopping dead in her tracks a few inches away from her driver's side door, she turns toward me with a mischievous look plastered on her face. "You've gotta go to your precious dance club tonight, don't you? Have you met Mr. Right yet?" A joking laughter seeps out at her own words.

I contain a smirk as I place my hand gently on Morgan's shoulder. Pity fills my gaze as I stare the younger girl down. "Do you think before you speak, Morgan?"

The laughter that was threatening before comes pouring out immediately after the words are spoken. Walking to my driver's side door, I shine more light on the conversation. "You're asking if I met the man of my dreams at a dance club? In case you've never been to a club before, they're filled with perverted wannabe cool guys that aren't Mr. Right material. Recommendation number one: stay away from them."

"Then why do you go?" The parking lot is barely lit, but you can still see Morgan quirk an eyebrow at my hypocritical words. Anyone would be the same way if someone told them not to do something when that very person was doing what they just said not to do.

"For a friend." Truth be told, I do many things that I'm not fond of for friends. Another truth be told, I do many things that I'm very fond of for friends.

"I see," Morgan mumbles as she unlocks her car door. Her slouched shoulders from the long day of work block half of her face from being seen.

Morgan's the best assistant I could ask for. It took

months after opening up my party planning business for somebody like her to apply. She fit every attribute I needed in a partner. She's punctual, polite, and can be ordered around without question. She knows her place at work, but she doesn't always know her place in my personal life.

When she puts her two cents in about my love life, I tend to get a little snobby, but I try to mask it by being motherly. Morgan's idea of Mr. Right is a pastor's son with good morals and strong beliefs in a higher being. I, on the other hand, go to a dance club on a Friday night. That should be enough said about how interested I am in finding a future husband.

"See you Monday morning, Morgan." With a sincere wave out of my open car window, I drive away without a second thought, forcing the discussion to pick up a different day.

The drive home is long and dreadful when the radio station always plays the same ten songs over and over again. With a tightening hold on the steering wheel, my annoyance boils over after having to listen to pop princesses and boy bands repeatedly. Gags of revulsion sound quietly in my head.

There's no time to sit and relax my overworked brain when I finally enter my house. Digging through the fridge and cupboards for a quick bite to eat leaves barely any time to change into different clothes.

The plush comforter that lies atop my queen-sized bed calls my name when I finally make it into the bedroom. I glance at the bed, then tug my body back toward the closet before settling on a pair of short black shorts and a tight teal top.

A puff of displeasure escapes through my mouth as I turn out the lights, leaving a few on for my return later this evening. The snap of the deadbolt locking into place causes the tiredness that already makes me groggy to thicken. "Just this one night," I whisper to myself, entering the car yet again.

I haven't been out dancing for at least a month now being preoccupied with work, so excitement runs through my veins at the same time that my limbs ache.

Four blocks away from the entrance is the closest parking spot. By the time I reach the block that the club resides on my feet already start to hurt, causing my strut to become more of a shuffle. Hoping that music lightens my mood is farfetched, but it's worth a shot.

The smug air suffocates any newcomer to the building, so many sweaty bodies in such close confines isn't appealing or any bit comfy. Dodging elbows along with the occasional protruding butt, which are all obstacles that I try to bypass, but not always successful at.

Instantly, familiar faces from afar make my frown of displeasure turn around for the better. Although one puts disdain into the emotional mixture. Juliet stands stiff as a board with her arms crossed tightly over her chest, throwing daggers with her eyes in my direction. Waiting it out is all I can do. It's all that I decide to do. She'll get over it in…one, two, three.

With a large step taken forward, Juliet leans closer to me. "About time," she hollers, making my eardrums rattle. Her blonde hair flies in several faces as she violently shakes her head in frustration. Some stray strands stick to my lip gloss.

Bursts of air rush out of my tight lips, all while trying to hold back any spit in attempts of getting her hair out of my mouth. All that happens is Juliet jumping backward from me when she regrettably gets spit on. When she does step away, relief from her hair goes away as well.

"Very funny," Juliet gripes. Her brashness puts a smile to my face.

"Sorry, I had your hair in my mouth, which was quite unpleasant, by the way." My hands swat at my face as the residual feeling of hair stuck on me remains. Flapping hands aside, I continue, "However, a girl's gotta work, so lateness is expected."

"I get it, I get it. Let's just try to have fun tonight," Juliet yells in my direction before dancing away.

The rush of the music gradually washes over me. Life becomes easy as the beat pulsates through every cell of my body. Any stress from work melts away as the loud melody mutes all senses. I didn't even realize that I started dancing until warmth from an unexpected visitor that's too close for comfort encompasses me.

Why guys find a cluster of dancing girls so intriguing is beyond me, but by some of their attitudes it seems as if they find it as a challenge and the challenge has now started. Two large, very warm hands place themselves on my hips.

Putting a pretty smile on my face without missing a beat, I spin around to look over the tall, scrawny man. His shaggy blond hair and unshaven face tell a story all of their own. Who knows how many girls have run their dirty fingers through those strands tonight alone? I wait for him to speak first.

"Did you have lucky charms for breakfast? Because you look magically delicious," he says loudly into my ear, so his deep voice can be heard over the music.

The things that come out of these guys' mouths every time are ridiculous and I don't have time to waste on them. I'm here for my friend and nothing else. Clenching his shirt collar between my fingers, I yank him down to eye level. Leaning in really close, my lips brush his ear. Anxiousness along with nervousness from my bold move rattles the man, causing him to stutter out useless words.

A sly smile spreads across my once highly glossed lips at the babbling idiot. "Why don't you run along and find me that pot of gold." With a push or more of a shove, I thrust him away. Except he doesn't move as far I would've liked him to.

His large, overbearing hands find my body once more. This time they're laid upon my shoulders for a few seconds before moving down my back and not stopping until my butt is cupped flawlessly in his palms. His mouth moves in reply, but anger causes me to go temporarily deafen and I don't hear a word he says. Like a normal everyday action my hand lifts in the air and swings, no second thought behind the act whatsoever. The only thing to stop it is that scruffy cheek of his.

"Bitch," he grumbles, rubbing his face. Not wanting to cause more of a scene, he swallows what little pride he has left and strolls away rejected.

After an additional two complete strangers approach me and four individuals approach Juliet trying their luck to impress us, the only thing I'm left with is a sore butt from their grabby hands. Why do I come here, I ponder.

Nothing can be easy when it comes to other occupants of the club and the same goes for friends too. "Thirsty," Juliet barks toward me from between two men, who nearly block her from view.

Somehow, I'm always the one who's designated to get drinks. Maybe it's because I'm dancing solo, or maybe it has something to do with the fact that Juliet's sister, Janessa had a one-night stand with the bartender. An abrupt nod of my head along with a salute in Juliet's direction tells her that I comprehend her orders, but also lets her know I'm not pleased about it.

The bar seems miles away when one has to duck

and bob around rude unmoving people. A sigh of relief escapes out of my mouth as I finally lean up against the bar.

"That tough, huh?" the bartender says, acknowledging my restless mood. A half cocked smile finds his face. However, it's his button-down shirt that's unbuttoned to reveal his smooth chest along with his well-defined muscles that demand all girls' attention. No wonder Janessa went for a joyride with that, I joke to myself. Although, looks can be deceiving.

"Tough is an understatement. Can I get a Cosmopolitan and a 7Up?" I only look him in the eye for a few seconds at a time, because I know he'll recognize me. The last thing I want is to get involved in Janessa's business.

He agrees with what he believes to be an enticing voice, but just gives the impression that he's trying too hard. Once the order is accepted, I turn around, not wanting to give the impression that I would want anything remotely close to a conversation to start up between us.

Propping my elbows up on the bar top, I scan the dark room, observing all the drunk people. It's when my eyes land on a certain stranger's face that my night has truly begun. There's no stopping my trembling fingers and the slight jerk of my shoulders. Not to mention the jello legs that are barely keeping me in a standing position. The bellowing thoughts rambling through my brain tell me to turn away, but I can't help but to keep staring at him, either in awe or fear.

It has been a while since I've been in this club, but when I am, he's always here. All those Friday nights he can always be found in the same spot just staring. Besides him constantly being here, I can't help but to spot him. Never has he once approached me, but you can tell by the look on his face that he holds himself back from doing so. His eyes give him away, the desire within him. It's not the first time I've seen that look. Their face betrays them by giving away what their brains are thinking.

A light tap on my shoulder causes me to jump. Feeling quite silly, I quickly grab the drinks that are on the countertop and make a dash for Juliet. Putting that creepy dude along with my absurd jumpiness aside, I try to look at the brighter side of things.

After several hours and several encounters later, the call of my bed summons me once again. Goodbyes roar out between us over the loud music before I exit the building. Stopping in the middle of the sidewalk, I slip off the high heels I forced myself to endure for the evening before starting the four block walk back to my car. The cool night air feels great against my somewhat sweaty skin, a breeze blowing strands of hair in my eyes.

The streets are dark and deserted at this time, causing my nerves to get the best of me. All the storefronts that line the street have darkened windows and eerie shadows play across the glass from the streetlights. The slow pace of my tired feet quicken when I spot my car in the nearby parking lot. Keys already clenched in hand and a quick press of a button, the door is unlocked and waiting for me to enter.

Before I can open the door it re-locks itself. My fingers slide off the handle as I just missed it. Standing still with my head hanging to the ground, I huff in annoyance. Why car security systems have to re-lock the doors after a certain timeframe of not opening the freshly unlocked door is beyond me.

My eyes slowly travel upward until they lock on a reflection in the window. I twist my torso, slamming my back up against the car door. The handle digs into my spine. Air gets stuck in my lungs and all the blood drains from my head, making me lightheaded. The bulge of my eyes and quiver of my bottom lip gives faultiness to any composure I'm pretending to hold on to. All I can do is stare into the empty lot as I try to comprehend what I think I saw, a second reflection in the glass.

Horrified to the point of suffocating myself from forgetting to breathe, I'm frozen in place. My shoes slip out from my numb hands as I'm unable to focus. The distant thud as they hit the pavement doesn't faze me the slightest bit. The dark hidden spots that aren't lit, a bordering tree line, and nearby buildings, all demand my speculation. Still gripping the collar of my blouse in hopes of it keeping my pounding heart from jumping out of its cozy spot in my chest, I manage to get into the safety of my car.

Images of that peculiar man from the club taunt me as I retrace my thoughts. His needy eyes, the messy shoulder-length brown hair, and an ashy pale skin tone under the lousy fluorescent lights sear themselves into my memory. "I did see him…right?" I ask myself as I speed out of the parking lot.

Comforting nonsense flows out of my mouth in efforts to convince myself I'm not crazy throughout the car ride home. It's not the first time that somebody followed me out to my car, but he's different from the other men. A sick feeling attacks my stomach, giving fuel to the crazy thoughts that find their way into my head. The dark look in his eyes tells you he wants something entirely different from what all the other guys want.

Stumbling bare feet prolong reaching the protection of my home and shaky hands fumble the key several times before successfully unlocking the front door. Just as quickly as I open it, I slam it shut. Completely out of breath from my overactive imagination, I try to compose myself for the night ahead, alone. "See…it's just your mind playing tricks on you and you lost a perfectly good pair of shoes because of it."

More than ready for a good night's rest even with nightmares waiting to haunt my dreams, I find my way to the bedroom. After a quick change into some pajamas I climb into bed. The doorbell unexpectedly rings throughout the house and a yelp escapes my mouth.

I tiptoe my way to the front door. My hands hover in front of me to balance my shaking body. The wooden floor boards creak beneath my weight. Not wanting to give my approach away, I tiptoe the rest of the way. Leaning ever so carefully against the door to peer through the peephole, I stare at an unwelcome guest.

The scratch of my fingernails sliding down the wooden door fills the house. That stranger who watches me on Friday nights from his distant corner at the club circles my front porch. It's that same pale face that I swear I saw reflected in the window. Now, he's standing outside my door, waiting for me to open it.

* * *

Maxwell

I arrive early at the club in anticipation of watching my future bride's body gradually start to sway to the music. My nerves start to get the best of me when she doesn't show up at her usual time. From the conversations I intentionally overheard, I'm certain she would be showing up tonight. The once good mood that engulfed me earlier disappears when I realize I'm stuck here surrounded by drunk, conceited people for no reason.

A young woman blocks my view of the door as she places herself right in front of me. A quick lick of her lips would give any normal man the impression of how easily it would be to take advantage of her. However, I'm as far from normal as anything gets. The seductive tone in her voice makes it extremely difficult to keep my irritation to myself. "You look like you could use some company."

Having no need for her company. I only want Charlie. "No thank you."

"Come on, handsome, you don't want a little fun in your night? I've seen you here before and you always remain alone…solo in this dark corner looking miserable. I can help you with that. I can give you quite pleasurable company if you let me." Her fake fingernails scratch down my thigh, intentionally stroking very close to my manhood. The way she bites her bottom lip as if she were in extreme turmoil over my refusal sickens me.

A flick of my wrist propels her hand away as if disgusted by it. I wanted to remain a gentleman by being polite in my rejection of her, but her stubbornness is proving to be stronger than the desperateness that radiates off her. "I'm fine without your company. There are many other men here who would love to have a girl such as yourself flaunted in front of them."

As if I told her to go whore herself around somewhere else, she straightens her back with a huff and stomps away. The high heels she's wearing slip from under one foot, causing her to buckle slightly as she spins out of view. I try to keep a smile of satisfaction from finding my face at the awful attempt of trying to make me feel bad for letting someone like her get away, but it's useless. A sly smirk forms across my mouth from her pitiful attempt.

Finally, an hour and a half later, Charlie enters the

unwholesome building. Her thick dark brown hair falls over her shoulders, occasionally blocking her from view as she bobs and weaves through the mass of bodies. Curves I've only daydreamed about are accentuated in the short shorts and tight top she decided to wear tonight. What should be sweaty palms grip the leather bench I chose to sit on.

In a room that's jammed with bodies and louder than necessary, I see only her, I hear only her. The sound of her breathing and pulse are the only things that can come close to calming my anxiousness when in actuality they make what little blood I have lingering in my dead body burn.

Remaining seated in the corner, I can only observe her from afar, patiently waiting until she decides to go to the bar. Grinding teeth and fists that clench and unclench are visible signs of my hatred of this place, of my wait. Thankfully, no other desperate women approach me.

Dishonorable man number one finds his way to Charlie within a matter of minutes. My ears perk up in efforts of listening to the conversation. Invisible shakes of my head due to confusion at the comment about lucky charms for breakfast is the least of my concerns. Unwillingly, my thoughts on how delicious she does look corrupt me. When the second man comes up to her, two sharp points protrude into my lower lip. The possessive creature slumbering inside is finding its way to the surface. Being in a dark secluded corner always works in my benefit.

By the time a third man walks away rubbing his head in confusion from her unexpected rejection of him, my fingernails leave faint red crescent moons in the palms of my hands. Opening and closing my mouth eases the ache that attacks my jaw. The pleasant sound of her disdain toward each of the strangers is like music to my ears. Pride takes over every inch of my body at the thought of my future bride and the confidence that emits off of her. Gratification at being the only one to conquer her untamed behavior, whether she likes it or not, is something I hold onto dearly.

With a quick swipe of my fingers through my hair, excitement comes over me when she finally makes her way to the bar. All I can do is stare at her back, waiting for her to turn around. If my lungs worked, I would be holding my breath with eagerness.

She always starts to her right side and works to the left. I sit to her left; I'm the last and only thing that catches her attention. Like all the other times previously, like the months prior, her deep brown eyes lock on mine. Her spine instantly straightens up. The fear that makes her become tense forces the blood in her veins to quicken.

I put pressure on the soles of my feet as if to test standing up. Nonetheless, I never do. The only thing I do is remain seated, staring her dead in the eyes. Never once have I been the first person to break the connection and I never will be. The jump of her being startled hurts my ego and my heart at the same time. She stares at me in fear not in awe, unlike most women. Just as quickly as she appeared she quickly disappears, walking away without looking back.

Her friend Juliet downs her liquor and my love takes her time with her soda. It takes much strength to rip my eyes away from her as several more greedy men approach her, but as her body moves up against a select few, fantasies blur my vision. The dancing bodies and awful smell of sweat that fills the air are gone. All that remains is an illusion of her and me, alone. That illusion will become a reality and a simple slap won't prolong it.

One attribute I have that has gotten me in many sticky situations is determination. Sometimes it's not the best characteristic one can have, but I've never regretted it.

By the looks of the men she chooses to keep her company it's not apparent what type of man she prefers. There's a mixture of hair color and a range of suntanned skin. However, they're all tall…much taller than her small five foot frame.

Against my better judgment, when she decides to call it a night, I follow her. Not close, but close enough to keep her in my view. Willpower to stay away from her is fading rapidly, quicker than I hoped. Any logic I have left disappears. Without even realizing it, I find myself standing right behind her as she stands by her car door. There was no intention of me allowing my reflection to be spotted in her window, but as she scans her own image, there's no missing mine hovering behind.

All I can do is sprint to a secluded spot across the lot to remain out of sight as she spins around horrorstruck. Her eyes wildly scan the area, searching for the prowler…searching for me.

The look of pure fear on her face that stares back at me will never leave my thoughts. Knowing that my other half, my bride who is meant to be by my side for all of eternity is terrified of me is devastating. She's all I live for and she fears me before even actually meeting me. From this moment on I know I have to fix this. I have to come clean and explain.

The squeal of her tires as she speeds away breaks my concentration of how I'm going to go about this. Tonight's going to be the night that tests her mental stability. Tonight she'll learn that she belongs to someone. Lingering scents of her perfume loiter in my nose and the glisten of the sweat on her tan skin try to replace the image of her petrified expression that's already planted itself in my brain. Soon those pleasant images will become constant and truthfully, I can't wait.

Gripping her shoes that she left behind, I arrive at her house before her. My feet begin to pace, wasting time until she arrives. With a few unnecessary deep breaths in efforts to remain composed, I practice my speech. "Charlie, my name is Maxwell Barnett and…and I want you as my vampire bride." My hands pound at my skull at such absurd words. "What the hell are you thinking?" I argue with myself.

Headlights shine down the empty road, indicating her arrival. I scrunch myself into some nearby brushes to conceal myself. My body doesn't relay any symptoms that my dead nerves cause, but my mind is racing with possible outcomes. The road ahead is going to be fairly bumpy for the both of us.

Rattling off number after number, I finally approach her house once reaching fifty. All I can do is stare at the door before ringing the doorbell. Once it sounds, the ring is deafening in the silent night. One foot follows the other and before I can stop myself, I'm making small circles on her front porch, waiting for her to answer or waiting for her to ignore me altogether.

Time seems pointless, because for people like me there's an overabundance of it, but not tonight. I only have three hours before the sun rises. That's three hours to convince her of the existence of my being. Of the existence of vampires.

Chapter Two

Charlie

An ever growing lump in my throat blocks any words that I would want to speak. Yet, after several swallows the blockage doesn't seem to waver, making my voice croak. "Can I help you?" The dark entryway and living room only make me more terrified. All this large open space is causing my imagination to run wild, wondering what's hiding in those dark corners even though I know the trespasser is outside.

I always considered myself a strong independent woman who would never be considered one of those stupid girls found in horror films who runs upstairs, putting themselves into a spot they're unable to get out of. However, asking a stranger who's on my doorstep in the extremely early hours of the morning—who I think is stalking me—if I can help him is falling right into the role of that oblivious girl. All I need now is for him to pound his hands on the door that is mere inches away from my face to scare the wits out of me even more.

His deep, smooth voice shatters the image of a knife slicing through the wooden divider from my thoughts. "Charlie, I was wondering if we could talk. I have something very interesting to tell you." The calmness in his words is completely opposite to the manic frenzy of my nerves.

"How do you know my name?" Without warning my vision begins to get clouded with blackness as fear boils up. Like hell I'm going to believe that 'I'm not going to hurt you' malarkey. The air that was starting to feel warm from fear suddenly gets icy. I can't stand near the door any longer. I can't be so close to him intentionally.

Taking a few large steps backward only to retake those very steps back to the door, I wait for him to reply. The outrageous thing is that I find myself anxious as to what ludicrous words he's going to say next.

"I have exceptionally well hearing. You recognize me from the club, right?"

"Yes." Too many emotions become overwhelming. People with all these emotions at once break and when no response is spoken, I crumble.

Taking a chance to look through the peephole once more with prayers chanting inside my head that he's gone due to the silence are crushed when I line my eyeball up to the small round glass peephole. His face nearly fills the entire view as he casually waits. Stumbling away from the door, I almost crash to the ground. A corner from the console table in the entryway jabs me in the back, forcing a grunt of pain to gush out from between my lips. With all this fear pumping large amounts of adrenaline into my veins, the pain lacks in significance.

"Charlie? Charlie, are you okay? I heard a crash…Charlie?" Concern thickens his voice.

Trying to gather as much of my composure as possible, I flatten my sleep shirt and pat my hair as if someone were watching. Embarrassment makes my cheeks flush. "Why don't you just leave and come back in the morning?" I holler at the door that's still several feet away from me.

"I can't. I mean I could, but mornings really don't work for me. I'm not going to hurt you if that's what you're implying. Take a look one more time. No weapons, my hands raised in surrender. I just wanted to talk to you for once, that's all."

One foot gradually follows the other, leading me to the front door. For some reason, no matter how fearful of him and beyond spooked that he mysteriously shows up on my doorstep, needing to look at him is at the top of my list. Needing to physically see him in surrender on my porch seems comical, almost masking the impending doom I felt earlier.

With shaky hands holding my body close to the door, but without touching it, I view him just like he stated. Hands raised in the air, no weapons in sight, and from the look of his T-shirt and jeans there's not a lot of room to hide a weapon anyways. But, my eyes are drawn to his right hand, which clenches my shoes that I dropped in the parking lot. It wasn't my imagination, he really was there…lingering. He waves ever so slightly and smiles, taking a few extra steps backward, allowing his entire body to be seen in the small opening.

Just about to take my eyes away from him in disgust, the unexpected happens. The porch steps behind him get closer and before he stops himself and before I can let out a squeal of warning, he topples down the front steps. All serial killer thoughts aside, I hurriedly unlock the door, bolting out onto the porch in efforts to see if my unwelcome visitor is okay. The last thing I want to do is accompany him to the hospital and I'm pretty sure the last thing he wants is for me to call an ambulance, which leads to the police.

However, once the bottom landing comes into view, I spot him sitting comfortably on the ground, waiting peacefully. My jaw drops in disbelief, but soon my shocked expression turns into a scowl. "You tricked me. You…you…" There were words I wanted to say, but my brain fought to pick the right one. I turn my body rigidly toward the front door, stomping back into the safe confines of my home unable to speak any of the insults.

"I didn't mean to, it's just that I want to talk to you," the stranger pleads, racing to the door before it has a chance to close. "It'll only take a few minutes of your night," he begs with his hand pressing against the door in efforts of keeping it open.

As he stands in front of me, I look at him, really look at him for the first time with all distance among us and the divider gone. Seeing him in the club is entirely different than seeing him here in the open night sky. The moonlight makes him look even paler. In contrast to his very ivory skin, his brown eyes and hair almost look black.

My eyes go from his face to his hand that's pushing against the door. I give him an evil glare in hopes that he'll get the hint and move all while my brain tells me to just slam the door in his face.

"Let me in, Charlie." His eyes bore into mine. He either is ignoring my anger or he's just too stupid to see it.

My hard stance goes limp as my tight grip on the doorknob loosens and my shoulders deflate. It's as if all the motivation and stubbornness that I hold so dear vanishes. He doesn't waste a second before he pushes the door wide enough for him to fit through before he quickly closes it behind him. Almost in a trance like state, unable to command my body to move, I allow him to guide me into the living room.

The pitch black room doesn't hinder his approach to the sofa that he sets me carefully on, whereas I nearly run into the furniture that fills the room. Sitting himself next to me on the cushions, he twists his arm back to flick on a nearby table lamp, partially filling the room with light. No matter how many times he looks away from me, I continue to stare at him, enthralled by something.

Not once do I break contact with him, be it looking into his eyes or touching his hand. Eagerly waiting for him to continue, I intentionally move myself closer to him. There's no care in world and nothing he can say can make this serene moment fade away. I'm not going to ruin it and I'm sure he's not capable of ruining it either.

He drops my heels on the floor by the foot of the couch before speaking. "Charlie, there's something important I have to tell you." His serious tone should worry me, but all it does is make me more curious.

Similar to an eager child, my head bobs up and down. Wide eyes, hair flying from the force of my head shaking, and teeth biting the corner of my lower lip show him just how I'm hanging on each and every word that exits his mouth. His voice causes my mind to turn to mush and I'm okay with that, I'm okay with not thinking but feeling. Silently, wish after wish floods the heavens, requesting for me to be able to listen to him talk all night, to be able to stare at him all night. Holding his hand tightly in my grip, all I can do is wait for him to explain.

His deep, raspy voice turns my legs into jello. "I've been watching you for some time now, Charlie. Waiting…" His free hand rises to my face as if to touch my cheek, but he doesn't. "I'm just going to say this and I want you to keep an open mind. Okay?" He waits for a response.

I nod my head, unable to find words.

He breaks the news as bluntly as one can. "I'm a vampire and you're my human."

What the hell did he just say? And just like the snap of one's fingers, the trance I'm in breaks instantly at his preposterous words. All those happy thoughts become insane and I turn red at such outrageous feelings. My hand that's clenching his now goes lifeless and his hold is the one to tighten as I try yanking the trapped hand out of his grasp. "Vampire? You're crazy, like seriously messed up in the head." My finally free index finger jabs my temple to further amplify the point made.

Scanning the floor, I try to recall my steps into the living room, let alone him accompanying me. However, no recollection of the events comes. Anxiety attacks my stomach and bile threatens to make an exit. "How the hell did you get in here?"

"That's not important. It's something special. Listen, Charlie, I know it sounds crazy, but it's true. Let me explain. You were born into a bloodline that belongs to me. You were born to nourish me, Charlie." He gently places his hand on my knee.

Even through my pajama bottoms, my skin crawls from the gesture. How things change dramatically, considering mere minutes before I would've loved for him to touch me…to stay with me forever, but now…now all I want more than anything is for him to leave.

"You've got to be kidding me?" My legs straighten as I bolt to my feet, walking aimlessly in circles around the coffee table. It sounds and probably looks as if I'm talking to myself, but I have to get these thoughts out of my head, because I'm on the verge of going insane.

Why in the world do I attract the most irrational men? Before I know it, he's standing right in front of me, his outstretched hand landing on my shoulder. All I can do is shake my head in denial, which travels down the entire length of my body, allowing me to wiggle out from under his tightening grip.

"Charlie? I know it's a lot to take in, but if you allow me, I can tell you as much as you wish to know. I'll try to make it as bearable and easy as possible to comprehend. I know I probably went about this the wrong way, but you needed to know."

As I take a few steps backward, the feel of his hand tugging at my T-shirt sleeve forces a shiver to ripple through me. I know more than anything that this conversation will be anything but bearable. He truly believes he's a vampire. Two choices cross my mind. One: play along and hear him out, or two: call him crazy and fight.

"Stop saying my name; it's creepy…creepy just like you, may I add. If this is some kind of sick joke, I'm not game. With that said, you can leave. Now." I wait, but he just stands there, staring at me. "I rescind your invitation, if you even got one to enter my house in the first place." My voice rises with anger as my hand shoots out, pointing to the door.

"I'm not some vampire that a Hollywood director made up. I don't need an invitation to enter a home nor do I sparkle either if that's the next question you're going to ask. We have more important things to discuss. Trust me, we'll get to my weaknesses and strengths soon enough." His voice took on a tone of annoyance.

"Oh, you're funny for a dead guy. That's if you're even dead. Listen, you're kind of freaking me out with this whole I own you thing. Please just leave me alone." My simple begs begin to sound like prayers. Staring at the floor, refusing to look at him is the only thing that keeps me…me, because every time I look at him something comes over me and I don't like it one bit.

"I'm not leaving until I explain our situation. You don't understand. I can't leave you, I will not leave you. You're my personal and only blood supply. You were born for this, you were born for me. Now, sit down." The authority in his voice demands all attention.

Without wanting to, my body complies with his

words and I go back to the couch. A mix of confusion and terror distort my face. Thinking he's doing me a favor, he tells me to relax. Gradually, my nerves calm and my breathing goes back to normal, abiding his words even though my brain is still in chaos.

"Would you stop with whatever the hell it is that you're doing?" I have no idea how he does it. All I know is that I just want it to stop. Before he has a chance to speak or worse make me stop speaking, I ask one last thing. "What's our situation exactly? I don't even know your name."

"My name is Maxwell Barnett and you, Charlie Preston, will be my vampire bride." He sees my intent to speak, so before a word could come out of my mouth he tells me to remain quiet and listen.

Not being one to take orders, I ignore his request, but as my mouth opens nothing comes out. Where there should be words, very foul words spoken in his direction, there's nothing but silence. Extreme heat from fear brings the bile that was threatening earlier to rise even higher.

"I'm sorry to have to control you like this, but everything I've said and continue to say is the truth. I'm a vampire and you were born to feed me. Each vampire is assigned a bloodline, holding possession over the humans within it. At any given point, we can choose a mate within that bloodline. Leading to the main reason why I'm telling you all this, Charlie, it's because I choose you."

Tears begin to run down my cheeks, but I quickly wipe them away. Being perceived as weak and crying over some idiot's crazy words is the last thing I want someone to see. I know he's a weirdo who believes he's a vampire, but I didn't realize he was this sick. Plan number one isn't going so well.

"You can speak now," he adds.

"Oh, thank you so much, Master. Are you done with the vampire politics? Can we get this over with? Are you going to kill me or not? I would prefer to skip the part where you bite me, leaving human teeth marks in my neck, seeing as I would love an open casket at my funeral. On the other hand, though, it would help the authorities catch you for murder." Laughter seeps out in between my words, but it sounds more manic than carefree.

Refusing to show him any fear and going against any better judgment, I stare him down. I didn't have to be staring at his mouth to see his lips curl without hesitation. My attention is instantly drawn to his mouth. The view of his perfect straight white teeth fills my vision, but soon everything changes. Sharp fangs quickly slide down, making me choke on my own spit.

Coughing hinders my breathing as I suck in several useless breaths, gasping for air. When I believe I can speak my voice betrays my strong composure as it cracks. "This is not funny anymore," I yell, truly scared, but at the same time mesmerized.

It's time for plan two to go into action; I have no other choice, but to run. I make a dash for the front door, planning to scream bloody murder in the middle of the street.

"Charlie, calm down." His gently spoken words stop me in my tracks.

My head swings from the living room to him, who's now blocking the exit. He extends his arms, trying to capture me. "How...what?" There's no amount of information to help me comprehend what just happened. He was in the living room one second ago and in a blink of an eye, he's in front of me, blocking the door.

Looking past all common sense that's trying to help

me decipher what just happened, I turn to the kitchen. There's no way I'm going to let his speed stop me from trying to escape again. Feeling like a trapped dog, I result to violence.

The sound of his slow footsteps taunt me from behind as I make my way to the kitchen. His calming words try to block any judgment that could find their way into my head. Wrapping shaky fingers around the handle of a knife, I swing around to wave it in his face. "Stop. Right. There."

"That can't hurt me, Charlie. Please, put it down. I have no desire to harm you, but if I have to force my hand just know that it's for the best." He takes several steps closer.

The blade whips through the air until it slices into his arm. More than thrilled that I actually cut him, only hopes of him understanding that I'm serious is all I'm left with. However, my hopes wither as I watch in shock the wound heal, not shedding a drop of blood. "This is not normal. What are you?" I demand, but with a severely unsteady voice.

"I told you, Charlie, I'm a vampire. What I am is a big part of your life now."

"My life…my life is normal and boring. Most of my time is spent at Jewish thirteen-year-old boys' bar mitzvahs. I am an intelligent individual who graduated from a prominent business school and started my career as soon as I had my diploma in hand. My calendar is booked months in advance for my services. I am not meant to be stalked by some crazy freak." The words desperately roll off my tongue, making me sound naïve as I try to explain my life all while waving the knife around. I've always been one to talk with my hands.

"You belong to me, Charlie, there's no ignoring that. It's in your blood. You won't be able to fight it for long. Your ancestors weren't very fond of me either. They left, forcing me to spend centuries tracking down the bloodline. I told myself that I would right my wrongs and find at least one human...one human who catches my eye. That's you, my darling."

"No. Nononononono."

"I'm sorry, Charlie, I truly am. You deserve a better life than this, but I'm selfish and I want you. And I'm not going anywhere. The blood in your veins calls for me just as much as I long for you at my side."

His words sink in. They sink in deep since they're right. There's this crazy little voice, the twinge in my chest, and numbness throughout my limbs all calling for him. "Not happening." My stubbornness is quite overpowering.

He clears his throat and continues as if my words mean nothing. "That will change. I can be very cunning when I want to be and I'll even throw in an incentive."

"Incentive for what?"

Frigid iciness freezes me where I stand as he strides up to me. He places his hand on my cheek, causing me to flinch at his touch. "Your promise to try to accept what we are to each other will not go unnoticed. My incentive for you is that I won't bite you without your consent, which is asking a lot out of me." He flashes his fangs at me before he quickly hides them with his lips.

"I'll never accept you, dead man walking." The words harshly exit my mouth as I raise my hand to slap him like all the other obnoxious men. Although, as my hand sails through the air, he catches it inches away from his cheek. With every ounce of might I have, I try to pry it out of his grip, but he just tightens his hold the more I struggle.

"I'm not fond of your reference to zombies, Charlie. I'm a respectable and well-mannered man, not some wild animal. Have I always been so patient? No. So why don't you stop testing that patience and let go of your fears. What's between us doesn't have to hurt." He releases my arm and just walks away, leaving me dumbfounded.

A steady flow of incoherent vulgar words rattle off in my head at his retreating back. The creak of the front door is what pulls me back into reality. He stops in the open doorway, looking back at me with those deep brown eyes. A sly smile spreads across his lips. "Sweet dreams, Charlie."

Incapable of looking away, I stare at the closed door for a few seconds. What exactly is that supposed to mean? Is he trying to be sweet? Or is he trying to scare me? Breaking into a sprint, I open the door, expecting him to be there waiting cockily, but to my dismay he's nowhere in sight. I still yell into the empty street for the need of having to have the last word. "Yeah, that's right, go back to the shadows."

The door slams shut and a huff is all I can manage. Words are unspeakable and actually thinking of said words seems even more incapable. Vulnerability taints my mind. Gradually, the rapid racing of my pulse slows and I take several breaths in while letting quivery breaths out. With a mental note made to call Morgan in the morning in efforts of striking up a conversation about going to church due to the fact of feeling cursed for some reason, I find my way back to my bedroom. There's nothing else I can do to make this any better, and hoping that I'll wake up tomorrow realizing this was all a dream is my best bet.

By the time I slowly walk to the bedroom, my heart stops pounding. A yawn escapes through my pursed lips as I crawl into bed impatiently. It's almost four in the morning and I need sleep, but unfortunately my mind counts all the windows and doors in the house. A steady debate on whether they're all locked puts me to sleep.

* * *

Maxwell

The shout of her words directed toward me brings a smile to my face. The shadows, my love, are exactly where I am and soon you'll be in the shadows with me, I mockingly think to myself. The sun will be up in an hour or so and that's the only thing keeping me in those shadows and not arguing with her further. For once in a very long time, I have a challenge and the anticipation of victory itches underneath my dead skin.

All Charlie needs to do is simmer down and accept her new reality, because it's not going to just disappear. Nonetheless, accepting this fate isn't easy. I didn't accept my fate with open arms and Charlie isn't either. Flashbacks of when I was in the same position as Charlie blur my vision as I casually walk down the street. I wasn't lured by an attractive female vampire wanting to make me her groom because she loved me. No, I was forced into the night by a greedy man who only cared for his own survival.

His selfish ways molded me into the heartless vampire I try not to be. I repeatedly tell myself that I'm willing to give her all the time she could possibly need to reach the right conclusion, which is that we belong together. Easier said than done.

Realism isn't a friend of vampires, considering everything about us goes against all human beliefs and proven scientific facts. Realism is what Charlie holds so close. For the sake of my sanity, wishes that she were one of those girls fascinated about vampires would make the situation more pleasurable. It would make things easier on the both of us, but she's anything but easy. In fact, I'm not even sure she's manageable, seeing as she cut me within thirty minutes of my arrival.

The need for her to be in control of all situations she comes upon is quite entertaining, though. Violence is a very vampire thing to turn to and the minute she turned forceful, I knew she would fit in my world effortlessly. Even so, her fitting in and her actually putting herself in a dead life are two completely opposite things. Now all I'm left with is the feel of her warm cheek against my dead, cold hand.

Time used to stand still, but now it seems to be passing me by quite quickly. There are many more things to discuss, if she likes it or not, and the small amount of hours in darkness seem to be pitting themselves against me. Sun filled days will only stand in our way for so long.

One of the most important tidbits of vampire information is how the bond is formed with their human, a very important part I chose not to share with her. After her outburst, I can image how she'll react when I tell her the bond has already started to take place without her consent. A simple skin-to-skin touch is all that's required to activate the blood…all that's required for her to understand that she lives for me as much as I strive for her.

She's a fighter, though. There's no doubt in my mind that she'll fight this tooth and nail, which leads me to the fact that this is going to take longer than it should, longer than I want it to. Wanting to control her so I can feed is overwhelming. A throbbing ache fills my body as my mind can't process anything other than 'eat, eat, eat.' The monster I try not to be rises to the surface, but I do my best to keep the blood thirsty killer at bay. I'm afraid that will only last so long.

What do the humans say...it will be like pulling teeth?

Chapter Three

Charlie

Tossing and turning in bed, I beg for my eyes to remain closed. A lazy half roll is all I can muster to stretch away the restlessness. Within seconds of my new found position, though, the sheet slides off, exposing my barely clothed body. The feel of a large hand trailing up my thigh causes my body to shiver with anticipation. I don't need to open my eyes to know who the hand belongs to. His hand keeps a steady pace as he glides his fingertips over my stomach to linger on my chest. Goosebumps break out over my skin from his tickling touch.

His lips touch my ear, and his seductive voice has an angelic tone as he whispers my name. "Charlie."

The need to be close to him gets to be too much for me to keep bottled up and my back arches in efforts of raising myself to my knees. However, when my head gets a few inches off the pillow he pushes me back down only to climb on the bed himself. His strong hands bend my legs at the knee. Loitering behind my closed legs, his hands rub at my knees and down my calves.

The dire yearning that wants out breaks through just the slightest when small points of pressure from his fingers walk down the length of my leg, causing a giggle to exit my sealed mouth. It's not until he grasps my underwear in his hand that my giggle episode fades into something serious. Without wasting a second, he yanks the thin lace fabric and tosses the now useless article of clothing aside. Even though a rush of air escapes out of my mouth when the loud tearing of the fabric fills the room, I feel nothing remotely close to pain.

Looking him dead in the eyes, I see something change. All playfulness vanishes and the look in his eyes turns into one of a predator. The tips of his fingers dig into my knees, ripping my closed legs apart. Taking as much time as he wants, making me wait for him, he roughly rubs my inner thighs. I'm positive that bruises would be left after our escapades, but since I don't bruise easily, there's no damage done. It doesn't take long for him to lower himself down to hover over me.

As he props himself above me, I can feel his completely naked body. He teases me by pressing himself against me, slowly moving his hips back and forth for a few seconds before moving away. A pounding in my eardrums from wanting his mouth to be upon mine fills the silence. The feel of fire courses through my veins.

Devoid of warning, he plunges himself into me. A smile of satisfaction finds his face from the sudden impact of his body slamming into me. Finally, his lips find mine and instantly I plunder the inside of his mouth. His newly extended, sharp fangs scrap against my tongue. A moan of pleasure rumbles deep in my chest. With each rock of his body, my fingernails dig deeper and deeper into his back, while my legs push him harder into me.

In efforts of holding back a moan to deprive him of any cockiness he could get from the pleasure he can induce, I bite my lower lip hard enough that a line of teeth marks remain etched in the tissue. When I finally release my lip from among my teeth the faint taste of blood fills my mouth. Just the smell of blood in the air makes his thrusts more violent. The force makes my breath rush out in the form of grunts and my body shudder.

That's all it took for me to reach the peak. Involuntary twitches attack my body as my legs demand for him to go deeper. Lost in the moment, I don't have time to see his need. As his body stiffens between my legs, he hurriedly pins one of my shoulders down while his free hand tilts my head to the side, exposing my neck. A quick scrap of his fangs against the sensitive skin lightens my mood before he plunges his teeth into my veins. Dark red liquid that doesn't make it into his sucking mouth trails over my shoulder, making a puddle on the bed sheet beneath me.

I leave faint red scratch marks behind on his back as he jerks his hips at a steady pace until his throbbing pulse of fulfillment stops. It doesn't take long for him to look at me with his fangs still extended, bloody mouth and all.

"You're mine forever now." The words don't seem to come out of his mouth as they echo throughout the room. The slow repetition of 'mine forever' tighten my chest.

A deep breath gets sucked into my unknowing lungs as I bolt upright in bed, clenching the collar of my sleep shirt. With my body drenched in sweat and still unable to catch my breath as it comes out in heavy gasps, I barely manage a few words in a hoarse, unsteady voice. "Holy shit…it was just a dream…holy shit."

Instantly, my fingers examine my neck in search of a bite mark. It was just a dream, Charlie, it was just a dream, I continue to tell myself. That devilish smile on his face as he left flashes across my eyes, his words repeating in my head, 'sweet dreams, Charlie.' That jerk knew I was going to fantasize about him and that makes me more livid than fearful. Frantically, I squint against the darkness in the room, searching for another pair of eyes, his eyes. Nonetheless, even though I feel like he's watching me, I'm alone.

A quick glance at the clock tells me it's a little after five in the morning and the sun's starting to rise. More than a little freaked out to go back to sleep, I crawl out of bed. My limbs still shake from the realistic dream. Even though I feel his touch lingering on my yearning body, I'll never admit that I'm attracted to a psychopath. I'll never admit being attracted to a monster.

The sun lightens the halls just enough to allow me to see any obstacles that stand in my way. Lacking sleep and being awoken suddenly impairs my reflexes and drowns me in grogginess. The empty semi lit living room seems like heaven and once I plop myself down on the plush couch some of my unease washes away.

The back of my hand rubs forcefully at the tender skin under my eyes as I lie on the sofa, watching nonsense on TV. A rug burn like sting encompasses my eye sockets and whenever my eyes well up with tears from having them remain open for so long it burns even more. My heavy eyelids fight to close and without wanting to abide, my body pushes my fearful mind aside. Blackness.

That free falling feeling tingles my arms and legs, and then the impact of the carpeted floor jolts me awake. A groan of pain escapes out of my dry mouth. My hand vigorously rubs at the spot that made contact with the floor. Instead of getting off the floor immediately, I contemplate what to do. Sleeping in my bed doesn't seem pleasant and sleeping on the couch is deadly.

There is only one place to ease this anxiety that eats at me. Work. And I get there in record time.

The familiar smell of the air freshener that fills my office building takes over my senses, making my fast beating heart simmer down. Passing Morgan's desk stops me in my tracks. I don't remember Morgan leaving her desk so messy Friday night. A shrug of my shoulders brushes it off due to my lack of attentiveness and being late in meeting Juliet. The need for coffee increases my slow pace to the break room. The chairs carelessly tossed in the small room and garbage lining the counter tops makes the confusion from Morgan's desk turn to suspicion. Someone was here this weekend.

Work is the best kind of distraction and I'm more than thankful that I have plenty of it to keep me occupied, but dread and panic eat at me. It had to be Morgan. No one else has a key. But why would she do this and who did she do it with?

Cup after cup of coffee only give a short-lived boost. As the sky gets darker, the greater the restlessness. I stretch across my desk in efforts to wake my stiff muscles back up, but as my hands reach out, my head touches the table and before I know it I'm resting on a pile of papers.

* * *

Maxwell

An overextended stretch wakes my body up. My joints twinge with pain and my muscles ache from malnourishment. Looking around the hotel room that's been my home away from home, my patience wears thin. It's as if staying in a stranger's home and having to watch your every step. The thick dark curtains that line each window are the only thing to resemble my home, the only thing to give hope to this retched place. The only thing that's pleasing is the fact that the streetlamps are beneath the fourth floor room, keeping any light at night nonexistent.

I find myself pacing the entire length of the room, entering a room and immediately exiting it. Boredom eats at me. I need to see Charlie even though I'll have plenty of her soon enough. Within minutes, I stand outside her home. All the lights are off and her friend Juliet continually pounds on the front door. Her panic settles into every inch of my body. If she has no idea where Charlie is when she should be at home something may be wrong.

More than thankful that I started the connection between us last night brings much relief to my strained body. I know exactly where she is. A grueling five minutes later, I stand outside an office building. The name of the business is in large black letters above the door, Little Miss Creative. A breath I didn't realize I was holding finally leaves my dead lungs as I stand outside of Charlie's business, her pride and joy she talked so fondly of the other night.

Bending down just outside the front doors, I pick up a fake rock that's mixed in with an abundance of real rocks. Occasionally, I peek through the glass doors of the brick building to make sure she doesn't spot me while I fidget with the stone. The back compartment on the rock opens easily to reveal a key that's hidden inside. There's an identical rock just like this one outside her house as well.

Flipping the spare key in my hand, I recall when it was placed here seven months ago. Charlie was unable to come into work due to an illness, leaving Morgan in charge. Instead of giving her a permanent key, Charlie requested that a spare be placed.

Unlocking the door as quietly as possible, my mind wanders back to her sick body. The flu attacked her immune system for days, leaving her helpless and immobile. Juliet and Morgan took turns checking up on her, along with bringing her soup. As soon as she accepts me, she'll never have the burden of illnesses again, but the way her attitude is, you would think she's willing to endure illness after illness to stay away from her fate.

Slow, steady steps lead me to her personal office. The door's wide open, but no lights illuminate the interior, indicating that she fell asleep before the sun went down. The lack of lights doesn't stop me from viewing her sleeping body hunched over her large desk, making her appear small in size. Papers litter the tabletop, along with a mug stained with coffee. Helplessly, I lick my lips due to roaming thoughts about her caffeinated bloodstream. Caffeine makes the blood take on a tart taste, as a grapefruit is tart to a human's taste buds.

Before I know it, I'm sitting contentedly in one of the chairs across from her. My hand slowly extends toward her arm that's lying above her head. Papers are still clenched between her fingers and strands of hair stick to her forehead. Inches away from touching her, a dim pool of light brightens a small portion of the room, followed by a blaring ringtone, which forces me to leave.

As she becomes startled, the sound of her crashing into the wall behind her fill the room. Grunts of pain can faintly be heard as she struggles to answer her phone. When the office becomes fully engulfed in light, I decide to leave the grounds entirely, wanting to keep the knowledge of knowing where she works to myself. If she suspects that I've been spying on her to this extent, she'll push me farther away, and the longer she fights me the harder it is for me to abide.

Reluctantly, I go back to my temporary home. With the door shut and latched, I head to the couch. My legs give way and I fall harshly on the cushions. Flipping the light on just out of habit, my hand brushes against paper at the base of the lamp. Now engulfed in a pool of light, an ivory envelope with curvy letters stares back at me.

I've been found and they know about Charlie. The High Council calls, making this ten times harder than I'm ready for. Than what Charlie's ready for.

Chapter Four

Charlie

The impact from me crashing into the wall makes the drywall sound as if it's cracking from the force. With hands flailing in the air scrambling all the papers, one piece somehow remains stuck to my cheek, which slowly falls off and lands in my lap after a few seconds of barely hanging on.

My dazed and confused voice answers the phone without knowing who it is since my eyes are watery from the bright light of the screen. "Hello."

"Charlie, where the hell are you? I was banging on your door for like fifteen minutes. I'm on my way to the police station to file a missing persons report." It isn't the concern or anger in Juliet's voice that makes me cringe, it's the sheer loudness of her voice shocking my eardrums, causing them to ring.

"Juliet, calm down, I fell asleep at the office. What time is it?" I rub at my eyes, trying to wipe away the blurry vision in order to see the clock myself, but it's just easier to ask.

"It's past nine. What are you doing at the office anyways? I thought this weekend you intentionally gave yourself off."

"I did, I just had a rough night last night and work puts my mind at ease. What's the emergency anyways?" The slur of my slow paced words would make anyone believe that I was drinking instead of working. Well, sleeping.

"Rough night, huh? Not to mention, what kind of weirdo gets relaxed by work?" Juliet says jokingly even though she just insulted me.

"Not what you think, Juliet, and work is very relaxing. My job doesn't involve whiny preteens, remember? Now what's so important that you're freaking out about?"

"Wow, you really did forget. The big party planner that turns into Hitler, who demands perfection along with following a precise timeline, forgot about her promise. Tomorrow is Harlow's birthday party. We were supposed to talk over plans tonight."

"Oh shit!" Sheer dread engulfs every inch of me at the realization that I forgot one of my friends' birthdays. I've known about this surprise party for over a month and somehow it only took a visit from a true weirdo to make me forget.

"Please, tell me you made reservations at least." Juliet might have been lighthearted moments prior, but now...now she's more than serious.

"Of course I made reservations. I called the same day you told me about the party. I just forgot that it's tomorrow. Trust me, I'll have everything done and decorated by five o'clock tomorrow night. No need to discuss anything."

"Are you sure? We don't need to decorate. It can be the first casual party that you coordinate," Juliet offers.

"Very funny, but I don't do casual. I'm going to clean up here and go home. If it'll make you feel better I'll even set my alarm to wake me up extra early." Which I'll probably need, but decide not to share with her for the sake of not arguing.

"I'll see you tomorrow then," Juliet blurts out before she hangs up without anything further to say.

If I felt pressured before, I definitely feel pressured now. Needing to make this party more than spectacular weighs my heart down to where I'm on the verge of hyperventilating. Somehow doing friends parties are more stressful than doing strangers parties and the crazy part is those strangers are the ones who pay me to do exceptional. Instantly, my fingers get busy by stacking all the loose papers that are scattered on the desk as well as the floor into a neat pile. Times like these would really help out to have everything electronically saved, but I'm old-fashioned and love the feel of a ballpoint pen in my hand.

Immediately, I arrive home to scavenge through all the closets for decorations. Thoughts of keeping the boxes and boxes of supplies at the office crosses my mind, but for some reason I find it easier to keep them at my house. Digging in each box only to end up tossing most of it aside, unable to use it, I gather only a few things that can be utilized.

The birthday girl, Harlow, has a very particular taste and in all of my years of doing parties, I've never done a party that would be approved by her. Juliet would be the best person to coordinate this given she's been friends with Harlow since they were children, but being a professional planner people's eye automatically travel to me. I only became friends with Harlow when Juliet and myself became friends. Harlow was included in the friendship.

After hours of gathering streamers and a bunch of other decorations, the pull of sleep calls. Falling face first onto the bed, my eyes close instantly. The need to change out of my clothes doesn't faze me and blankets are obsolete as I drift into blackness. Any fear from the night before is far in the back of my mind and even though a flicker of Maxwell crosses my thoughts, I'm still able to fall fast asleep.

It seems that just as fast as I closed my eyes it's time for them to open. The alarm on my phone goes off, indicating that morning has arrived and I stretch my well rested muscles in relief. No dreams, no unexpected visitors, just good old sleep.

First thing first is to change out of the clothes I wore yesterday. Something stretchy and comfortable fits my mood perfectly. I pull my hair up into a bun and put on some mascara and lip gloss.

Once entering the kitchen, I come to the conclusion that I still have a lot of work to do. Bag up all the party supplies, stop at the local party outlet, and make myself more presentable are key before I have to show up at the venue at least a couple of hours early to set up. Breakfast is fast and tasteless as my brain rattles through everything I need to do. Before I know it, though, I'm making several trips to my car, leaving me halfway done with preparations.

Three hours before the celebration is supposed to happen, I leave my house to make a quick stop to purchase balloons. With all errands completed, my final stop is the restaurant, one of the most trendy high-end restaurants in town.

I decide to park in the lot and walk instead of driving up to the valet. The large cream-colored building with tinted windows mocks me as I stare at it in my yoga pants and T-shirt. The servers are known to be quite sassy as they try to keep low scale individuals off the property.

With full hands, I spot an irritated Juliet by the doors. "What are you doing here?"

"I thought I would help." Juliet flings her hands out. She wants to help in her six inch heels and short mini skirt that barely covers her butt.

Without a choice, I have to agree. Even though her help will be useless and slow, I need all the hands I can get. "Okay, grab some balloons or bags from my car," I retort by bossing her around.

Juliet obeys my orders, but not without grumbling. She's no Morgan, that's for sure. Deciding to wait outside the front doors for her to return, a huff of exhaustion rushes out of my clasped mouth. Juliet waddles in her heels up to the doors with one bag and a couple balloons in hand, while I have more than three bags on each arm. Thank God the doors are automatic or else I would have to ask Juliet to open them with her mighty full hands. The two of us walk up to the hostess in silence.

The very tall blonde gives me a disgusted look as she takes in my outfit. She twitches her head, causing the hair that's over her shoulder to fly out. I'm not sure if she's going for the slow motion hair toss, but the over exaggerated fanning of her hair is barely within my tolerance level.

"Welcome to Junction 22. What can I help you with?" she greets us, not in a very welcoming tone, but greets us nonetheless.

It takes a toll on me to ignore a person with such a big ego, but in an equally perky voice that sounds just as fake as hers, I respond, "We have reservations under Charlie Preston."

"Right this way, Ms. Preston." She keeps her eyes on the floor while she speaks to me. Her strut down the hallway resembles that of a supermodel and her big feet stomp on the hard wood floor, forming echoes to be heard throughout the restaurant. The urge to mock her behind her back is overbearing.

Seeing this is my first time inside the business, I'm dumbfounded and amazed at the same time. I was expecting a secluded room, but after entering the dining area, I notice nothing is secluded. The kitchen is in view, as glass like windows are the only thing to shield it from the customers and the waiter's area is just a countertop, making a barrier at waist height.

A couple of hours before the dinner rush is to arrive leaves the dining space empty except for a few couples. Quickly checking my phone reveals that there are two hours before the guests are expected and with only a few minutes added on to that, Harlow will be arriving to be bombarded by the yells of 'surprise' in a packed dining area full of strangers. Sarcasm causes me to roll my eyes without even knowing it.

"Let's get the rest of the things and get this place decorated," I state in Juliet's direction, who in response slumps her shoulders at the thought of more work. "What? You said you would help. Take your shoes off and let's go."

"Yes, Master." Bending at the waist, Juliet bows in my direction. Her shuffling feet as she backs up reminds me of a retreating Igor.

All playful banter aside, I freeze. Those words bring me back to Friday night…okay, early morning when Maxwell showed up at my house. I called him Master as he ordered me to listen to him. Now is not the time to think about him, so I shake the memories aside. I haven't seen him since and I hope it stays that way.

Juliet already left the room to head to the car, leaving her heels right in the middle of the walkway. In a rush to join her before she starts asking questions, I trip on them, almost toppling down. The table that catches me screeches against the floor, bringing some unwanted attention my way, but I just straighten myself up and strut out of the room, knowing that some of the waiters will most likely talk behind my back.

After four trips, we have all the bags and balloons inside. The parties I organized for work usually take hours to set up, but within an hour and a half the corner is clad in gold and black decorations. Harlow is a year or so older than Juliet and myself. Since this is her last birthday in her twenties, I found it fitting to decorate in over the hill colors but still a classy combination.

"Please tell me you have a change of clothes," Juliet says, revolted.

"Do you think I'm stupid, seriously?" I hold up a re-usable bag that I set off to the side. Without saying another word to Juliet, I walk to the bathroom, annoyed by her pure witlessness. Who does she take me for, an idiot?

It doesn't take long for me to exchange my comfy clothes for some more fashionable clothing. For being such a fancy place you would think that their bathrooms would be exquisite, but they're as average as something you would find in any local mall. Curiosity grows involving the men's bathroom. One would think they would have an old man sitting there ready to hand you a towel after you're done washing your hands.

Looking at my phone one last time before making my way back to Juliet, knowledge that the guests should be arriving soon jitters my nerves. Sure enough, when I finally walk into the dining area in my dangerously high heels a handful of guests are talking amongst themselves.

As the minutes tick down, Juliet gets a text from Brock, Harlow's boyfriend, that they're five minutes away from the restaurant. Everyone gets themselves situated as they cram in the corner. All nerves are on edge with anxiety and excitement, especially mine.

The dining area is getting fuller by the minute, but the strangers' stares don't deter us from yelling 'surprise!' when Harlow walks in being led by Brock. A beyond ecstatic birthday girl plows into Juliet and me since we're right in front.

"Happy birthday," Juliet and I say at the same time in Harlow's tight grip. Her fake nails lightly dig into our shoulders, along with the occasional touch of her bare neck to each of our lips as she turns to give us individual hugs.

"Thank you, guys," she says shyly with tears in her eyes. Quickly blinking them away, she leaves the two of us behind to greet the other guests. Brock follows, giving me a thumbs-up as he passes, expressing his approval as if it's needed.

"Well, you did it," Juliet admits, crossing her arms gently across her chest after Harlow and Brock are out of sight.

"Of course I did it. Did you ever doubt me?" I answer. Juliet perks one eyebrow up with skepticism. "Really?" Juliet's lack of confidence in me is insulting since I get paid to do parties that are ten times more difficult than this.

Juliet's laugh ruins my train of thought. "Just kidding," she yells and runs away before I can come back with a snide remark.

Everybody is mingling and drinking, not to mention enjoying the great food, but all I can do is smile at people's jokes and hug various bodies that compliment me on the party, without really knowing who they are. In fact, I only know a small portion of the guests. An overwhelming need to glance around the rest of the dining area controls my brain and tells my eyes what to do.

There's people staring at our group in annoyance, along with curiosity. There's also people who are totally ignoring our presence altogether. My eyes however keep searching, as if they have a mind of their own. As if they were looking for something in particular.

When they finally stop at a table along the far wall

my heart stops beating and heat rises to my head. The top of my skull burns as all the blood rushes to the spot. Dizziness takes over just as my throat closes up, making me panic even more. It can't be. It just can't be. However, as the man turns ever so casually, I stare into his familiar dark brown eyes. Even from across the room, I can see him as clear as day. Maxwell.

* * *

Maxwell

Just the thought of The High Council in town puts me on the brink of insanity. The group of men that make up the council are considered elders. All of them are harsh, cold-hearted killers that are the oldest vampires alive, and I have a history that's not so pleasant with them. I reread the letter that was left for me several times, allowing memories from the past to fog my thoughts. The words that are written on the cream paper echo in my head.

> *Dearest Maxwell,*
> *We're so delighted to hear you've found your bride. We're more than excited to meet her. To insure that you follow through and collect what's yours for the taking, one member requests your presence at Junction 22 tomorrow evening. We expect to be impressed.*
> *Best wishes and happy drinking,*
> *The High Council.*

There's no doubt in my mind that Benjamin, the main enforcer of the council, wrote this heartless letter. Is he the member I'll be meeting at this Junction 22…I hope not. All I can think about is the repercussions I'll receive when they see how gently I'm handling Charlie. Once they see her disobedience, they'll force their upper hand, instructing me to change her against her will. Nobody ignores The High Council's rules. Nobody. If Charlie doesn't like my possession over her, then she definitely won't like the authority The High Council has over her as well as myself.

When they demand something of you, it's expected that you comply. It's known to every vampire that once you choose your bride or groom you must present him or her to the council. This person must be grateful for the life that's chosen for them. With my choice made, they now wait for me to present her.

If I had all the power in the world to keep Charlie's identity a secret, I would, but that's very unlikely to happen. The High Council knows everything and hiding things would just make it worse. However, I can keep The High Council a secret from Charlie. One more chance is all I'll give her to come around on her own. Otherwise I might have to force the situation along to a more pleasurable outcome. Sleep is the last thing on my mind, so I remain awake the rest of the night and following day. All I can do is wait until I'm to arrive at this restaurant to discuss Charlie.

When the sun finally falls the next day, I make my way to Junction 22. The hostess asks for my name and leads me to a table. To my surprise, a council member already awaits.

The man stands at my arrival. "Maxwell, so nice to see you again." His eyes look around and disappointment shows on his face, making him appear older than he is. "Where's your bride?"

"So nice to see you again as well, Eugene. My bride won't be joining us tonight. Her presentation's not ready. If that's the only reason for you being here, I'm greatly sorry for your displeasure."

Eugene extends his hand, motioning me to sit down before he starts speaking. "Your apology is accepted tonight, but it will not be again. I'm stuck in this town until I meet her. Maxwell, I know you very well and I'm instructing you to not prolong this, we all remember what happened before. Anyhow, we can catch up."

Eugene is one of the more tolerable men of the council. He has helped me get past certain obstacles and lessened my punishments. Even though I'm pleased that it's him here sitting across from me, I can't help but to be saddened as well. Eugene is known for talking very bluntly of his bride, his very compliant bride in efforts of making others jealous. Jealousy is the last thing I need right now when my bride refuses to speak to me like I'm not some crazy stalker.

"I can assure you the relationship between her and I is well-defined. I have the power in this blood bond and hold no interest in anybody else's." The ruthless words that exit my mouth come out effortlessly. With the appearance of The High Council, my animal instincts kick in. I'm her superior and she needs to grow accustomed to that, but I also feel the need to nurture her as well. Unfortunately, my entire being understands more than I ever have that this bond is more important than mere human emotions.

My attention is brought elsewhere as a group of people scream 'surprise' at a couple that just entered the dining room. With my senses off kilter from being instructed to embrace the cold-blooded monster within, I didn't realize that Charlie, my bride is here.

She stands in black leather leggings and a strapless dark blue top in the farthest corner of the dining room. Occasionally, she gets lost in the crowd of people she's surrounded by, even though most of the individuals gather around a certain woman who's a distance away from her.

Uncontrollably, I grip the underside of the table, praying that Eugene doesn't notice my lack of attention toward whatever it is that he's saying. The last thing I want is to draw attention to her. If Eugene were to notice my attentiveness to a certain girl, he'll come to the understanding that she's my bride. For there is no other reason to obsess over an individual if they're not your human. The repercussions of flat out lying to a high council member will be far worse than the nonexistent relationship between Charlie and me.

"Is something wrong?" Eugene questions, his cold gray eyes searching my face.

The words snap me back into reality. "No, I just find the humans to be quite fascinating throwing celebrations in honor of their birth."

"There's a reason why we only need one human, because they're useless and easily disposable. There's no need to be greedy when there's that one female or male who's born for you. Now, tell me about this girl. Is she everything you expect in a living being?"

I think carefully about my response, picking my words well before speaking them. "Everything and more." That sums it up very well in my opinion. She's everything I want and more than I expected.

Unwillingly, my eyes travel across the room to see her. She mingles with people, showing a true smile of happiness on her face. All it does is make me more determined than ever to get her to smile at me like that. I will make it happen. One way or another, she'll be happy with me.

Chapter Five

Charlie

Curiosity only grows as I stare at Maxwell and the unfamiliar guest who joins him at the table. The older man keeps on talking even though it's apparent that Maxwell isn't paying attention. As Maxwell ignores his friend, he also refuses to look at me as he sits stiffly in his chair. He only glances over in my direction once and it's a half assed glance at that. Maybe he got the hint, maybe he moved on?

Memories of his stone like body with lack of emotions, not to mention lack of blood torment my thoughts. Deep heavy pants hinder my breathing as beads of sweat accumulate along my hairline. It feels as if the world is crashing down and I need to escape. Rushing to the bathroom to breathe through my panic attack alone, flashes of his messy dark hair and deep brown eyes play behind my eyes.

The cold water that splashes on my face barely keeps me from falling completely apart. It's just a coincidence that he's here the same time I am…right? Patting my face dry, I examine my reflection in the mirror. The girl staring back at me is unrecognizable. Stark white face, blank eyes with a quivering bottom lip. Since when am I scared of anyone? A light tap to my cheeks brings some color to my face and I test out several smiles before exiting the bathroom.

Flattening my cobalt blue top with my eyes downward at the material, I inspect it for water stains. I didn't think I would run into anybody, because most people would move out of the way. There's always one person that's just as clueless, though. A grunt of pain slips out of my pursed lips as I slam into outstretched arms who force me to stop abruptly.

"What the—" I begin to mutter before my words are cut off mid-sentence when I finally look up at the person who allowed me to run into them in the first place. "Janessa, you scared me half to death."

"Listen, I need you to go get us more drinks," she says, getting straight to business. Her bright blue eyes that match Juliet's stare at me without blinking. You can tell that she's a little frazzled about something and this drink is her rock in keeping her grounded.

"Why?" I say, eyeballing her, but quickly come to the assumption without a reply due to a flash of guilt that crosses her expression. "You've got to be kidding me. This bartender too?" The words spill out of my mouth only to have Janessa nod in agreement. "What do you need?" Irritation blocks my better judgment, making me sound bitchy.

"Four cosmos. Thanks," Janessa informs me before prancing away. She quickly disappears around the corner before I can lecture her on her behavior.

Without wasting time lingering in the emptying hallway, I make my way to the bar. Stopping dead center in an aisle, I realize there's no way past Maxwell without directly crossing his path. There are two other routes, but with waiters serving customers, the paths are blocked. In order to get this done as fast as possible, I have to suck up whatever fear or hatred that's built up toward him and just walk past the man.

Deep breath in and held tightly in my lungs, which begin to sear with pain, I hold my head high when strutting past. In my peripheral view, I spot Maxwell. He refuses to look at me just as I refuse to look directly at him. Just to make things worse than they already are, my hips sway almost over extravagantly. Who does he think he is? Does he think he can show up on my doorstep and tell me he's a vampire, let alone his property that he wants to become his bride and then ignore me?

Common sense doesn't exist when thoughts that a dead man lost interest in you. I wanted him gone, out of my life and now that he is, I react like this. Leaning nonchalantly against the bar, I'm left waiting for my turn. Lingering out in the open and unaccompanied makes my insides turn. Feeling defenseless is an understatement.

No matter how fancy the place, the bartenders are always the same. This mid-twenty cocky bartender, who looks like all the rest with his half unbuttoned shirt, ignores an older woman who was waiting before I arrived, and asks me for my drink order. "What can I get a gorgeous girl like you?" His voice is swoon worthy, but his eyes that scan over my body give me the creeps.

"You can help her first, I can wait." The snooty tone in my voice is just a sliver of my annoyance. My thumb jabbing in the direction of the woman, who is now flushed with anger, is the frosting on the cake. Even though I want more than anything to get back to the party, get back to being surrounded by people instead of in plain sight all alone, I keep my manners.

He reluctantly takes her order and gives it to her in record time. I debate on how awful that drink is going to taste as the older woman walks away. With a look as if eternity has past, he fluffs his hair with his hand before leaning down so we can be eye to eye.

Holding back any disgust that continues to boil up, I show him nothing but charm. "I need four cosmos, please."

"All for you?" he asks. His eyebrows rise with curiosity.

"No, actually none of them are for me." The cocky tone finds its way back into my voice. "Although, I could use a drink right about now," I mumble under my breath.

"That's a shame, because I make the best drinks in town," he tells me. I just smile at his words and keep any thoughts to myself. Just another cheesy line that every bartender says...and honestly I've always had a better drink from a different bartender. He continues to search for bottles, mistaking my silence for speechlessness as he keeps the conversation going. "Are you a part of the party over there?"

I nod.

His eyes meet mine in the reflection in the mirror that lines the shelves full of alcohol. "Would you happen to know one of the other guests named Janessa?"

Here we go. "No, sorry. I only know the birthday girl," I lie.

He's almost done finishing the drinks when another customer approaches the bar. After a few moments the tall man's elbow touches mine. The ice-cold chill from his body engulfs me, causing all the blood to leave my face and all emotion to disappear. Dumbfounded, I stare at the empty space in front of me, intentionally making our reflection blurry.

Without even turning, I know Maxwell stands beside me. His pale hand slides toward me on the marble bar top, catching my attention. It quickly goes back to his side without touching me, but not before leaving a small piece of paper behind.

His handwriting is just as gorgeous as he is, especially tonight in his dress slacks, button-down shirt, and charcoal gray tie. A huff pushes the thoughts of him aside as I read the message.

Do not acknowledge me. Your life depends on it.

What? Is he threatening me? He has a lot of nerve to tell me that my life depends on whatever he says.

As the bartender finishes placing the drinks on a tray, he starts the discussion again, noticing the connection between his new customer and myself. "I can carry this over there for you," he offers.

"No thanks." My fingers clench the hard plastic circle the drinks are on.

"Are you sure I can't convince you to order a drink?" he asks one more time before I leave and don't look back. I just shake my head in response to his egging words. He turns to Maxwell. "What can I get you, sir?"

"I'll take a Bloody Mary."

The bartender grabs the glass and some of the bottles that are nearby and starts the drink. Like the drop of a hat something comes over me. "You know what, I will take a drink. Surprise me; just make sure it's strong. On another note, I believe he would love his drink to be extra bloody and maybe a Victoria instead of Mary. Marys seem too uptight," I interrupt, jolting my head in Maxwell's direction. What kind of vampire can drink Bloody Marys anyways? Is the bartender in on his secret and he adds a little something extra to it when no one's looking?

A smile of satisfaction finds the bartender's face. "Coming right up." He walks away to mix our drinks.

Vibrating in my back pants pocket stops a rant that's itching to be spoken. A short but sweet text message from Janessa demands to know where her drink is. A quick glance is shot toward Maxwell and I see his hands clench into fists. My own satisfaction fills my body as anger fills his. What the hell's his problem anyways?

The bartender arrives back with Maxwell's extra bloody, Bloody Mary and a small shot glass that I presume to be mine. No need to carry it over, so I pick it up and down it in one sip. My eyes involuntarily squint shut as the warm liquid burns my throat as it goes down.

A loud, raspy breath exhales through my still warm mouth and my voice comes out hoarse. "That was strong and hurt like hell, but it was good. See you later, boys." I walk with an extra pop in my step, knowing that both of them are staring at me. Who's playing with who now?

Balancing the tray with all the drinks on it takes great concentration and it feels like eternity before I can set it down on a clear tabletop. Instantly, the owners of the beverages grab them within seconds.

"Took you long enough," Janessa says with a smile. Nonetheless, she mouths a thank you in my direction before she vanishes within the crowd while taking large gulps of the alcohol.

Staring at the clock the rest of the night is all I can seem to do. When my eyelids get heavy with exhaustion and my feet ache with pain there's no better time to say my goodbyes followed by quickly dashing out of the restaurant to head home. With Maxwell preoccupied with his guest, I know he won't be able to follow, leaving me to feel quite comfortable as I exit the building.

There's no time wasted to change into my pajamas when I get home. With a quick wash of my face, the next stop is to bed. A long work week is ahead and I need as much rest as possible. A soft chant of 'sleep, sleep, sleep' brings my nerves down to a peaceful rest. However, when I'm finally at my most peaceful, his voice fills my head. Repeatedly he says those unbelievable words, my vampire bride.

Even though he makes every inch of my skin break out in goosebumps and causes the hair on my arms to stand on end, somehow the thought of him still makes my insides melt. His smooth deep voice makes my heart beat rapidly in my chest, but I don't know if it's from an unwanted attraction to him or how he could kill me with a twitch of his fingers.

His dark brown eyes torment me from behind closed lids. Images of his ashy gray, pale skin in the moonlight, contradict the pale, creamy skin that he appeared to have tonight. He looked normal. He looked as if he were anybody else, any other living anybody else, that is.

Deep down my subconscious knows that I'm not going to escape this. That I'm not going to make it out alive, or worse, that I'm not going to be able to stay away from him. Seeing him tonight with that strange man didn't make the situation any better. He had fear in his eyes as he sat across from the older stranger, just as I have fear in my eyes every time I look at him.

The small piece of paper that told me to pretend he didn't exist just draws up more questions. His actions are unreadable and unpredictable. His multiple personalities cloud my dreams.

* * *

Maxwell

It's easy for me to keep my eyes off her when she's across the room. However, it doesn't stop my senses from getting on edge when I feel her response as she finally realizes I'm here, in the same building as her. It takes everything in me to stay at the table and not chase after her when she bolts. My feet shuffle in anticipation of her reappearance.

Against my will I become even more rigid as she reenters the room, and my muscles twitch when she heads this way. Prayers sound in my head that she doesn't confront me, at least not right now. Keeping my eyes locked on Eugene as she walks past takes every ounce of self-control I have in order to not to grab her swinging arm.

Eugene seems oblivious to my inattentiveness as he talks about his bride. It's always the same, compliment after compliment in order to make others jealous of his well tamed bride. My eyes might be on Eugene, but my ears are on Charlie. The tips of my fingers dig into my knees from a tight firm grip that squeezes at the joints when I hear the bartender flirt with her. Even though his true desire is for a girl named Janessa, I can't help but to want to snap his neck.

I don't hear anything besides the words in my own head, the repeating words, she's mine. My restraint fades away, causing me to stand up abruptly.

"On edge, Maxwell?" Eugene questions. The skepticism in his eyes should make me fearful that I'm on the verge of being caught, but I don't have time for anything other than seeing Charlie.

"I just could use another drink. I'll be right back," I state before hurrying away. Slyly, I pull a pen out of my pocket before reaching the bar. In efforts of releasing some unwanted tension, I scribble on a napkin. When I'm finished, I purposely touch her elbow with my own. When her face loses all emotion, I know she realizes who's beside her.

At a slow and steady pace, I slide the paper in her direction and dismiss the huff she lets out as she reads it. The bartender finishes her drink order within seconds after my arrival. Relief washes over me as she rejects his offer of a drink, leading the man to turn toward me instead. Almost drastically her behavior changes after I order my drink.

Uncontrollably, my hands ball into fists as she orders herself a beverage. The emotions that are built up inside me pound away at the shield I try so desperately to hold up as she jokes about me wanting my drink extra bloody. It took me years to train my body to digest something other than blood. Some vampires learn to tolerate food, some learn to tolerate water, but I learned to consume Bloody Marys.

Knowing very well that Eugene is listening in on the conversation, I remain clueless to her banter. I even glance back at Eugene while she's busy flailing her hands around, giving him a clueless look as to who this crazy human girl is.

With the slam of two glasses on the marble bar top, my attention is brought back to the ever growing dire situation. My eyes close in defeat as she guzzles her shot of liquor. Alcohol taints the blood. It's like acid in one's mouth. She gestures a goodbye and I shrug a response at the bartender as his clueless look asks me if I know that girl, but I copy his expression of confusion. With my drink in hand, I grudgingly return to my seat.

"Did you know that girl?" Eugene asks me, his voice full of interest.

"No, just some drunk, oblivious girl who thinks everyone wants her. There are many of that kind of women in this town. My bride, on the other hand, completely opposite of that. She's kind, generous and very intelligent."

"Luck is on your side. My bride resembles a robot. She just goes through the motions and bends over backward to impress me." And he starts it up again. "This bride of yours sounds to be quite an equal to you. Not to mention, I have an impression that she keeps you on your toes."

"We're more similar than you can imagine and even though she's perfect in so many ways, we have our arguments."

Eugene continues to talk further about his bride. How she does whatever he asks of her, how she always overcompensates. My attention is still fully on Charlie, however, so anything he has to say doesn't stick. It would be more of a meaningful conversation if I had never heard the same words leave his mouth before.

Time stands still, but sooner or later Charlie calls it a night, causing my teeth to clamp together since I can't follow her. How I would love to follow her and question her about her actions tonight as I assume she would love to question mine, but I can't afford Eugene following me. If he were to find out that the girl I encountered at the bar was my bride and I didn't confess the connection, I would be in serious trouble, as well as Charlie.

Therefore, I say a few farewell words in my head. Until we meet again, my bride, until we meet again, I say to myself.

Chapter Six

Charlie

I tell myself encouraging and positive thoughts to help me get through my day. Nothing but relaxation and relief flow through me as I recline in my office chair with a coffee mug in hand. The silence of the empty office building adds to my comfort, although it doesn't last forever.

"Good morning, Charlie," Morgan sings as she pokes her head into my office.

"Must you every morning?" I say, annoyed.

"It is morning and your name is Charlie," Morgan retorts.

"It's how you say it, not why you say it, but anyways, good morning to you too, Morgan."

"Well, we have a big party on Saturday, so there's a lot to do. I'm going to get to work at the front desk." She ducks out of the open doorway.

"Not so fast," I yell, patiently waiting until she stands in the doorway again. "I need to talk to you about something. Sit down." My index finger points to the chair that sits across from me.

The discontent on her face as she solemnly drags her feet to the chair and restlessly plops herself down on the soft cushion causes the tension in the room to thicken. This is going to be an uncomfortable conversation for the both of us.

"Yes, Charlie," she mumbles, fiddling with her fingers, keeping her eyes locked on her lap.

"I came into the office Saturday afternoon, early evening and noticed that the office was...how can I word this...unkempt. I was wondering if you knew anything about that."

"Maybe. Most likely. I told him it was a bad idea." Her stalling lets me know she feels bad about what she did at least.

"Wait. What? You told who it was bad idea?"

"James. We've been seeing each other for a few weeks now after meeting at church. Anyways, we both have roommates and it was his designated night, but he refused for us to stay at his apartment, so..." She stops right in the middle of her sentence, fidgeting with the hem of her skirt.

I wait for her to continue in silence.

Her eyes roam all over the room, but never once land on me. "He said we should come here."

"What's so bad about him offering to come here?" Her refusal to continue leaves me no choice but to question her to pry the information out. I'm not mad at her for the poor choice she made, just disappointed.

"He kind of invited a few friends to tag along. I promise they didn't touch a thing. We all were in the conference room." Her palms smooth the fabric of the skirt. "The behavior that took place behind that closed door were irresponsible childish acts that shouldn't have happened," she blurts out as she sits stick straight in the chair.

Part of me is curious about what those acts were, but the bigger part of me doesn't want to go there. "Just make sure it never happens again and if it does, don't leave a mess behind. If he even says your place of employment, tell him I will personally have a talk with him. Don't make me take the spare key away. Now off to work. I need you to add calling the printer on your to-do list; we need more business cards and mailers." I watch her walk out and pray that the message got across.

What kind of boy wants to make out at his girlfriend's workplace and invite friends along? Not a typical church boy. Not to mention, that behavior from Morgan is completely unexpected. To take my mind off the group of partying adults in my office building, I start to work on my checklist.

First call is to the florists. After the third ring, a familiar voice answers the phone. "Bunches Floral, how can I help you?" a chipper male voice says.

"Hello, Justin."

"Well, well, well, I was expecting a call from you this week. How's our favorite Charlie doing?"

"Our favorite Charlie? Am I not the only one you know?" I love my conversations with Justin and his business partner, as well as life partner, Robert.

"The only female we know with the male name that's not a drag queen. Anyways, we're working on the order and we'll be there at the venue at noon for delivery. I have something better to talk about with you, a question really."

"Go on," I instruct.

"We're in need of a party planner and we want to enlist you."

"When you say we, you mean Robert and yourself? What kind of party can I assist you with?" My curiosity spikes.

"Of course Robert and me, who else? We're getting married." The excitement in his voice resembles a screaming woman. I can't help but to giggle.

"I guess I can fit my two favorite people in my calendar. Just email the information when you have it. Congratulations."

"Thank you, Charlie. We'll see you Saturday."

I hang up the phone and continue to move down my list of venders to call. Most of them I'm not looking forward to speaking with as much as I always am with Justin and Robert. A loud, long sigh exits my mouth at the thought of another party to plan. I wonder when I'll ever be caught up, but then again business is business.

Before I know it, the days separating me from the three hundred thousand dollar sweet sixteen party are dwindling away. Each day Morgan barely talked to me since she's still embarrassed at her outrageous behavior. When Friday afternoon finally arrives I'm wearing down and eager at the same time.

The sound of the office phone ringing forces my heavy eyelids to perk up. Before the second chime, Morgan answers it. Within seconds, though, her voice sounds through the tiny speaker on the phone's base. I roll my eyes and answer the phone with a perky energetic voice.

"Hello, Mrs. Monroe, what can I do for you this lovely afternoon? I assure you I'm working on your son's birthday party and will have everything you asked for by next weekend." Mrs. Monroe is a reoccurring client of mine. She would call me almost every day, making sure I had everything ordered and every last detail that she demanded met.

"I'm so happy to hear that, Charlie, but I hope what I say next doesn't ruin anything." Oh my, now what, I think to myself. "I really think Riley would love oompa loompas at his birthday party. Is that possible?" she asks, even though I know she's not asking, she's demanding.

You've got to be kidding me. She thinks that her two-year-old son would like oompa loompas at his birthday party. I can't imagine him even remembering his second birthday, but I have to do what the client wants. "Not a problem at all, Mrs. Monroe. How many exactly?"

"Four will do. I'll give you an additional six hundred dollars to hire them. I can't say that I'll talk to you next Saturday, because I'll probably call before then."

"Not a problem. Goodbye, Mrs. Monroe." I hang up and mumble to myself how it's beyond a problem and is a nuisance. Where the hell am I going to find four little people to hire in less than five days?

As if a light bulb went off above my head, I know exactly where I'm going to get some eager little people. Mid-dial Morgan appears in my doorway.

"What did Mrs. Monroe want?" she asks.

"Oompa loompas," I say, short and to the point.

"Oompa loompas?"

"Do not make me say it again. Yes, oompa loompas. If you don't remember, her son's second birthday party is next Saturday and it's Willy Wonka themed."

"Where are you going to find people to help you with that?" Her skepticism is daunting to my ego.

I raise the phone so she can see that I'm in the process of finding people.

"You mean to tell me you know little people?" Her disbelief is quite discouraging.

"No, I know somebody who's surrounded by little people all day. Juliet. I'm staying late so you can go home and get some rest, just make sure to lock the door behind you when you leave. See you tomorrow at The Liberty Hotel at eleven a.m. sharp." I pronounce those last few words implying that she shouldn't be staying up late doing who knows what with James.

I finish dialing Juliet's number and wait until she answers. "What do you want?" Her voice is charming yet full of inquisitiveness.

"I need you to do me a favor. One of my clients just

sprung some last minute details for her son's birthday party on me and you're the only person who can help."

"I like the sound of that. What do you need?"

"I need you to charm the drama teacher."

"Seriously? You know I can't talk to Wilson." The anger and embarrassment that fog her voice is the least of my concern.

"I need four students that have potential to be oompa loompas. There have to be mothers out there who think their child is the best and I'll pay them." My bribing voice overtakes any annoyance that grows deep within my chest. I know she refuses to talk with Wilson Geoffrey, the drama teacher, ever since she asked him out for drinks one day and he turned her down only to start dating the art teacher a few days later, but this is more important than a crushed ego.

"Really? Isn't there anything else I could do, like ask my students?" she offers.

"Listen, he turned you down over a year ago. I need striving wannabe actors not just any kid. All you have to do is relay the message and give him my email address. I'll talk with him further. I really need you to help me out on this, Juliet. There's no way I can hold auditions for little people on such a short notice. You're a junior high teacher; you're surrounded by short people who are starving for a little slice of stardom."

"Being painted orange isn't stardom," she states, unamused at how I'm referring to this as a professional gig. However, before I can counter her grouchy mood, she starts speaking again. "But, I'll do it for you…not for free, though. You owe me and as payment we can go out to dinner before the club tonight."

"About that…"

"Charlie, come on," she whines.

"I have an outrageous sweet sixteen birthday party

tomorrow that costs almost twice as much as my house; I can't afford to screw this up and go out tonight. You knew I wouldn't be coming every week because my schedule has picked up. Two weeks, I'll buy you the most extravagant meal you can think of in two weeks." Boy, she drives a hard bargain.

"Fine." She hangs up before I can say anything further like maybe simmer the tension that's obviously streaming off of her. She might be a sixth grade teacher, but she acts like a sixth grader herself sometimes.

I leave the office before nightfall to compel myself to relax and get as much rest as possible. More than aware that tonight is my dancing night, the night I usually see Maxwell, makes sleep difficult. However, unlike every other night this week his voice soothes me into slumber.

* * *

Maxwell

With my attention being put toward Eugene and The High Council, I don't have time to see Charlie within the week. It feels as though every cell in my body is on fire knowing that she's so close but yet so far from reach. I take the risk in trying to escape watching eyes to see her tonight at the dance club, recalling Juliet expects her to show up.

Doing everything inhumanly possible, I try to convince Eugene to make himself comfortable in the hotel he's staying at while I spend some quality time with my bride. He accepts my offer after much bribing and I instantly head out.

Sitting in my usual corner, I search the dance floor. It's later than I wanted to arrive, but when there's no sign of Charlie or her friends, I take a breath of relief.

There's just something about witnessing her enter the large over crowed room that pleases me.

With what feels like eternity later, I see her friends, including Juliet, arrive and indulge themselves with drinks. They dance to the music without missing a beat and when not a single one of them look at their phones or the door, a gut-wrenching conclusion that Charlie isn't coming causes my excited jitters to die. A quick glance at my watch tells me it's after two-thirty in the morning.

Standing up and straightening my shirt, I walk effortlessly through the crowd toward Juliet. She stops with a jolt as if I scared her. "Hello, handsome," she says as a greeting.

"Juliet, right?" I say, ignoring her flirting.

"Do I know you? I'm pretty sure I would remember if I ever saw a gorgeous man such as yourself."

"We've never met, but we have a mutual friend…Charlie."

"Of course, you're here for Charlie. Everyone's always interested in Charlie. She never mentioned you." There's a hurt scorn in her voice from the fact that I'm here for someone other than herself.

"It's a little secret between us, but a secret you're in on as well now," I reluctantly say.

"That girl is always keeping the good stuff from me. She's not coming tonight, some big party tomorrow. I'll tell her you were here for her."

"Not necessary, I'll see her soon enough." With that said, I turn away to leave the building, considering there's nothing for me here. The slightly cold air feels comforting against any exposed skin as I step out onto the sidewalk. There's also a relief from being away from Juliet's roaming hands. Even though I specifically stated I was there for Charlie, that didn't stop her from trailing her fingertips over my chest.

Charlie might be busy or plain out refusing to go to club anymore due to my assumed presence, but that doesn't mean I can't see her. Soundlessly climbing the steps of Charlie's front porch, I pick up the artificial rock and unlock the door. A smug smile spreads across my face at all the obscene words she would spew in my direction if she knew that I knew about this key, let alone breaking into her house.

Before unlocking the door, I take time to assess the inside. All the lights are off, leaving everything covered in darkness and then I sense her calm breathing, indicating that she's sleeping and not awake. At a quick pace I enter the house and make my way to her bedroom.

Before even entering the bedroom I see the outline of her unmoving body under the covers. Instantly, I go to her bedside, which allows me to examine every detail of her face; it lets me enjoy her beauty without her doubtful glare staring back at me. Clenching the blanket between my fingers, I lift it to see her curled body in her pajamas. Goosebumps break out on her bare skin. Within seconds, she grabs fistfuls of the blanket and pulls it closer to her face with incoherent mumbles escaping between her lips.

I side with my better judgment and let her sleep. Determined to leave the house before I change my mind and do something I'll regret, I head to the front door. As if this endeavor would be easy, her phone's ringtone blares throughout the house just as I pass the threshold of her bedroom.

I freeze and try to conceal myself in the dark hallway. Shuffles of her in bed can be heard; however, she doesn't wake up to answer the phone. I assume it's Juliet calling to inform her of me asking for her. So much for letting her sleep.

Slowly making my way past the kitchen table, my hand brushes against some of the stray papers. The small handwritten notes and schedules that fill the pages pique my curiosity. Picking up random sheets, I read through all her plans for this supposed party at the Liberty Hotel tomorrow night. At least Juliet wasn't lying about Charlie ditching.

I leave in disappointment and allow my mind to wander on the walk back to the hotel. Scenario after scenario fill my mind on how I can go about courting Charlie. Maybe I should be more old-fashioned. Maybe I should be more modern like the men who fill the streets in this day and age. Two completely different men and I have no clue as to which one I should become. Then there's the fact that if she's unwilling to give me a chance to have a civil conversation with her, I'll never know which she would prefer. So…maybe I have to be both.

Chapter Seven

Charlie

The blanket snuggly around my head is the only escape from the loud ringing of my cell phone. I toss and turn, trying to find a comfortable spot again after being woken up. However, a shuffle of papers coming from the kitchen sets my nerves on edge. Someone's in my house...snooping. As gently as possible, I slip out from underneath the blanket and tiptoe out into the hall.

My teeth clench together as I watch Maxwell dig through my papers that I left lying out on my kitchen table. You want to play dirty, fine, I say to myself. Making my way back to my room, I throw on some clothes. With my nerves on edge and my senses spiked, I hear the soft click of my front door. Waiting a few extra minutes before following him, I remember to keep my distance several feet behind as I duplicate his fast paced walk down the unlit sidewalk.

The night air has a slight chill and I'm thankful when he finally enters a hotel. It's one of the fancier ones in town, which makes me slightly grunt in response. He likes to live the luxurious life all right. I remain outside and peer through the glass doors, waiting for him to head to his room, but a man immediately approaches him, the same man who accompanied him at Junction 22.

As the man leads Maxwell away, I decide to change my plan of just following him to becoming more hands-on. There's not a lot of time to put my plan into action and I face the possibility of being caught, but the urge to dig my fingers in his things is overpowering. When

79

they're completely out of sight, I walk in, heading straight for the front desk. I stare at the man behind the counter, thinking about how I can charm him.

"Good evening, miss, what can I help you with?" His eyes scan my attire as he eyeballs me.

Not allowing my self-consciousness to ruin my chances, I put on my best act. "The guy who just walked in, Maxwell is his name…well, you see, he snuck me in through the back door and things happened that I'm not proud of. However, I left something behind. I need to get back in the room without him knowing."

"I can't help you with that. I'm only allowed to inform him and he can bring the things down for you or he can assist you in gathering them."

This is going to be tougher than I thought. "Listen, one-night stands are the worst ideas in the world and I can't look at him again." I see a wedding band on his left hand and try to play up my stupidity of not being able to settle down with one person. "I'm sure you think I'm a bad person just throwing myself on some man seeing as your married, happily I assume, but please spare me a little embarrassment. There has to be something I can do for you?"

I see him waver, just the slightest bit, but he's contemplating my silent offer. "Hmm, hmm? I plan some high end parties. A nice evening all planned out for your wife." I continue to ask, edging him toward the correct answer.

"My wife would be impressed if I gave her an anniversary dinner."

"Deal," I shout before he has a chance to change his mind. "Just find his room, make a key and nobody has to know about this, just like your wife doesn't have to know that I created the perfect evening. Maxwell Barnett." I wait. It kills me, but I wait.

He stares at me, knowing that what I'm asking of him is wrong and could get him fired, but within a few seconds, he taps at the keyboard of the computer and hands me a room key. "Room 218," he whispers.

Snatching up the pen on the counter and reaching over my boundaries to collect a piece of scrap paper, I scribble down the number to my office. "Call me during work hours. Just tell me about our secret key and I'll get you all set up. Thank you." I grab the thin plastic card from his hand before he can change his mind and make a dash for the stairs. Who would think that being a party planner would get you what you want.

My knuckles lightly knock against the door to make sure he's not back yet; with no answer, I slide the key card in. A rush of air bursts out through my tightly closed mouth as I quickly enter the dark room, praying that my knock wasn't too light and he's somewhere in here…staring at me.

Afraid to turn the light on to give my presence away, I dig out my cell phone from my waistband to light the way. Deeper and deeper, I go into the suite to start my search and once my phone lights up each room, I know he's not back yet. Time to get down to business. I haven't the faintest idea what I'm looking for, but I know something incriminating is here. There just has to be.

My mind's getting sleepy and my thoughts are screaming loudly inside my head to go home, but something inside me is forcing me to continue to look around. "You've been living here a while, haven't you," I whisper to myself.

I dig through drawers and closets, even suitcases. Nothing, I find not a single thing. I stare in defeat at a built-in bookshelf. I scan the books, wondering if he owns all of them or if they came with the room. An unwelcome urge draws me to one in particular. Unable to tear myself away from it, I remove it from the shelf. I rub my fingers over the soft leather binding, fanning out the yellowed pages before opening it to the first page. The title page, it reads The Travors Bloodline.

Could it be? Is this book about Maxwell's bloodline…my bloodline? Does a thing such as this even exist? I shove the book in my purse along with the key card, intending to read every last word in it as well as returning to this room to snoop some more. Sneaking down the halls of the hotel and peeking around every corner before I turn them is one of the hardest things I've done. My heart races with fear as thoughts of being caught fill my mind.

I take several sighs of relief as I unlock my front door and search the house to find it empty. I'm not the slightest bit interested in the book, because my eyelids demand my full attention. Changing back into my pajamas, I crawl into bed, trying to find that comfortable spot again.

Morning comes sooner than I anticipated and the clock is not my friend. Thoughts of being late cloud my judgment in picking out my clothes. With my face barely covered in makeup and my hair in the messiest ponytail ever, I reluctantly leave to start my day.

Adjusting my sunglasses, I stand outside The Liberty Hotel, keeping my sleepy eyes away from the shining sun. As the door attendant opens the door for me to enter the luxury hotel, I try not to trip as my full arms block my view. Morgan trails behind with her sighs of admiration.

Before I can reach the front desk, a woman steps beside me. "You must be Ms. Preston. I'm Daisy, the hotel manager that will be on shift tonight. I can show you to the ballroom. Would you like me to grab something?" I'm a little taken back that she knows my name, but I'm assuming the director of events relayed the message of my arrival.

She starts talking before I can say a word. Something about how excited she is. I, on the other hand, hope this party goes by fast, because my mind is elsewhere. All I can think about is that book I found in Maxwell's hotel room. I read the entire thing this morning, hence my tiredness and almost lateness.

The book consisted of what looked like diary entries. Who wrote them, I've no idea. The information on those pages opened my eyes to who Maxwell really is. A monster. On the walk to the ballroom, I will myself to think about the party that's ahead of me instead. There's so much that we have to do, I can't let my mind wander.

Daisy's voice breaks my thoughts. "Here we are. Is there anything I can help with?"

"No, my aides should be showing up soon," I say, dropping my bags on a nearby table. With a quick rub of my forehead in dismay, I walk away from Morgan and Daisy. "Let's get to work," I say, glancing back at my assistant.

Morgan smiles friendly at Daisy as if she knows her. Daisy just nods and politely smiles back before speaking in my direction. "The linens are folded and piled on the far table. When you're ready for the staff to set them just come find me." As she stomps out of the room, her clacking heels echo throughout the large empty space.

Without wasting time, we get to work. We barely stop our tasks as the florists, the lighting and the construction crews arrive. Not much later, the DJ and the aerial art performers finally arrive as well. Everyone's hard at work getting things done when I feel a vibration in my back pocket.

"Hello, Juliet." I'm uneasy about starting a conversation with her after the message she left me last night. I listened to it several times, thinking about what to say. I still don't have an answer.

"You never called me back, did you get my message?"

"Yes, I did get your message, but today's really hectic. I'm sorry that you feel angry, but he's not my boyfriend as you think he is. He's some crazy obsessed stranger that I want nothing to do with. I didn't find it important to tell you about him or anybody else for that matter."

"I wish I had somebody as hot as that obsessed with me. What's so bad about him anyways?"

I don't know; let me think...oh yeah, he's a dead bloodsucker that's almost three hundred years old. "It's hard to explain, just know that I would pry him off and hand him over to you if it were that easy. I have to go; I'll talk to you when I talk to you, which should be in a few days when you tell me you had a chit-chat with Wilson. Goodbye, Juliet." I hang up just as she starts grumbling.

By the time I end the call with Juliet there's less than an hour before the party is supposed to begin. With the lights set on dim, music filling the air, and the aerial dancers dressed as strippers hanging from their silk fabric, I know things are finally coming together.

With everything going smoothly, I grab the bag that I threw in the corner and go to the bathroom to change into clothing that's more appropriate. After I'm all dolled up, I run right into my clients on my way back to the ballroom.

An inner battle of keeping my facial expressions at a minimum from the sight of such a ridiculous dress the birthday girl is wearing takes a toll on me, but I put a smile of joy on my face effortlessly. She treats this party as if it were Cinderella's ball. I allow them to enter the room without me. Her parents approach me minutes later with looks of satisfaction.

"The guests should be arriving soon, please go make yourselves comfortable." I usher them back into the ballroom. I, on the other hand, hang out outside the closed ballroom door to keep guests at distance until we're ready to start. A number of minutes later, Morgan informs me that the birthday girl is concealed and ready for her grand entrance. I therefore let the crowd of guests that has accumulated enter.

Morgan and I stand in the back corner of the room, observing our work. I ignore the speech little miss rich pants makes to the crowded room. My head drops in my hands when her parents say their thank you as well. Any respect I have for my clients dissolves as neither my name nor Morgan's are included in the list.

Con number one for planning rich people's parties: no recognition. Pro number one for planning rich people's parties: free entertainment. Even though I'm at work technically, I still allow myself to have a good time, partially. Morgan dances in the corner by herself and I sing along to every song in my head.

I continually look at my phone. It states in the contract that at midnight myself and anyone else that's considered my staff leave. The clock reads ten pm. And my once happy mood dissolves at the thought of two more hours before I'm able to leave this hell hole. Being surrounded by sixteen-year-olds is not my idea of a good time, not to mention careless parents who allow stupid teenagers to become more stupid by letting them drink spiked punch.

Obnoxious, cocky teenagers are the least of my

worries as my feet start to hurt and sweat begins to gather in certain areas on my body. Silently, I beg for it to be done. When all hope's gone a cool draft encompasses my overheated body, making the remaining time seem manageable.

The air conditioner must have kicked on. But it's when a tip of a nose and the occasional touch of soft lips graze the back of my bare neck I know it's not the air conditioner. I should know by now that sudden coolness comes with a price.

I jolt around to face Maxwell. I have no idea what he said because of the loud thumping of my eardrums as blood rushes to my head. "What the hell are you doing here? How did you know where to find me?"

"I always know where you are."

"You were in my house last night, weren't you? I might be unorganized and messy with my papers, but I know they have been moved around." Without thinking, I jab my index finger into his chest.

His smirk makes my skin crawl. I decide to keep my detective skills to myself. He'll know soon enough about my findings. Just when I thought the night is almost done it seems to have just started since he doesn't look as though he's going to leave willingly.

* * *

Maxwell

The sight of her perfectly still body in a music filled room is disturbing considering every other time I saw her surrounded by music she was dancing. Although, tonight she's standing stick straight with her arms crossed over her chest. What a workaholic. Creeping up behind her, I can't help but to admire her body in yet another skintight outfit. The black and white dress gives an illusion of extra curves to her hips.

Careful to not touch any part of her, I lean in close. Unwillingly, the tip of my nose and lips brush her neck as my whisper startles her. "Oh, how I have missed you, Charlie."

Her shock and sheer stiffness disappointment me. All it does is push away any happiness I have in seeing her. The sound of hatred in her voice as she asks me how I found her makes anger of my own start to bubble to the surface. My reply of always knowing where she is doesn't make her any more content with my presence.

When she accuses me of being in her house last night, I can only shrug it off, being careful not to give any hint that I was in fact in her house last night. "Maybe." My response is short, without giving a concrete answer.

"You have to leave; I could get fired for you being here. This isn't my party. I'm not allowed to just invite outsiders to events, even though you're more than an outsider," she lectures.

Just then, a tall girl in a ridiculous short hot pink frilly dress approaches us. "I didn't know you had such a cute boyfriend." I watch as her hand casually lands on Charlie's shoulder.

She whips around to face the young girl. The sensation of her frazzled nerves put my own nerves under duress. This girl is just a child and Charlie's heart rate accelerates with each pump from her presence.

"He's not my boyfriend, just some party crasher that I'm about to escort out." Charlie's arm jolts backward manically, searching for me without her breaking eye contact with the girl standing before us. When she does finally grip my arm her nails scratch at my skin, but only momentarily before her squeezing grip turns to a shove. Just then, I realize that this must be the birthday girl.

I stand my ground and extend my hand to her. "She's just being harsh since she's not allowed to have my company here. I assure you the fault is all mine. I'm Maxwell, by the way."

"The fault might be yours, but the pleasure is all mine," the young girl responds.

Before she can say anything further, Charlie interrupts with her hands flying in the air. "Whoa there, you're sixteen and he's…old, too old for you. He was just leaving. Weren't you, Maxwell?"

"He doesn't have to leave. He can dance with me." The look of joy on this girl's face makes my stomach turn. Her fingers quickly latch onto my arm and begin pulling me out onto the dance floor. I fully intended to bring Charlie with me, but Morgan came rushing to her side.

Charlie leaves the room, but not before giving me a stern look. As if I would do anything inappropriate with this needy child. As the song finally ends, I slip through several bodies, thankful that a handful of boys her own age gather around her. There's only one place I want to be and that's looking for Charlie.

The halls of the hotel are long and empty. Stopping in one of the side aisles, I take time to listen for her. Her heartbeat. Her breathing. The unmistakable thump of her footsteps on the carpeted floor. As she rounds the corner that I reside behind, a smile forms on my lips. "Are you getting tired?"

Her startled body jumps at my voice. "How did you escape Justice?" she asks with her hand clenching her chest.

"Justice? What justice did I escape when I'm still on trial?" I say, playing along with whatever she's getting at.

"The sixteen-year-old birthday girl," she says, annoyed.

"Her parents named her Justice, creative. I slipped away when a few excited boys moved in on her. How about we go back and join Justice on the dance floor?" I find it more humoring than she does.

In a matter of seconds there's a flash of messy brown hair and a pair of fierce brown eyes staring me down. Her glossy lips purse to form whatever smart reply that brain of her is thinking, but a static filled voice interrupts. "Black Night, this is Muggle Born…where are you?"

She keeps still, ignoring her assistant with her finger still pointed at me.

"Black Night—" Morgan says again, cutting through the silence between us.

"Yes, Morgan?"

"I thought we were using code names? Anyways, where are you? Is the cleaning crew on their way?"

"I just got done asking for housekeeping; they should be coming shortly. Just make sure all the underage drunk kids are away from the scene, we don't need the cops here." Once she's done talking, she clips the device on her dress somewhere, somehow.

"Black Night, huh?" My laugh is muffled by trying to hide my amusement from her since I can physically see she's not in the mood for more of my jokes.

"Shut up. I picked that code name way before you came along and ruined my sanity."

"I know, but doesn't it make you a little curious?" The playfulness in my voice gives away the sheer pleasure of knowing that she's meant for me. "How about you give me one dance and I will leave."

Her bottom lip gets brutally bit by her teeth as she contemplates the offer. "I don't think so. If you refuse to leave, you can sit here and be as bored as I am." Without waiting for me, she spins around and heads back to the ballroom.

I catch up with ease. "If you insist." If she thinks I'll be bored in her company she's very wrong.

"I shouldn't be the only one to suffer," she grumbles.

I ignore her depressive tone and stay by her side. We enter the darkened ballroom to be stopped by whom other than Justice. "Where have you two been? Anyhow, dance with us."

"Justice, I don't participate in events I plan. Maxwell here already offered to dance and I told him the same thing. You can dance together…again…longer preferably," Charlie says as she tries to duck out of the conversation.

I grab her arm, swinging her around forcefully. "Not so fast, love, the birthday girl insists. There's no harm when the one that the party is for wants you to break your own rules." I pull her in close, staring down at her as I glide my hand across her cheek.

"You two are so cute," Justice says, walking toward the crowded dance floor.

Charlie starts to struggle in my grasp when Justice turns her back on us. I tighten my grip and force her to take unwilling steps into the crowd of people, weaving us through stumbling bodies to the middle where Justice waits for us. Right on cue a new song starts.

"Dance, Charlie." I persist. She stands stiff and shakes her head in refusal. "Charlie…if you remember, I can make you. I would prefer you act on your own, but if I have to force you to do something you don't want to do, I will," I whisper in her ear.

"Did you make Justice adore you so you can stay?" The dull emotionless tone of her voice stabs me in the chest.

"No, I can only influence the people within my bloodline. If only it were that easy to charm everyone, I would be able to get closer to you faster. I'm positive with your closest friends' approval of me you wouldn't be so cold."

"I'm cold. You're the one who's freezing to the touch. And I'm sure I would be more attracted to you if you weren't dead. Not to mention the not so hot part about you wanting to drink my blood. Total turnoff," she says in a hushed tone through gritted teeth.

Part of me couldn't disagree with her.

Just then, Justice barges in on the conversation and lifts Charlie's arms above her, urging her to dance. I can see the cockiness in the young girl's demeanor as she associates herself with Charlie. She finds herself lucky to be in correspondence with a beautiful, talented woman. I find myself in the same situation when I think about my bride as well.

Charlie finally gives in, and that infamous sway takes over her hips. Justice turns away to her own friends when she sees Charlie dance on her own, leaving me the only one to give her attention.

She keeps her distance from me, refusing to touch. My willpower breaks and I grab her waist, pushing her against me. She only struggles until eyes of speculation are on her and then she melts into me, not wanting to cause a scene. My fingertips glide over her shoulder, sliding down her back, leaving a trail of goosebumps. A wider smile forms on my face as her body shivers in response.

Without warning, her body lightly bumps against me, sending me across an imaginary line. Grabbing her arms a bit too aggressively, I feel my teeth extract along with the familiar ache. My lips desperately want to touch hers. Lost in thought, my nails unintentionally dig into her skin. I refuse to become aware of her struggling body trying to break out of my grip.

Her bare neck calls for my attention as I'm lost in this blood lust. I hear the pumping of her blood, which forces me to lick my lips. I hear her muffled voice as her body starts to jerk. With a quick glance at her moving mouth, not the slightest bit interested in what she's saying, it's the smell of blood that breaks my daydreaming.

The sound of the music is barely audible as I finally hear her words. "Maxwell, you're hurting me. Maxwell, please," she whines in a high-pitch squeal.

I let go of her immediately. Her own hands rub at her arms. As she brings her fingers back into view, I know where the smell of blood came from. My nails broke the skin on the backside of her arms, making her bleed. All I can do is stare at her apologetically while trying not to be infatuated with the tinge of blood staining her fingertips.

She grabs me aggressively and drags me off the dance floor. She looks around to make sure nobody is paying attention to us. "What the hell, blood thirsty much? Can you put those things away?" Her two index fingers make makeshift fangs.

"I'm sorry, it's just that…" There are no words to explain what I am going through, what I will continue to go through without her. "I got lost in thought; I can't promise it won't happen again."

"How touching."

"Can you honestly tell me you have no attraction toward me?" I know there is. The whole black night gave her away. It's just if she's going to admit it or not.

The hesitation as she thinks about how to word whatever it is that she's thinking is all I need. I know the dreams and thoughts that cloud her mind. The words she says have no meaning behind them. "You repulse me," she spits out, trying to convince herself just as much as she's trying to convince me.

A fanged smile flashes at her hate-filled gaze. "You can only lie to yourself for so long." I take her hand in mine, bringing it up to my lips. "I'll see you later, love." With a small kiss to the back of her hand, I leave the party with the sound of her racing heartbeat filling my ears.

* * *

The Travors Bloodline

August 5th, 1716

Transcriber: Fredrick Yearn

Maxwell George Barnett is born within the Freemore bloodline. Vampire Cornelius Herrington is possessor of all individuals who belong within the stated bloodline. At the moment Maxwell is one of eight persons alive who can nourish their owner. Thankfully, vampire rules state that blood lettings cannot happen until the individual is no longer a child.

March 17th, 1736

Transcriber: Fredrick Yearn

Pity grows deep in the pit of my stomach for Mr. Barnett who is now twenty years old. For the past four years Maxwell has endured the aggressive, inhumane behavior of the vampire that has control over him. Numerous feedings result in him being nearly unconscious. But the increased isolation is what's breaking the young man's morale. I've seen this happen to many donors in my years. It's frightening to see a spark of vengeance in a man's eyes.

September 13th, 1748

Transcriber: Alexander Rein

Maxwell suddenly becomes the only remaining human to feed Cornelius due to the deaths of the other two donors who remained. One illness related and the other was sentenced to death because of unlawful actions. Maxwell, age thirty-two (Pictured to the right) is unwillingly turned due to the growing infestation of small pox. With this Maxwell and Cornelius will be assigned a new bloodline, which I'm sure will be fully stocked with donors.

February 27th, 1776

Transcriber: Alexander Rein

Cornelius Herrington, Maxwell's maker has gone missing and is presumed dead after finding a pile of ash in the woods. Little evidence points to the assailant. Cornelius wasn't a very liked man, but Maxwell has the most motive in killing him. However, he is never tried for the death, but suspicious eyes remain on him. I witnessed the event occur and I will die with the facts of the brutal murder. My advice, don't underestimate Mr. Barnett.

June 3rd, 1776

Transcriber: Jonas Degolos

Since a conviction never occurred, Maxwell is now assigned a bloodline of his own, the Travors. I have counted seven individuals for him to choose from currently. None of which he holds any interest in at the time being. His behavior resembles the aggressive manner of the vampire that made him. He uses and tosses the limp individuals aside without a bit of compassion. I will remain watching him and his acquaintances.

May 23rd, 1851

Transcriber: Marco Longburrow

Speculation is once again placed upon Maxwell due to the death of friend Henry Mead's human consort, Prue Wendall. Prue was said to become Henry's bride within two weeks of her death. The High Council revealed information that Maxwell was the last person to speak with the young woman before she committed suicide.

With his growing forceful, selfish behavior toward the humans within his bloodline and now being blamed for causing Prue's death, Maxwell is sentenced to one hundred years without feeding. He is to spend his punishment in a square cell buried deep in the ground, blocked off from the sun but also blocked off from the rest of civilization.

His bloodline has been notified and they are moving to seek safety. No one is aware of where they will be going.

November 17th, 1954

Transcriber: Doug Reddington

I have found the Travors bloodline and with many marriages and births of children, two new bloodlines diverge from the main source. The first family line is now known as the Bloomburgs. The second line is now the Prestons.

July 30th, 1986

Transcriber: Doug Reddington

Gravely, I have been found by Mr. Barnett. He has been following me for several weeks now and I feel my time is coming to an end. My most recent finding is that, unlike the Bloomburg family line, the Prestons have birthed a child. I will not disclose any information about the individual because of the possibility of him gaining access to this journal.

Message to the next transcriber who takes over my duties: Do not underestimate vampire Maxwell George Barnett. He can be very deceitful and aggressive, but at the same time very cunning and humane. Keep the bloodline secret, for this baby is the start of saving humanity.

Chapter Eight

Charlie

The early morning sunrise wakes me up sooner than I'd like. Entry after entry from that journal kept me awake after arriving home last night. No matter how awful that book makes him sound, I'm stuck with him. No matter how much I force him away, he won't leave until he gets what he wants and what he wants is me dead by his side.

I get dressed as fast as possible, throwing the book in my purse. Hell-bent on a confrontation on my terms, I decide to head over to the hotel Maxwell is staying at. The cockiness that radiates off my body disappears once I enter the building. Since I kept that extra room key, I don't have to enter through the front door and humiliate myself again.

I hover outside room 218. He claims he's not some movie vampire, but I only see him at night. Stereotypes are all I'm left with and the best-case scenario is that he's here asleep, cowering from the sun. I insert the key card and wait for the blinking green light allowing me to enter. As quiet as possible, I open the door and close it just as carefully behind me.

The utter darkness puts my nerves on edge. My heart pounds against my rib cage as I approach the open doorway. With squinting eyes, I barely make out his sleeping body under a blanket. Creeping across the floor to the large window, I grab ahold of the dark curtains. Sucking one deep breath in, I tear them apart, not fully thinking through my actions.

"Good morning, love!" I yell, fully aware that once

the curtains are open and I make my voice known there's no going back.

I hear him grunt as he crashes to the ground. The bed keeps him in the shadows, away from the sunlight that now fills most of the room. I adjust one curtain to give him more shade so he can stand up and face me.

"You said you weren't a cinema vampire, but I see you're scared of a little sunlight. Are you okay?" I say as if I were talking to a child. My tone is degrading and most likely making him very mad, but I find power standing in front of the open window, a power he needs to know I have.

"Charlie? What are you doing here?" Anger distorts his voice.

It takes me a few minutes to collect my thoughts. I wasn't expecting him to jump out of bed in his underwear. I can't help but to gawk at his near naked body. I envisioned his body in a dream, but seeing it while I'm awake makes me react unwillingly. That fact that I'm beyond speechless and can't stop my eyes from wandering takes all the power I once had away.

A quick clear of my throat forces my thoughts elsewhere. "I wanted to surprise you like you surprise me, because how you feel right now with the sun threatening to beat down on you is how I feel every time you sneak up on me. Plus, you can only say good night and I really wanted to say good morning. Oh, and not to mention this." My hand plunges into the depths of my purse, searching for the leather journal. Once my fingers wrap around it, I wave it in the air like a white flag.

Disappointment plays on his face. He knows very well what's written in here and now he knows I know more about him than he wants me to. A side of him that he wished to remain unknown.

"When I questioned you being in my house it was

more of an honest statement, because I saw you…snooping. Then, I followed you. I was forced to bribe the man at the desk downstairs to give me a room key, which he did, obviously. Anyhow, enough of me divulging my secrets, this is about you." The interrogator in me is standing strong in the well lit room. Crazy thoughts of being a detective weave their way into my brain, but I silently laugh them away.

His laugh that fills the room, however, puts me in my place. He's more relaxed under my stare than I'll ever be under his, clothed or not. "That book describes the worst of me. I know you'll take this the wrong way, but we're more alike than I thought. You'll make a great vampire, Charlie, you'll make a great bride."

"I'll never be a murderer. Tell me, did you kill him…the man who wrote the last entry or any of the men who wrote those entries?"

"Only one, the last one. I had no choice. Vampires shouldn't be documented for all to read. When I found out who he was, I knew I had to get a hold of the book. I read the pages more than you have and I'm very displeased with my behavior, but I've learned from my mistakes."

"Have you? Some things that were mentioned in those pages describe you to a tee. They say what I think and feel about the…whatever it is that you are."

"A man, Charlie, I'm just a man. There are things that are different about me, but I was in your situation once. If you recall, I was human once too." I can see the hurt in his eyes. I can tell that some part of him wants to be human again.

Even with misery in his gaze, I refuse to go off topic. Or worse, feel sorry for him. "Who were those men who named themselves to be transcribers?"

"Just a group of men who found out about our

existence. They took it upon themselves to track us and learn how to rid the world of vampires. If you're worried about them still recording bloodlines, you can rest assure they're all dead."

His words calm me, but still make me fearful. I wonder how much participation he had in the murdering of all those innocent people. The thought of some stranger following me around keeping track of my every move and those I associate with is something I can't even stomach, but to kill them for it is a little too far.

"They mentioned a child." Curiosity gets the best of me.

"The infant mentioned was you. At that time they were forming a conspiracy against us and tried very hard to hide bloodlines. With my sentencing as I'm sure you read about, it was easy for them to conceal you. It still took me twenty-seven years to decipher their clues in finding you. I admit after reading those pages I grew weary that I was going to find you. Hunger does things to you. They thought you were special. I don't why, but they did and I told myself that I would track you down at all cost and capture you to find out. They wanted to classify me as an animal, and an animal is what I was willing to become."

His words stab me in the heart. I don't want to listen, but he gives me no other choice.

He continues to speak, staring off as if imagining himself in the previous years. "I wouldn't allow anybody to take what's mine away from me. He kept you from me and he paid the price. Even you, Charlie, should be paying the price of not feeding me, but the moment I saw you something changed. And though I don't know why those men thought greatly of you as an infant, I see you to be extraordinary for my own personal reasons."

"Personal reasons? Paying the price? I'm a living breathing human being if you recall not a piece of property." Irritation blocks my better judgment. After hearing that he was going to be some emotionless savage my guard goes up. It goes up thicker and higher than it already is. He starts to speak, but my finger goes up to silence him. "You think you can change what you are, which is a monster, by the way, to become what exactly?"

"A human man. My morals were broken by the vampire that turned me, causing my view on humans to be nothing but tolerable. That had to change. There was no way I was going to become like my friend Henry, using forceful tactics to obtain a bride." If I hadn't been staring him down as he tried to explain himself, I wouldn't have seen it. A small flinch his eyebrows made at the mention of Henry.

"You might not use force for a bride, but you're still a killer and you have threatened me more than once." It's like kicking him while he's down, but I can't stop my words from coming out.

"I would never hurt you, but I won't take no for an answer either. You will become my bride, Charlie. When is up to you, but you will be with me."

"I'm not talking about this right now. I'm not here to talk about you and me. I'm here to get answers." The rage that's growing inside me causes me to become flustered and most likely red in the face. I want to go, but I have one last thing to find out. "What is The High Council? They sent you away, who are they?"

"All you need to know is that it consists of a group of elders, the very first vampires to exist. They keep peace between our kind. You'll meet them soon enough."

"What's that supposed to mean? Why am I

supposed to meet them exactly? And I'm not your kind, so stop saying that. There's you and then there's me. Two different things, two very different kinds." I take a few steps forward, inching my way to the edge of the sunlight within the room.

I need to get away from his pleading eyes. Between being angry at him and visions of my dream I had of us in bed together overwhelm me. Trying to keep my eyes off the plush bed, I can't help but to glance at it several times. There's more questions to ask, but I have to leave and I have to leave now.

I stop short as he quickly moves to the farthest shadow, which happens to be inches away from the door. Even if I run, he would catch me. Even if I remain in the sun all the way to the door, he could still grab me and endure whatever amount of pain for a few seconds before his overbearing strength pulls me into the darkness.

"You can't keep me here. You want to be a human man that a human girl can tolerate," he nods his head in agreement, "then you have to let me leave when I want to leave. There's a fire exit out that window, do not make me use it." I keep my voice strong as I'm begging him to take my words seriously.

He bows the tiniest bit and waves his hand toward the door. I'm through the doorway when he begins to speak. "Charlie…" I turn around to face him. "Being my bride is not as bad as you think it would be."

I continue to walk to the exit without saying a response. There's no way in hell I'm going to be a walking corpse for him. Once parked in my driveway, I relax. Sanctuary…kind of. I plop down on the couch after locking the front door and double checking it multiple times before feeling at ease. With the whole day ahead of me, I contemplate what to do. After much thought, I decide to just sit on the couch and watch TV, trying to numb my mind. More like trying to forget what I heard.

When the sun starts to set my nerves get on edge and there's no food, TV show, or amount of locks that can shove the dread down. Fear of him showing up bashes against the same picture that keeps popping into my mind. Maxwell's unclothed body standing before me. Yearning, hate. Hate, yearning. This has to stop, but how?

* * *

Maxwell

I ponder on what just went down. Did I ruin things even further than they already were with her? Or did I help her understand me, where I came from? How far I came and how far I'm willing to go. That journal, though. Do I wish that she didn't come across it? Yes. But only because I should have been there to explain things. Now she has this image in her head that contradicts what I'm trying so hard to prove.

That book has traveled many miles and several cities, but I don't exactly know why I keep it. It doesn't tell a story I'm particularly fond of. An old friend of mine repeatedly told me to burn it and never look back. That one day it will come back to haunt me. Well, today is that one day.

A knock on the door breaks my concentration. The constant knock forces me to move even though I don't want to. There's only one person I want to speak with right now, but let's face it, she wouldn't knock.

I slip a pair of pants on since I'm still in my undergarments. Looking at the ground with sheer determination, I answer the door.

"I'm not intruding, am I?"

"No. Not at all. It's nice to see you again, Eugene. Come in." Stepping aside, I wave him in.

"Hum." His skepticism is portrayed in his voice. Instead of prying on the subject of my tiredness, he hands me an envelope and waits for my response.

The blood red stationary brings back memories, memories I wish not to be dug up. There's no need to ask what it is since I already know, but I do anyways for the sake of politeness. "What's this for?"

"I'm needed back and can no longer wait to see your bride. Therefore, the council has set a date for the presentation of her. I know you claim you're not ready and I won't question you, but this simple task has to be completed. It's the week after your friend Grace's party."

"Very well," I say reluctantly. I shouldn't be surprised that The High Council will put their grubby hands where they don't belong.

"Don't be so glum, Maxwell, if she's as great as you describe her to be, she'll be fine with the change of plans." He squeezes my shoulder before he exits the suite, leaving me in silence.

The door closes and when I sense Eugene is out of earshot, I grumble to myself, unable to hold back my words. They have to be said, otherwise they'll repeat in my head over and over, claiming all of my attention. "Oh, Charlie will be perfectly fine with the change of plans...since she never knew anything about the initial plans to start with," I mock.

I sit on the couch and debate how to carry out the final task that has to be completed before The High Council meeting. All I know is Charlie is not going to be happy, because blood is going to have to be shed.

Chapter Nine

Charlie

No matter how much I don't want another work week to start, it does. There are plenty of things to occupy my mind, but one thing keeps blocking my judgment…Maxwell. The screaming children at the birthday party I had this past Saturday kept me on my toes, though. The cries from the children made my head hurt and made it completely impossible to think about anything. However, the birthday party might have kept my mind in check, but Juliet kept my emotions in check.

She refused to call me about her talk with Wilson. She just sent an email that consisted of three words: you owe me. A few days later, I received phone calls from eager parents wishing to enlist their child for the party. She's still angry with me for refusing to tell her anything about Maxwell, not as if I have a choice.

After almost two weeks of surprising him in his hotel room, I haven't seen him since. All I can do to keep myself from going insane is count down the remaining hours to the next party. Thank goodness, it's tomorrow.

I walk into the office to see Morgan behind her desk hard at work. "I didn't think I was late," I say as I stop by her desk.

"You're not, I just came in early. I'm super excited about the party tomorrow night." She bounces in her seat.

"Morgan, are you sure? It doesn't start until ten in the evening; do you not have to go to church Sunday morning?" Any party that starts that late at night screams trouble and part of me wants to protect her.

"Yeah, but I'm going to stay as long as possible. I can't miss anything that happens." The innocent smile that spreads across her face makes me want to pinch her cheeks. Even though I feel the urge to treat her like my little sister, I don't.

"We'll see, Morgan." I tap her shoulder gently before I make my way to my office. My feet stop abruptly in the doorway. My eyes can't rip themselves away from the large wooden desk. "Morgan?" I hear her mumble 'yup' in reply. "Did you put this package on my desk?"

I hear her footsteps coming down the hall. "Package? I don't know anything about a package." She now stands beside me, staring at the blood red wrapped gift box lying perfectly centered on my desk.

"It wasn't by the door or delivered by a postal man and you just forgot that you put it in here?" I question her.

"I think I would remember if I saw that wrapping paper. I mean...wow; it reminds me of blo—"

"You can go back to work now," I say, cutting her off. I don't need her to tell me that the color of the paper reminds her of blood. The mention of blood only leads to one person. I walk over to the box cautiously and place it aside as gently as possible as if it were a bomb. Forcing myself not to open it until I get home takes a toll on me and drains me of all energy. I like to think I have an exceptional amount of patience, but that package taunts me.

I can't help but to stare at it all day. There's something about it that draws my curiosity in the worst way. Grateful once seven o clock rolls around, I grab my purse and head up to the front door, more than ready to have this day end.

Morgan is nowhere in sight when I make my way to the front of the office. "Morgan?"

"I'm in the back. Just a sec." Her hair is ruffled when she finally comes into view. A puff of air from between her pursed lips blows stray strands of hair out of her face. "Whew. Those boxes back there. Killer. Where's you box? Did you open it?"

"Oh, it still must be in my office. I'll get it tomorrow."

"Don't be silly, I can get it for you."

In a matter of seconds she reemerges with the red wrapped package.

"Thank you." A fake smile spreads across my face.

"Just make sure to tell me what's inside it." Her index finger taps the corner of the box.

"Of course."

"Goodnight, Charlie," Morgan says before walking to her car.

"Goodnight, Morgan." Not so gently, I put the box in the backseat so I don't have to stare at it on my drive home. The dark sky and limited streetlights keep me from spying on the box in the rear-view mirror. Nonetheless, once I lock myself in the comfort of my home, I can't help but to gawk at it once again. Sitting on the very edge of the couch, my eyes roam over the crisp red paper. Curious as to what's inside, I'm also fearful of what I'll find.

Shaky, unsteady hands extend outward to touch the wrapping. A frightful shudder washes over me just as two fingertips graze the paper the same moment the doorbell rings. My heart clenches in my chest, my lungs automatically get deprived of oxygen, and my joints freeze up as I will my body to answer the door. I assume it to be the worst person in the world since the sun just went down a little bit ago.

I don't bother in looking through the peephole. I just grab ahold of the knob and slowly open the door. A hand pushes against the wood and forces it to open faster, followed by them inviting themselves in.

"Is something wrong? You look like you've seen a ghost," Juliet says, closing the door behind herself.

Ghost...vampire, both are dead, does it matter. "Thank heavens. It's just you." I literally exhale in relief.

"Yeah, just me, don't be so excited." The sarcasm in her voice allows me to lighten up just the slightest.

"Not in a bad way. I'm actually glad it's you and not somebody else. Why are you not getting ready to go out tonight?" I know she should be arriving at the club in about an hour or so.

"I wanted to talk to you instead of partying like a good friend should do unlike the awful one I've been. Or am I intruding on something?" she asks, but plops herself on the couch without caring if she is or not. "What's this?" She grabs the mysterious package and shakes it near her ear as she tries to guess what's inside.

"I don't know. It was left at work for me today. Morgan doesn't recall anybody leaving it and she didn't move it, which makes me kind of scared to open it."

"Are you saying you don't know who left it?" she asks.

"Not exactly," I reluctantly answer.

"So you do know who left it?" she questions yet again.

"Most likely."

"Well, open it. I want to see what's inside." She throws the box at me and the corner digs into my chest.

Gradually and unnecessarily cautious, I tear away the wrapping paper. Hesitation stops me from lifting the lid of a white box. Juliet nudges my arm with her elbow, urging me to continue. With closed eyes, I lift the lid only to slam it back down as I hear Juliet's rush of air.

I need to hide whatever is in this box before she gets a better look at it, because there's no way I can explain anything about it. Without warning, she rips the box away from me and digs her fingers inside. I scrunch in on myself to hide from her stare as she pulls out the mysterious gift. I quickly take a peek. She stands up and lays a beautiful navy and black lace dress up against her body. Acting like a little school girl, she twirls in place, admiring the dress as if she's never seen anything like it before.

"This guy has spectacular taste. You hate him why?" She twirls some more, admiring the dress. A shrill whimper escapes her mouth as she went a little overboard with the spinning and crashes into the corner of my coffee table. Hobbling on one leg, she still manages to keep the dress perfectly lined up to her body.

Stifling a giggle, I ignore her clumsiness. "He's not all that he seems. Sure, he gives me a gorgeous dress, but he broke into my office to leave it for me."

"However bad you think he is, maybe you should give him a chance."

Her words cause an ice like freeze to paralyze me. If he didn't already tell me that he can't influence other people I would wonder if he talked to Juliet.

"I can tell that it's a bad topic, so I'll leave you to your thoughts." She drapes the dress over the arm of the couch and walks toward the door.

"Wait, you can stay. I would like it if you stayed." I would prefer her company more than being alone with my own thoughts. She wavers in the entryway, debating if she wants to stay. While she silently thinks about the offer, I grab the dress and shove it back in the box.

"Fine, but only because you asked so nicely. Along

with the fact that we haven't sat down and spent some quality friend time together in a while."

Tossing the box aside, I rush back to Juliet, who has laid herself down on the couch. She fumbles with the remote in her hand and just like that a never-ending debate of which onscreen hottie is cuter.

Hours later Juliet bids her goodbyes. Not expecting anything less from her, she reminds me that I have to feed her next week. With a wave and a smile, she drives away, leaving me alone. I refuse to draw attention to the dress and go straight to sleep. My eyes might scan the half open box that lies on the kitchen table with the contents peeking out urging me to look further at it, but I don't. I'm not giving him any more of my attention.

I'm eager yet apprehensive about the party tomorrow night and now knowing that Maxwell is lurking in the shadows makes sleep difficult. Staring at that dress and either admiring it or not only makes things worse.

I wake up later than expected, but since the client for the party tonight didn't request outrageous details, the set-up won't take long. What little they did want, I find to be useless, but they requested my help and I won't turn them away. With nothing better to do, I lounge around most of the day, waiting until it's time to get ready. Since the event is at the actual client's house, I change into my appropriate party attire at home.

The sound of hangers scrapping against the rod as I rummage through my closet fills the room. Nothing seems good enough. My mind wanders to the dress that still resides in the box on the kitchen table. I weigh the options and decide that I'll indulge myself. It's not as if Maxwell will be seeing me, this is at someone's house after all. He'd have to break into a stranger's home, which is entirely different than showing up at a public venue and party crashing.

I slip into the dress, grab a pair of heels from my closet, and look at myself in the mirror. The fabric clings to every curve and I begin to second-guess my decision as I start feeling self-conscious. You only live once. Walking confidently to the bathroom, I fix my hair into an up-do and apply a little blush. Thankfully, by the time I finish it's time for me to leave.

Having never been to the part of town the client lives in, I find myself wonderstruck. The gated community is one of the most high-end neighborhoods I've come across and some of my clients are very wealthy. I don't have trouble finding the address, but I do however have trouble finding a parking spot. The streets are packed as if the party has already started.

After finding a spot a couple of blocks away and making my way up the sidewalk, I spot Morgan loitering in front of the house we're supposed to conduct the party at. My pace quickens as I want to talk with her before someone sees us out here.

"Is this a joke? The party is here, right? Because it looks as if it has already started," Morgan asks me as I reach her with heavy breaths.

"You know what, go home." I take in her angered stare. "Morgan, listen to me. Go home and I'll talk to you later. I'll pay you as if you were here and if you leave without a snide remark, I'll pay you overtime. Understood." The possible outcomes that this party could have make that sisterly instinct kick into overdrive. Nothing good can come out of this and bribing Morgan to leave is the best idea I can come up with.

"Yes, captain." She hangs her head and walks toward her car.

I wait to enter until I see her drive away. Before I

have a chance to ring the doorbell or even knock the front door swings open to reveal a beautiful woman.

"You must be Charlie. You didn't have to send your assistant away. I realize you're confused and a little frightened about the start of the party before your arrival, but I assure you everything is fine. My name is Grace, by the way." She waves me inside her home and as the door shuts behind me, I know something is not right.

Her demeanor, her smooth, seductive voice. She reminds me of a certain someone and a pit of dread forms in my stomach. As I follow her to the backyard, I scan her slender frame and her flowing golden blonde hair.

Once the backyard comes into view I know I'm over my head. I see several individuals already dancing and drinking. They're all dressed to perfection and their movements are extremely crisp and elegant. Looking at all the creamy pale bodies that fill the spacious yard makes my heart beat harder and harder. I feel my hands get sweaty as my mind yells for me to run. I'm relieved that I sent Morgan home, but now that leaves me to face the trouble alone.

* * *

Maxwell

"Maxwell, relax. She'll be here. I'm paying her, so you better be grateful. I know why she resents you, though, tricking her into a trap. Think about your actions, there has to be another way."

"There's no other way, Grace. The presentation is next week, six days from now, to be exact. I have no more time to waste. If she wishes to remain a human until she's ready, then this has to happen and it has to happen now." I thought many times about what I have to do and how exactly I should go about doing it. No matter how many different ways I think of, I know Charlie and she won't take it lightly.

Grace leaves me to my thoughts as she speaks with the other guests. When I see her walk inside with a tight nod of her head in my direction, I know that my bride has finally arrived. As a way to blend into the crowd, I mingle with others by holding useless conversations with various individuals I don't even know. All my attention's brought to the back porch where I hear Grace compliment Charlie.

"You're as beautiful as Maxwell describes you to be," Grace says kindly, putting herself on thin ice.

Charlie's body immediately goes stiff with the mention of my name. "You...you know Maxwell?" she stutters out.

Grace nods and points in my direction. I drop my head before Charlie's eyes connect with mine. Boy, Grace doesn't waste time in calling me out. Within seconds, I stand before the two women. "I see you're wearing the dress I gave you."

"You broke into my business, so I won't thank you. You had something to do with this whole party, didn't you?" The vindictiveness in her voice causes me to cringe. Maybe now that Grace gets to see a glimpse of how overbearing Charlie is, she'll finally understand why things are so complicated between us.

I bow my head with regret. "Yes, you were hired on false pretenses."

"You tricked me into coming to a vampire party. This event was scheduled ten months ago, ten months, Maxwell." Her voice rises with anger.

"I think I'm going to leave you two alone," Grace interrupts.

"Maybe we should go somewhere and talk about this without drawing in everyone's attention. There're a lot of capable ears here; our differences shouldn't be their entertainment." Grabbing her arm very gently, I lead her back inside the house. She doesn't detest the gesture, so I don't release her or say a word as we go up a flight of stairs and walk toward the room I asked for.

I wasn't expecting one door to be open on our way to the end of the hall and knowing what's taking place inside, I try to rush past it. However, Charlie stops in her tracks. Tug after tug on her elbow to urge her to follow proves to be pointless. The damage is already done.

I step alongside her and peer into the room. Two fully unclothed bodies in a very private activity can be seen clear as day. The girl is covered in her own blood since the vampire that I don't know very well has bitten her several times in many locations. The sheets are stained red and small puddles accumulate on the floor. Screams of pain escape the girl's mouth as nothing but moans of pleasure escape the vampire's blood filled mouth.

In a rush, I slam the door shut. With my arm wrapped tightly around Charlie's waist, I pull her fighting body to the last room and lock the door behind me. "We have to talk," I say.

Her somewhat shaking body that refuses to look at me makes me regret the actions that I am about to take.

Chapter Ten

Charlie

I shut down. My brain freezes, unable to register what I just saw while my emotions paralyze my body. No matter how much my feet refuse to move, Maxwell's brute strength pushes me along. Silence fills the room he leads me to. But silence is soon replaced with the click of the door locking.

"What's going on, Maxwell? Why did you bring me here?"

"She'll be fine." His calm voice puts my nerves even more on edge. I can picture his statue like body guarding the door.

"Stop with the bullshit, Maxwell. I could give a crap if that girl leaves the room alive or not. This isn't about some other vampire's carelessness; this is about that empty look in your own eyes. I thought you were trying to be a better vampire. I thought you were trying to be more humane." I still have my back to him, refusing to look at those mischievous dark eyes.

"There's something you need to know. Need to do if you like it or not."

"What the hell is that supposed to mean?" I swing around, finally looking at him. The sight of his fangs makes my fingers tremble. I want to scream, but only a whimper comes out as fear squeezes my lungs.

His hands jolt out to grip my arms as if what he's about to say will scare me even more than I already am. He takes time choosing his words, speaking slowly. "Charlie, do you remember asking about The High Council and I told you that you would meet them sooner or later? Well, they're requesting your presence in six days. You have to be presented as my bride and in order for the meeting to remain in our favor one thing needs to happen."

I don't know what to say. I have many things to say but to choose one is impossible. One foot after another, I slowly walk backward, slipping out of his grip. His fingertips clutch my elbows, trying to keep me next to him, but he eventually allows me some space. Carefully rounding the bed not breaking eye contact, I get as far away from him as possible. More than anything I want a greater amount of distance between us than he's permitting as he carefully follows each of my steps. The sharp corner of the nightstand jabs into my lower back, telling me there's no space left to go.

He must be able to see my body quiver with fear as he moves his hands to the tops of my shoulders, trying to steady me. My heart pounds so loud that my eardrums throb and my hyperventilating makes me lightheaded. His fingers press harshly into my bone, trapping me in front of him. "This doesn't have to hurt, Charlie. Just hold still and I promise everything will be fine."

Fine? Everything will not be fine in my opinion. What happened to not digging those fangs into me until I wanted you to? I lean away from him, bending backward over the nightstand as he slowly slants toward me. The lampshade of the lamp that sits upon the table behind me presses into the curve of my back, tipping it over.

With my instincts kicking in, I reach my hand behind me in search for the lamp base. My stretching fingers frantically grope for the base before it falls off the table entirely. As soon as my fingers wrap around cold metal, I swing. The heavy object seems light in my grip as it soars through the air.

The force of the hit vibrates through the lamp up my arm. Taken by surprise, Maxwell bends over, holding his head in pain. I see my chance and make a dash for the door, but luck isn't on my side as my fingers fumble with the lock. As Maxwell becomes silent, blood rises to the top of my skull. Panic makes the worst of a person come out. My fists pound wildly on the door as my screams finally escape my mouth.

A growl of anger sounds behind me. His voice comes out harsh and strained. "No one will come running, Charlie. You're at a vampire party in a gated community."

And just like that I find the Maxwell that was described in that journal in the room with me. A monster more so than man.

Shuffled footsteps play with my head. I press my back up against the wooden door. Fear incapacitates me, but that doesn't stop my eyes from meeting his. His casual walk in my direction taunts me as he lightly dabs the gash on his forehead. The thick, tangled mess of hair covers parts of his face, making him appear more menacing than he already is.

He runs his hand through those tangles, letting me see his glare in full. A small dribble of blood runs down the side of his head. The wound is deep and gruesome. It looks as if it should produce more blood than it is.

"You're bleeding?" I say with a barely audible shaky whisper.

"Vampire 101, love, we tend to hold blood in areas that cannot be covered up. The head, neck, and hands remain seen by human eyes; therefore, blood accumulates there to keep one looking alive." He looks at me with those devilish eyes.

The cruelty in his voice as he continues sends chills through my body. "You know, Charlie, I was going to be easy on you, but seeing you still don't trust me, there's no better way to get around this. We'll have time to fix our relationship; you'll have eternity to learn to love me. As I'll have eternity to forgive you for your stubbornness. Not to mention that you made me bleed, twice."

"First time you didn't bleed. And you're going to make me bleed, you idiot. So it's even," I yell back.

"Look at me, Charlie," he demands.

I shake my head violently, refusing to listen to his commands.

He ignores my words and continues with his rant. "What did I ever do to you to make you hate me so much, besides love you?" He steps in front of me and grabs my jaw, forcing my head to lift in efforts of making me look at him.

"I can't do this." His fangs are no longer extracted. As I stare at him all I see is a man. An average, normal, heartbroken man.

"Charlie, relax." His voice puts me at ease. "That's right. Relax."

With those words everything becomes a haze, but a welcomed haze.

* * *

Maxwell

As if some imaginary switch is pulled, Charlie's feisty behavior disappears and all I'm left with is a woman that will do whatever I say. Part of me is relieved, but at the same time part of me is sickened. It shouldn't have to be like this. And as I stare at her while she presses her warm cheek into my palm, I debate on going through with what needs to be done.

She won't remember exactly what happened, but

it's better than her looking at me with tear filled eyes as she glimpses the monster that lurks just beneath the surface. Her hand remains tightly clenched in mine as I lead her to the bed. "Charlie, sit down." My hand slips out of her as she places herself at the edge of the bed. I kneel in front of her, taking her hands back into mine. "Do you remember what I told you about The High Council?

She nods anxiously at me.

"They need to see a connection between us. They need to see that you...that you love me." It kills me to say those words. It kills me even more as she squeezes my hands tighter.

"I'll do anything for you, Maxwell. Anything." Her words toy with my feelings. It's not real. "What do I need to do to prove to you, to them that I love you?"

With ease, my teeth extract. Showing them to her in full. She would normally pull back or quiver in my grip, but this time she doesn't. Instead, she places her lips on mine. If I were to pull back my influence she'd be furious with me. Using her isn't what I want. If I wanted to do as I pleased with her and feed whenever I felt like it without having a deeper connection with her we wouldn't be here. I wouldn't be a frantic mess preparing for our visit with The High Council.

Lost in my own thoughts and fighting certain urges, I don't realize her hands aren't touching me anymore. Opening my eyes, I see her fumble with the back zipper of her dress.

"Charlie."

She ignores me. Just as I'm about to tell her to stop, she folds down the collar of her dress, exposing her neck and shoulders. Her hands continue to pull the fabric further. My hands encompass hers, forcing her to a stop before she uncovers herself too much.

Letting go of her hands, I cradle her head in my palm. She follows the gentle push of my fingertips to lean her head to the side. The pulse of her veins under the thin, tender skin causes an ache all over my body. It's been so long since I fed. Either forgetting or not caring that Charlie isn't the true Charlie, I let my instincts take over. My lips instantly go to her neck. The warmth that radiates through her smooth skin is breathtaking.

A laugh erupts from her mouth. "That tickles, Maxwell."

Her fingers tangle within my hair seconds before she pushes my mouth harder upon her neck. The tips of my teeth pierce the skin from the force. There's no wince of pain. No second thoughts. She just leans her head further to the side, allowing my mouth more room to bite.

Seconds tick by as I just linger over her neck, resisting the urge to take advantage of her. But once the sweetness of her blood touches my tongue, bringing it life, it's over. I plunge my teeth in the curve of her neck as deep as they'll go. Her body tenses before it goes limp. Fear races through me. What if I drank too much?

The slow beat of her heart fills my ears as I lay her on the pillows. Relief washes over me, but it doesn't last long.

"So you took the easy way out. How did it feel to bite into an empty shell?" Grace says as she stands behind me.

"Not now, Grace," I threaten.

"The council will see past whatever act she'll put on to save her own ass. It's either standing up to her or them and from the looks of it, it's not her."

"You think I don't know that, Grace? I at least bought her a little time."

"Well, aren't you the charmer every woman wants." Sarcasm is one of Grace's strong suits.

"Is it okay if I let her stay here tonight?" I ask, ignoring her.

"Sure. Why not?" Her sarcasm strikes again.

"Don't be scared. You two will get along quite fine, believe me. I'm going to go clean up." I pass her on my way out. Her words, however, follow me down the hall.

"I'm not scared of a little girl. And she'll just love to be my BFF when she gets her senses back. Oh, you're the vampire that set me up. Hey, take a look at this big bite in my neck because I showed up for a party I didn't need to. Yeah, best friends. Forever."

A smile spreads across my drying red lips. My reflection in the bathroom mirror is horrendous. The freshly wet blood red lips give my skin a ghostly white tone. Dried blood starts to crust on my face from the head wound she gave me, which flake away at my touch. I spot Grace in the corner of the mirror. She decided to follow me to taunt me some more.

"Do not try to make me feel bad about this, Grace. You know better than anyone does what The High Council would order if she arrived with her smart-aleck attitude. Not to mention that the bond has only formed to a certain level due to simple skin-to-skin contact. They would order me to bite her right there and depending on how much she disrespects them or myself they would order for her to be turned on the spot."

I see Grace waver. Even though she wants to criticize me for my actions, she understands. "I came here to get a washcloth and a bandage for her. Not to criticize you."

I collect the damp washcloth and bandage before leaving the bathroom. "I can do it. Why don't you go deal with the rest of partygoers? They should be getting ready to leave soon."

"Very well," she says before heading downstairs.

I clean up the bite mark and hide it from view with the bandage. Guilt makes the air thick and my head foggy. I remain in the room with Charlie while Grace decides to stay as far from her as possible.

The sound of latches snapping into place means only one thing. Sunrise. Grace never has been one to sulk in a basement or tomb during the hours of daylight, so she vampire proofed her home. Every place that lets in the moonlight at night gets barricaded with aged, thick wooden shutters she had carved by some elderly man in Venice decades ago. I made this room light tight last night before Charlie arrived, but as the minutes ticked by I could almost see the wood brighten from the sun's rays.

Sunrise is the worst. An ache takes over the body. The pull of sleep tugs at your eyelids. Vampires don't have to sleep, but it reminds me of my human days and I've grown accustomed to it. More than anything, I want to be awake and in the room when Charlie wakes up, but I need to move around to get rid of this restlessness that's starting to take over my limbs, so I join Grace downstairs.

Chapter Eleven

Charlie

A moan escapes my dry, chapped lips as the stabbing pain of a migraine throbs from inside my skull. Almost zombie like, I whip the blankets off me, intent on getting some pills to ease the throbbing, but stop short. The room spins in a slow circle, causing my body to sway along with the imaginary movement. In order to ease the nausea that attacks my senses, I anxiously rub my palms over my thighs.

The once smooth fabric of the dress that I wore last night is now damp from sweat and layered with wrinkles. "I'm going to kill that man," I mumble as my feet shuffle across the floor.

I reach the corner of the room where my bathroom should be. The backs of my hands rub aggressively at my eyes. Where the hell am I? I'm nothing but a bunch of nerves as I look around the room in search of the door. Or any clue as to where I am. The sudden movement of my head causes a twinge of pain to run down the length of my neck. Thinking I pulled a muscle, my hand automatically goes to rub it out. But when I feel a plastic like square patch my blood starts to boil. And when my fingers apply two points of pressure that twinge of pain comes back.

It doesn't take much for the flashbacks of last night to flood me. I'm still at the house that enlisted me to coordinate a party, a party that they didn't need me for. A vampire party. And Mr. Barnett bit me.

Set on a mission, I speed walk downstairs in search for Maxwell. He took a piece of me, it's only fair that I take a piece of him. The clink of a glass sounds from the kitchen. Expecting to see Maxwell, I see the startled expression of the woman who requested my services instead.

I'm sure I look like a mad woman and once my words harshly spew out of my mouth, I sound like a mad woman too. "You." My finger points at her in hatred. "You helped him attack me, didn't you?"

"Maxwell," she shouts.

"You knew what he was doing. You. Vampire."

"Maxwell. Someone is awake...and not happy."

"Charlie, leave Grace out of this. She's an innocent bystander," Maxwell says from behind me.

I jump around to face him. "Innocent? She's innocent?"

"Calm down. Let's talk this out," he says as he slowly approaches me.

"Calm down? You bit me, you fiend!" I yell back at him.

A distant laughter that I assume to come from Grace makes matters worse. I'm not sitting here talking to him. Just the fact that he bit me is one thing, but not being able to remember what happened after I smacked him in the head with a lamp is scary all in itself.

"Charlie, we can talk about this. Let's just go back upstairs," Maxwell pleads. He blocks my path from getting anywhere near the door.

"Upstairs? You mean the little room you trapped me in so you could have a snack."

"Oh boy, she is a firecracker," Grace mumbles behind me. Her giggles fuel my anger.

"Grace. Shut. Up. Charlie, calm down. Look at me." His words are caring but stern at the same time.

And that's when it hits me. "I can't remember what happened because you did something to me. Your freaky vampire mojo. You know what, I don't want to talk. I can't stand to be in the same room as you." I shove him to the side and thankfully he lets me.

The front door is within reach when I hear him call my name. "Stay back." My hand flies out to stop him from getting closer. "Leave me alone." My fingers fumble with the lock. God damn locks and my jello fingers.

"Let me." Within seconds Maxwell is by my side, pushing my hands aside. He easily unlocks the door, but he doesn't open it. "Charlie, before you open that door, please know that I'm truly sorry and I hope one day you'll understand and forgive me. At best, let me explain."

My eyes glare at the floor. Tears threaten to flood my eyes, but I hold them back. Just as I'm about to look at him, he places his soft lips on my forehead. When I finally get the courage to stare back at him he's gone. With a grunt, I swing open the heavy wood door. The sunshine from the morning rays burst into the house. I hope I never have to come back to this place again. And the slam of the door behind me hopefully lets those two dead bodies inside understand that as well.

I make it home in record time. Even though no one was staring at me through their car windows and no one is out on my neighborhood streets, I still tug at the collar of my dress to hide the bite mark on my neck. Its throbbing feels as if it were sending out some fantasy sign to flash above my head. Look at me. Look at me. This one got bit by a vampire.

I don't remember much about last night, but Maxwell telling me that I'll be meeting The High Council in six days. Being a weekend I don't need to go into work, but while I'm gone I can't let Morgan be by herself. Maxwell didn't bother on telling me where we'll be going or for how long we'll actually be gone. I need to call in reinforcements, because I don't think Maxwell will just let me decline the invite.

"Hello."

"Good afternoon, Dave." I hear his laugh over the phone cutting off my greeting. The rumble that comes from a throaty chuckle puts a smile on my face momentarily.

"Charlie, what a pleasure to hear your voice. What can I help you with...you need me to come over and clean your pipes?" He never ceases to amaze me.

"I beg your pardon? I called to ask you if you would stay and help Morgan at the party that's this coming Saturday. I have to attend a very important meeting and I don't know if I'll be back in time."

"This meeting, is it a business meeting?" I could hear the curiosity in his voice. His tone let on that he thought otherwise.

I find my way to a mirror and carefully peel off the bandage to reveal two deep, nasty looking puncture marks. "Of course it's business, my life revolves around business." I feel bad for lying, but there's no way I could tell him that a vampire was taking me to be presented as his bride to a whole bunch of other scary ass vampires. I didn't want to go in the first place and I certainly don't want to talk about it.

Waiting for a response takes a toll on my nerves, especially when he remains silent for so long. "Listen, Morgan trusts you. You know my deadlines better than anyone does. You can keep the authority there without me being present." I speak professionally and unemotionally attached. Out of all the options I could have thought of, I result to calling Dave. An ex-boyfriend that I should hate to the core.

"Fine, but I need something in return," he replies.

However, I know that attitude. I'm all too familiar with that macho man tone.

"Go ahead." I now become the one that's curious.

"You let me take you out to dinner when you get back."

Crap. "Juliet and I are having a girls' night when I get back." It's the first thing that pops into my head. It's a totally false story, but it doesn't have to be.

"Do you plan on dying a few days after your return? I didn't put an expiration date on it, it just has to happen. Deal?" He remains persistent.

Nervous laughter exits my open mouth. I think about his words. For all I know I will die a few days after I get back. I can only hope I don't die while I'm there. "I guess I have to accept it if I want you to help Morgan...so I guess it's a deal." I could have sounded happier about it, but I'm anything but happy. Getting tricked into a date is the last thing I need right now.

We say our goodbyes. I keep the phone up to my ear and listen to the dial tone, not fully understanding the consequences of what I just agreed to. I don't know how I can turn down Dave gently without having to admit anything remotely close to a relationship with Maxwell. How can I tell someone that I'm stuck with a man I despise who is impacting my entire life...and afterlife?

As the day comes to a close and the sky gets darker my tolerance fades. I dig through my drawers in search of a permanent marker. With a blank sheet of paper in hand, I scribble down a few words. A smirk grows on my face as I tape it to the outside of the front door.

Trying to go about the rest of my night like a normal person, I take some leftovers out of the fridge for supper. My heart beats faster, my breathing deepens, and the muscles controlling my hands seem to weaken no matter how hard I try to ignore what's happened. What's happening. As it becomes darker outside the threat of Maxwell's appearance taunts me. With every little creak I hear, I become on edge.

When I hear unmistakable creaks coming from the front door, I freeze up. My mind's been playing tricks on me for a while now, so when I swear that I heard the porch steps creak from pressure of one's feet, I brush the accusation aside. However, my reflexes didn't convey what my brain was trying to tell it. Without warning, my numb fingers loosen on the plate I'm holding and I watch it fall to the tile kitchen floor in slow motion. The loud clatter as it shatters on the ground snaps me out of my nightmare. "Shit," I mutter to myself.

A loud sigh fills the room as I drop to my knees to pick up the bigger pieces; I clutch them in my hand as I try to gather as many shards as possible. There's no time to register the following events that unfold. All I know is that the front door crashes open and in a blur Maxwell is there standing in my kitchen, hovering over my kneeling body.

I squeeze my hands into fists at the mere sight of him. The sharp stabbing pain in my left hand breaks both of our silence. Maxwell kneels down beside me, cupping my bleeding hand in his. "Charlie, open your hand."

I look down to see red lines running down my arm and dripping on the floor. The broken pieces of the plate dig into my palm. Somehow, this fresh bleeding wound doesn't faze me as a constant sting attacks my neck, reminding me of the deep puncture marks the monster—that's trying to be caring—left behind. I would sit here for eternity, refusing to do as he says. Nonetheless, my hand opens up to reveal three pieces of china stuck into my skin.

"This may hurt," he says.

I'm not even sure I'm listening to him. The blood that runs down my hand stops my brain from working. All I can picture is Maxwell with a bloodstained mouth, lapping up the trails that continue to flow steadily. There's no additional warning as a sharp stab shoots up my arm from Maxwell yanking out plate piece after plate piece. The amount of time it took for me to jerk my hand away from him, all three pieces are already removed.

I stand up and hold my hand against my chest. The warm blood soaks through my shirt, but I'm determined to keep it away from him. His hands gently touch my elbow as he helps me to my feet and still touches me as he tries to keep me sturdy on my wobbly legs. I need answers and I need them now. I aggressively back away from him.

* * *

Maxwell

"Let me see your hand." More than anything I want to lecture her on her carelessness, but my voice comes out slow and calm in efforts to ease the situation.

"No. What the hell are you doing here? Did you not see my note or do you just not care. Haven't you done enough damage?" The disgust in her voice feels as though a knife is shredding my insides.

"I did read your hate letter and I was going to go, but then I heard a crash. Note or not I had to see if you were okay. I might have pushed you too far, but you're the one who's making yourself bleed all over the floor. Now let me see your hand."

"No!" she yells as she squares her shoulders all while blocking as much of her hand from view as she can manage.

I force breaths to tame my anger because my patience is wearing thin. "Charlie, right now, you might need stitches. Let me see your hand."

"Stitches, sure act as if you care that I might need stitches. Let's be honest with each other, I can see your blood thirsty stare that seems to be unable to break away from my bleeding hand." She shakes her injured palm in the air, drops of blood splattering to the ground. "This is all you're after, blood. This is all you care about, not me, just what's inside. You see it spilling out and you can't stop yourself from thinking what a waste."

"That is not true." And that is the truth. It might seem as if Charlie is nothing but an attractive walking talking blood bag, but she's more than that. "I know what I did was wrong and it's going to take some time to gain your trust, but you're more than blood to me. You mean more to me than my own survival. I'm on the verge of begging here, Charlie. Let. Me. See. Your. Hand." I walk slowly toward her as I speak. She doesn't back up or try to run away, she just stands there.

I grab her hand with the intention of examining her wound, but before my eyes can focus on the cuts beneath the oozing blood, I see her uninjured hand soar through the air. A slight sting radiates across my cheek as I allow her open hand to make contact with my face. "I deserved that." I see her hand swing again. The force makes my head turn to the side, but the pain becomes nonexistent. "I might have deserved that one as well."

When I see her hand go for a third hit I catch her at the wrist. "Enough. I get it, Charlie, you're mad…I get it. I'm mad at myself too, but you'll understand sooner or later that I did what I had to in order to keep you safe, in order for you to remain human for as long as you wish." I let go of her hurt hand to catch her knee that's in the process of getting ready to strike me as she refuses to hear my words.

"Charlie." The authority in my voice startles her. I push her knee down so she's standing on both feet again. I barely straighten my back before she rips her hand out of my grasp; with both hands in fists, she begins to pound on my chest. Her bloody palm leaves streaks on my shirt. Doing nothing but standing there allowing her to get her anger out, I tell myself I deserve every punch, every jab and I undeniably deserve to be called every foul name she mutters out.

As she grows tired, I catch her hands, pinning them against me. My eyes go to the bite mark on her neck and notice shiny spots of fresh blood line the small circles. She's been picking at it. She yanks one of her hands free once again and pulls the collar of her T-shirt up to cover her neck from view. Looking straight into her eyes, I can't help but to notice speckles of blood that cover her face. I can only assume mine does as well.

I lower her cut hand, opening it to reveal her sliced palm. "I don't think you need stitches, but it needs to be wrapped tightly to apply some pressure in order to stop the bleeding," I say after a few seconds.

"In the bathroom is some gauze. I'll go..." She takes long blinks, refusing to look at me.

"Let me." In the snap of one's fingers I arrive back at her side with the bandages. I ignore her shocked stare and gently grab her uninjured hand and lead her to the kitchen table so I can nurse her wounds. The silence in the room is broken as the microwave beeps, signaling that whatever is inside is done.

Barely touching her hand as I wrap the gauze bandaging several times around her palm is all I can do to try to make this mess better. She winces a few times when I pull the wrapping tight. As soon as I add a few pieces of medical tape to secure the end, she pulls her hand into her lap once again, hiding it from view.

"Why don't you go change and go to bed? I can clean this up," I offer.

"I'm sure you would love to clean up my spilled blood," she says in a cocky tone.

I cut her off before she begins her ranting again. "Charlie, not again."

"Am I becoming a vampire?" She struggles to say her last word as if it were poison in her mouth.

"No."

"Do not lie to me, Maxwell. You keep so many secrets and tell so many lies, for once be honest. I know you said some mumbo jumbo earlier about me staying human longer, but tell me the truth."

"Not yet. It takes more than a bite to turn a human. You're just weak from the blood loss. You need to eat and rest." I stand up, grabbing her elbow, pulling her to her feet. "I will plate your food and bring it to you. Just go lie down."

She gives me a skeptical look, wanting to refuse the offer, but I know she wants to lie down more than anything. I leave her once we reach the doorway to her room. The microwave continues to beep and I open the door, annoyed by the noise it keeps making. I pull out a steamy glass container that holds some kind of casserole. In search of a plate, I open cupboard after cupboard. After giving her enough time to change and crawl into bed, I make my way to her. Being a gentleman, I knock on the doorframe to signify my arrival.

Her small voice is barely audible. I walk in the dark room and place the plate on her lap, along with placing a glass of water on her nightstand. Without a word said, I leave her to eat while I go clean the blood. The temptation to lick any drops is overwhelming. Putting my index finger tip to my lips, I waver. If she spots any staining on my lips she'll know I did exactly what she said I wanted to do. I'm stronger than the pull of blood. I went one hundred years without an ounce of blood. I can wait a little longer.

I decide to go check on how she's managing her food. However, I barely make it through the doorway when I hear something wheezing through the air. As the sound gets louder, my fast reflexes react to the threat at hand. Effortlessly, I catch the empty plate just as it touches the tip of my nose. "Throwing things, Charlie." She doesn't stop keeping me on my toes, that's for sure.

The inhale and exhale of her breath fills the room, along with the disappointment that accompanies it. I assume it's to calm herself and keep her hateful words at bay. I allow her time to speak. "Just because I let you help me doesn't mean in the least that I forgive you even a little bit. You attacked me, Maxwell. You attacked me with intention. You had it all planned out and I had no other choice than to be the helpless victim."

"It's not like that. It's true that the party was a setup, but it was supposed to be fun. You were supposed to get to know Grace and a few other kind vampires that I've known many years." I see her squinty eyes glare at me, but if she's hell-bent on knowing why she became a victim I'm more than willing to tell her.

"Eugene, the man you saw me with at Junction 22 is on The High Council. He came up here to meet you. He was called back and since he didn't meet you due to your disrespect toward me, The High Council stepped in. They scheduled the presentation against my will. You do as they say, Charlie, or bad things happen."

I can hear her heart race. I know she has many questions, but the longer I stare at her ghostly pale face the more I listen to my better judgment. "We have plenty of time to discuss the cruel-hearted men that the council consists of later. Right now you need rest." With that said, I turn away and shut the door behind me without waiting for a response. One final stop at the kitchen sink to drop the plate off and then I head to the front door. She'll thank me soon enough.

It only takes a few minutes of walking down the bare streets before I reach the hotel. The cold breeze that whips through the trees doesn't faze me besides the obvious fact that it ruffles my hair, occasionally blocking my vision. The houses I pass on Charlie's block show just how oblivious the world really is. Lit windows showing carefree individuals cause regret to build up inside my dead body. I'm taking the bland human life away from Charlie and deep down I know she deserves better than a vampire's life, but I can't let her go. Selfishness is something I can't shake away.

Finally, entering my secluded room, I stay in the darkness. The only sound that fills the air is the drumming of my fingers and the low hum of the steady traffic from below. I pushed her too far and I'm not sure I can get her back. She was in my grasp and then The High Council had to push their authority on me. Now I'm barely able to keep her from slipping through my frantic fingertips.

Chapter Twelve

Charlie

I lean back in my chair behind my desk, thinking about how exactly I should tell Morgan that I'll be gone on a business trip for a length of time that I'm unsure of and that she's not able to come along. Her puppy dog stare is going to torture me, but she and I both will have to face disappointment.

I see her stand enthusiastically in the doorway. She almost skips to the chair in front of me. "Yes, Charlie."

"You're awfully happy today. Is there something I'm not aware of?"

"No, just stuff with James." She crosses her legs only to uncross them. She repeats this several times and after the third time I get annoyed. Her love-struck mood makes me want to gag. I place my hands on the desktop in front of me, intertwining my fingers.

"Oh my gosh. What did you do to your hand?" She gasps.

I see her extend her arm out as if to touch mine, but I slide my hands back onto my lap. "I broke a plate last night, nothing serious."

Morgan sucks in a breath and has a look of sheer horror on her face as she eyeballs me. "Your...your neck."

Shit. I forgot to cover my neck up.

"There's two holes that look like—"

I cut her off. "Oh, it's nothing. I went to the dermatologist about these sunspots I had. They cut them out, is all." I move my hair over my shoulder to cover the bite mark. "Listen, I called you in here to discuss something other than my wounds or how awful the party was on Saturday night."

"The party was bad how? What did I miss?" Morgan asks enthusiastically.

"Nothing that you needed to be there for. No police was called and no fights broke out. So it was just not the kind of style most of the parties I schedule have." The disappointment on her face is annoying. If she only knew. "Now, you've worked for me for a while now and I'm extremely grateful for your dedication. I could hope that one day you'll take over if anything were to happen to me."

"Oh my God, Charlie, are you dying?" Her face is horror-stricken and the concern in her voice makes my heart unintentionally skip. I find it comforting that she would be somewhat devastated if I died...more like when I die.

And the lies roll off my tongue. "No, I'm not dying. I have an important meeting on Friday that I have to attend. I won't be back in time for the party on Saturday. I called Dave yesterday and enrolled him to assist you."

"What meeting? I've been making most of your appointments." Here start the questions.

"I don't know much about it, because it was just sprung on me. I'll tell you all about it when I get back. Enough said about the topic." I know I'm being rude, but I want this conversation concluded before it even started.

Throughout the rest of the day at work I feel guilty. Morgan's ecstatic about her interpretation of a promotion. I don't know how she would react if I told her I didn't have a choice in giving her this believed promotion. The next couple of days go by slow.

Within an hour after telling Morgan of my supposed business trip I decide to leave. "Morgan, I'm heading out."

"Okay. I'll see you tomorrow," she says without looking at me.

As soon as I get home, I head straight into the kitchen to start my apology for Juliet. I bake a dozen chocolate cupcakes, frost them, and add my finishing touches. Bold letters in white frosting decorate the tops of a few of the tiny cakes. As I stare at the desserts lined up in a box, I read the message I spelled out. Sorry.

I close the lid and quickly return to my car. Being a Tuesday, Juliet is bombarded by her students' school work, so I know my visit will be unwanted, but yet much appreciated. I drive slowly, procrastinating my arrival. I've never been one to deliver bad news. Taking some well-deserved deep breaths, I gradually make my way to her front door. The time between when I ring the doorbell and her opening the door feels like eternity, but really is only a couple of seconds.

"Charlie, what are you doing here?" Surprise and concern show on her face. Now I know how I must have looked when she surprised me at my own house a few weeks ago.

"I made you cupcakes." I make my voice perky and gentle to ease into the disappointment she's in for.

She grabs the box and waves me inside. "What's going on?" Her bored tone throws me off guard. She's on to me.

"Nothing…well, not nothing, just something came up and I'm not going to be available to go to dinner and the club on Friday." I speak fast, hoping that my still chipper voice makes her less mad. Before she can reply, I race over to her and open the box, allowing her to read my message.

I view a hint of a smile on her face and I know she'll forgive me sooner or later. "I promise when I get back we can have a girls' night. You can come over and we can do each other nails or something. I'll even stock my pantry with your favorite food." My last word comes out in a singsong manner, trying to win her over. I wag my eyebrows at her, praying that she agrees and saves me the lecture.

"Apology accepted. Since you're here, care to organize some of my papers? It'll be part of your apology."

"Sure, only if I get a cupcake, though."

"I guess I can part with one," she replies as she places a large stack of paper in front of me. She quickly states what she expects of me and leaves the room. When she finally comes back she places a cupcake on the coffee table, one for each of us.

I hide a yawn as my body involuntarily stretches. Both of our attention is brought to the clock. "Holy crap, you've been here for three hours. I need sleep and so do you." Juliet claims.

I agree with her. My body aches as I stand up from hunching over the papers for so long. I've no idea how she can manage doing this all day. Like a good hostess, she walks me to the door, rubbing her own back as well.

"I'll call you when I get back." I wave profusely as I walk to my parked car.

I think about this expected presentation on Friday as I lie in bed trying to sleep. I keep telling people I'm leaving for a meeting and stating that I won't be back in time for certain events, but truly I don't know if we are even leaving the state. Maxwell's lecture about The High Council just makes me more fearful. I wrap the blankets tighter around me, praying that they give me extra comfort.

* * *

Maxwell

As soon as the sun set, I left Grace's house. I wanted to be as far away from there as Charlie did. But with a few days past, I have to go back. A bad mood accompanies me as I make final preparations for my unwanted trip. As if I own the house, I enter through the front door without knocking. The quietness that lingers within the halls is upsetting. Where is she, I say to myself as I search the first floor with no luck. However, the open patio door in the kitchen gives away her location.

I instantly spot Grace's pale body that seems to glow slightly in the darkening sky in a swimsuit with sunglasses on, lying on a lawn chair. "Do you think I can get a tan from the moon?" she asks as I stand alongside her.

"The moon's not even out yet." Is that why she's in a bikini? She's trying to get a tan?

"I know the moon's not out yet, you idiot, that wasn't the question. What do you want that's so important it can't wait for another day?" Annoyance distorts her voice.

"I need to ask you to do something."

"I made that poor girl hate me because of you, what more can I do to ruin a friendship I haven't even had a chance to build yet?"

I didn't even have to say that it involved Charlie. Grace is just that good that she already knew. "She's out of the house at the moment. I need you to go pack her luggage and bring it with you when you leave tonight."

"She can't pack her own bag why exactly?" Her cocky tone starts to irritate me.

"She thinks we're leaving Friday not tomorrow. She won't have time to pack. Just do it, Grace."

She jumps up from her lounge chair and gets in my face. "I can see why she doesn't like you very much. You owe me." With her hateful words spoken, she struts away to change.

"Remember to not touch anything that you don't need to. I don't need her to realize somebody was in her house," I say in her direction before she gets inside. The slam of the patio door is all I need for a response. I quickly leave to finish the plans I had scheduled for tonight.

Within a few minutes, I arrive at an apartment complex. A gentle knock is all it takes for the sound of footsteps to rush across the floor to the door. I took watching Charlie's life very seriously and with that dedication to find out as much about her as possible, I learned important factual information about those that surround her. Such as where Morgan lives. I get the sensation of the young assistant looking through the peephole in the door in front of me as Charlie did the night I told her about her future. Morgan, unlike Charlie, opens the door to greet me kindly.

"You're friends with Charlie, right?" she asks.

"You remember me?"

"How can I forget?" I see her blush as she admits something she wishes she didn't.

"You can call me Maxwell. I'm going to tell you something, but I need to know if you can keep a secret, Morgan?" She nods eagerly. "I'm going to keep our Charlie company on her trip, but I'm surprising her by leaving tomorrow instead of Friday like she assumes we are. I just wanted to inform you of the change and ask you to keep it a secret. Can you do that for me?"

I watch her jitter as she tries to find her words. I might not be able to influence her as I can with Charlie, but apparently Charlie is unaware of my charm. "Of course I can. She'll be angry at first, but she'll love it."

"I'm sure she will...and thank you. I'm positive we'll see each other again." I walk away satisfied. Morgan's words are spot on, Charlie will be angry. However, I'm not sure she will love any aspect of the trip.

With Grace packing Charlie's bag and Morgan aware of the soon absence of Charlie, all I have to do now is wait until the sun sets tomorrow. I go back to the hotel and count down the hours.

Chapter Thirteen

Charlie

Morgan acts strangely at work the next day. She constantly smiles in my direction as if she knows something I don't. Every time I try to talk to her she scampers off claiming to be busy or she pretends to be on the phone. She still doesn't admit to hiding anything even after the phone rings loudly in her ear, catching her in her lies.

In order to ignore her peculiar behavior, I stay in my office. I was planning on staying late to get as much work done as possible to make up for my departure, but at six o'clock Morgan leaps through my doorway. Her booming voice that fills the room causes me to fumble my pen as my body convulses in a tremor from fear. She runs over to my desk, piling up all my papers, insisting that I head home. My brain barely has time to register what's going on before she starts pushing me out of my own chair.

"What's going on, Morgan? You've been acting weird all day. You're not having your boyfriend over here again, are you?" Keeping some authority in my tone, I intend on scaring her into telling me her secrets.

She shrugs her shoulders. "No. I would never have him here again after you specially stated not to. Just go home, get some rest, and I'll see you later." She winks at me as she holds the messy pile of papers in her arms.

I guess authority isn't going to work with this situation. Not wanting to be smothered with her eagerness, I heed her words and home.

What's that girl hiding, I ask myself on my drive

home. The sun starts to set by the time I walk through the front door. Even though Morgan forced me to leave the office, I have to admit that I'm quite tired and relieved to be home. First thing first, pajamas followed by food, followed by mind-numbing TV. Midway through my evening plans, things take a turn for the worse with the sound of a familiar voice.

"Do you seriously find this show funny?"

Leaping up from the couch, my empty bowl falls to the floor. A shameless yelp escapes my gaping mouth. I turn around to face Maxwell with my eyes closed and slowly huff in response. His bland words imply he's unimpressed by my lifestyle or mere interests in human things for that matter. Somehow, almost accidentally my brain connects the dots from Morgan's odd behavior at work earlier today to this unexpected arrival of Maxwell.

"I'm going to ignore that and ask two questions of my own. First, why are you here exactly? Second, why do you think you can come into my home whenever you please? My house is absolutely not your house." Irritation distorts my words.

"I'm here to pick you up; we have a plane to catch within the hour." There's a twitch of his upper lip as if he wanted to smile, but thought better of it.

My eyes get bigger as I take in what he's saying, completely dumbfounded at his words. "Plane?" I know I must sound like an idiot with my one word response and my bulging eyeballs.

"Yes, plane, Charlie. We're leaving for the presentation; remember I told you about this days ago."

"What? You told me that it wasn't until six days. That's Friday, Maxwell. Not today." My arms sail through the air in disbelief. Even though I'm flabbergasted by his behavior once again, my mouth continues to ramble on. "There you go with your lies again. Would it kill you to be honest?" I'm furious…no, I'm more than furious. The need to punch him again washes over me.

"You can express your anger and I'll plead for forgiveness when we're in the air." He sounds bored as he blandly pleads with me. "Now, please get ready, we have to go."

"I have to pack."

"No need. Grace stopped by while you were out and packed for you. It's already at the hotel waiting for us."

The slow grind of my teeth blocks out the buzz of anger that lingers in my eardrums. I'm sure he can hear it, but to make sure he knows how I feel exactly, I show him my lovely middle finger before entering the bedroom. Grumbling silently to myself, I pull on a pair of jeans and a top.

Just as I slam my closet doors shut, Maxwell graces me once again with his unamused voice. "Dress warm."

I reopen the doors and grab a cardigan as well as a jacket, slightly mumbling his words, mocking him and his so called sincerity.

"May I ask where it is that we are going or is that a secret too?" My attitude turns sour and I'm not sure that it'll get any better.

"Rattenberg." He takes in my confused stare. "Rattenberg, Austria. We have an over nine hour flight ahead of us."

Yup, not getting any better. "Austria…the vampire council lives in Austria." I stop in front of the door, trying to wrap my mind around what's so wonderful about Austria.

Maxwell strides alongside me. "Rattenberg is very unique. The Rattenberg mountain blocks the small town from the sun's rays in the Winter season and even in the other seasons sunlight is very limited. It's the perfect place for vampires to live a semi-normal life. Now let's go, we can't be late." His strong fingers encompass my upper arm and lead me toward the door.

Great, three things I just love will surround me: coldness, no sunlight, and tons of bloodsuckers. The slam of the front door ruins my train of thought, but as we stand outside on my front porch, I struggle slightly against his grip. We remain standing facing each other and I begin to think that he's about to lecture me on something, but it turns out to be much worse. He pulls a key out from his pocket with his free hand and locks the deadbolt on the front door. I give him a questioning look, but before I have a chance to say anything, he places his index finger up to my lips to hush me. "We don't have time right now."

I slap his hand away and scold him anyways. "You stole my key. Who the hell do you think you are? We don't have time my ass, we have all the time in world," I yell as he drags me down my driveway. I almost don't realize that we're completely past my car.

We reach the end of the driveway and a black vehicle comes into view. "I arranged for a driver." He opens the door for me and I enter, as if I have a choice.

The fear from flying and The High Council make the car ride seem like forever. The churn of my stomach along with the nervousness of meeting all these new 'different' people keep me silent on the drive to wherever it is that we're going. Not to mention being in such close proximity to Maxwell puts my nerves on edge. Admitting that I'm attracted to him makes the sickness that burrows in my gut even worse.

I have no idea if I was holding my breath, but when the car finally comes to a stop, I inhale deeply. Jumping out immediately, I gulp the fresh night air as if I would never breathe it again. The scenery before me is anything but what I expected. We're not in an airport parking lot.

I must have a shocked expression on my face, because Maxwell feels the need to explain. "Did you think we would be taking a regular plane? I can't take the chance that we would come across daylight on the way there."

The anxiety that I had before is now tripled in size. "Umm, yeah. You mean to tell me that this is a vampire owned airplane."

"Council owned airplane." Is all he says before he walks away, entering the plane without me.

My heart skips a beat and my breath hitches as I try to catch up to him. My chest begins to constrict, thinking about being left alone with so many vampire employees. I enter inside the dimly lit interior, instantly becoming off guard as I see a few of the seats occupied. They barely lift their heads to acknowledge me and that's fine by me.

The slap of my hand from covering my mouth is louder than I intended it to be, but as I pass a young girl whose forearm is sliced open, I become repulsed. She bends it so the trail of blood drips into a large container. I must have come to a stop in front of them, because the man that's dressed in a business suit looks up to meet my eyes with a smile on his face. A smile that doesn't sit well with me as his fangs push against his lower lip.

Almost in a trance from such horrific behavior, I don't notice Maxwell striding up to me before it's too late. Yet again his fingers harshly grip my upper arm and yank me away from the scene. My head bobs from the force. "Staring, Charlie," he whispers to me as he waves his hand to the row we're to sit in. I'm surprised he didn't throw me into my seat.

"I didn't mean to, it was just so awful I became horror-struck. Maxwell." I hate how many times he says my name. Goosebumps break out across my skin from the sound of his voice saying those few letters. In efforts of disturbing him as much as he disturbs me, I say his name in return, hoping that one day he'll understand how annoying it truly is. I sit down in the window seat, although there's no difference in my seat compared to the aisle seat since there's no window to make it an actual window seat. A quick cross of my arms, I refuse to talk the whole way to Rattenberg.

Plane rides are almost like car rides. If they're long enough drowsiness takes over. Although there's no way in hell I'm falling asleep on this plane. I wish I would've remembered my iPod to block out the thoughts that scream in my head. Music numbs the soul and right now everything needs numbing.

Lightly, Maxwell's cold elbow nudges me. I wither into my own seat, trying to get farther away from him. My eyes catch a glimpse of his extended hand. Don't smile, Charlie, do not smile. I don't want to, because giving him the satisfaction will somehow give him the upper hand, but my God he is a savior. With what I hope to be lightning fast reflexes, my hand jolts out to grab my iPod from his clutch, instantly placing the ear buds in my ears.

He leans in close. "You're welcome," he says before I get the songs to start playing. I put a phony smile on my face and crank the volume up. I have no idea when or how he came to have it, but deep down I'm extremely grateful and I let the argument that would've went on between us fade away as a thank you.

The bumpy landing indicates that my hours of being trapped on a plane with a whole bunch of vampires and their drones has ended. I'm expecting to look at something similar to a cabin in the middle of nowhere surrounded by hills of white or rundown centuries old buildings, but when I depart the plane there's no buildings in sight. At all.

"We're a few minutes away from the hotel. Just a short car ride and we'll be there," Maxwell reassures me.

I shiver from the coldness as we make our way to a waiting car. I'm not all too familiar with the weather in Austria, but the air is crisp and the ground has a light coat of snow covering it. Maxwell wraps his arm around my shoulder to shield some of the cold air that eats at my warmth. "As if your ice-cold body could warm me up. I mean really, it's like hugging a snowman," I say as I shrug my shoulders in efforts of knocking his arm off.

I see the disappointment in his eyes as he occasionally glances at me and just like that I start to regret my words. What am I thinking, screams in my head. Clearing my mind takes priority over everything else. I try to think about something other than hurting Maxwell's ego and feeling bad about it, but the nagging feeling doesn't go away. Almost in a daze, I enter the car. No words come out of my mouth on the way to the hotel.

The sky is dark and the shadow of a large mountain that lurks just beyond the many rows of houses and buildings makes the sky look even darker. The few houses or businesses we pass shine brightly. Each one is in weathered condition, three stories tall, and narrow. Within seconds you feel like you're in the old world. The buildings start to get fewer and dense forest makes everything else disappear, which only makes the hotel look more glamorous once it comes into view.

Spotlights shine onto the building as well as illuminate from inside. It's massive in size as several wings go off in different directions. Garden like sitting areas have snow covered benches, cute trees, and statues that line the building. Such a place doesn't look like it would belong somewhere with no sunlight, or in a place that looks to be centuries old.

My eyes slightly bulge as I look at the woman behind the counter. She's dressed in very German looking attire with a billowed sleeved white shirt under a tight lace-up black corset vest. She greets us with a wide smile on her face. "Willkommen in Rattenberg Posthotel. Was führt Sie zwei Liebe Vögel hier?"

A hum of confusion slips through my lips. I didn't realize that no one would be speaking English here.

"Sie spricht nur Englisch," Maxwell says back to the woman. The foreign language flows effortlessly off his tongue.

"Englisch. Ja," the clerk replies directly to me.

"Yes. English."

In a heavy accent she could possibly repeat what she already asked. "What brings you two love birds here to the Rattenberg Hotel? Anniversary? Honeymoon?"

It's extremely hard to understand her, but as she talks to me as if I were a child, I understand fully what she's getting at. An abrupt unexpected cough bursts from between my lips at her words. Spit lodges itself in the wrong pipe, causing me to have a coughing fit. Gasping for breath, my hands grope my throat as if it would help the oxygen in.

"Are you okay, love?" Maxwell asks with sheer compassion.

I give him the most evil stare I can muster at the moment since I can't find my voice.

He turns back to the woman behind the counter. "She'll be fine. We're here on business. Aber es gibt immer Zeit für ein wenig Romantik." Maxwell tries to hide a wink, but I catch it. And when they burst out laughing it just makes it worse.

Deciding not to be the butt of the joke anymore, I walk away. How could I not realize that people would be speaking a different language? I feel like a fool and just a few seconds ago I looked like a fool too.

The laughing stops with my retreating body. "The reservation is under Barnett."

"Elevator is around the corner and the two of you have a pleasant stay here." I keep my back to the lady. I bite my tongue to keep my hateful words to myself about her ridiculous outfit. As many more staff passes me, I understand that each employee has to wear it against their will, but I was angry that they were laughing at my incompetence of only being able to speak English.

Maxwell's arm goes around my waist. "This way, love."

"You know I'm only letting you touch me because people are staring." A phony smile plays across my lips as other guests pass us by.

"Understood."

Standing outside the elevator doors waiting for them to open seems as if time becomes still. A mixture of words rattle off in my head as the elevator travels up to the appropriate floor. Trapped. Liar. Bloodsucker. Run. Relax and breathe never once popped up. Before the metal doors open Maxwell looks at me with pleading eyes. "In your dreams," I say in a rough raspy voice. No mile high club and absolutely not whatever making out in an elevator is called either.

"Is something bothering you, Charlie?"

"Just a little taken back by the fact that no one's native language is English."

"We're in Austria. Their native language is

German. Most people know English, so it shouldn't be a problem."

"And you just so happen to be fluent in German."

"I'm fluent in many languages, Charlie. Maybe if you sat down and had an honest, civil conversation with me, you would know that."

Burn. And it stings, but the sting doesn't last long.

"An honest, civil conversation? Well, let me see." I rub my chin and stare him down. "Firstly, none of our conversations are honest, because you are the one who's not honest. You either flat out lie or keep crucial details secret."

"Secrecy is not lying," Maxwell interrupts.

"Close enough. And that last time we had a civil encounter, which should have been at that party I was hired to do, ended up with you taking a bite out of my neck. So I'm sorry if I can't be civil with you. You fiend."

"You have a point."

"Damn right I have a point." Just then the elevator dings, signaling that we reached our floor.

Silently, we walk down the deserted hall to our room. Maxwell must be scorned by my honesty and I'm too furious at his stupidity to talk to him. He opens the door to a room halfway down the hall and bows his head, urging me to enter. Suck up.

Nervousness, anxiousness, not to mention the jitters wash over me unwillingly. The minute I stepped foot on Austria ground I've been a total wreck. I don't know if it's the impending meeting with The High Council, the close confines with Maxwell, or being in a country that one way or another can't help me if they tried.

Entering the large kitchen like space, I begin to wonder if we have separate rooms…we better.

"You should go change and rest. We're going to

have some busy days ahead of us," Maxwell says, catching me off guard. He struts past me to the living room. I watch him casually drop himself onto the couch.

"Days? How many days?" I screech.

"We'll arrive back home Sunday evening." His calm voice sends chills yet again down my spine. He's so laid back about being here for three days, not to mention that we're here a day early. I want more than anything to shake some sense into him as he lies there with his arms crossed behind his head.

I mock his carefree tone and walk through the closest door. Thank goodness it's the bedroom. Unfortunately, since I found the bedroom right away I have no idea if there's another one. The large spacious room is just as gorgeous as the rest of the hotel. I see my luggage off to the side, but when I see it beside a bag I don't recognize my chest tightens. Spinning around ready to stalk into the living room to see if there's another bedroom, I slam into Maxwell.

I rub at my nose. "There's another room, isn't there?"

He shakes his head.

"You've got to be kidding me." I stomp away toward my luggage; I pick it up aggressively and throw it on the bed, snickering to myself as I unzip it.

In the corner of my eye, I see Maxwell leaning up against the doorframe. Like a mad woman my hands dig and dig into the suitcase. "You said Grace packed this bag?"

"Yes. Why?"

Article after article of perfectly folded clothing becomes a mess as I continue to search for some clothes that could pass for pajamas. "Grrraaacccee!" I hiss.

* * *

152

Maxwell

"Something wrong?" I ask. The irritation in her voice as she yells Grace's name is more than humoring to my ears.

"Something wrong...something wrong! This is what's wrong, Maxwell." She pulls out a skimpy nightgown that's mostly see-through. "You had something to do with this, didn't you? She packed lingerie as my pajamas. First there's only one bed and now this."

"I just instructed her to pack what was necessary, not what I would want." The effort I have to put forth in not smiling or laughing takes a great deal, but I remain calm and unfazed by Grace's joke. I walk up to her and place the thin fabric between my fingers. A smile spreads across my face, ruining my demeanor. I can't help the words from slipping out of my mouth. "You had this in your drawers?" My eyebrow perks up in speculation, wondering if I'm missing some crucial piece of information. "And who did you plan on wearing it for? Or should I say who have you worn it for?" Curiosity is killing this cat.

Her hand rips the fabric out of my grip as her left hand punches me in the shoulder. She whimpers in pain, cradling her injured hand while I stand there insulted, but pain free. Flexing her hand to ease the pain, we both notice faint red smudges start to deepen in color as the wounds from her bone crushing grip on broken plate pieces begins to bleed. Her words are forced through what I assume to be stinging pain. "For your information, these aren't mine."

She holds the tiny fabric up by its brand new tags. "Huh." Is all I say before I walk away to let her change.

"Care for a pillow? A blanket maybe?"

153

"For what reason exactly?" I know what she's getting at, but I decide to give her hopes that she is going to get what she wants. Which she isn't.

"For you to be more comfy on the couch, you idiot." Even though she's resulting to name calling, the anger that should have been in her voice isn't there.

"No need, love."

"Oh, there is need...love." The disgust as she calls me love is classic and I'll never forget the roll of her eyes and the sneer of her lips as she said it. "You are sleeping on the couch," she adds to make her point even more clear.

"Oh yes, I am. I mean, especially after I know you're going to be wearing that." I can't help but laugh. For the first time in a long time a laugh rushes out through my hard lips and for a second I'm carefree and relaxed.

This little bickering between us is getting me more excited than it should. Her stick straight posture with her hands on her hips in disapproval is highly entertaining. Her cheeks are starting to flush from embarrassment, but her eyes give that infamous evil glare, so I offer an alternative. "You can always wear one of my T-shirts. Think of it as a nightshirt."

"Hahaha, you would get turned on more if I were to wear your shirt." Her fake laugh only makes me smile wider.

"You're probably right. Take your time on deciding what to sleep in while I go and thank Grace...I mean, go and lecture Grace about her terrible judgment. I'll be back in a few minutes." I strut out of the room, holding back my laughter the whole way to Grace.

After three soft knocks on her door, I lean against the wall across the hall until she opens it. The need to smile or laugh at Grace's outrageous behavior eats at me, but I remain serious. "You're not making it any easier on yourself to start this so called friendship up with Charlie. She's furious with her nighttime apparel."

"You ruined that already, so she'll have to learn to like me for the vampire I am. She hates me already, so I should make her hate me a little more before I reel her in with the best friend talk. Plus, it's only a nudge."

"It's more like a shove than a nudge."

"Fine, I shoved. It's not like she's not bound to shove back. Now you tell me what was the bloody gauze about in her trashcan, friend. The smears looked like slices." Her attitude changes instantly. She might claim to be a very good friend to me, but she cares for Charlie just as much as I do.

"She cut herself on a broken plate Sunday evening. She's fine." I'm not going to tell her that she cut it due to my presence. "What time is the meet and greet tomorrow?"

"Noon, in conference room number four."

"Well, I really should be going. I'll see you tomorrow, and fair warning, watch out for Charlie." I nod my head and with a slight smile, I exit the room.

I purposely leave Grace early in hopes of catching Charlie before she goes to bed. The sound of her humming in the bathroom fills the suite. Sneaking around the corner, I can't help but to spy on her. The sight of her in the same see-through lingerie she was tossing around earlier is all I can see. My eyes can't seem to tear away from her nearly naked body dancing around as she brushes her teeth. For someone who hated the concept of wearing that particular piece of clothing she sure seems happy in it.

Her scream pierces my eardrums and most likely all occupants in the nearby rooms when she catches me watching her. "Holy shit, Maxwell." Her hands grope her own body, trying to cover up all the bare spots. "Are you spying on me?" she demands. Before I have a chance to answer, she shrieks at me again. This time it's more agitated than frightened. "Would you stop looking at me?"

I look at the ground to make her feel better. What she doesn't know is that I will see her in that again.

Either making light of the situation or making it worse, I pull my T-shirt off as well. Instantly she becomes even more uncomfortable as she takes in my bare chest. Her heartbeat increases and just like that I get antsy from the sound of her quickening pulse. Disappointingly, at some point in time when my eyes were on the ground, she grabbed a towel to cover herself up.

"I'm just getting ready for bed." I sit on the edge of the mattress, slowly taking my socks off and then stand briefly to take my pants off. Folding them in my hand, I toss them to a nearby chair, followed by gradually crawling under the blankets without giving Charlie a second glance. Trying to make her more comfortable, a flick of the light leaves the room completely black. "Are you coming?"

"I think I'll sleep on the couch," she says before tiptoeing toward the door.

"Charlie, I promise I won't bite. Just lie down and get some rest." I make my words sound like a plea.

A groan comes out of her mouth, putting yet another smile on my face. I have no idea if she realizes that I can see her as clear as day in the unlit room, but I have no intention of informing her of that. Secrets are not lies.

She throws a temper tantrum like a toddler in the open doorway as she struggles with accepting the offer. Her feet stomp wildly and her hands ball into fist only to swing at the air. Amongst the battle between herself, she loses the towel. The sight of this grown woman barely clothed throwing a fit is more than hysterical. Taking her time, she gathers up the towel from the floor and waves it through the air in a manic frenzy. A cracking whip from it slapping against the doorframe doesn't stop her from continuing and it's the whip of it striking the edge of the bed that causes me to choke on a laugh.

She stops in her tracks, staring wide-eyed at me. "You can see me, can't you?" Her voice sounds extremely agitated.

"Just a little bit." I'm unable to make my words sound believable.

"Maxwellllll!" she growls.

"What? You…you sounded as if you needed to relieve some tension, so I kept my mouth shut. Are you ready for bed now? It seems you got your exercise in for the day." I feel the blankets lift up to my side, accompanied by warmth that radiates off her body. She harshly tosses and turns before she finally turns her back to me, snuggling her head into the plush pillow.

"Oh, for future reference, when my mouth is closed it doesn't always mean that my eyes are. Can you remind me in the morning to thank Grace?" I know my words don't comfort her, but I couldn't help it.

The sound of the slap as her hand hits my bare chest echoes throughout the room. "Could you at least pretend that it hurts?"

"Oh, the pain," I say as blandly as possible.

"You're a terrible actor."

"And you're any better?" I grow curious at her statement. I'm most likely thinking too much into it, but maybe she's coming around after all.

"Have an awful night, Maxwell." There's no sign of laughter or humor in her voice.

"Goodnight to you too, Charlie." The conversation ends after my final words are spoken. Usually, she needs to have the last word, but after what just happened, I'm sure she's done for the night. Therefore, I just lie in bed fully awake, thinking about the partially naked girl next to me, completely unable to sleep...as if I could. The sun's setting and this is a vampire's prime time.

Chapter Fourteen

Charlie

"Charlie…Charlie, wake up." I ignore Maxwell's whispers by burying my head into my pillow. His voice sounds too close for comfort, but when my forehead is scratched by something that feels similar to facial stubble I freeze up.

My mind analyzes the scene before my body starts moving. My head's not nuzzling into a pillow, it's snuggling into Maxwell's shoulder. As the feeling to the rest of my body starts to perk up, I find myself curled up against his cold rock hard body all the way to my toes. My arm drapes across his bare chest, my leg intertwined with his. What seems like minutes, but most likely is mere seconds later, I leap backward, swearing under my breath.

My body over jumps and is on the verge of falling out of bed altogether, but Maxwell's strong grip pulls me fully back onto the mattress. "What did I do?" I point to myself in shame and immediately blame him instead. "What did you do?" But the blame settles on my shoulders as I contemplate if I actually could have done something. "Please tell me I didn't do anything stupid. That you didn't make me do something we both regret again." My head falls into my hands, afraid to look at him. I swear I didn't do a thing, but as my mind races. Trying to recall last night, I come up empty-handed.

"I didn't do what you think I might have done. I let you sleep. What is that you think you've done?" He winks at me with a large smile on his face, which part of me finds repulsive, while another part finds sexy.

I whip the blankets off me, refusing to remain this close to him. Standing alongside the bed, I point my finger at him. "Just because I wake up draped over you doesn't mean a thing."

He nods with skeptical eyes, not believing a word I'm saying.

"Will. Not. Happen," I yell as I walk around the bed to the bathroom.

"What if I told you that you said you loved me? What would you have to say then?"

I have no idea if he's telling the truth or not. I mean, I can't remember a single thing that happened last night because I was so tired. For all I know I did say those words in my deep sleep, but I'm not going to admit that. "Then I would have to call bullshit. Maybe you were the one dreaming last night."

"Well, if I was dreaming, I would have to admit that my dreams came true when you woke up in my arms. Although, if you were talking in your sleep, your dreams must have been fairly strong to force you to rub up against me. Either way it proved to be a pleasant morning." He barely finishes his sentence before his laugh grows stronger.

"You're not going to let this go, are you?" An answer isn't necessary, but I still have to ask it.

"Not in the least." Without warning, he turns on the bedside lamp. The smile that is on his face makes me stumble into the doorframe of the bathroom. His sharp fangs glisten in the light. They seem to mock me as I stare at them. Then I remember I'm in Grace's opinion of sleepwear.

"Hungry this morning, are we?" I say before quickly turning into the bathroom and slamming the door. My head thumps against it in defeat. A groan of agony fills the large room as I realize that my clothes are out there. I stay in the room for as long as possible, but eventually I gather my composure and slowly open the door. The light is still on, but Maxwell is nowhere to be seen. Instantly, I start my pursuit to my suitcase, tiptoeing as fast as possible.

The blood in my head drains, leaving me lightheaded, and I stop dead in my tracks as I hear Maxwell's voice coming from the living room area. All I hear is him thanking someone as I take the last few steps to my luggage. With the suitcase in hand, I turn around, ready to race back to the confines of the bathroom, but my luck runs out.

"I see you finally left the bathroom. Your breakfast arrived."

"Breakfast? You ordered me breakfast and it miraculously got delivered in the matter of minutes?" I don't believe his lie.

He walks out of view only to return with a tray full of food. "I had breakfast scheduled for delivery before we arrived. Now change and have something to eat because I have to discuss something with you." He walks away, leaving me alone in the room.

The clothes were perfectly folded in the bag before I went crazy on them last night. It takes a while, but I settle on a pair of jeans and a sweater before heading into the living room.

I see Maxwell lounging on the couch, pretending to pay attention to some TV show. Without turning around to face me, he tells me to eat and join him when I'm finished. All I can do is pick at the food to start with, but with one bite at a time the plate gets emptier than I expected. My head drops in acknowledgment that I have to have a serious conversation with him. My heart gets heavy just thinking about what it could possibly be about.

Leaving a cushion between us, I wait for him to speak first. Not to my surprise, he moves closer to me. He takes my injured hand in his and gently rubs at the bandage. "I'm truly sorry about this," he says, looking at the white gauze that wraps around my hand.

"That's what you wanted to tell me? You're sorry for busting into my house and making me accidentally cut myself? You're forgiven. Is that what you want to hear? I'll say it just so you'll stop with the pity party." I'm forced to keep my hand in his because his hold gets a little tighter when I try to sneak out of his grip.

"No. We have a meet and greet today at noon and I need you to be on your best behavior."

"Best behavior! What am I, your dog?" I interrupt.

"Let me finish," he says with a hint of anger in his voice. I lower my head, taken aback by his harshness. "Charlie…I'm sorry, it's just that The High Council will be present and I need them to like you. You need them to like you."

His free hand goes under my chin and lifts my head up until our eyes meet. "Can you do that? You need them on your side, you need them to believe that you love me and that one day you would love to become a vampire. If they sense any type of betrayal or hostility before or during the presentation tomorrow, things could not go in our favor."

I can sense the fear and regret from Maxwell. If he's scared of The High Council, I definitely should be. "Fine," I reluctantly say.

"Why don't you practice? Try talking positively about me. How about you try telling me you love me?"

"I said fine; don't push your luck. You want me to trust you, so why don't you do it in return?" I stand up and stalk away. I have no idea what this meet and greet is all about, but I pray that I get through it alive.

I go back to the bedroom. With nothing better to do, I look at the clothes Grace packed for me. I'll admit she does have good taste. A light tap on the door before it opens a crack lets me know that my alone time is ticking down.

"You should get ready." Is all he says before he shuts the door behind himself.

My heart starts to race and my hands unwillingly become sweaty, so sweaty that I have to change my bandages because they're becoming damp. It takes a shorter amount of time than I would've liked, but with the most attractive dress in the suitcase and my hair cascading over my shoulders, I exit the room. "How much time is left before we have to leave?" I ask Maxwell, whose back is toward me.

He turns around, staring at me in what I assume to be approval. "You look—"

"Save it. When do we have to leave?" I don't want or need his compliments. My nerves are on overload and I just want this to be over with. There's absolutely no room for any jitters or excitement Maxwell will add by expressing how I look in his eyes. I can handle Maxwell, but a whole room of vampires is more than I can manage.

"We should leave now if we don't want to be late." He walks to the door and opens it for me.

The halls appear to be empty as we walk side by side. Once we reach a certain point, he suddenly loops my arm around his. My injured hand rests on his forearm and his large hand instinctively rests on top of it. "Here we are. Are you ready?"

"No, but let the madness begin," I say in the best happy voice I can muster up. My nerves are a jumbled mess right now and the feeling as though I could throw up at any second keeps me from saying anything further.

We walk into the full conference room with nothing but pleasant looks on our faces. Maxwell leads us through the crowd of bodies. A wave of belief rushes through me as I see living, breathing human beings mixed throughout the room. Sadly, stiff pristine vampy bodies overpopulate the room.

"Breathe," Maxwell whispers as he leans in my direction.

I don't even notice that I'm not breathing. Each forced breath I take matches the aimless steps forward. Nowhere ready to talk to anyone, we come to a stop. Grace's face comes into view. She has a polite smile across her lips. More than anything I want to yell at her for the trap she set for me, but I have to be pleasant and caring, so I kindly smile back at her.

"I'm sorry about what I did. I hope you can forgive me," Grace says as she lays her hand on top of my shoulder.

"Maybe," I say blandly. I know I'm supposed to be happy and what not, but I can't help the bitterness that fills my voice.

"You're quite the rebellious one. I have a pleasant feeling that we're going to get along just fine." She laughs, finding humor in something that I must be oblivious to.

"There are many introductions to be had. We'll talk to you later, Grace," Maxwell says in the most businesslike manner.

The show is about to start, I say to myself and in a trance, I follow Maxwell's lead through the people, only stopping or greeting individuals Maxwell acknowledges.

"Care for something to drink?" he asks me.

I numbly nod in response. He turns away, but I clutch his arm tighter, refusing for him to leave me. I've never been one to be frightened in being surrounded by strangers, but this is too much…this is too scary.

He wraps his arm around my waist and whispers in my ear, "You'll be fine; no one is going to hurt you." With that said, he breaks my grip and walks away.

I barely have time alone to assess the room before three happy-go-lucky humans approach me. I smile in return at their excited expressions. One of the two young men is the first to introduce himself. He extends his hand. "I'm Aiden." I shake his hand in compliance. His free hand goes to his chest as to point to himself. He then points to the young woman next to him. "This is Paige and this is Eddie." His hand then lands on the second young man.

"Nice to meet all of you. My name is Charlie." My voice comes out as if I'm a robot on autopilot, but I can't help the nervousness that continues to consume me. I mentally shake myself. These people are happy about becoming a vampire, happy to be with a vampire.

"So you're the reason we're all here. You're the one being presented as Maxwell's bride," Paige spews out.

"Paige, get a hold of yourself," Eddie says through clenched teeth as he jabs Paige with his elbow.

"You know Maxwell?" I ask, growing very curious.

"Paige here has had a crush on Mr. Barnett for a few years now. She would kill to be in your shoes," Aiden informs me.

"Since I can't physically be in your shoes, I'll have to settle for the next best thing." She cheers. She nearly knocks me off my feet as she throws herself on top of me. She crushes me in a hug.

I pat her back gently, praying that she'll let go…soon.

She holds me out at arm's length. The sudden moment causes my head to bob. "We'll just have to be BFFs."

What? She wants to be best friends. Not what I was expecting to happen out of this meet and greet, but it's way better than what I did have in mind. I smile profusely at her as I pry her hands off me.

"Is there a problem?" Maxwell asks, walking up behind me with my drink in his hand. He wraps his free arm around my shoulders, looking over the three people who stand in front of him.

"No, I just made some friends. Who would have thought that would happen." I turn toward him until my back is to the three sets of eager eyes. I lean in close, pretending to fix Maxwell's tie. "Let me fix your tie, honey," I say in a fake nurturing tone. Looking up to meet his eyes, I mouth the words 'help me' before turning back around, grabbing the glass from him.

"Well, we have a lot of people to meet still, so we must be going," Maxwell says toward Paige mostly. I watch her eyes slowly blink in admiration. Give me a break, I huff to myself.

We make it a whole two steps before Aiden's voice stops us. "Charlie, we were going to ask if you would like to join us in the restaurant for a bite to eat tonight. We don't get to meet a lot of other…" He pauses, searching for the right word.

"Blood donors," I say for him.

"Yes, that exactly," he says through a laugh.

I never thought I would ever have a conversation that consists of calling people blood donors, but I guess there's always a first time for everything, and I can't wait for this first time to done with. "Sure, I'll scamper down at seven, how about?"

They all nod with joy and I thankfully walk away. I down the glass of whatever it is that Maxwell brought me.

"Nervous much?" he asks as he takes the empty

glass away from me.

I'm more than willing to reply, but we come to a standstill once again as a man comes to block our path. I stare at the familiar face before me.

"Maxwell, it's so nice to see you again. And you must be Charlie." He turns his gaze on me as he extends his hand to shake.

Wide smile. Check. "The one and only. You must be Eugene." Pleasurable tone to my voice. Check.

* * *

Maxwell

"I'm so sorry that I wasn't able to meet you when you were in town. I'm quite the busy girl back at home." The fake tone in her voice is nerve-racking and I can only hope he doesn't pick up on it.

Eugene stands there for a few seconds without saying anything. I grow weary waiting for him to reply. "Are you sure we haven't met before? You look familiar."

Charlie instantly becomes tense as we both come to the same conclusion; he remembers seeing her at Junction 22. "I don't think so. I would've remembered meeting such a handsome man as yourself."

I pull her closer to me, almost crushing her. She pats my chest, reassuring me that she has this under control, but I'm not sure her flirting can get us out of this if Eugene connects the dots. "Not as handsome as this one here," she says as she looks up at me, continuing to take the reins of the conversation. As if we have this all planned out, our eyes met. Without warning, she kisses me.

"I don't know what we were all worried about, she seems perfect. Well then, I'll see you tomorrow at the presentation," Eugene says as we break our kiss. He then turns away and immediately starts having a conversation with some other vampire.

I try to examine the look she gives me, but she quickly looks away. You can tell just by glancing at her that she feels ashamed of what she did, of what she had to do to save herself. "One more person, then we can go if you'd like," I say. My mind starts to wonder if she means anything she's saying. Our previous conversation of how well she can act plays in my head. I want to believe she enjoyed that kiss.

"Hell yeah, I want to go. I want to go as far away from this room as possible. By the way, what would he be worried about exactly?" she finally replies as she puts some space between us.

"Not a clue." I'm a terrible liar, but before she can call me on it, I change the subject. "Now, the last person you have to entice is Benjamin. You could consider him the leader of the council." We come to stand in front of a group of people who are lined up to speak to him.

I gently shove Charlie into the line with not so comforting words. "Make sure you bow. Why don't you say something in French to him as well?"

She pushes against my hand, refusing to enter the line. "What? I don't know French. What if he starts talking French back to me?"

I give her a little harder shove, forcing her into the line and stand off to the side to wait without instructing her how to go about the situation. She needs to think on her toes and from the heart, because Benjamin will know if I've instructed her how to behave. He seems to be able to sense lies and withheld secrets one would have. I have no idea what he's going to say to her, so my words are pretty much useless.

There aren't enough minutes in the world to prolong

the inevitable. Before I know it, she's standing in front of the overbearing man. He towers over her in height as he stares down at her with his usual stern look.

She jolts out her hand stiffly and bows in his presence. "Monsieur, it's such an honor to meet you. My name is Charlie Preston. I'm Maxwell Barnett's future bride." I hear her say.

He holds her hand in his longer than I would like, but she doesn't let on how it scares her. "Oh, Mr. Barnett has picked himself quite the charmer. It seems he's quite the lucky man," Benjamin replies back.

"Quite lucky indeed," she says with a smile on her face.

"I'll be looking forward to seeing you tomorrow, Ms. Preston." He lets go of her hand and she rushes away from him. As she approaches me, I put on a smile to mask my worry.

I make eye contact with Benjamin as he continues to stare at her. She must be aware of his stare as well, because she engulfs me in a hug. Burying my face in the curve of her neck that the bite mark is on, I feel her tense up with fear. My hand glides up her back to pull her dark curls away to reveal the still present bite mark. I have to give the spectator what he wants.

Her nails dig into my back as to warn me when she feels the touch of my lips upon her neck. I release her hair to hide my face from view. "You did it," I whisper in her ear.

I feel her instantly relax. "Did you ever doubt me? You questioned my acting skills last night. I felt the need to show you." Her words make me laugh, but stab at my heart. Some part of me doesn't believe that this is all an act. At least that's what I want to believe.

"Let's go." Taking her hand in mine, I escort her to the doors.

She exhales in relief at my words and tightly holds my hand in return, but as soon as we are far enough away from the conference room, she breaks away from me.

"Was it so hard to adore me?" I ask once we enter the elevator.

"Do you really want me to answer that?" she replies in annoyance.

I remain silent on the walk back to the room. I know she's been put through a lot in a little amount of time and I won't make things worse...for now. We enter the room to her cell phone ringing. The sight of her running for her phone in her high heels is interesting to watch, but I get to the phone first, holding it out of her reach as I read the name that's across the screen. Dave.

I decide to answer it since I'm curious as to who this Dave is. "Hello?"

"Who's this? Where's Charlie?" he asks me.

"Charlie's a little indisposed right now. I can certainly tell her that you called, Dave."

Charlie immediately rushes toward me in frenzy. With no other choice, I hold out my hand to stop her. Her forehead meets my palm. Anger causes her arms to swing viciously at me along with a few choice words. But her perfectly fixed hair, strapless dress, and those high heels cover that anger with a humorous image.

Giving up the fight early, she becomes completely still as she whispers through rigid lips. "Really mature, Maxwell, really mature."

A smile unwillingly falls upon my lips. Her eyebrow fights against my palm to arch up in what's supposed to be a demanding look, but as my hand blocks her eyebrows from view, I don't acknowledge her gesture.

Dave continues to talk in my ear. "So this would be

the infamous Maxwell that visited Morgan last night. Funny how Charlie never mentioned you, but yet she lets you accompany her on a mysterious business trip."

I know the second those words exit his mouth that I'm officially under his skin. He spit out my name as though it were venom and I find great pleasure in that. I have what he wants. "I'm her best kept secret. We have a lot of things to handle today, so I really must be going. I'm sure we'll get the chance to meet at some point, Dave." I hang up without waiting for a response. A mere human man is of no importance to me or my bride.

"Why did you do that? Are we jealous?" Her questions turn into accusations.

"Jealous? Of him? Not in the least. You'll be with me in the end." I don't mean to sound cocky, but it's the truth. There's no way that she's going to choose this Dave over her destiny.

"Give me my phone back."

"No more phone on our trip. You need your pretty little mind in the game or you can falter, resulting in you becoming my bride tomorrow. Then this Dave is definitely out of the picture."

That evil glare dons on her face once again as she doesn't like either of the choices I lay out for her. "Dave's already out of the picture, Maxwell. I'm going to take a bath before I go out tonight." She walks to the bedroom door, but stops before she enters.

"Who is he then? And why does he think he matters?"

"Someone who's in my past. Someone who thinks he has a place in my life like another person I know."

"And why would that be?" She's hiding something.

"I might have agreed to a date after I get back."

"A date? Why would you do that, Charlie, when you are being presented as my bride?"

"I didn't want to, but Morgan needed the help and even though we have a rough, untrustworthy past doesn't mean that I don't trust him to help her."

"Morgan is a big girl."

"Not that big. She needs help and I obviously won't be back in time. Going to dinner with him is the price I have to pay to be here with you, so think about that."

If you look at it that way, I guess it is my fault that she's going on this date. But the fact that she has a past with this man is the part that disturbs me the most. I let the subject go as she walks away toward the bathroom.

The rush of the water drowns out her rambling as she argues with herself. I now have one more thing to add to my list when we get back. Find out exactly who this Dave is.

Chapter Fifteen

Charlie

The minute the water touches my chin relaxation takes over every inch of my body. I close my eyes as the warm water surrounds me. I felt ashamed of this dinner date with Dave, but I had to do what I had to do. Maxwell is jealous and he shouldn't be, but I'm not going to stop him from thinking that. As far as he needs to know I'm going on this date because he brought me over here.

I know Maxwell has this idea that coming here will bring us closer together, but part of me refuses on making him right. I'm not ready to admit that I think he's attractive. I'm not ready to lose whatever it is that I lose being with him, be it my beating heart or humanity. My head gently rests against the rim of the luxurious bathtub with heavy eyelids.

Quietness mixed with the lightweight warmth the bath gives me is a bad combination. I shoot up from under the water, gasping for air. I fell asleep only to wake up fully submerged. Water runs in thick trails down my face and my once dry hair is now soaked. My hands automatically wipe away the water from my face.

To make matters worse, I nearly slide back under as Maxwell bursts through the door. I instinctively scramble to cover myself up, only to realize that most of my bubbles have disappeared. "Would you learn to knock!" I shriek at him.

"I heard you struggling and I…" It's the first time I hear him at a loss for words.

I raise both my eyebrows and bob my head, urging

him to finish the sentence. As the seconds pass, I get annoyed. "Well, as you can see, I'm not drowning, and Casper the friendly ghost is not present, so you can leave the room."

I see him try extra hard to not look at me, but occasionally I see his eyes bearing down on me. "Oh and try not to be in the bedroom, I'm going to be getting out." I shoo him out the door with my hand, several drops of water dripping off my fingertips, landing on the floor.

As soon as the door closes, I hop out of the tub and wrap myself in one of the fluffy white towels. Even though I instructed Maxwell to leave, who knows if he's actually going to listen. I cautiously exit the bathroom to enter an empty bedroom. Grabbing the clothes I've been eyeing up earlier, I lay them out on the bed and speedily towel dry myself off. I return to the bathroom clad in only my undergarments to face the mess that my reflection is bound to show.

A small smile stretches across my face as I hear Maxwell knock on the bedroom door. I shut the bathroom door, just leaving it open a crack before I give him the okay to enter. "I had some food delivered if you're interested."

Really, even though he knows I'm going downstairs to a restaurant, he ordered me food. I tell myself to relax. I know he's just trying to be nice, trying to be a gentleman. "Hand me my clothes that are on the bed, please." I stick my hand out the crack of the door, waiting for him to put the articles in my palm.

I mistakenly look out the opening as my fingers wrap around fabric to meet Maxwell's darkened gaze. His roaming eyes don't hold my attention for that long due to his straight tense mouth. He's trying to keep his fangs hidden from view. In a rush, I pull the clothes through and shut the door. Even though I'm annoyed by his behavior, I'm thankful for his effort. And I wanted to torment him with the whole Dave issue, but I'm not willing to go that far in teasing him.

I'm expecting to find him waiting in the bedroom for me, but once I exit the bathroom he's nowhere in sight. With little searching, I find him sitting at the table across from my food. He immediately stands up in my presence.

"You know you didn't need to get me food. I was planning on getting some downstairs, unless…you're depressed that I didn't invite you to come along and you're trying to make me late," I say mockingly.

"You still can ask me to join you."

"That would make an interesting evening, but no thanks. It's going to put a toll on me the way it is without watching Paige goggle at you. I mean, you might falter at the presentation tomorrow and things might not go in our favor." I can't help but to laugh as I tell him his own words.

He, however, just stares at me blankly.

"Oookay then, I'm just going to eat." I look away from his emotionless stare and take bite after bite. I don't overstuff myself, just enough to hold me over.

"You still have some time left before you have to go. Do you want to watch some TV?" I know something is going on because he's acting excessively nice. Nonetheless, I agree. I follow his gesture and sit on the couch beside him, but not too close. I expect him to ask me if I have anything in particular I would like to watch, but he hoards the remote.

Once I hear that familiar theme song, I can't help but to smile. He's gloating in satisfaction, but I just can't stop the smile from getting wider. "Shut up, you broke into my house when I was watching this yesterday." He just shrugs, allowing me to put all my attention on one of my favorite shows.

Once it's over, Maxwell finds his voice again. "I honestly don't know what you see in that show."

"Humor, corpse…humor. Why are you being so nice? You know this getting me food, watching my shows, trying to be a gentleman with fangs is not going to get you whatever it is that you want."

"I can try."

"What exactly are you buttering me up for?" One of my eyebrows perks up as I think about what I just said. "Wait, that sounds bad, considering you butter things that you eat and you eat people, so I shouldn't talk about buttering me up. What do you want?" I decide on the bluntest way of saying it.

"Nothing, I just thought I would act like any other human man. Cons—"

I cut him off because that's all I need in order to call him out on his slip-up. "You're jealous of Dave," I say as if I were playing a game of Clue and am calling out the killer. I don't need an answer. I can see it all over his face. I saw it on his face earlier. "There's just something he and every other living, breathing man is always going to have over you…something that's incredibly hard to compete with, a beating heart."

I look at the clock on the wall; it reads two minutes to seven. "Well, would you look at the time. I got to go. Don't be sad, Maxwell; there are some things you have that he can't compete with either." I walk away with that said. With my hand twisting the doorknob, I think I'm in the clear, but before it's open just a sliver, he appears beside me with his foot stopping the door.

"Maxwell," I say in a threatening tone.

"What is that exactly? I am dying to know." He tries to look smooth and seductive, ignoring my warning; however, his words tear at me.

I hold the laugh back as long as I can, but it explodes through my tight lips. "Dying to know, oh so cute. Like a puppy…a vicious puppy, but a puppy nonetheless." I shove the door open against his foot and walk out into the hall. "I always wanted a puppy. I promise to be back before ten, Father."

"Very funny, Charlie," he hollers down the hall at me. I enter the elevator before I hear the door close. I just hope he gets the hint and doesn't follow me. The last thing I need is eyes glaring at me while he eavesdrops on the conversation I'm sure is just going to be great.

At first, I don't spot the trio when I enter the restaurant and I'm more than willing to back out and face Maxwell instead of looking for them. As if life cannot for once go in my favor, I see Aiden jump up and down. The sound of his voice echoes through the restaurant as he shouts my name.

I put on the most genuine smile and walk over to my new found friends. Aiden pulls out a chair closest to him for me to sit in. To my joy, Paige sits to my other side. Aiden waves his hand at the bartender for another round of drinks and within seconds four tall glasses of something alcoholic, I presume, arrives at our table.

Paige is the first one to speak. I watch her blonde hair bounce as her head bobbles. Her bright blue eyes bore into mine for seconds at a time. "Are you excited for the presentation tomorrow? I can't wait until it's my turn."

"Of course. Maxwell is…" I pause, trying to find my words.

"Perfect. Gorgeous. Prefect," Paige says dreamily.

"Exactly. Perfect." Way too perfect for me. He deserves better than me. He deserves someone like Paige who's willing to jump head over heels for his attention, for his love.

"I would love to have him. He could use and abuse me, but I wouldn't care," Paige continues.

"Get over yourself, Paige," Eddie chimes in. His hand flaps in Paige's face to bring her back to reality.

"You know what, I think I'm just going to have water," I say, getting up from my chair to head over to the bar. I get my glass of water, finding relief from being away from them, but as I turn around hoping to take one last breath before I join the group, I run into Aiden. I see the water splash in my glass; luckily, he doesn't get any of it on his shirt, because who knows what he would do.

"Everything okay?" he asks.

I nod in compliance.

"I can see you don't care about Maxwell as you say you do."

"That's not—"

"Shh. No need to try to convince me. It's fine. I'm not going to tell. It wouldn't be the first time that a presentation was called and one of the parties didn't care for the other. Most of the time it's the human who dislikes the vampire. Beauty, health, and eternal youth don't appeal to everyone. There needs to be that connection. A physical attraction," he says in a throaty whisper.

What the hell did I just get myself into? "I appreciate that, but it's not necessary. I love Maxwell, truly I do."

"I love my vampire bride too, but vampires aren't known for having just one bride or groom. Or one donor either. My vampire bride was off obtaining another groom before we had to come here. Hopefully, the next time we meet we'll both be exceptionally cold." His fingers glide across my cheek. Before I know it his mouth is over mine, taking me completely off guard.

I shove him away, disgusted at his immature behavior. "Aiden. I'm with Maxwell and there aren't any other donors or brides. We treat this living and 'unliving' relationship very seriously."

"Right. Sorry."

"Is there a problem here?" Grace says, making the situation even more awkward than it already is.

"No," I reply.

"Charlie, would you care to sit and talk? I mean, if you don't mind leaving the company of your friends, that is."

"Of course," I say back to Grace. "Aiden, tell Paige and Eddie it was nice talking with them, but I really should sit down with Grace."

Aiden walks back to the table defeated.

"You're going to tell Maxwell, aren't you?" I whisper as we make our way to a table.

"I really do want us to be friends and I want you and Maxwell to be happy together, so no, I won't tell. It'll be our little secret."

I smile at her effort, but part of me doesn't trust her. The same part that doesn't trust Maxwell. The vampire part.

"I don't think Maxwell has ever showed an interest in anybody as he does in you. Don't believe that idiot. Just because each of their vampires are bloody awful doesn't mean that all of us are."

"This whole presentation and The High Council…I just want to go home."

"Soon enough, but until then I'll let you in on a little secret. I hate The High Council just as much as you, just as much as Maxwell." I can tell by the look in her eyes that at some point in time they did something awful to her. "You don't know how much you resemble him; he despised the man who changed him." I never would have compared the two of us, ever.

"Would you tell me about it? I mean, your hate for The High Council. If you don't want to, though, I understand," I ask as kindly as possible.

I watch her look at the tabletop as she gets lost in recalling the memory. "It was many, many years ago. I just met Maxwell a few years earlier, in fact. I remember the look on his face when I introduced him to Alexander. At the time picking a bride or groom to him was a waste and when I told him that Alexander was to be my groom he laughed in my face." She laughs quietly, lost in thought. "Alexander was the most humble, honest man and he too didn't want to become a vampire such as yourself. I waited a total of three years until he agreed to start the transition. I bet you're wondering where The High Council comes in." She stops, waiting for my reply.

All I can do is nod my head. I'm thankful that it's enough for her to continue.

"Alexander went to collect some donors who belonged to our new bloodline, but while he was gone a naïve young girl ran to The High Council claiming that Alexander bit her. It was against every vampire law written and unwritten, claiming that if you bit another vampire's property you will be sentenced to death. Benjamin being all 'I am your king' demanded for me to bring him Alexander. When I said that he has been gone and was not responsible for that girl's bite, I was told that I was lying to protect him. They knew he would have to show his face sooner or later, so they waited. He was spotted walking back into the village with four donors."

I have a feeling I'm not going to like the ending to this story. I swallow the lump in my throat and continue to listen.

"The High Council sent the humans away. They told me that I was to go back to my original bloodline because there was no need for a new one. At dawn Alexander saw the sun again. Mind you, he was not turned for very long and he still remembered what the shining rays looked like. It made it worse, of course. The fresher the vampire the longer it takes to die. I was more than willing to refresh my memory of the sun's rays. However, I was forced to hear his agonizing screams as he slowly burned."

She drops her head, finally showing emotion. Although I don't see tears, I know she's hurting. She raises her head with an awkward smile. "Maxwell was the one who stopped me. He called it saving me." She laughs again the same way as before, short and abrupt. "At that moment I didn't agree, but now I'm more than thankful. Anyways, a few days later the girl who claimed Alexander bit her begged for forgiveness at the feet of Benjamin. She said that her vampire told her to say that after he bit her."

My jaw drops in disgust and my heart aches for her loss that she shouldn't have had to endure. "Of course the human girl was unharmed, because it was not her fault in Benjamin's eyes. She was put under a trance that us vampires like to use sometimes. As for the vampire, well, when dawn arrived he was next to see the sun again."

"Grace, I'm so sorry. I didn't mean to make you talk about it, I was just curious." I can't help but to keep apologizing. I have no idea if it makes it better, but I have to try.

"I have had a difficult time picking a groom again. There will be no one like Alexander. No need to apologize, if anything it makes you understand things better. Just take what I told you and think about it. I might be Maxwell's friend, but he's just as caring and sincere as any other human. He knows better than anyone, including myself, that to turn someone means that you really have to care for them and you have to be willingly to take the heartbreak that may follow."

I remain silent, not intentionally, though. I just can't find the right words to say.

"You have a big day tomorrow, you should get back. It's after ten and I'm sure Maxwell is waiting for you," Grace says before I have a chance to say anything, even if I had something to say.

"You're right." However, one question pops into my head. "Grace, who turned you? Do you still talk to him or her?" I know I'm out of bounds, but I have to know.

"Times like these I really don't have a choice. All I can say is that he's closer than I want."

I know she's not going into it any further, so I finally tell her goodbye. I hear Aiden and Eddie yell their goodbyes as well, but I just wave at them as I walk out of the restaurant. I don't think twice about Paige not being present at the table. I figure I'll see her again before I go back home.

Between Grace's miserable past and those three who can't wait to die, my emotions bear down on me, bad...guilty emotions fill me to the brim. After turning the corner and a matter of a few doors away from the room, I see Paige walking down the hall.

She fluffs her hair as she greets me. "Charlie, is it that time already? I missed everything."

"It's fine. Grace came down and snatched me away to talk. Why are you up here and not with Aiden and Eddie?"

"Oh, I had a little job I had to do. Nothing to

concern that pretty little head of yours. I should be getting back to the boys. See ya later." With heavy feet, she quickly walks away.

That was weird. Not thinking too much into it, I finish making my way to the room. I'm expecting to see Maxwell with a stern look on his face and his arms crossed sitting at the table when I walk in, but after walking around the kitchen and living room areas, he's nowhere in sight.

I try to peer through the crack of the bedroom door; it's open no more than an inch or so, leaving it completely pointless. I quickly push it open to reveal something that connects dots that should never be connected. I take in the scene before me perfectly, even though several candles dimly light the dark room. My bad emotions just get worse.

* * *

Maxwell

I hear the door open and the soft tiptoe of feet. "Charlie, you're here early. Just make yourself comfortable. I'll be right out." In a rush I get out of the tub. I've been soaking in hot water to warm my body temperature up so I'm not so cold to the touch.

I exit the bathroom wrapped in nothing but a towel. Charlie lies in bed completely covered. A pile of clothes is at the foot of the bed. This special night is going better than I thought it would. I lined the room with candles and have romantic music playing in efforts to show her that we belong together, that loving me isn't all that bad. There might be a monster lurking inside me, but it will only protect her instead of hurt her. She's right, secrets are just as bad as lies.

I crawl into bed, stopping mere inches away from

her naked body. "I must say I'm quite surprised at your turnaround."

She scoots toward me. Her buttock rests against my manhood.

"Oh, Charlie, I love you so much," I whisper in her ear. But that's when I see all this blonde hair hiding under the pillow. I shoot out of bed, gathering to towel to cover myself up.

"I know I'm not Charlie, but you can call me whatever you want," the young woman says. She sits fully exposed on the bed.

I stutter in search for her name.

"Paige. My name is Paige and I've loved you ever since I saw you."

"Aren't you supposed to be downstairs with Charlie?"

"Grace came and took her away, so I thought I could come here and visit you. I just want you inside me one time. I want to feel your teeth rack across my body."

"You need to go."

"My vampire won't know and I certainly won't tell him. This week he's with Courtney and next week he's with Autumn. By the time it's my turn with him the bite will be healed. Please," she begs.

"I said leave." The hatred in my voice makes her tremble.

"But—"

"Now." I point her to the door and reluctantly she obeys my orders.

She dresses in a matter of seconds and rushes out of the room. Women such as herself shouldn't be donors, shouldn't know of the existence of vampires. Desperation of that degree can get you killed.

Lost in thought, I don't hear the door open until it's too late.

"I must have missed something pretty good. Didn't I, Maxwell?" Charlie says in an accusing tone.

In a rush I pull my pajama bottoms on. "Charlie."

She doesn't allow me to say anything further. "Don't Charlie me. I know what's going on here. You have perfect timing, I must say."

"What are you talking about? This is for you. I wanted to show you how much I love you. How much we belong together."

"Do not lie to me. I saw Paige in the hall. Her ruffled hair, sloppy clothes, and only three doors away from our room. Looks like you got done with whatever it is that you were doing with her just in time."

I walk up to her to offer some kind of comfort, but she steps away from me. I will kill that Paige if she ruined my chances with Charlie. No one will stand in my way and if anyone does they will pay the consequences.

"Yes, she was here to seduce me, but I sent her away. I've been bathing in hot water for who knows how long so I wouldn't be cold for you. I thought you were back early and she hopped into bed before I exited the bathroom. She covered herself up completely, tricking me in thinking she was you."

"And you just thought that some lovey-dovey music and candles would make me jump into bed?"

"I'm optimistic that you'll come around."

"That's nice, but I'm pessimistic. You want to know why? For this very reason. You can't get hurt if you expect the worst of people. I've been here, Maxwell. I've been through this all already and I won't be the loser again." She takes in my confused stare. "And he's just as stubborn apparently as you are."

"Dave." Dave cheated on her? Just another reason to kill him.

"Ding ding. I'm over this." She turns for the door.

"You have to care to get hurt." At that moment I know she cares. She's just pushing me away before I realize it. I block her way to the door and grab her arms, planting her in place. She has no other choice than to look at me.

"I can't do this."

"Why? Why can't you let me in, Charlie? I'm not going to hurt like you think I will. You have to give me a chance to prove that. You can't let people like Dave ruin your life."

"It's not about Dave. It's about Paige."

"Paige? She's nothing compared to you."

"She's everything. You deserve someone like her. Someone who will do whatever you want whenever, wherever you want it. That's not me. I'm damaged goods. Why do you think Dave did what he did if I was so great?"

"Dave's an idiot. And I don't want somebody like Paige. I could have someone like that if I wanted it, but I don't. Sit."

"No." The obnoxious tone in her voice is beyond irritating.

"For the love of Jesus Christ, Charlie, just sit down." My hands run through my hair from her stubbornness.

With a defeated look in her eyes, she abides.

"After my sentencing I went in search of the Travors. I traced family lines and came across the Bloomburgs first, but there was something telling me to keep looking. Searching. That's when I found the Prestons. Not soon after coming across your great great grandparents and what not, I found a transcriber. He was hiding something and I wanted to know what. So I waited for the perfect time. That's when I read the journal. That's when I read about a baby they thought to be special. You. I knew I was searching for you. I found you just over a year ago and I haven't let you out of my sight since."

Her head snaps up to look at me. "How touching but yet so creepy. You're just fascinated with the concept of me being 'special'."

Without warning, I grab her face between my hands, applying just enough pressure to hold her still. My mouth finds hers and needfully I kiss her. She struggles under my grip. Her hands pound at me, but I don't let her go. After a few seconds she goes limp. Her unmoving lips start to press against mine and just like that she kisses me back. I lean her backward until she lies on the bed. Pressing up against her gets me more excited than it should. My teeth extract and pierce her bottom lip.

A sharp breath from her breaks the kiss. She stares at me shocked as her tongue licks at the small wound.

"Charlie, I didn't mean to, it's just…"

"A vampire thing. I get it."

"I don't need—"

"It's my fault. I shouldn't have...led you on." Her head falls in her hands. "This is so embarrassing. How did I do this last time? Oh, that's right, I wasn't fully there."

"Just get some rest. It's fine."

"No, it's not. Let me do this." She pulls at the hem of her shirt. She's trying, she really is, but you can tell it's taking a great toll on her.

"Charlie. Look at me." Once her eyes are on mine, I order her to listen. "This is not necessary, Charlie. Now get comfortable and get some rest. You won't question or remember any of this. Understood."

She nods her head as if in a daze. And just like I

commanded her to do, she does. She strips off her clothes, pulls on a T-shirt that she digs out of her bag, and crawls into bed. Not soon after, I follow.

I lie in bed with a smile on my face, but it doesn't last long. I resorted to influencing her once again, but this time it's for the better. It might be awkward to be lying in bed with what Grace refers to as an empty shell, but I wasn't going to have her endure something she would regret again. At least I'm making progress and that's all that matters.

Chapter Sixteen

Charlie

Sleep was peaceful and I guess much needed as I slept late into the day. Maxwell didn't bother to wake me and now I'm left with little amount of time before the presentation begins.

"You're nervous, I understand, but nothing terrible is going to happen." Maxwell rubs my arms, trying to calm me.

"What exactly is going to happen? I mean, what's the purpose of this presentation anyways?" Part of me wants to know and the other part of me is scared to death to find out.

"Think of this as our engagement celebration."

"Engagement celebration, but you didn't ask me to marry you." Marriage? He's comparing this to marriage.

"I can if that will make it easier for you to accept. You're my bride, Charlie, in the eyes of vampires and in the human terms."

"A dead bride, not a bride in a gorgeous white dress."

"Is that what you want? To walk down the aisle in a white dress in front of every single person you know?"

"Maybe. Is that so hard to believe?"

"No." He remains silent for a bit. I'm just about to say something when he starts to speak again. "After this we can go back home and you won't have to worry about impressing anyone or have death looming over your shoulder. I'll give you all the time you need to decide when to start the change." He changes the subject quickly. Maybe it's because he can't truly give me that big wedding.

I go with the change of conversation. I don't want to talk weddings with Maxwell. "I need to find something to wear."

"I have something for you already," Maxwell says as he walks past me straight into the bedroom. I'm going to question his intentions when he stops in front of the large oak armoire in the corner of the room, but I remain quiet as he opens it widely. He pushes several clothes that I assume to be his to the right and reaches deep inside.

He pulls out a long black dress bag on a thick plastic hanger. I can see the muscles in his forearm flex from the weight. My heart races as he slowly unzips it. I have no idea why I'm so anxious. Please don't be a white dress. Please don't be a wedding dress. After he removes the bag it glides gently to the floor. Finally I'm able to view what's hidden inside. A gorgeous black silk mermaid style evening gown with pink corset top stares back at me. Fabric that flares out in the form of a train of sorts from the waist down creating a slender silhouette.

"You…you want me to wear that?" I'm speechless at its beauty, yet also speechless about the presentation once again. "A formal gown. Maxwell, what are you not telling me? There is no engagement celebration in the world where a person would wear this fancy of a gown."

"It's a very formal event. I'll let you get changed. Grace brought shoes and accessories from your closet to match. They're over by the dresser."

I don't get a chance to refuse or demand that he answers my question of what he is hiding from me, because he immediately walks out and shuts the door. Mumbles of terror spill out of my mouth as I shimmy into the dress. I twist my arm as far back as it can go only to hang my head in defeat. I have to ask for assistance in zipping up the last two inches or so.

Sitting as best as I can on the edge of the bed, I put on black studded earring and silver and black bangle bracelets along with a pair of black heels on before I face the music. "Maxwell," I say into the empty room with my back to the door.

He immediately enters within seconds as if he were waiting right outside. "Yes, Charlie." There's a seductiveness to his voice that I'm sure is intentional.

"Zip me. Please." I feel his ice-cold fingers touch my back as he grasps the zipper. It sends a shiver down my spine.

"Are you cold?" he asks.

"No, I'm not cold. It's from your fingers touching me. They're like ice cubes." I spin around to face him. I ignore his love-struck stare. "I have to fix my hair."

"Make sure you put it up. You need to show everyone your..." His fingers trail along the side of my neck that he bit me on.

"I feel more like a piece of property than a bride. Except instead of a hickey it's two puncture marks that have been bit into my flesh."

"Well, you are mine, love. And sometimes I bite." He removes his shirt as he replies back. He takes in my annoyed gaze. "What? We have about forty minutes left to get ready before we have to leave. I can't always spare you from admiring me, although I do enjoy it." His smile puts butterflies in my stomach and causes my heart rate to accelerate, which causes me to forget his owing me a comment.

Pushing the feelings down, I roll my eyes and grumble to myself. "I'll bite you," I say in a hushed voice in the bathroom doorway, unable to keep my mouth shut.

"And I'll be looking forward to that day," he jokes.

With a loud exhale, I slam the bathroom door. I glare at my reflection, inspecting every last inch. A small swollen lump on my bottom lip draws my attention. Where the hell did that come from? I shrug it off as to biting it in my sleep. By no means have I ever been good at fixing my hair, but after several different tries I manage to put it up in a slick high bun. A light tap on the door breaks my concentration.

"Charlie, are you almost ready? We need to get going so we're not late to our own celebration."

I open the door to find Maxwell leaning up against the doorframe. My heart speeds up at the sight of him in his sleek black suit and pink tie that appears to match the pink of my dress. This is more like prom than a wedding. A small smile plays across his face. "What's so funny?"

"Nothing, I'm just excited." He grabs my arm and drapes it over his as we walk to the door. "How's your hand?" he asks, picking at the white bandages that still wrap my palm.

"Fine, it's scabbed over. I thought I would keep it hidden, because it doesn't look appealing."

He remains holding my hand through the elevator ride, the lobby, and out of the hotel altogether. Occasionally, I try to slip my hand out of his grip, but he tightens his fingers around mine, not allowing it. A sleek black car waits for us outside the front doors. I didn't realize we would be leaving the hotel, otherwise I would have grabbed a sweater of some sort.

The car ride is short, but my nerves make it feel like hours pass. Maxwell remains holding my hand, gently caressing it the whole way. Immediately after the car stops Maxwell assists me out. The first thing I spot is an extravagant mansion like manor. Maxwell waits a few seconds before he starts to walk toward the large building.

"Who lives here?" I ask in hushed voice.

"Benjamin." The word comes out almost hateful.

Maxwell's pace quickens as we make our way up the front steps. I stop abruptly, trying to collect a small sliver of tranquility before I have to endure whatever it is that is about to happen. The hold he has on me breaks and he involuntarily takes a few steps without me. I watch his hand jolt out into the air as if it were searching for mine. His hand trembles just slightly, but as soon as his fingers wrap around mine, his strong grip doesn't waver again.

A tall man with a monstrous look to him answers the door before we can knock or ring a doorbell. I can only stare; his complexion looks almost greenish to my eyes. His voice is loud and thunderous. "Welcome, Master Barnett." He opens the door wider and waves us inside.

I turn toward Maxwell to ask what that is…who that is, but he shakes his head just a fraction and continues to guide me down several halls. We stop outside a set of engraved wooden double doors. I observe the terror in Maxwell's eyes. It's barely visible. You would have to be looking for it to see it. I only spot it because my face most likely holds the same fearful expression.

"It'll be over soon and then you can relax."

"That…that dude was green…like green green," I say, completely baffled. All Maxwell does is nod in response. "Why?"

"I don't know why, Charlie, too many peas maybe. Can we get back on topic?"

"And what would that be?"

"If you call them by their names they'll be impressed."

"I don't know their names. To be honest I don't

even know how many of them there are." My mind races. I have no idea if I can remember any information under this stress.

"There are five of them. You already know two. Benjamin will be in the center, to his right will be Eugene and next to Eugene will be Oliver. To Benjamin's left will be Duke and next to Duke will be Robert."

I nod my head, forcing each name to soak in. I repeat the names in my head. Oliver, Eugene, Benjamin, Duke, Robert. Maxwell pushes the doors open and several eyes turn toward me. My body freezes up, my limbs refuse to gracefully bend, and the sound of my heartbeat pounds in my ears. However, I keep repeating the names. Oliver, Eugene, Benjamin, Duke, Robert. I'm sure a few eyes can see Maxwell kindly push me along. The doors slamming closed behind us makes me jump, making the situation even better.

I don't know what came over me, but with all those unfamiliar eager eyes staring at me I can only panic. There are a few faces I recognize in the crowd of people, but not enough to make this dread that burrows in my gut subside.

Maxwell moves his grip from my hand to around my waist. He leads me up to a row of five throne like chairs. I identify Eugene and Benjamin instantly. Eugene smiles kindly at me, but Benjamin gives me a harsh, cold grimace. Can he see I'm scared? Can he tell I don't want to be here? Be with Maxwell?

I remain silent, waiting for Maxwell or one of The High Council members to speak first. I see four women and one man sit off to the side on my right. I recognize Grace, who sits in the middle seat. She smiles briefly at me before her eyes go back to the five men who demand everyone's attention without even speaking. I can't understand why those individuals are separated from the rest of the crowd.

Maxwell's low voice pulls me out of my thoughts. "We can start, Benjamin."

Benjamin's gaze moves to me. I didn't know if I should speak or not, but I decide to anyways. "Nice to see you again, Benjamin." I shift my gaze over to Eugene. "Eugene," I state with a slight nod of my head. I intended to introduce myself and state the other members' names like Maxwell told me to, but Benjamin's commanding voice stops me.

I become stick straight as he calls a start to the presentation. Maxwell's arm that's still around my waist tightens, trying to calm me as Benjamin addresses the room. "You have all been asked here to witness the start of the eternal merging of Maxwell Barnett and his future vampire bride, Charlie Preston. In this everlasting life as a vampire they have agreed to trust and love each other as equals. Forever."

My heart thumps wildly in my chest at his words. My palms are starting to sweat, causing the bandages on my left hand to become damp and cool, which starts to make my scabs itch. Benjamin continues talking, oblivious to my inner battle. "The next time we all gather for Maxwell and his bride, Ms. Preston will be one of us. She will bathe in the moonlight and feed on life."

Oh my God, I think I'm going to be sick. Time stands still as Benjamin and Eugene take turns talking. I block out what they say, afraid to hear it. Maxwell's strong arm keeps me standing upright. I imagine the sunlight washing over me as I inhale deeply, getting completely lost in my anti-vampire daydream. Eugene's voice at close proximity rips me away from my safe sanctuary.

"Charlie, may we ask you some questions?" Eugene asks, standing in front of me. He holds out his hand and I have no choice but to place my hand in his. I feel Maxwell's fingers trail along my back as I slip away from him. A look over my shoulder to gain some strength from him seemed like a good idea, but once I meet his darkened stare it doesn't help. Deep down I know he can feel my fear, but there's nothing he can do to help me. I'm stuck defending myself.

Eugene walks me up to stand in front of Benjamin before he leaves my side. The feeling of being naked engulfs me as five sets of questioning eyes scan my body from head to toe. Benjamin's once loud, overbearing voice speaks in a gentle, soft tone toward me. "Ms. Preston, by arriving here with Maxwell you are accepting your fate as a vampire. By doing so I am to assume that you know and trust him very well."

With a lump growing in my throat, I just nod my head in acceptance. My eyes dart between the five men as I try to guess the outcome of this conversation.

"You know of Maxwell's violent past and the punishment he was given. He has been known for being merciless to his past donors. Has he been volatile toward you in any way?" I look at the man who speaks the question. If I remember correctly his name is Robert. His honey-colored eyes bore into mine as he waits for an answer. He looks well-groomed compared to the other members with their unshaven faces.

I take a deep breath, trying to buy myself some time to think of something great to say. "I'm very aware…" My voice cracks, allowing them to hear my fear in case they failed to see it. I clear my throat as quietly as possible.

"It's okay, Charlie, we're not here to judge or punish. Go on, my child," Oliver assures me. I can't help myself from comparing him to a pirate. His disheveled black hair, his thin moustache that lines his top lip, and his chin has the illusion of being pointy due to a goatee, but his nurturing words are nothing but that of a caring individual.

I brush off the child statement and speak my words in a gentle, steady voice. "I'm very aware of Maxwell's past and he has assured me many times that he has changed over the years. From what I heard," more like read, I think to myself, "and from what I have seen, I know for a fact that he's no longer that cold-hearted monster people perceive him to be."

My gaze lands on Benjamin. I see his eyes linger on the bite mark that's clearly visible. "Was the bite by choice?" Why are they asking me these questions? Benjamin stares at me with narrow eyes, waiting for an answer to his inquiry.

My hand goes up to my neck, grazing the bite mark. The two small punctures have been healed for some time now. Only two scabs that are flaking away remain. I'm tempted to pick at them, but decided against it because I don't want to listen to Maxwell bicker. "If you're suggesting that he forced me to endure this bite against my will or put his vampire charm on me, you would be wrong. We talked about it for some time before the deed was done."

I can tell Benjamin is getting annoyed with my heartfelt answers. Nonetheless, I'm not going to slip up and he can't ask me questions all day. "Are you aware that you are the only female who has been born in your family line? All the women in your family have been married to direct descendants, but you're the first daughter born for decades."

What? Maxwell just talked about this last night before I fell asleep. He said that none were for the liking and now I know why. He didn't want a groom, he wanted a bride. I guess that the women who married into the family weren't good enough. With that said I know exactly why everyone found me so special.

"Very lucky, isn't he?" Benjamin asks.

I try my hardest to keep my facial expression happy and light, but his words claw at me, leaving deep grooves in my heart. Without wanting to, thoughts of Maxwell's deception and lies gradually fill my mind. For all I know he wants me to be his bride because I'm his last chance. The last woman he can take advantage of. I see a small smile on Benjamin's mouth as if he enjoys the possibility of his words tearing Maxwell and myself apart.

Benjamin's eyes break away from mine. He stares at the people behind me or at the wall. Abruptly, his hand stretches out as his voice fills the room. "Grace, darling, would you gather the ceremonial supplies?"

Grace? Darling? I watch her as she jumps up and almost runs toward him with a silver bowl and a small dagger. Unintentionally, I take a step back. I come to a stop when I bump into a tall, muscular body behind me. Maxwell once again wraps him arm around my waist and pushes me forward. My eyes widen as I see the light reflect off the metal blade.

Eugene holds the silver bowl as Benjamin stands in front of Maxwell. Without being asked, Maxwell holds out his free arm. I want to look away more than anything, but my curiosity forces me to gawk at what plays out before me. Benjamin places the knife's point in the middle of Maxwell's wrist. In one fluid motion, he drags the blade all the way down to the tip of Maxwell's middle finger. I watch as dark blood oozes out of the long slice. It looks almost like syrup as it drips into the metal bowl.

When Benjamin stands in front of me, I begin to sway on my feet. Maxwell keeps me steady, but my insides are a mess. I think for sure that my heart will rip out of my chest and land on Benjamin's feet. With the heat that rises to my head, I find it incredibly hard to speak. I allow Maxwell to grab my left hand. He unwraps my bandages with ease. I look down at the scabbed over cuts. I have to agree with Maxwell about re-injuring an already injured hand instead of leaving me with both hands sliced open. Benjamin briefly looks from my scarred hand to Maxwell as if accusing him of doing this.

When Maxwell asked me earlier about how I was healing, I had no idea that this was why he was asking. I squint my eyes shut as I see Benjamin raise the dagger. I feel the cold metal tip dig into the middle of my wrist. I suck in a breath and bite my bottom lip as the searing hot pain radiates up my arm as the blade slowly works down the middle of my hand. I refuse to whimper or cry from the pain in front of these people.

When I feel the sharp point run off the end of my middle finger, I open my eyes. Glancing down I see blood that's lighter in color than Maxwell's cascade into the bowl. The stream that pours out of my hand flows faster and looks thinner in consistency.

Before Eugene takes the bowl away, Maxwell starts to re-wrap my now fresh wound. He puts my hand against his chest. The thought of his crisp black shirt getting a blood stain on it crosses my mind. The thin layer of bandages is not enough to soak up the flowing blood. His arms encircle me, causing my hand to get pushed into his chest harder. I start to feel his shirt get sticky and wet.

He whispers in my ear, "Almost done. You're doing well, Charlie."

"The presentation will be concluded with a kiss," Benjamin declares.

With each word Benjamin speaks the more I hate him. The feel of Maxwell's fingers gently wrapping around the back of my neck makes a trail of goosebumps break out over my exposed skin. My eyes quickly find his. Before I have time to process, which is for the better, Maxwell places his mouth upon mine. His lips are smoother than I expected. He pulls me in tighter, deepening the kiss. The small cut on my bottom lip twinges with pain as he slips my lip in between his lips. My chest presses up against my hand that still separates us. My hand throbs in unison with the thumping of my heart.

Maxwell finally pulls away. He nods his head to Benjamin and the others before turning to leave the room. I leave my hand on his chest because the coolness that emits from him feels nice on my wound. We walk out the large wooden double doors that we entered all too long ago, leaving behind whispers and prying eyes. Shock stops any conversation that could start on the way back to the hotel.

* * *

Maxwell

I have no idea what has come over Charlie. The pained look on her face says it's more than just her hand hurting. We enter our room with her arm intertwining with mine, but as soon as the door slams shut, she rips her arm away from me. I brace myself for the storm that's about to come my way.

"You need to explain yourself," she says in a calm voice.

"I know I should have told you about the kiss…and

about the bloodletting, but I knew it would only make you more nervous."

"Not that, Maxwell. You need to explain what Benjamin said. I waited for you to say something about it first, but you remained quiet the whole ride over here. Is it true, that I'm the only female that's a direct descendant from the Travors bloodline? That you're ending my life because I'm your last chance at having a lover?" She spits the last word at me, extremely disgusted by it.

"Charlie, stop," I demand.

As usual, she didn't hear me or she doesn't care as she continues to accuse. "Oh, I'm special, all right. Not for anything other than being a girl." Her hate-filled glare doesn't waver.

In a blink of one's eyes, I come to stand in front of her. "Charlie, stop." I watch her body go rigid when I demanded that she stop, but within a few seconds, she loosens up. Her eyes move to stare at the ground midway through my explanation.

"Why does Benjamin dislike you?" she abruptly says.

"That's not my story to tell."

"Not your story to tell. I don't care whose story it is, this is about me pretending to know everything about you—when I clearly don't—to the man who hates you and most likely hates me too. Amuse me, whose story is it to tell?"

"Grace's."

"Of course. Well, Grace has some explaining to do herself. However, you're just going to have to betray your friendship and tell me. You might answer the questions I have for her, but I think she would understand. Now tell me why or I leave. After everything I went through because of you, this is the least you can do." I can tell she means business. I have never heard such anger in her voice before.

I reluctantly tell her what she wants to know. "Benjamin dislikes me, because Grace found a friend in me. When everyone thought I was cruel—"

"You were cruel," she interrupts.

I correct myself. "When everyone saw how cruel I was, she still saw the best in me. Benjamin, however, lost her trust and companionship when he took a second bride and he grew jealous." I feel better after saying the words. I examine the confused look on Charlie's face. Before she can ask, I answer her question. "Grace is Benjamin's first bride."

I wait for her to process the information. "You and Grace?"

That's what she got out of what I said, Grace and I together...intimately? "No, we're merely friends. He blames me for giving her courage on taking a groom, Alexander. He blames me for helping her love someone other than him. He hates me because the woman he loved at one point in time, maybe still does, prefers to be with a murderer than him."

"I watched her jump at his words. She's still loyal to him."

"She has no choice but to obey him at events such as these." It kills Grace more than anyone will ever know to be Benjamin's like a little lap dog. He takes advantage of her since he knows that she has to obey, which leaves Grace physically and mentally drained.

"His questions sounded like he knew...like he knew I don't want to be a vampire."

I want to breathe a sigh of relief once she speaks the words. I thought she was going to say he knew she didn't love me. Benjamin certainly didn't help smooth out that bump. "I assure you, Grace is on our side. She would never deceive me and she would never put you in harm's way."

"I don't like him. Maybe even more than I don't like you right now," she claims.

"You just don't like me right now? Meaning that you'll forgive me for getting you hurt and pushing myself on you?"

"Yeah that. What other things are you keeping to yourself?"

"I'm not hiding anything. I didn't find it important and it's not. I wanted you not for blood."

She cuts me off. "Let's be honest, Maxwell."

"Okay, maybe a little for your blood," I rephrase, but her arching eyebrows say otherwise. "Fine, at first for a lot of your blood. Is that better? However, once I saw you—"

"Spied," she corrects.

"Spied, whatever. I knew you were more than just a feeding. I've been through this already, Charlie. Nothing is more important than how I feel for you. Either you believe that or not."

"Okay."

"Okay? You believe me? Or okay you still hate me?"

"I don't hate you, Maxwell. I want to, trust me, I do, but I can't. You're just too cute when I put you on the spot." Just as she finishes, her stomach growls.

"You must be starving."

I watch her nod in approval. Within minutes I get lunch ordered. "It'll be here in fifteen minutes. You should change."

"Maxwell?" Charlie asks, standing in the bedroom doorway. She starts speaking when I look her way. "I need help with the zipper again." She sounds annoyed, but I, on the other hand, am quite grateful.

She turns her back to me and within seconds I reach for the zipper. I try to keep my cold fingers off her warm body this time around as I unzip it to a point where I know she can reach. She turns around to face me just as I let go of the dress.

I hold my hands up to her to show my innocence. Her skeptical eyes scan my hand that has been cut open not long ago. The wound is completely healed now. Only the dried blood that stains my palm shows any indication that I was injured at all. Deciding against saying anything, she turns back into the bedroom and shuts the door in my face.

The fifteen minutes fly by and I take her food from the room service personnel, only to have it sit across from me on the table as I wait for Charlie to exit the bedroom. When another knock raps on the door, my senses go on overload. Everyone knows that the rest of the day is for Charlie and myself to be together…alone.

I open the door without looking to see who it is, assuming it to be Grace even though she knows better. Without warning, a tall woman throws herself on top of me. Her dark wavy hair covers my face. A glass bottle that's tightly grasped in her right hand smacks against the doorframe. A sickening feeling takes over my body as her fingers bury themselves in my hair.

"Benjamin sent me," she whispers in my ear. I feel her cold lips touch my neck. Her hand harshly tugs my hair, stabilizing my head for a fraction of a second. That second is all she needs for her mouth to find mine.

I try to pry her off me, but the harder I push the more she latches on. Seeing that she's a vampire, overpowering her takes some effort. "Stella," I mutter out as her mouth still presses up against mine.

"You know this woman, Maxwell? Would you mind introducing me?" Charlie yells from behind me.

The woman detaches herself from me to look at Charlie. I can sense Charlie's anger. "Why exactly did Benjamin send you here?" Charlie asks with severe pronunciation to each syllable.

The woman's hand tightens around the neck of the bottle. "Benjamin said you wouldn't mind. He said that Maxwell might be getting blood from you, but he's not getting all of his needs met by the great Charlie." Her blue eyes move to gaze at me. The words come out in a purr. "Come on, Maxwell, it will be like the old days."

I can hear Charlie stuttering in rage as she searches for her remark. I can only imagine what she's going to say. The stomping of her approaching footsteps tells me to move aside. I assume she's going to stop at my side to embrace me, telling this sleazy woman to get the hell out, but as she comes into view, I see her arms crossed over her chest.

"I think I'm going to have a chat with Grace. I'll leave you two alone for a while," she spits out while she stares Stella down.

I watch Charlie propel herself forward to shove past the unwanted woman, but I catch her by the elbow. "Not so fast, love. Stella here will be the one on her way. I think she gets the point and realizes her services won't be necessary. Go and tell Benjamin that he needs to keep his nose out of others' personal lives and that my needs are very well met." I slam the door in Stella's face and walk back into the kitchen area with Charlie still in hand.

It takes great effort to hold back my anger that vibrates through me. Benjamin is going too far in his tactics of trying to separate Charlie and myself. Did he really think I would choose Stella over Charlie? It's true that years ago when I saw the donors within my bloodline as food and nothing else I engaged in sexual activities with Stella. However, Charlie is the only woman that my fantasies revolve around now and she'll soon be the only vampire who will fulfill my desires as well.

I push Charlie onto the chair by the table; the tray of food sits in front of her. "Eat," I tell her.

"I lost my appetite." I watch her as she tries to hide her hands under the table as they ball into fists, but she winces in pain as her fresh wound splits open wider.

"Charlie, you didn't eat breakfast this morning. You have to eat, don't punish yourself because of Benjamin. He sent her because he knew you would react like this. Now prove him wrong and for once do as I say."

"What did she mean when she said like the old days? You know what, never mind, I don't want to hear it." She bolts up from her chair; it falls over from the force. She storms past me, but once again, I catch her by the arm.

Aggressively, she yanks her arm out of my grip. "Don't. Touch. Me. I get it, I really do. I'm not stopping you, Maxwell, go have your fun. I don't love you like she does, obviously." The words come ruthlessly out of her mouth and she speedily walks into the bedroom to slam the door behind her.

I immediately go to the door only to find it locked. Wiggling the knob profusely, I begin to pound on the door out of rage. "Charlie, open the door." I wait. With no response, I continue to pound on the flimsy wooden door and demand her attention. "Charlie, open the door right now."

Silence.

"She's my past, Charlie, and nothing more. Haven't I proven to you that my past is in my past, that I'm not the same person I was then? Don't you think if I was still that person we would be here? That you wouldn't have more than one bite mark? That you would you still be alive for that matter?" My fists pound on the door. When she doesn't respond my head drops to the door with a thud. How can I prove to her that Stella is not who I want or who I want to be with for forever?

I hear things crash behind the door.

"I will break it down," I threaten.

"I'd like to see you try," she retorts.

Her silence and backtalk brings the monster out in me. And after a minute or two of peace I slam into the door at full force. Creaking and cracking fill the rooms as the door proves to not be able to hold up to my strength, but if she wants me to break down the door, I will, and I might just lay down some ground rules while I'm at it. She wants the old Maxwell, she just might get him tonight.

Chapter Seventeen

Charlie

I stomp my way over to my suitcase and throw any loose articles in before I harshly zip it up. Great one, Charlie, try not to be a complete bitch and still get scorned. I mean, who would look twice at me with Stella in the room? She has similarities to mine, but they look better on her. She's skinnier, taller, more mature looking, and the best attribute she has is that she's already dead. I deserve this, I tell myself.

Sitting on the corner of the bed, I allow my head to fall into my hands. I can feel fresh, warm blood seep through my bandages and smear on my face, mixing with my tears. In the middle of arguing with myself, the pounding starts again. I didn't bother listening to Maxwell's speech. Part of me doesn't want to hear his apologetic words, while part of me believes what he says to be more lies.

I laugh to myself as I hear him threaten to break down the door. But he's completely serious because seconds later he crashes through the door. Splinters of wood scatter across the floor and fly in air from the sheer force.

"What. The. Fuck," I say as an afterthought. My body is still glued to the bed.

"You wanted me to break down the door."

"No, I didn't," I interrupt.

"Yes, you did. You said you can try. Well, guess what, love, I don't have to try. I can and I did. Do not ever do that to me again. Do you hear me? I won't let anyone or anything come between us, including a damn door. Understood?" Maxwell bickers as he walks into the room and begins pacing.

"I didn't mean it literally. It was a figure of speech. Calm down."

"I don't think you understand, Charlie. You drive me crazy and it takes a whole lot of self-control to not be who I was. Do you want that side of me, Charlie? I'm not proud of what I did in the past, what I did with Stella, but I try to change every day. Try to impress you every day and when you keep pushing me away it drives me mad. It turns me into this."

His features go from hard to soft in the matter of seconds when he sees how much he's scaring me. His hand stretches out to me, expecting me to take it as he speaks in a nurturing tone. "Let's get you cleaned up."

With the refusal of me moving my hand into his, he grabs it himself. I shuffle my feet all the way to the bathroom. My body goes rigid as he picks me up and sits me on the countertop. His head shakes from side to side as he wets a washcloth. I refuse to look him in the eye when he grasps my chin firmly to lift my head up. Roughly, he wipes at my left cheek and forehead.

"You got blood all over yourself," he mutters. Once he's done, he grabs some clean bandages and re-wraps my left hand. "Are you going to say anything, Charlie, even if it is to yell at me?"

"Did you love her? Do you still have feeling for her?" Once I speak the words, I instantly regret it.

"Do I really need to answer that? I never loved Stella. She and I only...how can I say this without making things worse...I'm not proud of the person I was in the past. Stella was just as cruel as I was and we added fuel to each other's hateful fire. I'm not that person anymore and her behavior, her attitude hasn't changed after all these years. She's not you and she never will be."

I can feel myself start to forgive him. He's trying awfully hard to convince me and no matter how hard I try to fight it, I find it sweet. "When can we go home?" Part of me wants to fix the tension between us, but a bigger part of me wants to go home. This place has been nothing but disaster.

"We can leave tomorrow afternoon."

"Really? That easy?"

"It's only a day earlier than I planned, but since I did bring you here a day early. Now, go eat before your food gets cold."

"Fine." I start to slide down off the countertop, but he catches me and helps me the rest of the way to the floor. My body slides down his. "I get it, Maxwell. You don't love or even like Stella anymore. And I'm going to ignore the fact that it eats at me that you two were together. And that bothers me to no end that it bothers me." I walk out of the bathroom, through the bedroom and sit down at the table without so much a glance back at Maxwell.

I mean, did I expect Maxwell to have never looked at another woman in his life? Did I really expect that he wouldn't have had intimate relations within his three hundred or so years on this planet? Maxwell sits across from me, his eyes boring into me. The last thing I need is for him to start his speech about how his past is in the past. Or even worse, bring up the fact that I admitted to having feelings for him.

I see the corners of his mouth lift as he's about to speak, so I force words to flow out of my mouth to stop whatever it is that he's planning on saying. "What are you looking at? Are you hungry?" My eyes widen as I realize what I just said.

"If you're offering, I could have a bite to eat." He

winks at me.

"I didn't mean it that way. It's just that I'm eating and you're staring at me. It felt wrong not to offer but since you don't eat food it's a useless comment." My eyes go back to my plate and I take a few more bites before my stomach turns into knots. What an awful attempt at dodging an unwanted conversation.

"Do you want to watch some TV or go down to the bar later this evening?" Maxwell asks when he sees me push the tray away. He's willing to do whatever I want, but all I want to do is lie down.

"Would it be awful of me to say I just want to take a nap?" I reply.

"Not at all."

I have to walk past him in order to reach the bedroom. As I get closer his arms twitch at his side. I glance over my shoulder as I speak to him, but don't make eye contact. "And I guess I'll be leaving the door open."

I strip off my jeans and T-shirt and slide into bed in just my bra and underwear, completely careless of the possibility of having spying eyes on me. I sigh as my head falls onto the soft pillow, only to toss and turn several times before finding the perfect spot. Inhaling deeply, I unwind in the fresh scent. What I didn't realize is that my head lies upon Maxwell's pillow.

My eyes slowly open as I feel a cold nudge. I just groan and move over, relaxing in the coldness that lingers under the blanket. I don't know how much time passed or if it's morning yet, but Maxwell's voice wakes me up. My cheeks flush as I realize I'm draped over him once again.

"Holy shit. I didn't know...I didn't mean to." I can't finish my apology or even piece my words together properly as I stare at the sticky blood that puddles on the bed sheet and Maxwell's chest. My still bleeding hand sticks to his abdomen.

"Charlie, it's okay. It's just some blood. We can put more bandages on it and change the sheets. Just let me take a shower first." He's being overly calm. I bet inside he's going crazy.

"But…you're covered in blood." My voice gets shakier with each word I try to speak.

"It's not the end of the world. This isn't the first time I've woken up covered in blood."

My eyes go wide imagining the massacre he caused and his body lying in the middle of it, gloating with glory.

He quickly starts the conversation back up to take my mind away from the awful scene that plants itself in my brain. "Probably shouldn't have said that. Relax, it's not what you are most likely thinking. Allow me to shower and then I'll change the sheets. You can re-bandage your hand, preferably with more layers."

He jumps up from the bed and within seconds the bathroom door closes. I slide my way out of bed, holding my bleeding hand against my chest. Aimlessly, I walk around the room in circles, leaving a trail of droplets behind me that soak into the carpet. My bandages are in the bathroom where Maxwell happens to be. I can completely understand why he would want to shower as soon as possible. He's thirsty and having my blood taunt him must be crushingly painful, but I can't stand here and bleed all over the place. With one deep breath, I make my way to the bathroom door. The sound of the shower head comes from behind the closed door. If anything the shower curtain should conceal him.

I knock anyways. The knocks are good and strong even though he has his super hearing. Patiently, I wait and knock again only to wait again. There's a small puddle of blood at my feet that's growing in size the longer I stand out here. With no other choice, I brace myself and walk right in. Steam fills the room, making it hard to see. Wafting my hand from side to side, I begin to make out a body standing in front of me.

My jaw drops at the sight. Abruptly, I turn to run out of the room only to smack into the doorframe on the way out. The sting from the brunt force to my shoulder makes me stumble, but I catch my footing and lean over the bed.

My eyes squint shut, trying to get the image of a naked Maxwell out of my head. Right about now I wish the image of him lying in the middle of bloody bodies would come back. No matter how hard I try or how many times I tell myself to forget, the image won't go away.

The image of Maxwell staring right at me not bothering to cover up any part of his completely naked body begins to taunt me. The details are crisp and fresh in my mind as I replay the scene over and over again. His slick, wet body, and his shocked yet cocky expression on his face as I entered the room unexpectedly.

"Charlie, I didn't know you were going to come in or I would have had a towel. Are you okay? It sounded like you hit your shoulder pretty hard," Maxwell asks, his voice full of concern.

Slowly, I turn around with my eyes closed, afraid that he rushed out of the bathroom without bothering to cover himself up.

"You can open your eyes. I have a towel on."

"I didn't mean to walk in on you like…that." I wave my hands at him to specify his nakedness. My hands unwillingly hover over the lower half of his body, which is now covered up by a white towel that he wrapped around his waist. I wanted him to understand that I didn't mean to see his 'business'. I have a hard time looking him in the eyes.

A small laugh from Maxwell catches my attention.

"What?" My tone is demanding and shaky at the same time.

"So innocent. Let me bandage your hand."

What the hell is that supposed to mean? Innocent. He thought I was innocent because I freaked out at the sight of his naked body. It was shock not innocence. It's not like I'm a virgin. I've seen naked men before.

Layer after layer of soft fluffy white gauze covers the nasty painful wound while I bicker with myself. It's beyond me why they would slice a human's hand from wrist to fingertip. Whenever my hand bends just the slightest you can feel the splitting of the skin. It isn't deep, but it still makes daily functions irritating.

"I can imagine how uncomfortable it is. If there was anything I could do to help ease the pain, I would," Maxwell offers. His tall frame towers over me as he stands in front of me. Water drips from his wet hair and body.

"I'm going to dry myself off and then change the sheets, so just sit tight for a minute."

It doesn't take him long to emerge from the bathroom completely dry and in some pajama bottoms. I've never witnessed his abilities first hand, but as he moves with ease at an insane pace I finally get to. His movement is swift yet flowing as he appears by the bed then disappears from the room with sheets in his hands seconds later, only to have the fresh crisp linens on the bed before I blink twice.

A giggle escapes my mouth as he bends with a wave of his arm as he gestures for me to lie back down. I slap my hand over my mouth at my girlish behavior.

"Your chariot awaits, my lady," he says in the most cunning, deep voice.

I crawl into bed with a smile spread across my mouth. I stifle groans of pain when I put pressure on my wound as I make my way to my pillow. Maxwell places his hand on my back to comfort me. The expectation of a chill doesn't come. Only comfort and relief wash through me. An idea pops into my head about how he can help with the throbbing pain of the cut. "Maxwell, can I ask something of you?"

"Anything," he quickly replies as he pulls the blankets over me. His words seem a little too anxious.

"Can I…" I can't believe I'm going to ask him this, but if I want to be able to go back to sleep, it needs to be done. "Can I rest my hand on your chest…shoulder?" I quickly correct myself. My head nods and shakes every which way as I grow more and more embarrassed. "I mean, your shoulder is fine. The coolness of your skin makes it feel better. Unless you want to go get me some ice."

He slips under the covers. "Well, from what I'm informed of by you, I myself am like ice. Really, Charlie, you don't need to ask." His fingers lightly pick up my injured hand and place it on his chest. Right over his heart. His hand gently lays on top mine, pinning it in place. The soft thump of his heart beating doesn't come. His emptiness starts to make me feel empty.

"Maxwell?"

"Yes, love?" he replies back. His eyes are closed, but I know I have his complete attention.

Curiosity is getting the best of me. "Couldn't you just give me some of your blood to heal me?"

"I wish it were that easy. I could and it would, but you would become vampire."

"Oh."

"It will heal. It will take time, but it'll heal. Turning into a vampire to get rid of an annoyance won't go away so easily. Get some rest."

The cold that emits off his body numbs my tender hand and for once I abide by his words more than willingly.

* * *

Maxwell

I haven't slept for at least a day or so, because of the excitement of being this close to Charlie. It's not necessary to sleep, but it allows me to cling to my once human self. Charlie gave me the perfect opportunity to make her into the vampire that she's going to be one day. I could've tricked her and offered her the relief she is so looking for from her wound, but I just couldn't do it.

Before I know it, morning arrives. Even though this town doesn't receive direct sunlight this time of year, I can still sense it. I slip out from under Charlie's hand to get a head start on getting dressed. There's business that needs to be handled before we leave this afternoon.

Charlie wakes up a few hours after me. She walks out of the bedroom fully clothed, looking well rested. "What time do we leave?" she asks, overly anxious.

"The plane will depart at two this afternoon." The clock on the wall reads nine. "That leaves you three hours to try to occupy yourself."

"That leaves me? What about you?" The sound of concern in her voice is barely recognizable as it's laced with annoyance.

"I have something I need to take care of before we go back home." I don't want to tell her that I intend to confront Benjamin about his tactics last night. The quarrel he wants to start is between him and me. Charlie doesn't have a place in this. She shouldn't have even been brought into this century old battle. "Why don't you go and visit with Grace? Last night you mentioned you were going to go have a chat with her. I assume you want her to explain the unwanted relationship she has with Benjamin. You can also inform her that we're leaving today as well."

She agrees with a nod of her head. With breakfast eaten and an hour before I have to send her to Grace, we sit on the couch, completely oblivious to each other. I can tell she's lost in thought. Her stern lips give away what she's thinking about. Stella. That's where she thinks I'm going. Even though I can clear her insecurities away by admitting where I'm going, I don't. She would only offer to come along, which is out of the question, and I kinda like this jealous side of her.

The hum of silence is broken as I touch Charlie's thigh. She sucks in a breath at my touch. "Let me walk you to Grace's room. I'll come get you when I'm finished."

"What if she's not there or she's busy, then what?"

"She'll be there." I know that Charlie is carefully insinuating that she wants to come with me, but I can't allow that. There might be more than just words thrown at each other.

I usually don't bother in knocking when it comes to Grace, but seeing as I don't have a key to her room, I have to wait until she answers the door. Her footsteps are slow as if she knows it's us and she's dreading the conversation that's going to be brought up.

"What a pleasure to see the both of you again. Come in, Charlie, I know you're dying to question me about yesterday's presentation." Grace's perky voice has a sourness to it.

She holds the door open, waiting for me to follow inside, but I shake my head. I look as far into the room as I can. When I see Charlie nowhere in sight, I continue in a hushed voice. "I'm going to pay Benjamin a visit. He sent an unwanted present to my room last night and he needs to learn a lesson."

"A present? That's more than what I get."

"He sent Stella to my room last night, Grace." That one name is all I have to say for Grace to understand how far her once vampire husband went in ruining her friend's relationship. I walk away from Grace, who hovers in the open doorway. All that's on my mind is getting to the council estate.

Once again I'm greeted by the Sylvester. No matter how many times I see him I still can't comprehend his green complexion. When Charlie asked I had other things on my mind, but I truthfully don't have a logical answer. It's infrequent to see someone as unique as him. His deep set voice makes him more monster-like. "Master Barnett, The High Council is unaware of your visit."

"I realize that, Sylvester, but Benjamin has some explaining to do."

The library seems like the worst place ever for someone who has not learned a thing over the past few hundred years. However, there he sits elegantly in a large wingback chair with a book open, although I believe it to be just for show.

"Maxwell, I had a feeling I would be seeing you again. Without Charlie, I see. I assume things didn't go well last night." The way he says his chosen words makes me sick and feverish with anger.

"As if you wouldn't know how the evening would conclude," I spit out.

"I suppose you're right. I knew it would hinder the

fake relationship you have with your soon-to-be bride, but when Stella came barging in here with her high heels clanking on my marble flooring I was a bit disappointed. The fish didn't take the bait, but there's always next time seeing as you're in my pond."

"Leave Charlie and myself alone. If I see that whore one more time, because of your orders, you will pay." If my cheeks could flush with anger they would. If my heart could beat, it would be pounding against my ribcage.

"Who are you kidding, Maxwell. You come in here and blame me for your bride's trust issues. You can fool the others. Hell, even she can fool the others, but not me. I know she doesn't love you, although she might start to realize now that she might. You can thank me later for that, but she's not willing to die for you. With one look at her I know she's repulsed by vampires. After everything that's happened in the past you think you would learn to pick a girl who loves what you are not despise it. We all know that doesn't end well."

"She will be my bride and she will be happy with eternity. I'll be better to her than you were to Grace, because let's face it, this is all about Grace. You can't bear that she disowned you. Let alone the disrespect you got for killing Alexander. You think you would be the one to learn that revenge can't level the playing field and betrayal can never be forgiven. You interfering with Charlie and me just makes Grace hate you more. Alexander might be gone, but she considers me and Charlie her family now." I stand my ground and stare Benjamin in his eyes. I'm ready for a fight if he wants one.

However, when he just stares at me in disbelief, I turn to leave him with his regrets. Almost through the door, his voice brings me to a stop. "Was there a threat mixed in your words, Maxwell?"

"No, there's no need to threaten you; you're doing just fine in ruining your self image. One day the council will see you for who you really are. For the time being, I'm just telling you where you stand. Be honest with yourself, Benjamin. If it wasn't for your loss of Grace, you wouldn't even know I exist in this vast ever growing vampire population. Have a good day, your majesty." Storming out the doors, I refuse to look back.

Benjamin's digging his own grave and I want to make sure he knows I'm here to fill the hole after he falls in it. The discussion between him and I didn't last as long as I thought it would, so when I see the perfect little shop on the car ride back to the hotel, I decide to stop. Charlie's not expecting me back for a few more hours, therefore I have enough time to browse for an ideal gift.

At a slow pace, I make my way to Grace's room. Grace opens the door in better mood than she did before. Maybe Charlie is rubbing off on her or more like Grace is rubbing off on Charlie.

"I'm not interrupting anything, am I?"

"No, just some girl talk," Grace replies.

"You know we're leaving today, right?"

She nods her head in disappointment.

"You're free to join us on the flight back," I offer.

"I wish I could, but in the eyes of The High Council I'm Benjamin's bride and therefore I can't leave until the presentation is fully concluded," she retorts.

"Fully concluded, but isn't it done?" Charlie asks, rounding the corner.

"For you and Maxwell it's done, but there usually is a celebration that all the vampires attend to mingle. I would leave, but I can't." Grace's happy demeanor fully changes for the worst. No matter how much I tell

Benjamin to leave Charlie and me alone, I can't save Grace from his evil ways.

"I wish I could make things better," Charlie offers, patting Grace's shoulder gently.

Grace smiles kindly back, but doesn't speak a word. Letting her get her peace before she has to face The High Council again, I lead Charlie out of the room.

"A vampire gala of sorts is happening tonight?" Charlie says as soon as we enter the elevator.

"You sound like you're interested." First, she wants to leave as soon as possible and then she hears that there's going to be a party resulting in her wanting to stay.

"Maybe." Is all she says as she looks at the floor. Her eyes are toward the ground and the tip of her right foot grinds into the lush carpet that covers the elevator floor as if she's weighing the idea.

"If you want to stay, Charlie, we can, just say the words." There's no way I want to be at that party, but if Charlie wants to, I will. I'm so deep in my own misery that I almost miss the quick nod that Charlie gives me as an answer. "I said say the words, not agree with them."

"I want to go to the party." Her childish whine makes me smile. "I'm just a little bit curious." She holds up her index finger and thumb, leaving a little gap between the two to signify her little bit of curiosity.

Trailing behind her without saying a word, I follow her to kitchen table where she plops herself down on a chair. Her stiff back tells me everything I need to know. She's determined.

"Are you sure this is the best idea?" The words could cost me, but I have to ask. I have to make sure she fully understands what she's saying. A glare is all I need to back down. "I'm just saying, Charlie. I thought vampire parties didn't agree with you considering what happened last time. Nonetheless, if you want to go, we will. The party starts at eight."

"Oh, we're going," she says as she stands up from the kitchen chair. She struts over to the couch, falling onto one of the cushions.

She's never shown this drive before, but I do find it quite pleasing. I sit next to her while she rests her eyes. I don't have to wake her when it gets closer, because she wakes herself. Sitting back, I watch her jump off the couch and prance to the bedroom, rubbing her hands together.

She pokes her head out the doorway. "What would be suitable to wear?" she asks.

"These parties can be very revealing." Is the best way I can explain it. The women wear the shortest skintight barely visible dresses and most of the men have either their button-down shirts open or no shirt at all.

A squeal comes out of Charlie's mouth in excitement. "Grace packed the perfect dress."

Oh Jesus. I can only imagine what Grace packed that would be appropriate for this party. I refuse to degrade myself and follow the unwritten rules of seduction for this event. I have been to four prior to this. Let's just say I was young and naïve. I took every advantage made available from inviting two women with me one year and neither one of them escorted me back to my room, because they were passed out in the corner from being fed on too much.

The clicking of heels pulls me out of my flashback. She clears her throat several times to get my attention. It's not as if I don't want to see her in this supposed dress, but I know that some part of me is going to want her to cover her up. Just the thought of searching eyes scanning her body makes what little blood I have boil.

The thoughts I had about people's eyes violating her are proven correct as my own eyes react that very way when she comes into view. The metallic silver and black dress barely reaches mid-thigh and the deep v-neck shows excessive amounts of cleavage. With her hair pulled up to show her slightly tan flawless neck—except for the fading bite mark—and shoulders, I begin to feel aches in more places than just my mouth.

"Do you need to get ready?" she asks, totally oblivious to my inner battle of bedding her right now.

I unbutton a few top buttons on my shirt. "All ready." I don't want to go to the party any more than I did from the start, but I look at the bright side of things. The most beautiful woman alive will accompany me.

"Let's go tell Grace we're attending," Charlie speedily says, hanging on my arm.

"Very well, but just know that things might not be pleasant at this party." There's much more I want to say. There are things that happen at these events where vampires from all over the world attend. I don't want to scare her or ruin her happiness, so I keep it to myself. I just have to be on guard at all times.

Chapter Eighteen

Charlie

We reach Grace's door and I'm just about to knock when Maxwell grabs my hand to stop me. "What?"

"Let's go downstairs to the party. We'll surprise Grace there." He can't hide his emotions from me. I see concern etched into his features, tense lips and narrowed brows.

"What are you not telling me?"

"She has company and I think it's best not to disrupt them."

"Who?" I know he knows who's in there.

"Benjamin," he reluctantly says.

"Is he being cruel to Grace?" After hearing that Benjamin takes advantage of Grace, I can't help but to want to give him a piece of my mind. There is part of me that wants to call him out on sending Stella to our room.

"He's in the middle of scolding Grace and it wouldn't be best to make things worse." His eyes are cast down to the floor.

"What!" I bellow. Maxwell's hand clamps across my mouth to keep me silent.

"He's yelling at her because she let us leave. Even though she's not loyal to him, he still demands her to be. In the eyes of The High Council she's expected to be devoted to him and their rules. He apparently wants us here and Grace let us slide through her fingers."

I can't sit here and let him ream Grace out because of me. While Maxwell left earlier today to do whatever it was he had to do without me, I really got to know

Grace. The similarities between the two of us are outstanding. Her life was not pleasant and she found light in the dark world she was trapped in because of Benjamin. Her light was Maxwell and Alexander.

I yank myself free from Maxwell's grip and pound on the door. "Grace," I scream at the door. A quick sideways glace toward Maxwell to see his angered glare is all I have time for before the sound of footsteps gets louder. The look on his face is all I need to know that what I've done doesn't sit well with him. "Listen, I'm not going to stand back and let him win. Now, are you with me or not?"

"Only if you do what I tell you to for this to work as well as you want it to."

"Deal," I agree faster than I should have. I can only imagine what he is going to instruct me to do.

Within a few moments the door swings open to show us a hesitant Grace. Her eyes light up at the sight of us, but quickly dim down.

"Surprise," I cautiously say as she looks from Maxwell to me.

"What are you doing here? I thought you were leaving," she asks in a hushed voice. She puts extra emphasis on the word 'leaving' as if she's secretly telling us to go.

Maxwell tips his head toward me. "She wants to go to the party, Grace." His words are strained. I know he blames Grace for bringing the party to my attention in the first place, because if she didn't we would be almost home by now.

"Grace, I'm in the middle of a discussion with you. Tell your meal to find you at the party," Benjamin shouts from somewhere inside the room.

Heat rises to my head, and gradually the feeling takes over my whole body. I push past Grace to storm into the room to confront this ungrateful man. With his back to me, I have the advantage. The feel of Maxwell's cold body lingers closely behind me. I glance back, silently telling him to back off.

"Good evening, Benjamin. I understand you're giving my dear friend Grace here a hard time about my unexpected departure."

He whips around at the sound of my voice. The look of shock mixed with disgust on his face as he stares down at me creates a sudden urge to punch him. "What a pleasure to see that you are still here." He beams at me.

I can see through his fake façade. You would think that after hundreds of years vampires would be able to conceal emotions better. "It's not a pleasure, however, to see you, Benjamin." I, on the other hand, keep a smile on my face and my voice very calm.

I hear the sudden intake of breath from Maxwell and Grace. The look of hatred on Benjamin's face is all I need to continue. "Your sick joke last night was unacceptable. I'm much harder to get rid of than you assume. I hope you have fun tonight and wish you all the luck in the future." I want to tell him he'll need it, but I decide against it.

Maxwell wraps his arm around me to escort me out of the room with Grace trailing behind. My heart can't stop racing as adrenaline fills my bloodstream. I can't believe I just did that. Putting my life in danger for vampires is the last thing I would expect myself to do. Maxwell's rumble of a laugh vibrates in his chest.

"I can't believe you just did that. He hated the three of us before, but now...now he definitely despises us," Maxwell finally responds to my actions.

"Is that bad? Should I have kept my mouth shut?" Nervousness takes over my voice. At first, I wanted to stand up for myself, to find inner strength and tell myself that no human or vampire is going to make me cower in the corner. However, after the words have been said…maybe it wasn't the best idea.

"Are you kidding me? Hell no! He deserves getting put in his place by a human, by a tiny female human nonetheless," Grace replies from behind me. Her laughter fills the semi empty halls.

The closer we get to the party the more I regret even wanting to come. Woman after woman passes me by and I force my eyeballs to remain looking forward. Their attire barely covers their pale bodies and the occasional flash of bare breasts causes me to shudder. The female humans are just as tasteless. The male guests either have open button-down shirts or deep v-neck T-shirts on, but there's the occasional glimpse of a man who's completely shirtless. No wonder why Maxwell didn't want me to attend the party.

We stop a few feet away from the doors. "Charlie, I need to tell you something."

"I'm going to go find somebody…anybody," Grace interjects. She quickly walks away as if she knows what Maxwell is about to say and refuses to be around when whatever it is goes down.

A questioning look glues itself to my face as I try to figure out the cryptic message. It doesn't take long for Maxwell to explain. "There are going to be things behind those doors that you're not going to be fond of. I need you to remain calm and keep your words to yourself."

"What's that supposed mean?" My voice comes out more scared than I want it to. Maxwell turns away and gently nudges me to follow him, but I refuse. "What's that supposed to mean, Maxwell?" I say in a more strict tone.

The deep breath he takes lets me know it can't be good. "Feedings are meant to be in private...but...it's expected of us to draw blood tonight. There are some vampires who get carried away, though. Don't be surprised if you see people with bite marks, multiple fresh bite marks." He intertwines my arm with his and leads us through the dreaded double doors.

I know I should have thought about this party more. Imagining what I agreed to earlier when Maxwell told me to do what he asks of me makes my stomach turn. No matter where I am or what I'm doing, I've always bad judgment.

The dimly lit room puts my nerves on edge. Who knows what's lurking in the unseen corners of the room. Just the thought of 'feedings' going on around me makes my eyes stay fixed on the ground. Although, either my eyes are playing tricks on me or I can make out puddles of red liquid that spot the tiled floor.

Managing to get through the crowd on merely trusting Maxwell, I try to focus on things that are more important. My breathing lessens the further inside the room we get. When an unexpected body jumps in front of us, I become startled. Maxwell's grip gets tighter as he feels me literally jump and stumble in my high heels.

"Charlie, I didn't mean to scare you." The man's voice is nurturing, however unwanted. My eyes go up the man's body, starting at his feet, up his legs, over his shirtless chest, to meet his soft brown eyes...Aiden's eyes. There's no mistaking the four bite marks I spot instantly that are randomly placed on his body.

"You found her. I was wondering if you were coming," Paige chimes in as she bounces over. She looks at me with her doe eyes, trying to be sexy, but it takes a toll on me from not slapping her. She purposely tried to sleep with Maxwell and now she's playing bestie to me. But it's her dress that keeps me silent.

I become speechless as my eyes frantically try to find somewhere else to look. I finally decide on looking at Maxwell. When my eyes finally put him in view, I see he's already staring at me. With my mouth still hanging open and my eyelids taking extra long blinks, I think about what to say. "Um…" My head shakes in disapproval and my hand automatically goes to cover my mouth. "I…yea."

The words slowly leave my mouth unintentionally. They don't make sense, which isn't a surprise because my brain can't comprehend why someone would leave the confines of a secluded room looking like that, wearing something like that. All I can do is stare at Maxwell, praying he'll be the one who's able to get us out of this awkward situation.

"I think Charlie is trying to say that we have to find Grace," Maxwell says in the duo's direction, but without looking at them.

"Yea…yea." I just can't find words. My head bobs in agreement as Maxwell leads us away. When I know we're a safe distance away I finally talk. "Her dress was mesh; it was mesh and nothing else. I mean, it was all out there for everyone to see. Mesh. Maxwell. Mesh," I blab like an idiot. However, no matter how fast I looked away from her I couldn't miss the nasty bite mark on her neck that was oozing blood down her shoulder.

"I warned you."

"You warned me when we were standing at the vampire feeding orgy's doors. I should've known. Nothing is ever easy with you vampires. Look at what I got myself into again." I wave my hand at my surroundings. The room is filled with vampires and humans barely wearing clothing. All the humans have drinks in their hands with smiles on their faces, but no matter how big the smile or the drink they can't hide the still bleeding bite marks that cover their bodies. As for the vampires that fill the room, they drunkenly laugh as they tap their kegs with legs and wipe at their smeared blood-stained mouths. I even notice several limp bodies that line the edges of the room.

"At least she's wearing more than she was when she showed up in our bed."

"Not making it easier, Maxwell."

"Understood. I shall never bring it up again."

"That's right. Now, let's find Grace."

Before we have a chance to find her, she finds us. "How are you holding up?" Grace kindly asks as she walks up from behind me.

"Great, just great. The smell of blood in my nostrils is pleasant and the half naked bodies are not making me uncomfortable at all."

"Not so well, I take it," she says, finding the hidden truth in my words.

"Ya think," I snap. "I swear I saw someone with bites down the length of their arm. The blood from the top one just blended into the one beneath that and the one beneath that one." I know I'm rambling, but the words just won't stop pouring out.

Grace's hand slaps Maxwell's shoulder as she says her parting of ways. "Benjamin's here. That's my cue to go and eat in peace, as well as your cue to get this one contained."

"Furthermore, that's our cue to not eat in peace," Maxwell adds. He ignores my confused expression. "You remember when you agreed to do as I ask?" I shake my head slowly at his words. "Do you want to ruin everything we've done to keep your humanity for as long as possible? He knows, Charlie. When I left you with Grace this morning I went to go talk to him. And your little outburst didn't make it any easier for him to digest."

Relief mixes with despair. At least those nagging thoughts of Maxwell going to see Stella while he left me with Grace are smothered. My confused or fearful gaze doesn't stop him from continuing.

"He told me you can fool the other members of the council, but you can't fool him. He knows you don't want to be a vampire. He knows you don't want to die for me. Just one bite and we'll be back on top."

"One bite, one bite in a place like this means death. Do you see those limp bodies that are lining the wall? They'll probably bleed out by the time anyone thinks of looking for them."

He cuts me off, speaking over me. "I would never kill you without being able to start the transformation and I wouldn't do that here. I would never hu—"

"Hurt me, you would never hurt me, says the man who trapped me in a room and did his vampire voodoo on me. I still have the bite mark from before. You want me to have puncture marks all over me like these freaks. I have to go back to work, you know? I already had to lie to Morgan when she spotted the first bite. Now you want me to hide another one?" My words get louder and angrier by the time I finish.

"I understand you're frightened, but you'll be fine. Do I need to seduce you with my vampire charm? This isn't just for me, it's for you too." Those dark brown eyes silently beg me. His shaggy long hair creates shadows on his face to exaggerate his depressed features.

That's what he calls it, charm. This trip has cost me nothing but blood, sweat, and tears. I punch him in the arm. He's unfazed by the action, which just makes me even more agitated. "I hate you," I say through gritted teeth. The words are easy to say, because I'm angry with him that yet again I am tricked into getting bit. However, my heart pangs just the slightest amount at my hurtful words. My head plummets into my cupped hands from frustration. This inner battle of wanting him as close to me as he can be and loathing him is tiring.

"Let's get this over with," I mutter.

"You know, if you were happier about it, it would hurt less," Maxwell says in a husky voice. In a blink of my eyes, his fingers are around the back of my neck. With a sudden jerk of his hand, I'm forced to look at him. He rests his forehead against mine, the tips of our noses touching. The entire surface of my body begins to tingle and my breathing gets rigid. My brain is screaming inside my skull, but my vocal cords refuse to function. Once his mouth touches mine any chance of words coming out are lost.

His soft lips push against mine. The movement at first is gentle and caring, but the longer I don't protest the more forceful he gets. The breaths I'm able to get aren't enough for my lungs. The inside of my chest burns as his yearning gets rougher and rougher. He breaks the kiss, leaving me breathless. His head instantly buries itself in the curve of my neck.

"Relax…breathe in…breathe out." His warm breath touches my neck as he whispers his words. Goosebumps break out along my exposed shoulder and a tingle runs down my spine.

I do as he insists, I breathe in…I breathe out. The feel of his mouth on my neck makes me involuntarily tense up.

"Charlie, relax. Trust me." His lips graze my ear as he speaks each hushed word slowly.

My eyes close as I let his deep voice calm my senses. Maxwell's mouth finds my neck once again, except this time it's wide open and I can feel the scrap of his fangs. I clear my mind as I wait for the pain. The pressure of his jaw clenching down is accompanied with a pinch.

It is as if something snaps inside of me, altering my views of Maxwell as a vampire altogether. I get dizzy from the thrill of his pressing mouth. His tongue massages my neck to pump more blood to the fresh puncture marks. An urge of wanting to feel pain takes over my body. I can't accept that him biting me is satisfactory. No, it has to hurt. My uninjured hand tangles in his hair and gently tugs. Without thinking, I nudge his head into my neck. Sucking in a sharp breath from the unexpected pain from his teeth burrowing in deeper doesn't stop me from feeling ecstatic. As he drains me of life, I can't help but feel alive.

* * *

Maxwell

The warmth coming from her body as she presses against me is intoxicating. I can feel my ice-cold body start to heat up in spots. It's a weird feeling, but I welcome it because it tricks my subconscious into thinking it's a step closer to being human. As she tugs a fistful of my hair and urges me to sink deeper into her neck, my fingertips dig into her skin. The sound of her hissing breath in my ear as I crush her only adds to my excitement.

Lifting her off the ground, I spin us around, so we're facing the direction that Benjamin is located in. I know he watches us and I want to see the look on his face. Within seconds after averting my gaze, I see him with clenched fists glaring at us. My mouth still suctions itself to Charlie's neck, and my hands slide up and down her body. The curve of her butt fits perfectly in my palm. If I stretch far enough, I can touch her bare thigh.

With Charlie's hands still latched on to me, it gives us the reaction we're hoping for. Benjamin breaks the stare he has on us and storms away with his second bride, the bride he chose over Grace. Grudgingly, I detach from Charlie. Sticky blood gathers in the corners of my mouth, but I quickly lick it away before I look at her.

"How are you feeling?" I ask, afraid I took too much.

Her hand goes to her head. Her eyes squint closed. "Just a bit dizzy is all." The words come out with a sigh.

I know she's not used to the withdrawal of blood and this isn't even a regular basis. Some vampires feed from their humans three times a day, just as a human eats three meals a day. "Let's get you something to drink," I instruct her.

She seems as if she's in a daze as she follows my lead with her fingers gripping my forearm. By the time we arrive at the bar Charlie seems to be getting better. She slaps her hand on the bar top and asks for a shot of something strong. Her voice takes on a slur as if she's already drunk.

"I think my love here will have a glass of juice," I say, correcting her.

"That's probably a better idea," she mumbles out as she agrees with me.

We make our way over to the corner where Grace is located. Once she comes into view we see her sitting next to a chipper young man. He has his pink button-down shirt open, showing his hairless tanned chest. At first glance, I see five bite marks on him. Charlie immediately plops down into a chair, totally oblivious to the leaking blood bank on the other side of Grace.

"If I recall you seem to be in better shape than the last time he sunk his fangs in you," Grace jokes.

"What I'm willing to do to keep my beating heart," Charlie replies, matching Grace's joking tone.

Just as I am about to offer for us to leave, Paige runs up to Charlie. "I requested a song and I want you to join us on the dance floor." Her blonde hair whips as she sways her head. If I could vomit, I would. This Paige is the complete opposite as my Charlie and I don't want any aspect of her rubbing off on Charlie or worse yet…tainting her. She's insecure and desperate as she flaunts herself in front of everyone. She treats herself as her vampire treats her, like meat.

"I'd rather not," Charlie says in a snobby tone.

"Oh my God, Maxwell told you. I'm so sorry. I was just...I mean, when I saw you kiss Aiden I thought I had a chance with Maxwell," Paige whines.

"What? You kissed Aiden?" I abruptly say, interrupting their conversation.

"No...yes, but not how you're thinking I could have."

"I saw it, Maxwell. It was entirely Aiden putting the moves on her," Grace chimes in.

Charlie's eyes light up as she hears the next song play. I can tell she doesn't want anything to do with Paige, but the pull of the song is winning her over. Not to mention that she doesn't want to argue with me further. "Fine, but we are not friends," she reluctantly states.

"Agreed," Paige reluctantly abides.

Without a word said, Charlie jumps up and runs to the dance floor with Paige trailing behind her. I try to stop her, but Grace grabs my arm to stop me. Aiden and Eddie meet them at the edge of the dance floor. She stays in full view. Aiden's brave enough to glance at me as he grabs Charlie's hand to twirl her around. My fists involuntarily clench and unclench. The feel of warm blood gathering in my palm snaps me back into reality.

I watch her as I used to when she was at her favorite nightclub. Except if I were to kill a man here no one would look twice. The only one I would have to answer to is Aiden's vampire, but I'm sure she wouldn't mind. Grace's hand still clamping down on my arm breaks my train of thought. Her strong grip pushes me back down into the seat Charlie occupied.

"Let her dance. You have nothing to worry about," Grace urges.

"I'm not here to watch her dance, Grace. I've watched her dance with fools for quite some time." My temper is starting to get the best of me.

"Settle down."

"You're blood drunk, Grace. Don't lecture me." My words cut her off.

Grace stands in front of my face, blocking Charlie from my view. She leans in extra close, and both her hands find their place on my shoulders. Her fingers painfully squeeze the muscle lining the bone. "The connection has been made for a while now or am I wrong? Since that first touch many things have happened or am I wrong? She didn't kiss that fool. That fool kissed her and she hated it. She was repulsed and shocked at the same time."

"She still doesn't want to become a vampire." Saying the words makes it more real. The truth can hurt greatly when it's spoken aloud.

"Don't be such a baby. You're just blind, you think so little of yourself. You can't see how she looks at you. You think she was just acting a little while ago when you bit her. She'll come around sooner rather than later. Just be patient even though I've never known you to be.

We didn't want to become a vampire, so why are we so quick to make her one?" she lectures.

I go to retort a smart comment, but she refuses to hear my words.

"Shut up," she orders before she bites aggressively into her meal's wrist.

I hear the snapping of cartilage and the gush of blood. Left with no choice, I stare in the direction of a dancing Charlie. To my dismay, when I finally get the will to look directly at her I see something I least expect. She points at me with her index finger. It starts to curl in toward herself, gesturing me to join her. When I don't move she runs over to me.

"You don't want to dance with me?" she says in a sad school girl voice.

"If you're doing this to upset Benjamin further, rest assured that he's gone. We can actually leave whenever you please."

She grabs both of my hands and tries to lift me off the chair. The chair itself drags across the floor a few inches from her determination. I come to a stand so she doesn't have to keep struggling. She brushes herself off with a huff. Taking my hand one more time, she leads me to the dance floor.

"I'm doing this to be nice if you must know. And to shove it in Paige's and Aiden's faces."

Knowing that she's dancing with me to make others jealous is an interesting concept, but I'm curious if there's another reason. "Are you really doing it to be nice or are you starting to like me?"

Her laugh sounds like music to my ears. Her wide smile makes me feel alive. There has never been anyone in my lifetime that has made me feel anything remotely close to how I feel when I'm with her. She just shrugs her shoulders, refusing to answer.

I dance to the upbeat music and the occasional slow song. To feel her body close to mine again puts all my worries aside. More than once Aiden tries to steal her away from me, but Charlie just laughs in his face and turns away. Her behavior pleases me more than I want it to, but I don't say anything to make it stop. Except when a yawn escapes her mouth I put a close to the night.

We walk side by side down the halls. We still have a ways to our room when she starts grumbling that her feet hurt. Right in the middle of the hall, I watch her whip off her heels. The smack of her back against the wall as she loses her balance puts a small smirk on my face. Oh, how graceful she is.

Once she reaches my side, I lift her up in my arms. Her scream of surprise echoes throughout the halls. "Maxwell, put me down," she protests.

"Would you stop squirming before I drop you?" There's no way I would drop her, but maybe the threat of falling on her face will get her to settle down. "Just lay your head on my shoulder and relax," I add.

She doesn't listen to me right away but within a few seconds her head is upon my shoulder. By the time we reach the room, she's sound asleep. I carefully place her in bed and slip off her dress. I have no time to admire her body as she grabs the blankets and utters the word 'pervert' in my direction.

I read the clock before I crawl into bed next to her. Just a little past midnight. Placing my hands under my head as I try to fall asleep, I hear Charlie's voice. Her words put a smile on my face. "Goodnight, Maxwell."

Chapter Nineteen

Charlie

Utter joy rushes through my body when The High Council plane's engines hum to life. I sit in the same windowless window seat with my iPod blaring in my ears and Maxwell's statue like body next to me. As we soar into the sky, I can't help but to be glad that we're leaving the Posthotel Rattenberg behind…forever preferably.

Maxwell's ice-cold fingers graze my cheek as he plucks one of my ear buds out. "Yes?"

With a flick of his wrist, my phone comes into view. His fingers clutch down on it, leaving fingerprints on the screen. I harshly rip it out of his hand and instantly turn it on. Dread and fear turn my annoyed attitude into something more, much more. "Thirty-six missed calls…fifty text messages. Seriously, Maxwell, as if it were possible you just created more work for me. Thank you," I say in a snooty manner.

"My pleasure."

"My pleasure," I repeat in a whispered voice shaking my head, mocking him. My eyebrows scrunch together as my eyes squint with anger. I shove my ear bud back in and turn the music even louder. The flight back seems to take longer than it did to get to damned Austria to begin with. Maybe because it has something to do with the impending doom that's waiting for me at home.

Thinking that turning to my phone for comfort would settle my nerves is one of the worst ideas I have. One after the other is the same message said many different ways. 'Charlie, I'm worried about you. Please call me.' Fifty missed texts from Dave. I sigh to myself. Way to go, Maxwell. I thought I would be able to blow him off...not anymore.

When that familiar bumpy landing alerts me of our arrival some of my tension is released. Nonetheless, I still have to endure the car ride back home. Unlike leaving for Austria, coming back is different. We're accompanied by Grace this time. She sat several rows away from us on the plane, but now she sits to my right, sandwiching me in between her and Maxwell. As if life could get any better or worse for that matter.

Grace stays silent, staring out the window, refusing to acknowledge either of us. Even when the car pulls up outside my house and I tell her goodbye, she just waves her hand sheepishly at me. Maxwell, on the other hand, offers to walk me to my door, but I decline. "Maybe you can see what's wrong with Grace instead." My hand goes to his shoulder. I pat it lightly before grabbing my luggage from his hands. "Don't worry, I won't get jealous." With that said, I walk away, leaving him behind me.

Halfway to the front door, I start tapping at my phone. With one short message sent to Morgan saying that I'm home and I'll see her at work tomorrow, some of my regrets go away. My limbs start to feel heavy as I walk through the house. The loud thump of my luggage as it hits the kitchen floor makes me realize how off my senses are. It's already quite late and most of my day was spent on a plane. I decide to go to bed in order to get some rest for the storm that's brewing for me tomorrow.

Surrounded by the plush comforter, my body loosens up. My eyelids close automatically, my head nuzzles into the pillow, and my feet wrap themselves in the excess blankets at the bottom of the bed. Sweet dreams of nothingness occupy my numb mind. Occasionally, my fingers tug the blankets closer to my body without my brain telling them to. An imaginary chill nips at any exposing skin.

A stretch along with a whisper of rise and shine, I get ready to face the music. Once I get into the parking lot outside my business, a smile comes to my face. I'm back in my comfort zone instead of being surrounded and tested by vampires. The silence in the office building at first is overwhelming, but within a short period of time I grow accustomed to it. Sinking into my large office chair, my hands skim the top of my desk.

"You're finally back, I see," Morgan kindly says, standing in my doorway as she usually does.

"Jesus, Morgan, stealthy much." The words come out louder than I want them to and my hands involuntarily shake like crazy from being startled.

She flat out laughs in my face. Moments later her hands clap together as she clears her throat. "How was your trip with Maxwell?"

"What? How do you know Maxwell? I assure you I went on my business trip alone." My heart pumps faster and faster, trying to keep up with the blood that rushes through my veins as I lie straight to her face.

"You might be a terrific liar, but I have two eye witness accounts that say otherwise."

"Two?" I can assume that Dave told her or she was present when Dave called expecting to talk to me but got Maxwell on the phone instead.

"I am quite envious of you, successful business woman…a sexy romantic boyfriend."

"He's not my boyfriend." Words come spewing out of my mouth. They shouldn't have been the first words to speak, but I couldn't help it. Sounding like a little school girl adds to my embarrassment, but something in me refuses to admit it. The thought that I'm dating a three-hundred-year-old man or have romantic feelings for a walking corpse is…gut-wrenching.

"He came to my house the night before he whisked you away. He wanted to make sure I didn't freak out at your disappearance since he was planning on leaving a day or so earlier than you expected." She winks at me, causing my stomach to turn. "I mean, I don't believe in having intimate relations before marriage, but he is…breathtaking."

"Morgan!" I'm not sure if I sound more surprised or horrified at her words.

"It's the truth. I'm willing to turn my back on what I believe for one night with him. Me, Morgan, the girl who has been going to church every Sunday plus many other days in between since she was a wee tot. The girl who, let's be honest, acts as if she's physically wearing a chastity belt. I don't let a single person besides myself go near the button on my pants."

Laughter erupts from my mouth. I clamp my hand over my lips to stop it. It's awkward enough listening to her talk about herself in the third person, but for her to worship Maxwell is disturbing. I already have one person on my radar who worships the ground Maxwell walks on and hopefully I never have to see her again.

Morgan stops dead in her speech and gives me a stern look, ready to interrogate me. "What's so wrong with him, Charlie?"

"It's complicated."

"What's complicated? You're the prettiest girl I know. Don't give me that look, Charlie." She waves her finger in my direction. My lips clamp together in defeat. "Flawless tanned skin, thick dark brown hair, big doe eyes, and the perfect frame for any man to carry around." She counts the list of things off on her fingers as she says each item.

"Morgan," I say in a testing tone.

"Let me finish. I haven't even got to the best part yet, the part where you have two men after you. Oh, that's right, two. They're not just going to go away; they're waiting for you to choose."

"Morgan, please. Isn't there work that has to done? I know I'm super behind." Changing the subject seems like the best outcome of this conversation. If only it would work.

"There's plenty that has to be done, but let me tell you what I went through while you were gone on your romantic getaway with Maxwell that you no doubt probably ruined."

I stand up abruptly; anger and confusion block my better judgment. She's going too far into this. What happened to my assistant? What did Maxwell do to turn her against me?

Morgan's demeanor changes like a snap of one's fingers once she realizes that she crossed a line. She continues to speak, though, but her tone is more understanding and friendly than lecturing. "Did you talk to Dave yet? Did you know he was here every day, pacing your office after that phone call he had with Maxwell?" She walks out of the room, leaving me dumbfounded, but then she peeks her head back in.

"Oh and he's stopping by today." With that said, she finally makes her way to her desk.

What? I want to scream it through the whole office building, but I resist. The last thing I need is a confrontation with Dave. However, I don't have a choice. Either I face him here or face him at home. Remaining at my desk for as long as possible trying to immerse myself in work, I wait. The little numbers on my desk clock flip, indicating it's now four o'clock.

A soft knock sounds on my door, causing my insides to turn, but to my dismay Morgan enters the office. "I just wanted to let you know Dave's here to see you now." She walks up to the corner of my desk and leans against it. "Oh, let me fix your scarf." She walks right up to me and tugs at the fabric that's wrapped around my neck.

Panic rises and I can feel the flush of redness creep up my face. What's she going to say when she sees a second set of puncture marks hidden under there? I can't say I went to a dermatologist again considering I wasn't even home and was supposed to be on a business trip…not like she already caught me in that lie, but still.

"Is this new? I've never seen you wear it before. In fact, I've never really seen you wear any scarves."

"Yeah, I'm not really a scarf person," until now, I think to myself, "but, I saw it lying in my closet this morning and thought what the hell."

Once her hands drop from the fabric, relief washes over me.

"I'll send him in," she says before turning toward the door.

A sigh of liberation rushes out of my mouth after I hear her receding footsteps. If she did see the new set of teeth marks Maxwell left behind, she didn't pry the subject. Thankfully.

One problem passed only to be followed by another. Dave enters my office and shuts the door aggressively. One would jump at the gesture, but I've been waiting for it to occur for several hours now. Once I actually make eye contact with him, I can tell he looks tired and stressed. For what reason is beyond me.

"Why didn't you call? Hell, even text me when you got back?"

Here we go. "Dave, we're friends, right? After everything we've been through together, we're still friends. If it makes you feel better, I didn't call or text Juliet either."

"You contacted Morgan."

"I texted Morgan, because she's a direct employee of mine. My absence is her responsibility. She has to open and close the business, not to mention she has to take care of all the events that I miss. You, on the other hand, have nothing to do with this place anymore."

"You go on a trip with some stranger and your whole attitude changes."

How dare he accuse me of changing? If only he knew what I have to juggle. I'm surprised I can keep half of my sanity intact. "We all know what this is about. Fifty text messages, Dave, come on."

"I don't like him, Charlie."

"It's not your choice. You've never met him, so those words mean nothing to me. If you're going to stand here and lecture me, you can go. Now." There's no way I'm going to get stuck in this conversation. I'm not going to stand back and allow another man to try to conquer my life, especially when this one already had a chance.

"I think I do have a say."

"Really, Dave, how do you figure? You expressed your feelings for me years ago, then started dating a client of mine behind my back? That doesn't sound like a person who deserves a say in anything." If he thinks I'm going to forget him telling me how spectacular I am and then totally ditch me to sleep with some rich bratty girl, he's extremely mistaken.

"I learned my lesson, you know that. I begged for forgiveness for months." His freckled suntanned hand slides through his sandy-blond hair in regret.

"Only after months went by without a word. And that so called begging for forgiveness only came after that rich bitch realized she didn't want to date a construction worker. I think you are just learning your lesson now, because you realize someone else wants what you can't have. What you already had, but didn't want. Now please go. I'm too old to play these games." My arm shoots out, pointing him toward the door.

"You still owe me a date. I don't care if we're at a crossroads right now, but I helped Morgan out when I could have said no. The deal was a date and this Friday you will accompany me at Junction 22." I can tell he means business and no matter how much I fuss there's no getting out of this. He takes my silence as submission. "I'll pick you up at seven." Without anything further to say, he leaves.

I hear Morgan tell him goodbye, but he remains silent and just...leaves. It was awkward and extremely uncomfortable for the both of us to admit our pasts involving each other, but it had to be done. I looked past his heartless actions years ago, remaining his friend to prove to him as well as myself that I'm the bigger person, and it still looks like I am.

* * *

Maxwell

"Grace, do you mind telling me what's wrong? I mean, even Charlie realized something is bothering you and she doesn't pay attention to either of us half the time."

"I'm going to be leaving for a while." A tear escapes her eye and runs down her cheek.

"Leaving for where?" I have an idea where she plans to go and no matter how awful I think the idea is, I keep my mouth shut.

"Home."

"It's not going to be plain fields and forests with our little village smack dab in the middle. It's a large city now, Grace, with the sun's rays shining down on masses of humans."

"You think I don't know that? Cambridge, it's called Cambridge. I have had plenty sleepless nights to do research, to figure out where I'm going to stay. Most importantly, where we used to live. Aren't you the slightest bit interested? There's a library where our cottages used to be, Maxwell, a library." She sounds fascinated with the thought of a library being where her home used to be hundreds of years ago.

"Cambridge…" I say the word as if it were poison in my mouth, "has been nothing but cruelty and pain for me. If you were smart, you wouldn't go back either." I don't mean to insult her in any way, but to bring back such gruesome heartbreaking memories is ridiculous. What type of person would ask to relive the worst period of their life? Grace refuses to acknowledge me. "I'll be here when you get back," I reluctantly say.

I'm about to tell her there's no need for me to leave when everything I need is here, when everything I need is in the form of a tiny smart-aleck girl by the name of Charlie, but the car pulls to a stop in front of her house, and she immediately exits. Peering through the tinted windows, I notice that she doesn't look back as the car starts to drive away. The last image I see is her wiping her tears off her cheek.

I wait a few days to tell Charlie of Grace's departure. With the sun finally down, I make my way to her house, but I end up leaving instantly when I see her car missing. There's only one place she would be at being the hard worker she is. I glide through the office building's doors. To my surprise, Morgan stands behind the front desk.

"Maxwell." Her voice cracks as she says my name. The nervousness that plays in her speech makes me slightly nauseated. I nod my head in her direction. "Oh yeah...of course, Charlie is in her office."

I feel her eyes on me as I make my way down the hall. I stop short of Charlie's door as I hear her talking to someone. I assume she's on the phone since I don't hear or sense another person in the room. With nothing else to do as I wait for her to finish, I eavesdrop on her conversation.

"How do you know about that?...Well, he's in for a rude awakening. I don't know who he thinks he is...Hahaha, very funny. The only thing he's going to get from me is possibly my fist in his face."

That's enough for me to grow extremely curious. I step into her office and close the door gently behind me to immediately sit across from her in one of the chairs by her desk.

"Juliet, I'm sorry. I have to go. I'll see you Saturday night at my house." She hangs up the phone in annoyance. "Maxwell, what a not so pleasant pleasure to see you. Please tell me I don't have to travel across the country again to meet more dead people."

"That bad, huh?"

"More than you know."

"Care to talk about it?"

"Not really, seeing as it's your fault to begin with."

I get straight to the point. "I came here to tell you that Grace is leaving for a few months. She wishes to visit our hometown."

"Where exactly would that be?"

"It's known as Cambridge, Massachusetts."

The wheels turn in her head as she thinks about that piece of information. "I don't feel the urge for another road trip, so I guess I'll see her when she gets back. It took you four days to find that out?"

"No, I wanted to wait until she was gone just in case she changed her mind. I know you don't want to talk about it, but I'm dying to know who you want to punch in the face."

"Curious, are we? Well, thanks to you taking my phone away I got trapped into going on a date with Dave tomorrow evening." Hatred laces her voice.

"You're also having Juliet at your house on Saturday?" I'm growing very disappointed. All these events are hindering my time with her.

"Yes, so don't show your face at my house. That's the last thing I need. Is there anything else? I'm just about ready to leave."

"No, but I can come home with you."

Her laugh fills the room. I have no idea what's so funny, but I have a feeling she's laughing in my face. "There's that cute little puppy again."

"I'll take that as a yes then." Her facial expression disappears and is replaced with shock. "You called me cute and referred to me as a loyal companion."

"That's not what I meant." I love how her arms wave frantically and her head bobs as she tries to deal with her humiliation.

Morgan stares at us with an overly excited smile on her face as we leave. Refusing to go away and sitting myself in the passenger seat of her car, I invite myself to her house. Charlie slams the gear into park once we get into her driveway, most likely getting some of her frustrations out. Turning toward me with a very serious look and a wagging finger in my face doesn't make it easy to keep a straight face as she lectures me. "No funny business, do you understand?"

I nod obediently, but the words that put themselves together in my head are saying anything but. I really should tell her about the bond we have between each other. How she will not be able to resist me for much longer. Silently I follow behind her, watching as she disappears into her room only to reemerge in her pajamas. Without acknowledging me yet, she makes herself supper and plops down on the couch. The click of the television tells me that she's going to continue to ignore me.

Sitting as close as possible next to her, I look at her. Her eyes don't budge from whatever pointless show is playing. She takes four bites until I finally open my mouth to speak.

"Charlie, I need to tell you something."

Her limbs freeze up and her mouth hangs open, waiting for the forkful of food, but her hand no longer moves. In fact, her breathing seems to have lessened, her eyes refuse to blink, and her fingertips belonging to the hand that clenches the bowl are turning white from pressure.

"Again? What more is there to tell?" Her strained voice proves her strong persona to be fake.

"Do you like me, Charlie?"

"That's asking me a question, not telling me something."

"I'm getting there. First, you have to answer my question. Do you have feelings for me, Charlie?"

"First it was like, now it's feelings. Fine, Maxwell. Yes, I like you. There, I said it, now what do you have to tell me?"

"Do you love me?"

I hear a moan of frustration rumble in her chest.

"I know you do and you know it too. There's something you need to know…about a vampire and their humans. There's a bond that connects them together; this blood bond is activated by a touch. The more contact a vampire has with their donor, the harder it is for the individual to resist."

"To resist what?" Her retort is flat and I can tell she's scared at my words.

"To resist me, Charlie." I lean in to kiss her, but she jumps away.

"You mean to tell me I'm going to love you whether I like it or not? These feelings that I keep pushing away will just get stronger and you want this…you want a fake relationship?"

"It's not fake, it's in your blood. Every cell in your body strives for me. You won't feel happy or complete without me, as I don't feel complete without you. Give into me, Charlie; let the blood that courses through your veins and heart lead you to where you belong."

"Death, that's where they're leading, Maxwell, to death. I want you to leave."

I try to talk some sense into her. I try to tell her that it's not fake or forced. She needs to understand that she was born for me. Nonetheless, her stubbornness won't let me get a word out, so with my head toward the floor I abide by her words and leave without having her to demand it twice. With one look back before I close the front door behind me, I look at her.

The sadness and fear that fills her engulfs me as well. "I love you, Charlie. Just know that my feelings are real and that the bond doesn't influence me. This connection between a vampire and their donor only helps to accept me. Some humans have been known to form some sort of lust for their vampire, but not truly love them. Only you can love me, Charlie, nothing can make that happen. Your feelings are only amplified by the bond not being fully created." With that said, I shut the door gently and walk home.

I debate with myself if I shouldn't have divulged that information, but no matter how much I want her to love me and accept her fate as my bride, I couldn't lie to her any longer. She has to start understanding that she's going to be my bride…that she is going to die for me. Even through her anger, I did get the information I was searching for. She does love me and as I told her, the bond doesn't create love. It just helps it along. She's just scared and too stubborn to admit it.

Chapter Twenty

Charlie

Why is he even trying to be a gentleman? He said it himself, I really don't have a choice. Lying in bed staring at the ceiling unable to sleep, just allows me to ponder my sense of despair more than I wish. It forces me to sit wide awake in my dark room, obsessing about Maxwell. How I want him to touch me, how I want to hear him say my name one more time. I could so kill that man.

When I jolt awake from my alarm clock, I realize I must have fallen asleep, although I'm not sure at what hour the exhaustion took over. Moving my tired heavy limbs, I gradually get ready for work. I used to love work, that's until Morgan called me out, creating thick tension that hovers between us now. I highly doubt she would be praising Maxwell so much if she knew he is dead.

The whole car ride my brain tries to register what my dear ancestors had me born into. Did they seriously think Maxwell wouldn't come looking for what he thinks is his? A shiver runs down my spine. Maxwell believes I'm his property—even if he won't flat out say it. Hell, I'm the man's food source. All this time, I've looked past the fact that he's a blood-sucking monster who's three hundred years old, only to have it slapped back in my face. It's hard to explain, but I don't care he's a vampire and that's the part that scares me.

I stop at Starbucks to get a peace offering for Morgan. Balancing the two cups as I unlock the front door is tricky, but I get behind her desk without a spill.

The wait I endure is agonizing, but small sips of my latte calm my nerves.

She walks in a few minutes later with a confused look on her face. "Something wrong, Charlie?" she asks as her hazel eyes continue to question me.

Holding out the still hot cappuccino I got her, I allow a smile to find my lips. "A peace offering. I know it's a little late considering you lectured me four days ago, but things between us have been…awkward. I just want you to know that I thank you for your insight and telling me what I already know, what I didn't want to admit. However, I need time to process Maxwell. He's not as charming as you think he is. Dave either."

Morgan's smile is all I need to know that she understands and to some extent accepts my apology. "Now, if you excuse me, I have tons of work to do before I'm forced to go on a date with Dave." Holding my cup high in the air as a salute of some sort, I walk away.

The clock ticks away the minutes, and the sun slowly starts to set, leaving my office dark and my eyelids tired. Laying my head on my desk and closing my eyes, I repeat in a hush voice, just a few minutes.

"Charlie, Charlie, wake up." A soft, nurturing voice slowly makes reality set in.

When I start to feel a nudge that gets more aggressive with each tap, I whip my head off the desk. "I'm up, I'm up," I repeat more to myself than who I now know to be Morgan.

"Dave's here for you and he's not happy."

I rub my head, trying to get rid of the slight headache that's growing under my skull. "What time is it?"

"Five minutes after seven."

"Shit, no wonder he's not happy. Send him in." I

watch Morgan leave the room only to be replaced by a flustered Dave.

"You fell asleep in your office when you knew that at seven o'clock I was going to pick you up at your house." I can almost feel the anger radiate off him. His blond hair seems more ruffled and his face is gradually turning a shade of red.

"It's not as if I did it intentionally. These past few weeks have been pretty stressful, making it extremely hard to sleep. I'm up now. We can just go straight to the restaurant."

"We're late. Junction 22 doesn't take in late guests, but I called and our new reservation is in twenty minutes thankfully."

"Just enough time to get there if we leave now." My palms slap at my dress in efforts of straightening it out as I stand up.

"What the hell happened to your hand?" He takes a few steps toward me, reaching for my still injured left palm.

I didn't even realize that he knew nothing of my first incident, making him even more shocked to see the white gauze encasing my hand. Although, when he showed up in my office the other day to force me into this date I had the injury. He must've been too pissed to notice.

"I had a mishap a few days ago. Nothing important, you can ask Morgan about it if you want." My shoulder bumps into Dave's arm as I walk past him; the dire need to get out of this room starts to make me sweat. "Can you lock up, Morgan?" I holler at her as I rush out the front doors.

"Sure can. Have fun." From what I do manage to hear before I get too far away, her voice sounds overwrought as if she's not pleased with this date either.

What is she so upset about?

Turning toward my car, Dave harshly pulls me toward him when he finally catches up. "We're going in the same car. This is a date, after all. We can get your car later."

Can this 'date' get any worse? Staying completely silent the whole way to the restaurant, my fingers can't help but shake. Thoughts about how I would prefer to be going to this so called date with Maxwell flood my mind. I can't help but find myself wishing that I was in his company instead of Dave's. Snap out of it, Charlie, snap out of it.

Dave repeatedly tries to hold my uninjured hand and loop my arm through his on the short walk to the entrance of the restaurant, but I refuse by keeping my arms tightly at my sides. The familiar hostess leads us to a table. When she sits us at the same table that Maxwell and Eugene were sitting at when I was here for Harlow's birthday party, I realize that this date can get even worse…much worse. Just sitting across from the spot that Maxwell occupied only makes my thoughts turn to daydreams as I catch myself envisioning Dave as Maxwell.

With our drinks ordered, I allow the menu to take my mind off the awful situation I find myself in once again. I know the menu by heart considering it's not that complex and only bears a few items on it, but it's better than focusing on Dave, who sits and stares at me, expecting something to happen.

He's the first to break the silence between us. His hand tips the menu down to reveal me cowering behind it. "We need to talk."

Those words, those dreadful words. How many times am I going to be told by a man nonetheless, that they need to talk me? "Go on." Annoyance fills my voice without me wanting it to.

Before he answers me, the waitress comes back with our drinks and takes our order. Only when we hand our menus over and the young gal walks away he decides to talk. "How was your day prior to falling asleep at your desk?"

That's not what I was expecting him to say. He's trying to make this as civil as possible. "Busy, I have a lot to catch up on. My days away weren't even close to a vacation. All it really did was create more work for me."

"Since you mentioned it, what exactly did you do when you were at your meeting?" The skepticism that his voice is laced with turns my contempt mood sour. He knows it wasn't a business trip as I insinuated before I left and I don't blame him. He calls and talks to a man he never heard of before or met, who's accompanying me. Anyone would instantly question why a stranger would assist me at a business meeting instead of one of my own employees or someone who's familiar with my business.

"Nothing important, potential clients."

"This Maxwell knows them then, I presume."

"That would be the reason why he came along. Can we talk about something else or maybe not talk at all?" As if the heavens finally open up, our appetizers arrive. I take a few bites without waiting for him to ask me his next question.

To my surprise, he lets me eat. Conversations that surround us draw my attention away; my eyes search each table, refusing to look at Dave. An arm reaches over me to take the empty plates away; for the first time tonight I look at the waitress's name tag, Lily.

Wanting Lily to stay at the table as long as possible to get rid of this awkward silence that looms between Dave and me, I can't help but to stare after her as she walks away. She disappears into the kitchen after she waves toward the bartender, the same bartender from my previous visit as well. Several people crowd the bar; the overconfident bartender flirts with all the younger girls and acts macho in front of the male customers. He acts extra friendly to a man who leans against the countertop, laughing at his jokes and tipping drinks in favor. The stranger's almost shoulder length brown hair looks awfully familiar. My shaky hand gropes for the glass of water I ordered.

"Charlie, are you okay?" Dave's hand lightly caresses mine.

My eyes remain on the back of the stranger's head at the bar. I praised the heavens earlier, but now...now the gates of hell have opened as the man at the bar turns his head the tiniest bit. I know that face anywhere with its strong jaw line, smooth pink lips and let's not forget its creamy pale skin tone. His hair conceals his eyes, but I don't need to see those deep brown eyes to know I'm staring right at Maxwell.

A sharp jerk of my hand shakes Dave's clenching fingers from me. Almost as if it's in slow motion, my hand hits my water glass that I was inches away toppling it over. When the cold liquid runs down the table and puddles in my lap I abruptly stand up from my chair. Several people turn to look at me, all except Maxwell. He just straightens his towering six-foot frame from his hunched position. Lily rushes over with towels, but I don't allow her to help.

"I'm just going to go to the bathroom and fix myself up." I reach the hallway leading to the bathrooms and whisper, "Now." Knowing Maxwell is listening.

Tick tock...tick tock.

"You do know how to get everyone's attention in a crowded room, don't you?" Maxwell's cocky voice finally comes around the corner I'm waiting behind.

"You," I say in the most accusing manner.

"Hold on a second, you're mad at me as if I was the one to spill water on you in your very sexy dress, by the way." A smirk spreads across his mouth as his fingertip traces one of the cutouts in the dress.

Angry at him and myself, I shove him. Except he doesn't stumble or budge from his stance, which is mere inches away from me. My hands pound at his hard chest as incoherent words stream from my mouth. "You jerk, y-you jackass. What the hell are you doing here?" My teeth forcefully grind together, distorting my rant.

"This is a public place, Charlie. I happen to be here on a date as well."

"What." It's not a question, but a blunt statement, causing my hands to fall from his chest. Emotions and bad acting give my hurt feelings away. My blood races through my veins.

I stare at him wide-eyed when he starts to laugh in my face. "Calm down, my love, I'm just joking. Now you know how I feel when I watch you at that table with him." A quick nod of his head points toward where Dave sits.

As a low moan rumbles in my chest, my hands ball into fists. Unintentionally, I shake them in his face with rage. Who in the world does he think he is anyways? I'm so mad at him I can't even think straight, let alone put any words together.

The coldness of his touch as he rubs my arms soothes my anger; I've been waiting for that coolness to engulf me for days. I physically shake myself from the thought. I don't want to die, I don't want to die, I chant to myself.

"I'm sorry I upset you, but this date is a waste of your time and it's wearing my patience thin."

"You did not just say that. Do you not listen to me when I talk to you or do you just stare off into space?"

"You're implying that this date is my fault?" One of his hands leaves my arm to point to himself in astonishment. "If I recall, you agreed to go on a date with him to help Morgan out."

Just him saying the name Morgan brings even more irritation to the surface. "Don't even say Morgan's name again, that's a conversation for another time. Don't you for a second forget I know you visited her at her apartment. How you even know where she lives is beyond me, but your sly ways are growing old. Back on the subject of Dave, if you hadn't answered my phone when we were in Austria or took my phone away for that matter, I could have ignored him."

He remains silent, taking in the guilt he should be shouldering.

Before he has a chance to speak, I continue my speech. "You know what, I don't need a response, I don't want a response. How about that? I'm going to sit back at that table in my wet dress and finish this date I'm stuck on because of you. So think about that." My feet take three steps away from him before they turn around, leading me toward him again. "No showing up tomorrow. Is that clear?"

When he nods his head just once, I try to walk away for the second time, but after turning away I turn back toward him with my finger inches away from his face. "No more spying on me either. Understood?"

He nods again and this time I tell myself to be strong and walk away. However, just as I turn around, Maxwell's strong fingers grip my upper arm, spinning me around to face him yet again. As I make eye contact with him, I know what's to happen next. I can start talking or shove him away, but for some reason I act startled and let the events play out. Within seconds, Maxwell's lips touch mine.

"Let that help you remember who you're supposed to be with," he says before letting me go.

With wobbly legs, I make my way back to a nervous Dave. His saddened expression just makes matters worse. The only good thing that happened while I was gone was our food being delivered. The touch of my plate is still hot, meaning that it hasn't been sitting here long.

"Is something wrong? I never remembered you being so clumsy."

"Nothing. I just thought I saw something. Can we just get this night done with?" I know I hurt his feelings with my rude attitude, but there's this nagging feeling eating at me that he expects something to come out of this, be it a stronger friendship or a romantic relationship. The only way I know how to prevent a conversation pertaining to either of those two concepts is to eat.

With the tab paid not soon after, the seat belts buckle us into another uncomfortable situation. Plenty of stoplights decide to turn red on our way back to my car. When Dave turns the radio louder at the start of a particular song, I can't help but to wither in the seat, searching for its hidden meaning. Magically a light switch flips on as the chorus blares through the speakers. The words sear my eardrums.

I take a chance to glace at Dave. He lip syncs the words perfectly. Something about you belong to me and being his sweetheart. Uh-oh. Thank goodness the parking lot outside my office building is starting to come into view. He parks next to my car, keeping the engine on and the doors locked. I snap the handle a few times to tell him to unlock the doors without saying a word, afraid that my bad attitude will just create more problems.

"I'm sorry," he blurts out of nowhere.

"For what exactly?" I want to ask if he's sorry for keeping me trapped in here or forcing me to go on a date with him, but I decide against it.

"For everything. You were right before with the whole 'someone else wanting what you had' thing. I never intended for this, for these feelings to come back." His fingers fiddle against the steering wheel and his eyes don't leave the dashboard.

"Good to know. You can unlock the door now. Please."

"You don't understand. I'm trying to be compassionate and understanding." His voice rises with anger at my refusal to accept his apology.

"No, you don't understand. I don't need your compassion or understanding. I already forgave you and you need to move on. There's only friendship in our future and to be honest that's me being generous. Now, if you excuse me, I have to go home." With my fingers wrapped around the door handle, I wait until I hear the click of the locks.

Exiting the car as fast as possible, I refuse to look back. All I can do is shake my head in disbelief on my way back home. The date itself didn't last that long. I get home before nine. Changing into my pajamas, I watch a little TV before I try to go to bed. No matter how many meaningless TV shows I watch, several hours later drowsiness doesn't find me.

Forcing myself to try to sleep, I make my way to my bedroom. At least tomorrow will be better, I tell myself as I lie beneath my comforter once again, staring at the ceiling. It is only when I feel a chill in the air that my body completely relaxes and my eyelids close in expectancy of sweet dreams.

* * *

Maxwell

If she is expecting me to leave, she's wrong. However, instead of making her even madder, I sit behind her. This cockroach named Dave has not the slightest clue who I am, so when he makes eye contact with my wandering eyes he has no idea I'm thinking of the most efficient way to kill him.

First thing would be to break each one of his groping fingers. Next would be his knees so he couldn't kick at me, make a distance between us or run away like a coward. With his screams shredding my eardrums, I would finish him off due to annoyance. The feel of his neck snapping beneath my fingers solves my problem. Although as he licks his lips while he stares at Charlie, my Charlie, I begin to contemplate ripping his throat out with my pointed teeth just to watch him gurgle on his own blood.

When I see them start to rise, I quickly duck behind a nearby corner to watch them leave. Since I don't have a car to trail behind, I keep pace with them from the shadows. Knowing where exactly they are going, I allow myself to get there first to find the perfect hiding spot that conceals my spying eyes yet again.

Unwilling, my teeth extract, digging into my lower lip and my nails form bloody crescents in my palms. The over willing sense of fear and annoyance coming from Charlie as she jiggles the locked door handle tests my willpower. One pointless breath after the other keeps my feet planted in the dark corner I hide in. All I can do is stand and watch as she gets irritated and then angry. When she finally exits the car relief calms my nerves. It takes every ounce of self-control I have left not to follow her home.

Grace has already left on her trip of redemption or whatever it is she plans on proving to herself, leaving me alone with nothing to do but go home. Lying in bed, I debate whether abiding Charlie's demands are worth it or not. If I do, I don't get praised, and if I don't, I get yelled at…as usual.

When I told her my patience was wearing thin, I was being completely serious. I don't know what I have to do to get her to see me as the gentleman I am. A light rapping on the door forces me to get out of bed and put my sour mood behind me, but when I open the door to no one my bad mood resurfaces. I don't think anything of it and slowly close the door before going back to lounging around.

After I fall into the plush sofa, the doorbell rings again. In efforts of catching the pranksters, I rush to the door, violently swinging it open. No one once again stands before, but I do however scare a young woman with dark blonde hair who's walking toward me down the hall. It couldn't have been her seeing as she hasn't reached my room yet.

"I'm sorry if I startled you," I say as she walks past me. I catch a glimpse of her name tag. The Liberty Hotel, Daisy.

"It's okay. I've been told that there are kids in the building playing tricks on all the occupants," she replies, smiling kindly at me.

"Good to know." I shut the door, but remain at the ready for these supposed kids to come back, but after several minutes nothing happens. They must have gotten scared away.

Time slowly goes by. Night turns to morning, morning turns to afternoon, and afternoon turns to night.

Chapter Twenty-One

Charlie

Completely engulfed in cleaning and organizing, I lose track of time. The doorbell chimes throughout the house, putting a stop to my manic frenzy. Almost skipping to the door with my hands rubbing together with anxiousness, a shriek of excitement greets my friend at the door. I stare at Juliet, who holds up two large bottles of wine, one in each hand. She invites herself in and immediately goes to the kitchen to put the bottles in the fridge.

"So what's on the schedule for tonight?"

"No idea. What do you feel like doing?"

"Well...I did bring my favorite movie to watch." She waves a DVD in front of my face.

That's the best movie she could find. I do have to say that it's better than another movie I can think of, but Warm Bodies...a zombie love story. It's just the thing I want to see right now, a dead man who tries to be as much alive and human as possible for his attraction to a living breathing girl. This is some sick joke or a really bad dream. Maybe just maybe I'll wake up and laugh at myself.

"Why don't you get ready? I'm just going to get some snacks ready."

Minutes later I join Juliet on the couch. The movie is already at the title screen, waiting for the play button to be pressed. I force myself to endure the movie as if it's going to be a chore, but it's anything but. To my astonishment, I laugh, cry and by the end of the movie I grow disappointed that it has to come to an end. With all my attention put on the TV, I didn't even notice that Juliet drank my soda along with a majority of the chips.

Both of us stand up to stretch our stiff limbs in our pursuit to the kitchen for refills of chips and soda. Halfway there the doorbell rings. Juliet looks at me with a full mouth of chips from the now empty bowl, her eyes asking the question of who's at the door without her physically saying a word. I shrug, completely frozen. The thought of Maxwell showing up here tonight out of all nights when I told him not to makes me bite my lip in anger. Juliet races to the door before I can get a handle on my emotions.

I can feel her swallow the mouthful of food as she brushes crumbs off her shirt. "Can I help you?" Juliet questions our visitor after she opens the door just a crack. From where I stand, I can't see who it is.

"Is Ms. Preston available?" His deep smooth voice stops my heart. The searing in my lungs lets me know I haven't died of a heart attack…yet. With a chill shivering its way through my body, I can't help but to fear the man behind the door even though I have no idea who he is.

One foot goes in front of the other, leading me closer. I hover to Juliet's right side, staying unseen by our mystery guest.

"Maybe, why?" Juliet says bluntly.

"If I could come in and talk to her."

"Sorry, no boys allowed tonight," Juliet quickly retorts back.

"Maybe she can come out for a walk. It's quite a beautiful night."

"I'm sorry, but who are you?" The rudeness that makes Juliet…well, Juliet starts to seep into her voice.

"I'm a friend of Benjamin and even Maxwell." The way he said it sounded like he added Maxwell's name

Krystal Novitzke

on at the end to justify his visit, not because he's an actual friend.

I see Juliet's eyes veer toward me, searching for some kind of clue that I know this man, but I just shake my head. Any friend of Benjamin is not welcome here and if he truly is a friend of Maxwell he must not be that important because Maxwell never introduced us. His voice is new to my eardrums. I know for a fact that I didn't hear it when we were in Austria.

Juliet takes my silence as her clue to get rid of this man. "I really don't know either of those people, so no offence, but no can do. Maybe you can come back in tomorrow afternoon. See ya." She slams the door in his face, ending the conversation.

"Where in the hell do these people come from? Who is Benjamin and why did you lie to me about Maxwell?" I cower from the agitation in Juliet's voice as she turns her snarl on me.

"I'm sorry. I can't explain the relationship between Maxwell and me because I don't know how. It's complicated." I keep on telling people the same thing, it's complicated. Truthfully, there's no better explanation and it's not like it isn't completely honest.

"And..."

"Benjamin is an old, long time friend of Maxwell's. I only met him once." Well, I only wanted to meet him once, I think to myself.

"I don't know if Maxwell is expecting any other friends of his to show up, but this one didn't ask for him...he asked for you."

"I heard."

"I think this is my cue to go home. You need to call your secret boyfriend and talk about your unexpected visitor."

"What? You're going to leave right after a

268

psychopath just knocked on my door?" I'm somewhat frightened to stay here by myself, although her company wouldn't help if that man comes back anyways.

"If I stay, therefore I might resort to drinking and I might drink way too much. Waking up with a hangover is one thing, waking up with a hangover and body aches from sleeping on a couch is just asking for feeling like hell. I'll talk to you tomorrow to set up another girls' night, I promise." With a quick hug, she heads out the door.

I watch her car leave the driveway and disappear down the road. Looking at the mess that covers the tabletops makes my lazy gene kick in. I don't know if being in my pajamas is making the bed call my name or not, but I decide against cleaning the mess and try to go to sleep. However, just because I feel the pull of sleep doesn't mean that sweet dreams follow.

Nightmares haunt me. Even though I didn't see the man who gave me an unexpected visit, I imagine him. First, I'm conducting an event I'm failing at miserably, ruining the party and all eyes turn toward me with glowering scowls on their faces. Instantly, I can pick out his face staring back at me in the surrounding guests. He was nothing but a shadow with no features whatsoever, but I knew it was him.

I only toss and turn from that dream to be thrown into another one, the most common dream known to man or woman. I'm running for my life that's threatened by an imaginary figure and no matter how fast I run or how hard I think I'm running due to my exhaustion, the killer just gets closer. I'm running for what seems like miles without seeing one single person. The dream's ending is no different than it is to anyone else. Right before this unseen stranger goes in for the kill, I wake up.

My ears start to ring from my cell phone blaring, the screen partially lighting up the room. I begin to wonder if this unexpected call or the typical dream's ending is what woke me. With my eyes getting watery from the bright light of the screen, I try extra hard to read the name of who's calling this late at night. Giving up, I just answer it.

A familiar voice starts talking before I say anything. "Charlie…Charlie, are you awake?"

"Janessa? What's going on? What time is it?" My eyes are closed, wanting more sleep since my nightmares kept me awake almost all night.

"It's Juliet…she's in the hospital. Can you come down here...you know, to keep me company?" The occasional sniffle of her nose is the only evidence I have that her tough front broke at some point in time, resulting in her crying.

"Yea, I'll get dressed and be there in…where exactly am I going?" My voice is dazed from lack of processing the information I'm just told. Part of me thinks this is a dream.

"I'm in the ER's waiting room. I'll fill you in when you get here." I'm left with dial tone.

I put the yoga pants I had on earlier and a long sleeved top before retrieving my cell phone again along with my keys to leave my house in a blur. I don't even remember driving to the hospital, parking the car, or walking inside. It's when I see Janessa, Harlow, and Brock huddled together in the corner of the waiting room that reality hits me.

"Man, you look like crap," Brock jokes when he sees me heading in their direction.

"Thanks for that. It isn't every day that I get woken up at two in morning to an urgent call telling me to go to the emergency room." Normally I would have a better comeback, but tonight I'm not in the mood for a fight. He's right anyways. I probably have dark circles under my eyes, my hair isn't brushed, and I don't even know if my clothes are matching.

"Harlow, Brock, why don't you go home and rest? I'll call you tomorrow morning to tell you Juliet's room number," Janessa says in our fellow friends' direction. After they leave the room, she turns to me, gesturing toward a chair. "I know she would want you here when she wakes up."

I don't bother asking why Harlow and Brock were here only to immediately leave after I get here. "What happened?"

"A neighbor of hers called 911 after hearing her screams coming from inside her house. The elderly woman claimed to see a shadowy blur rush out the front door. Whoever it was, was long gone by time the police got there."

"Attacked her, someone attacked her?" My knee begins to bob up and down, bouncing on the ball of my foot. Nervousness or something that can be perceived as the jitters masks my panic. A shadow with inhumanly speed…friends with Benjamin…a vampire.

"The police didn't give me much information when they questioned me the second I got here, but they said that the front door had been ripped off its hinges. They're keeping it under surveillance for the time being. They didn't even take anything or anything of value that we know of; they just went in there and…" Tears begin to stream steadily down her checks.

"What kind of shape is she in?" I'm not sure I want to know, but sooner or later I'll be allowed to see and I want to be prepared.

I remain silent waiting until Janessa is ready to speak. "I don't know."

"Well, I'll sit here and wait it out with you." I'll do exactly that. I put my feet up and wiggle in my seat, finding the perfect spot. The spot doesn't remain comfortable for long and hours pass by with Janessa and myself changing positions several times or just pacing the waiting room floor.

Somehow Janessa and I fall asleep lying across the rows of chairs. A light nudge on my shoulder wakes me up; a small puddle of drool dampens my sleeve. A woman in a white lab coat greets me. "You're here for Ms. Anders, correct?"

I see Janessa's already awake, waiting for the nurse to continue. I nod due to my dry throat closing up. "She's been moved to a room in the intensive care unit, room 316. I'm afraid that only family can go in at this time, but I'm sure that one of the nurses will give you a chair to sit in outside her room if you'd like." She says the last part mainly to me, because even though Juliet and I are close, I'm not family.

"That would be great, thank you," I reply back.

"How is she?" Janessa barely manages to get out.

"She's been beat up pretty badly. She has a broken Radius, a mild concussion, and significant bruising covering portions of her body. She handled surgery to fix her break very well and as far as the doctors can see there is no internal bleeding. She did however have to have a blood transfusion, which isn't common with injuries like hers, but...this may sound odd, but she has two puncture marks on her neck."

She was bit.

The nurse leaves us to find the room on our own. To my surprise when we reach Juliet's room, I find a chair outside the door, waiting for me. I prepare myself to sit in this chair all day just as Janessa prepares herself to sit in whatever chair that lies behind that door all day as well. The nurses are extra nice as they bring me a pillow for my head and a blanket to fight the chill within the halls. Janessa steps out of Juliet's room several times, trying to get in touch with their parents, but to her disappointment, she's unable to contact them.

"No luck," I say before she disappears in Juliet's room again.

"They're probably busy; they left the country on separate business trips a while ago." I expected her to talk further about the subject, but her eyes remain on the tiled floor and just as fast as the conversation ended, she entered Juliet's room. I never met their parents and honestly I never really heard either of them talk about their mother or father.

Before I know it morning arrives. Well, a decent time of morning. Several people stop by and leave throughout the day, but I stay. I stay through the sore butt, the restless legs, and the pounding headache. I have to be here when she wakes up. I have to see if she remembers who did this to her. To have the time pass by faster, I call Morgan and even Dave to tell them the news. To my surprise, they arrive at the same time with flowers in hand.

"You look…well…" Morgan searches for her words.

"I know, I know…awful, right?"

"You've been through a lot and if you looked all gorgeous I would begin to wonder about your friendship with her," Morgan adds, trying to comfort me.

"Thanks." I haven't even looked at either of them since they walked up to me, but Dave kneels next to me, moving his head to cover the spot on the floor that I'm intently staring at. "Yes," I say to him.

"I brought her flowers," he says.

"Janessa can take them in her room when she comes

out." I wanted to tell them how I'm not allowed in her room yet, but a frazzled Janessa exits the room, stopping my words.

"She's awake." She yelps as she rushes past us in search of a nurse.

A nurse and a doctor followed by Janessa enter the room. I stay seated until spoken to. Time stands still as I wait with Morgan and Dave for someone to exit the room and give me the okay to go in. Janessa exits the room with a sense of relief. She looks more relaxed, but there's still pain in her eyes.

"How is she doing?"

"She's alive. I told her you're here. You should go see her."

I linger in the doorway of her room. Even though I know her injuries, I'm not ready for what I see. Tons of tiny tubes connect to various parts of her body, pumping all kinds of clear liquid in her. The occasional beep of machines monitoring her heart rate and blood pressure break the overwhelming silence in the room. Her right arm is in a cast and dark purple splotches better known as bruises cover a large portion of her body. Well, her face, neck, and right arm that peaks out of the plaster, since those are the parts that are visible.

"Juliet." One word, just one lone word is all I can get out.

"Green eyes," she mumbles.

"What?" I know what she said, so I don't know why I asked her to say it again.

"Green eyes," she says clearer.

"Ms., we need to talk to your friend." I didn't even hear the door open, but I stare at two police officers that barged in on my time.

"Yes, of course," I say toward the uniformed men. I look at Juliet one more time before I leave the room.

"I'll be right outside," I tell her.

I wait by pacing the hallway while Janessa rocks herself back and forth in the chair I've been occupying all day. Once the officers exit the room, they walk in my direction. "Ms. Preston, may we have a word?"

I nod.

"We understand that Ms. Anders was at your house last night. Is that correct?" one of the officers asks.

"Yes."

"And a man showed up at your house, but Ms. Anders answered the door. Now did you see that man? She claims he was the one who attacked her."

"No. I wish I had, but I didn't. I'm sorry I can't help you."

"Understood. If you see anything or hear anything that you think would help in this investigation, please let us know."

"Of course," I say stiffly as they walk away. I go back to pacing and taking turns talking to Juliet before she goes to sleep. If I'm expecting to get any information out of her, I'm greatly mistaken. All she remembers is green eyes.

* * *

Maxwell

There she sits half asleep in a chair in the hallway outside what I assume to be Juliet's room. I overheard the short conversations she had with Juliet's sister to understand why she's here. Slowly I make my way to her side. With my hand squeezing her shoulder, she takes in my presence.

"Maxwell, what are you doing here? How did you know…who called you?" I can't tell if she's surprised or angry with me showing up.

"Charlie, you have company this late?" Janessa asks as she exits Juliet's room.

"I thought it best to take Charlie home. She insists on staying here, but she's no good to anyone tired and sore."

"Right," Janessa agrees.

"But—" Charlie begins to protest.

"He's right. You should go home, get some rest. She's not going to be discharged for a while. You can come by and see her tomorrow," Janessa states.

"Come on." I lift her up by her elbow. Once she's standing beside me, I wrap my arm around her and lead her down the hall. "To be honest, you should've been the one to call if someone were to telephone me."

Like the typical Charlie, she interrupts me. "I don't have your number. I didn't even know you had a phone."

"There are other ways besides a phone to let me know you're distressed about something, although it would help to let me know about what it pertains to."

"What's that supposed to mean? Why are you here? You don't know Juliet, so coming here to show concern for her is uncalled for."

"I'm here to comfort you, Charlie. I'm here because I felt your strain, your despair. I had to know you were okay." My hands rub her arms to calm her.

Her expression immediately changes as she thinks about something. "How did you know I was here?"

"It's something I can do, what every vampire can do. It's not important. All that matters is that I'm here for you."

"Explain about what you can do." She sounds bored or irritated, maybe both.

"You might not like what I have to say, but just understand that it's a benefit. Please hear me out till I'm finished." Her eyebrow perks up, urging me to continue. "The bond between a vampire and his donor is strong."

"The bond," she says mockingly, interrupting me when I told her not to.

"Charlie, I told you to hold your remarks back."

"I have a problem with obeying orders. I thought you already knew that."

"This bond has saved lives. Many vampires and humans are thankful for this connection. I'm here to offer you support for the anguish you feel over Juliet. It'll let me know if you ever become harmed."

"Oh, that will come in handy when Juliet's attacker comes back for me."

"What do you mean?" What happened to Juliet is awful, but I assumed it was just a break-in gone bad.

"There was this man who came by my house last night while Juliet was over. She answered the door, was snobby, and he left. Well, only to return and beat the crap out of Juliet."

"Did you see him? Did he say his name?"

"No. There was something about his voice that terrified me, so I cowered behind the door. He said he's Benjamin's friend. He also said he was your friend, but it didn't sound genuine. It sounded as if he knew I was listening and wanted to throw me off guard."

"He's a vampire."

"Yeah. He even left a reminder behind. A nice set of fang marks in her neck."

"I think you need to stay at my place for a while." There's no hint of romance or playful banter as I speak the words.

"What? No."

"At least for tonight." Why does she always have to fight me? She admitted it yesterday that she has feelings for me, so why is she acting like this? How serious do I need to get for her to understand that she's not safe?

"Why can't this vampire drama ever end? I just want it to end."

"I can make it end, Charlie. You just have to embrace your place at my side and become my bride. You won't have to be scared or helpless ever again." There's no better way to say it. She wants safety and I can give it her, but I'm not too sure she's willing to pay the price just yet.

She crosses her arms and gives me that stare as if she's wishing me dead, but hidden in those dark brown eyes of her is genuine fear that she desperately tries to mask. "You're the one who got me into this mess in the first place and I'm just supposed to let you kill me before this stranger does?"

"Charlie, please. When I 'kill' you, you won't be entirely dead. When he kills you, you'll be gone, and instead of still seeing the people you care about, they'll be attending your funeral."

She remains standing there, biting her bottom lip to prevent any insulting words from coming out of her mouth. She's trying to be strong and not let her emotions get the best of her, but I can see through her façade.

Her retreating stomping feet is all I get for an answer. I watch her harshly push the elevator button. "Is there anything else you can do that doesn't lead to me dying in any way?"

"You'll need to stay by my side, especially at night. Since they are a vampire you'll be safer during the day, but you still need to be close."

With her shoulders relaxed, I know she heeds my words. I lightly kiss the top of her head.

A woman to Charlie's right makes eye contact with me. Her long exhale is audible to everyone's ears in this small metal moving box. I swear I hear Charlie whisper under her breath, oh please. I grin in the older woman's direction, which causes her to fan herself with her hand. I bury my face in Charlie's neck; her messy hair covers my face. "Now why can't you be more like her?" I jokingly whisper.

I feel her tense up against me. I know I struck a chord with her, but I'm at the point where I'll mention every little thing to make her understand that she's envied by many.

Charlie abruptly grabs ahold of my hair before I have a chance to back away. "I know what you're getting at and it's not going to work." She lets go of me and turns toward the woman right at as the elevator's doors open. "He bites," she says as she slips out.

The woman looks at me in shock, but curiosity. "Fetish, really," I say before I weave through several people to catch up with Charlie.

We walk side by side in silence the rest of the way out of the hospital and through most of the parking lot. That is until she twirls her keys in her hand, but I snatch them away and reach the driver's side before her. Refusing to enter the car and to sit in the passenger seat, she hovers outside the window. I lean over and push open the door from the inside, just in case she was expecting me to be a gentleman by opening the door for her, but I highly doubt that's why she grinds her teeth together in annoyance.

Eventually she enters the car. "Why are you driving my car exactly?"

"You're stressed and need sleep."

"You really aren't in a position to tell me what I need. There's one concern I have. What if we get pulled over by a police officer? You don't have a license. Are you just going to look at the officer and say that you're a three-hundred-year-old vampire and cars didn't exist when you were alive?"

"Very funny, Charlie. I promise I won't get pulled over. I've been practicing driving for a while now. Can we change the subject to something more pleasing? Like how many cups of coffee have you had today?"

"What does that have to do with anything and how do you know I even had coffee today?"

"I can smell it on you." It's intoxicating.

"Is that a problem?"

"No, coffee is quite delightful."

"You drink coffee?" Her question makes me smile.

"No."

"Then how do you know coffee tastes delightful?"

"Think about it, Charlie, coffee has caffeine and caffeine goes into the bloodstream."

"Eww. Spare me the gross details next time." Her laugh makes me smile.

Five minutes away from the hotel in which my room resides in, she falls asleep. Effortlessly, I carry her limp body inside, laying her on the bed. Unwillingly, I pace the length of the room, thinking about how I can protect her from unwanted attention. Every so often, I check on her. Her tense body puts dread in my hollow heart. Therefore, I strip down and curl up against her to offer the only comfort I can. Instantly, her body relaxes with a shiver as the cold from my skin surrounds her.

Her mouth can lie, but her body can only tell the truth. She intertwines her fingers with my own hand that lies over her stomach. She wiggles beside me, inch by inch getting closer. When my face falls in the curve of her neck once again, she nudges her head closer to mine. A sleeping Charlie is one of my favorite versions of her.

Chapter Twenty-Two

Charlie

The pitch black room doesn't make my escape any easier. After prying Maxwell's arm off me, I slip out of bed in search for the door. I contemplate opening the curtains, allowing me to see where the exit is without bumping into furniture, but I decide it would be best to have Maxwell continue sleeping. So, with my eyes open as wide as possible, which is useless, and my arms outstretched before me to guide the way, I start the treacherous walk.

I hold my breath with each tiptoe across the floor. The fact that I probably look like Frankenstein crosses my mind. The rattling of something on top of what I believe to be a dresser echoes throughout the room as I walk face first into it. The point of my hands protecting me from that very outcome proves worthless as I underestimate the fact that my brain doesn't register objects until it's too late. My body goes rigid until the object becomes silent again. Wishful thinking of if Maxwell does wake up he won't be able to see me…another pointless thought.

"Charlie, what are you doing exactly?" Humor fills his voice.

"Nothing." I don't know what else to say besides the fact that I've been caught.

"It's quite amusing to watch, but I figure I'll save you some time or pain and let you know that you are nowhere near the door."

What? Not even near the door? All I have to do is round the bed and take a few steps forward. A huff of annoyance puffs out between my lips. How in the hell am I going to get out of this room when I can't see a thing? I would flip the light switch, but that's by the door and if I were by the door I wouldn't need the light switch to begin with. To be honest, I would open the window to wipe that smirk off Maxwell's face that I know is present without visually seeing it, but I'm not even sure I can find the window.

"Do you wish for me to help you? If you don't want my help, I'll warn you that there's one more piece of furniture you are most likely going to run into."

I hang my head in defeat. "Can you help me?" I mumble.

"I'm sorry, what? I didn't quite hear you, can you say it again?"

I raise my head to stare at him. Well, I think I'm staring at him. "Can you help me." I don't say it as a question. It isn't a question so to say, as agreeing to a last resort.

Before I can finish exhaling my anger from him mocking me, I feel the iciness that always accompanies him surround me. His hand clamps down on my forearm. "I thought you have super hearing to go along with your super human speed."

"I do," he says overconfidently.

"Then why did you make me repeat myself?"

"I just wanted to hear you say it again. Don't roll your eyes at me. It's not every day that I hear the great independent Charlie ask me for help."

I forgot he can see me. "You're dressed, right?" The chill from his body is extra strong, making me second guess the amount of clothing he's wearing.

"I have some articles on. I was sleeping right next to you before you escaped my grip. You didn't notice if I was wearing clothes or not?"

"Well, there was a blanket in between us since I probably started to show signs of hypothermia." I laugh in his face with over exaggerated expressions. He finally starts to lead me out of the room.

The rest of the suite is lighter than the bedroom, although everything is still shrouded by darkness. I can at least make out objects and my own extremities. Therefore, I look from Maxwell's hand to his face, back to his hand again. "You can let go now."

"Where are you going?"

As far away from you and your half-naked glory is what I want to say, but I decide against it due to him probably getting the wrong idea. "To work. Well, home to change, then to work." As if it were any of his business.

"Are you going to the hospital?"

"Of course."

"Promise me you'll leave work and be inside the hospital before the sun sets." I can't ignore the concern in his voice or the somber look on his face.

"The sun is high in the sky. I'm fine."

"Promise me." The seriousness he portrays straightens my spine.

"Yea, yea, I promise." I'm sure the grumpiness in my voice shows on my face.

"I mean it, Charlie."

"I said I promise, Maxwell. What else do you want me to say…yes, Father, or better yet, yes, master." I bow to him like a well-mannered slave.

Roughly he grabs me by my elbow, bringing me upright to face him. I wince with pain, but regret it instantly. I slap his chest with my free hand as I bellow. "Ow, you jerk."

"I know you would rather die than admit you want to be with me, but you don't understand how close that is to becoming true. When that sun is close to setting you need to be in a well populated area. We'll discuss further arrangements later tonight. I'll meet you at the hospital."

He still has a grip on my arm and he doesn't seem to be letting up. "Can I go now?"

"Remember, Charlie," he says as he lets me go.

"And where did you park my car? So I'm not wandering the streets looking for it."

"Your car is in the parking ramp across the street. First level, right side, four cars inward."

Quite precise, isn't he. I make a dash for the door and just as I expected, I'm stopped.

"Maybe a kiss for good measure before you go."

A laugh finds its way out of my pursed lips. "Good measure? What's that supposed to mean exactly?"

"For you taking my words seriously. For protecting you." He's completely serious as he expects me to agree with him.

"Are you serious…you can't be serious…right? You must be confused or something, because I wouldn't need protecting if it wasn't for you. So you and your good intentions can go fly a kite right now." I rip away from him and begin to pace the floor.

I mutter to myself. My hands shake wildly in the air due to my rising anger. "I can't believe him…I-I just can't believe that man. Mr. Tall Dark and Heartless wants a kiss as if he deserves one. Juliet's sitting in the hospital not because of me," I say aloud as if I were the only one in the room.

"I'm right here, Charlie." I can only imagine how annoyed he is at my talking to myself.

"Shut up," I bark at him as I stop to point my finger in his face. My eyes drift to the table that's beside the door, which is a few feet behind Maxwell. "Where are my keys?"

He begins to dig in his pocket to withdraw my keys. Dangling them in the air above my head, he smiles at me. I can hear his mouth spread apart. The sound makes me furious. With my anger taking over every cell in my body, I tackle him. Repeatedly, I jump up, trying to catch the clanging metal keys he taunts inches away from my outstretched hand. His laugh only makes me angrier.

A flood of curse words spew out of my mouth as I grow tired of his game. As quick as possible, I give him a small kiss on his cheek.

"Not good enough."

"What?"

He grabs ahold of my waist and tightly hugs me before his mouth is upon mine. I want to pull away so badly, but at the same time, I can't find it in me to break away from him. My arms stay at my sides stick straight with my hands balling into fists from his grabby hands, but my willpower doesn't last long as the urge to bury my fingers in his hair grows stronger. A trance takes over my body, letting my brain scream at me, but not allowing it to have the power to stop my limbs from moving.

One hand tugs at his hair, while my other hand slides over his sculpted chest. In all truth, no matter how many times I say my snide comments, I don't feel at ease without him near. As he squeezes his arm tightly around my torso, he lifts me off the ground and quickly stands me back on my feet. Thankfully, he breaks the kiss. I stand mesmerized with my eyes still closed.

I clear my throat, physically shaking myself. My hand jolts out face up in anticipation of my keys. Maxwell refuses to hand them over. "Keys...now," I demand.

"Say please." He taunts me yet again by jingling my keys above my head.

He's still pushing it. He got what he wanted and now that doesn't seem to be sufficient enough. "Keys. Please," I say through gritted teeth. With the cool metal of the keys in my hand, I immediately leave.

In a rush, I make my way to the parking ramp. Sure enough, right side, four cars up there's my car. The drive to my office is comforting. The space away from Maxwell lets me think instead of feel. Once I arrive I see Morgan's car out front. Late. I'm late.

"Charlie, I thought you would be at the hospital," Morgan says as soon as I enter through the door.

"I would love to, but it wouldn't do either of us any good. I'm going to try to catch up on some work."

Truth is that even though there are several things to do, I can't seem to concentrate on any of it. Strands of my hair fly as I flip through pieces of paper, trying to settle on one task at a time. It seems as if only an hour or two at most went by, but with a quick glance at the clock, I freeze. "Crap."

Gathering my belongings as fast as possible, I sprint out the door, yelling to Morgan on my way out. "Got to go to the hospital. See you later."

Shit…shit…shit, I grumble to myself. There's no way I'm going to be inside the hospital by sundown. The drive from my office to the hospital is fifteen minutes away and the sun is almost completely set. I can't even think of the lecture I'm going to receive from Maxwell. Prayers of him not being there waiting for me fill the car in the form of repetitive chants.

* * *

Maxwell

I don't waste time after Charlie leaves to phone Eugene. If anyone is aware of a vampire seeking revenge on Charlie, he would know, especially if it involved Benjamin. However, if he does know of Benjamin's plans, the outcome would be the same as if he didn't know. Eugene might be a council member and be treated with high respect, but no one can put Benjamin in his place alone. All council members would have to be on board and for that to happen they would all have to be conscious of Benjamin's plan.

After requesting to speak with Eugene to his assistant, I'm forced to wait through a series of more rings. Finally, his voice greets me. "Maxwell, what an unexpected surprise. What can I do for you? I assume everything is going well with Charlie?"

"Well, that's what I'm calling you about, Charlie's well being. Someone attacked her friend the other night after showing up at Charlie's house requesting to speak with her. He claimed to be friends with Benjamin and myself, but didn't say his name."

"I don't see where I can help you, Maxwell. Without a name I'm as in the dark as you." The curiosity and concern in his voice come across as genuine.

"It's not important, I can handle him. The reason why I'm coming to you is because I need to know that Benjamin isn't behind it. Charlie may have stepped out of line and I know that he can be reckless sometimes. It wouldn't be the first time he overstepped boundaries."

"I heard about that. She is quite the firecracker, but I assure you Benjamin isn't scheming of her demise. After he requested Grace to return, we have been keeping a close eye on him."

"Grace? She told me she was going back to our hometown." She lied to me, all that research she told me she did was fake.

"She's very much here in Austria and not in Massachusetts. I just had dinner with her last night to calm her nerves over Benjamin's ill manners. I'll keep an eye open for any such thing, but as I said before, Benjamin isn't behind it. He has his hands quite full at the moment."

"Thank you, Eugene."

"Before you go, Maxwell. Have you received the package that Grace sent over to you?"

"No."

"Well, maybe later today. Good day, Maxwell."

I hang up after I hear the faint click of Eugene disconnecting the call. As if I didn't have enough to worry about, now I have to add Grace to the list. I understand why she didn't tell me, though. She knew I would overreact and not allow her to go. And what is this package she sent me about?

No matter how much I want to look out for Grace, I know I can't. Right now my first priority is Charlie. Keeping her safe and alive for as long as possible is enough to handle. I look at the clock multiple times, sometimes seconds apart, wishing for the time to go by faster. The hours before the sun goes down are physically excruciating.

Without a second's thought as the sun's rays set, I set out to leave the hotel. Before reaching the doors, the personnel at the front desk stop me. "Mr. Barnett. A package arrived for you moments ago. Would you like me to keep it until you get back?" the man states.

"No, I'll take it now." I take the very small box out of his outstretched hand. Grace's handwriting stares back at me. "Thank you," I say before retracing my steps to the front door.

Once outside, I peel open the package and put its contents in my pocket, keeping a note she wrote in between my fingers. Before leaving to meet Charlie, I stand off to the side and read it.

> *Dear friend,*
> *It is very likely that you know by now that I'm not back in our hometown, but in the company of The High Council. Take this gift and keep it with you. I'll be in touch.*
> *Grace*

Minutes later, I enter the hospital and gradually make my way up to Juliet's room. When I don't see Charlie sitting in the hallway, I assume she's inside. Although, when I meander by, peeking inside, there's no sign of Charlie. Juliet sits upright in her bed half-asleep, watching some show on the TV.

I go back to the parking lot to search for her car in hopes that she's somewhere else within the hospital gathering food or coffee before she accompanies her friend. My eyes lock on each parked car, followed by the next…hers isn't in sight. I told her many times to be inside by sun down. Either something is wrong or she's blatantly ignoring my requests, which are to keep her safe.

A nerves habit of racking my hands through my hair usually calms me, but not this time. The feeling of the rough bricks behind my back as I lean up against the building is the only thing that reminds me of where I am. If it was not for the bustling of all the visitors coming and going along with a few staff members heading home or making their way inside to start their shift, I would surely do something irrational. I pace the length of the building to release some of this tension.

Her voice sounds from behind me. "Maxwell, I'm so sorry. I know you made me promise and I didn't mean to lie, I just got preoccupied at work. Please don't yell at me, but I'll take it if you do…well, some of it." Her voice is strained and she's panting for breath as if she ran at full speed. Spinning around, I see her bent over. Her arms are resting on her knees, supporting her upper half.

At least she knows she did wrong and she apologized for her irresponsible behavior. The fact that she agreed to allow me to lecture her is quite refreshing. "You could have been killed," I finally say to her.

"Killed? I think that's going a little too far. If this mysterious man was going to come after me or kill me as you say, then he would have caused a traffic accident and it would have ended up involving more than just me. I need to sit down. Can we go inside, please?" Her kindness and good mood force my anger to disappear.

"We'll discuss your reckless behavior later. Right now let's go see Juliet." More than anything I want to scold her for her carelessness, but I stop myself. She still huffs, trying to catch her breath from her sprint and I can't argue with someone who doesn't have enough energy to breathe, let alone talk back.

We walk arm in arm to Juliet's room and to my surprise she allows me to enter with her. Shock and embarrassment distort Juliet's face as she sees me stand before her. I know this can't be the best situation for us to meet, but I'm glad that Charlie is finally allowing me into her life. Nonetheless, anything pleasant about this visit is minimal, because the black and blue, broken Juliet just makes this worse.

This could have happened to Charlie or worse.

Chapter Twenty-Three

Charlie

Everyone in the room is speechless. Juliet's eyes move from me to Maxwell just as my eyes move from Maxwell to her. "Juliet, you met Maxwell before." I want so badly to say that he's the reason she's injured lying in a hospital bed, but refrain against it. Even though Maxwell got us neck deep into this, he's the only one who can get us out.

She nods her head in agreement. The sound of her dry throat clearing fills the room. "Yes, of course. He's your secret boyfriend, the one who knows the man who attacked me." Sarcasm laces her words as she puts the pieces of the puzzle together herself without me mentioning the connection.

"If that's how you want to put it, yes. And no, he doesn't know the man, but he's going to do everything he can to find out who he is." The less she knows the better; I wish I could say the same for myself.

I, on the other hand, know that the only reason Maxwell is going to even try to catch this vampire is because he's after me. The tension in the room is thick, too thick for my liking. "You know what, I'm going to get some coffee and a snack from the vending machines downstairs. Do you want anything?" I look at both of them only to be polite as I take a few steps toward the door. Maxwell follows my lead. "You can stay here and get some juicy dirt on me from my best friend," I say to him, holding up my hand, stopping him in his tracks.

"Twizzlers," Juliet demands before I finally depart the room.

I look one last time at Maxwell; his expression is a mix of worry and dread. I'm forcing him to stay in the room with someone he doesn't know and doesn't want to know. At a steady pace, I pass doctors and nurses until I reach the corridor that the vending machines are down. Seeing it's somewhat late in the evening, most visitors are gone, leaving these halls vacant. My footsteps echo, playing tricks on my ears. It sounds as though I'm not the only one in these deserted halls. The lights flicker above my head, causing me to catch my breath.

With the little nook that holds the variety of machines full of choices within sight, I make a run for it. My shoes squeak against the tiled floor as I screech to a stop. A nurse, who seems to be just as petrified as I am, swings around at my surprising arrival. Unlike her fear, which is caused by me scaring her, my own fear is brought on by these creepy halls. "Sorry, so sorry," I apologize.

"These halls can be spooky late at night, believe me. I've asked the maintenance crew to fix that light for weeks now and they continue to ignore me," the nurse says in a comforting tone. "It's like they're waiting for someone to get murdered before they do their job," she jokes, although I don't find it funny. Watching her leave, I can't help but to be relieved.

"Waiting for someone to be murdered? Who says that to a stranger?" I whisper to myself when I know she's long gone, leaving me alone in the dank nook.

I can't believe I scared that poor woman due to my own paranoia. It does make me less regretful that she scared me in return. However, all I can think about is Maxwell's words of staying in well populated areas. These halls are anything but well populated. I start my coffee while I search the various machines for the lucky one that holds Twizzlers. The reflection of the hall behind me shows on the glass locking away all the food. I try not to pay attention to it, because I haven't had the best of luck with reflections. Tonight proves to be like all the others. A man strides behind me. A flash of green eyes is the only defining attribute I see.

Instantly, my palms rub harshly at my eyes as my brain tries to tell my pounding heart to relax, that what I just saw was my mind playing tricks on me. Although, it isn't that easy…it never is. With shaking hands that barely contain the coffee in its cup and crush the licorice, I race away from what is starting to feel like a death trap. My eyes watch the brown liquid swish in the cup as I make my way back to Juliet's room or at least a hall that has more people. My friend's words of 'green eyes' repeat in my head.

"Jesus." Coffee spills out of the cup and onto the floor. Some of the hot fluid drips onto my forearm. My nose and forehead ache from making impact with something hard, but with my hands occupied, I can't rub at my face to ease the pain.

"Charlie, are you okay? I felt the spike in your heart rate and I got worried. I didn't mean to run into you and spill your coffee." He lifts my hand to observe the burn that disguises itself as a faint red mark on my arm. "We can put some ice on it when we get back to Juliet's room."

"He's here…I saw him, the man with the green eyes…I saw him, Maxwell. Green eyes. Juliet can only remember green eyes and I saw green eyes behind me in the reflection of the glass." Tears are on the verge of spilling over the brim of my eyes. I don't know what's wrong with me, I never cry or show weakness, but knowing that someone put your friend in the hospital for no reason at all only makes being brave harder.

Maxwell takes my coffee out of my hand and wraps his free arm around me. "It could be anyone. If it is him, he won't do anything, not here…not in a hospital."

"Yea, heaven forbid that I get stitched back up before I have a chance to die." My words are muffled due to the fact that he's smothering me against his chest. I try to make a joke out of the situation, but it doesn't work.

Gradually, we make our way into Juliet's room. Maxwell looks over his shoulder the whole way there, but Mr. Green-Eyed Stranger doesn't show his face again. I put an apologetic smile on my face as I hand Juliet the crushed package of Twizzlers. All she does is raise her eyebrows in amusement before she rips the package open.

When I turn around I see Maxwell's back to me. He stands in front of the sink in the room. Just as fast as the water turns on, it turns off. Maxwell moves my coffee to my unburned arm and proceeds to place the ice-cold paper towel on the burn mark. Instantly, the cold soothes the fiery burn.

"What the hell happened to you? The machines downstairs attack you or something?" Juliet questions me.

"I spilled my coffee on myself. It's nothing, I'm fine," I say, trying to take my arm out of Maxwell's grasp, but he refuses to let go.

The three of us are lost in our own little worlds. Maxwell stares at my arm, Juliet chews her licorice, and I silently sip my coffee.

After four pieces ate and questioning eyes staring at me, Juliet speaks with her still raspy voice. "I get to leave on Wednesday." She shakes her arms in the air…well, one arm in the air with excitement. "I want you to come over and help me settle in." It'll be three days that she's been in here by the time she gets discharged.

"Settle in? It's not like you're moving into a new house. Are you?" I'm confused at her words. Does she mean keep her company?

"I should after what happened. I only have one arm, Charlie, one arm for two months. You need to feel sorry for me…I feel sorry for myself, if that helps."

"I didn't say I wouldn't help you. You don't know how awful I feel about you only having one arm and a purple face. I'll vacuum your floors, do your dishes and whatever else you need help with. Almost whatever else you could possibly need help with," I correct myself. Who knows what she's going to ask me to do.

"You're going to do my dishes? How sweet, I wasn't going to ask you to do my dishes, but since you offered." Her hand goes to her chest, covering her heart as if she's touched by my offer. The cocky smile on her face counteracts her genuineness.

"What were you going to ask me to do? I can see it, it's written all over your face. Come on, what is it?" Preparing myself for the worst possible thing, I patiently wait.

"Nothing worse than dishes. There're a lot of splinters of wood all over my foyer and living room, so I was going to ask you to sweep my hard wood floors and…"

"And what?" I say, getting slightly annoyed.

"Janessa says there's dried blood on my kitchen floor." She says it so fast I almost don't catch it.

"What? Why can't she clean it? She's your sister, after all. I mean, you two have the same blood, don't you?" Cleaning blood, her dried blood off the floor is not the worst thing I thought of, but it's pretty high on the gross list.

"She almost passed out thinking about my broken arm yesterday. Why do you think she's not here?" With her bottom lip puckered out, she resembles a begging child.

I thought I owed her; however, she now owes me. "Fine, I'll be there Wednesday. Call me when you get discharged. I'm going to go home to get some rest before I have to turn into a housemaid." I give her a gentle hug and a kiss on the cheek. "I'm glad you're okay. See you later."

As soon as we're close to exiting the building, Maxwell breaks the silence that lingers between us. "It could have been much worse. She's in quite well shape for having an encounter with a vengeful vampire, if I might say."

"Really?" I don't know what else to say to that besides the fact that he's right. She could be dead or in a coma or paralyzed. But a broken arm, a head injury, and being covered in bruises is bad enough.

Without warning, Maxwell's arm jolts out, forcing me to a stop. He stands stiff as a board, staring into the nearly empty parking lot. There's a mix of shock and anger on his face. I look into the parking lot, trying to spot what he sees, but give up soon after. It's pitch black out here, and if the object or person isn't in the glow of the lamp posts, there's no way I'll ever be able to see it.

"Give me your keys, Charlie," he says, barley moving his lips with his eyes still staring out into the lot.

"What? Why?" He's not telling me something and part of me thinks that if I demand an answer I'll get one.

"I'm taking you home, Charlie, just give me your keys," he says, facing me head-on. His voice is uneasy.

Dropping my keys in his open hand, I allow him to walk me to my car held tightly in his grasp. Almost at the passenger side door is when I see it, a silhouette leaning against one of the nearby trees that line the parking lot. Involuntarily, my fingernails dig into Maxwell forearm as the person leisurely walks into the closest pool of light that one of the lamp posts creates. His green eyes stare at me from afar. A sly smile spreads across his lips as he nods our way.

Maxwell has his back to the man and before he can turn around, he's gone.

"He...he..." I mumble.

"Yes, Charlie. Let's just go."

Once he slams the door shut, he stands there with his back up against the door and stares off in the direction of where the green-eyed stranger just was. I shuffle in my seat, trying to get a good look at the expression on Maxwell's face. However, before I can figure out which way I have to turn my body, Maxwell makes his way to the driver's side.

I can't help to stare at the lamp post the green-eyed man was under as we leave the parking lot. Seeing the parking lot get farther away eases some of the strain of my tensing muscles. My head falls against the seat and my eyes close in relief.

* * *

Maxwell

"You are taking me home and not to your place, right?" Charlie questions me as we get onto more populated streets.

"I would prefer if you stayed with me."

"I can't stay with you forever, Maxwell," she claims, completely irritated by my mentioning the idea of staying with me.

"I beg to differ." Unwillingly, I abide by her unspoken words and drive to her house. The radio is the only noise that fills the car all the way to her house. I can tell she's nervous and uneasy, but she remains quiet, battling her thoughts herself.

We reach her house sooner than I would have liked. "At least stay in the car while I check the house over," I tell her. Her hand lingers on the door handle while I talk, but eventually falls back onto her lap.

An exhale of her breath ruffles her hair that falls in her eyes.

"Stay put," I tell her before I finally exit the car. The door quietly shuts as she starts to reply, but I ignore her and make my way to the front door.

I hesitate on the front porch, listening for the faintest noise. Besides the hum of the insects outside, it's completely silent. I cautiously enter the house and to my relief no one lurks within. With an extensive search of every room, every little hiding place proves just that, completely empty.

I barely step outside the front door before she starts yelling in my direction. "Well?" She stands outside the car, leaning against the hood.

"I thought I told you to stay inside," I retort, trying my hardest to keep the anger out of my voice.

"I thought I told you a lot of things too, but you never seem to listen either." Her arms are crossed over her chest as she snaps her answer at me.

"You can go inside, but I'm staying with you as long as I can, which will be until a few minutes before sunrise."

She walks right past me to enter the house. "I'll allow it," she says with a smirk.

A smile of my own creeps onto my lips at the thought of her believing she has a choice in the matter. Instantly, she goes into her room to change into her pajamas. When she finally sits next to me on the couch, she has her hair up in a ponytail, along with a tank top and plaid bottoms on.

"Care for something to drink or eat?" A laugh explodes out of her mouth and chases the silence away. "Just thought I would be a good hostess, but not that good." She continues to laugh as she turns the TV on.

Hours go by with her eyes glued on the TV and her mouth shut. She doesn't even bother covering up her yawn. "Well, I'm off to bed. Feel free to watch whatever you want and make sure to lock the door on your way out."

I don't hear the bedroom door close, so I assume she left it open. The glow of the TV fills the living room, but even though it's on, I don't pay attention to what the moving picture is illustrating. Trying to get as comfortable as I can on her couch, I prepare myself for the boredom that's bound to happen during my wait until sunrise. I dig out a cell phone from the depths of my pocket. Flipping it in my hands, I debate whether Grace sent it for a reason or if there's something going on in Austria that I'm unaware of.

The sound of a trashcan crashing to the ground from outside startles me as well as Charlie. I shove the phone back in my pocket and leap from the couch.

Within seconds she comes running out of her bedroom. Her voice is breathless from her fear. "What was that? Is someone here?"

To ease her fear as well as my own, I stride up to the front door. I think I would know if a vampire prowls outside, but that's not always the case. Carefully, I open the door to reveal an empty front porch and a deserted street. All except for a woman walking her dog. I witness her pick up the trashcan her pet must have knocked over.

After shutting the door and purposely taking a few

minutes before I speak, I tell Charlie the verdict. "Someone's dog tipped over a neighbor's trashcan. Go back to bed."

"Does green eyes have a dog? It could be a trick."

"Why would a vampire have a dog, Charlie? It's enough to watch humans who have long life spans die. Having a dog is just asking for depression."

"Oh. Right." Her eyebrow perks up. "I guess you have a point. Maybe you can stay in my room with me…you know, like sit on a chair in the corner or something."

"Sure." I waste no time following her to the bedroom.

She points me toward a bench that's up against one of the walls. Sitting there watching her sleep brings some peace to my mind. At least having her in sight makes the stress I have diminish a little. Her breathing becomes slower and deeper as she finally drifts off. Trying to avoid the squeaky floorboards, I exit the room when I feel a soft vibration coming from inside my pocket.

I answer the phone casually. "Hello, Grace."

"I see you got my gift," she happily replies.

"And why exactly did you send it to me?"

"Because I don't know when I'm coming back." The words are strained as she forces them to be said.

I really could use her to help me figure this out. To help watch over Charlie. "And what is it that you are doing there exactly?"

"Nothing important. How's Charlie. Alive?"

"For now. Although there's someone who could possibly want her dead, besides me."

"I'm gone for a week if even and all the good stuff happens."

"It's not good, Grace. Someone showed up at her

house the night her friend Juliet was over."

"So...."

"That very same person, or should I say vampire, attacked Juliet that very night. She's in the hospital, thankfully alive."

"Who was it?"

"Don't know."

"I'll keep an open ear, but—"

"You're busy. Yes." The squeak of a floorboard from behind alerts me of a second pair of ears listening. "Grace, I'll discuss this with you when you get back." Quickly, I put the phone back in my pocket. Without turning around, I address Charlie. "Spying now, love."

"Spying...not listening to orders, it's just another thing you tell me not to do, but you can't seem to stop yourself from doing either. Where the hell does a vampire get a cell phone?"

"Grace sent it. She thought I would appreciate her keeping contact while she's gone. Us vampires have to adapt. Now back to bed."

"Us, vampires," she argues with me.

"Go back to bed, Charlie," I argue back. I spin her around and force her feet to take steps toward her room.

It takes quite a bit of nudging to get Charlie into bed, but once she does, I tuck her underneath the covers, along with placing a kiss upon her forehead. She grunts in disapproval, which forms a smile on my face as I walk back to the bench in the corner. She stares at me from underneath the blanket, making sure I don't sneak off again. After an hour or two, she finally falls asleep due to exhaustion.

I remain on the bench until a few minutes before sunrise as I said I would. Reluctantly, I lock the door behind me and race to the confines of the hotel. The lock of my own door just makes me think about the snap of the lock on Charlie's front door. Tomorrow she's going to be demanding answers and I don't know how to explain any of this.

Chapter Twenty-Four

Charlie

Number one thing I like about mornings in my own home, no Maxwell. The sun shines on my face as I walk to the mailbox to gather my mail. Already clothed for work I sit at the kitchen table to enjoy some breakfast as I look at the letters I received. A wide smile forms on my face as I see a letter from Robert and Justin, my flower experts.

Eagerly, I tear into the envelope to read what other than an invitation to their engagement party. A tiny bit of disappointment seeps into my good mood because I thought they wanted me to help them with their wedding. I haven't had a chance to check my emails in forever, so for all I know there's an email from them waiting for me to reply to. To my surprise, a corner of a second piece of paper that is still wedged inside the envelope peaks out. A small laugh fills the silent room as I read a message that Justin wrote.

You better have this date available.

After finishing my breakfast, I gather my purse and keys to make my way to work, double checking several times that I remembered the invitation and my calendar before I leave. The sole of my shoe slides as I turn away from the door. Wondering if I dropped anything, I look around my full hands. Sure enough, right there still under my foot is an envelope.

In a rush, I pick it up and shove it in my purse. My anxious heart calms when I park in the lot in front of my office building. As expected, Morgan hasn't arrived yet and the quietness the empty building offers me is much needed.

I haven't been in my office fully enjoying what I do for a while. Only one thing is on my mind and that's contacting Robert and Justin about this engagement party. While I wait for my laptop to boot up, I dig out the invitation. Along with it comes the envelope I slipped on.

I tear it open without looking to see who it's from. It feels as if the blood coursing through my veins freezes the minute I read the short message written on a single piece of paper that was shoved inside. The crisp white stationary paper slowly floats down to my desktop as my quivering fingers can't hold on to it any longer.

I brushed it off earlier as dropping it by accident, but a little voice in my head tells me otherwise. After examining the front and back of the small black envelope, it only makes my suspicions greater. There's no stamp on it indicating that it was even mailed. Someone left it intentionally on my doorstep, but when? No matter how hard I want to take my gaze off the note, I can't.

You're next.

Life seems to be crashing down on me and when my ring tone blares from inside my purse, I can't help but to twitch from fear. With shaking arms along with numb fingers, I barely answer the phone.

"Charlie, where are you? Are you okay?" The panic in Maxwell's voice probably matches my own if I could actually speak. "Charlie, answer me," he pleads.

"I'm at work." I manage to get out.

"What's wrong?" he asks, but when I remain silent

he continues to talk. "Charlie, we have been through this before. I know when something is wrong. Now tell me before I come find out for myself this instant."

"The sun's blazing outside…you would die…wouldn't you?"

"Possibly, but I would risk my life to save you. Tell me what happened."

"A letter...just a letter. I thought I dropped it, but after opening it, I know I didn't drop it, Maxwell…it was left for me."

"Charlie, calm down. It's just a letter, it can't be that bad. What does it say?" His stern voice creates more panic.

"You're next."

"And you think it's from the same man who showed up at your house and attacked Juliet?"

"Who else would leave me a note saying you're next?"

"It could have been left before sunrise." He tries to reason with me.

"I got my mail and went back inside to finish getting ready. There was no way I missed it going to the mailbox and coming back inside. Not mention I would have heard it hit the porch if I dropped it. It was maybe fifteen minutes to a half an hour the most I was inside before leaving." Going over the scenario just makes it more obvious. Just as obvious as the message is.

"You should leave work and come stay with me until we figure this out."

"I can't, I have too much work to do."

"Work isn't important if you're dead. You said it yourself. I can't save you during the day. A living breathing human being is working with him. The game has changed and I need you to understand that things just got worse."

"Charlie?" Morgan calls from the front office.

"Morgan, I'm in here," I yell back.

"Listen, I have to go. Morgan just got here. I can get pepper spray or a Taser to put the odds in my favor if I get attacked during the day. Trust me, if I have to, I can take on a human. Plus, they would be stupid to come here."

"You're thinking too greatly of yourself, Charlie, and you could get hurt. No meeting new clients today. Please watch your back and I'll see you come nightfall in your office, so wait for me there."

"I'll do just that. See you later." My farewell is short and brief to Maxwell as Morgan hovers in my doorway.

"I'm sorry. I didn't realize you were on the phone."

"No big deal."

Morgan remains in the doorway, shuffling her feet.

"Is there something you need to tell me?" I wave my hand to one of the chairs in front of my desk. "Take a seat."

"I do, but I know you're going through a lot, so…I understand if you say no. It's just that James and I are planning a little trip this coming weekend. We're planning to leave on Friday, but if you need to be with Juliet and can't arrange the party this Saturday, I don't have to go."

"No, you go on your trip. I can orchestrate the party. I'm seeing Juliet tomorrow, so I'll let her know I'll be unavailable." And there's no way I'm asking Dave to help out in my absence again.

"Awesome." She gets up from her chair and heads to the front desk.

The work that's piling up keeps my mind from wandering to dreadful thoughts. As disgusted as the letter makes me, I shove the paper back in the envelope and harshly stash it in my purse. Pleasant hums from the computer draw my mind to what I'm here to do, plan and organize parties. Robert and Justin's engagement party is at the top of that list. Several emails and outlines later, things for the scheduled party on Saturday along with my dear friends' party are gradually being completed.

As the work load gets less, my attention starts to stray. As my office gets darker, my heart feels as if it could break out of my ribcage. I'm not sure if it's my nerves due to the impending nightfall or anxiousness to see Maxwell causing my irrational behavior. Nonetheless, with or without an answer, night covers the city and Maxwell soundlessly enters my office.

"Are you ready to leave?" Maxwell says, sitting in one of the chairs across from me.

"Holly shit, Maxwell, do you want to give me a heart attack?" He knows what a wreck I am with this letter materializing on my doorstep in broad daylight and then he goes and sneaks up on me.

"Morgan let me in. I didn't think it would be a problem. I sent her home, by the way, seeing as we're going to be leaving as well."

"Leaving to go to my house, right?"

"No, to mine. It's not safe for you there, Charlie. The sooner you realize that, the safer you'll be. Please don't argue with me, I'm doing this for you…I'll always do everything I can for you."

"There's no need to explain, I get it, but I need to go to Juliet's tomorrow with or without your approval. So don't you think it would be best for you to go and search the house tonight than me to go there tomorrow…alone?"

"Point taken. We'll stop there tonight for you to get a change of clothes, but then we are going back to my suite."

"Not what I meant."

"I know." Is all he says before picking up my purse.

The feeling of being a sitting duck puts me on edge. He holds out his hand for me to take and without thinking I tightly latch on. We remain quiet the whole way to my house. The music from the radio sounds like it's miles away.

I didn't even realize that we arrived at my house until he opens my car door. Carefully, he sits me on the hood and tells me to wait until he checks the house over. Like the night before, it's all clear, but I can't approach the house without Maxwell placing himself at my side.

"I won't let anything happen to you. You know that, right?"

All I can do is nod my head. After we enter the house, I double check the door to make sure it's locked several times. I have no idea why I'm so hell-bent on locking my door, it's not as if the wooden divider would deter any unwanted company from entering. "What?" I say annoyed at a staring Maxwell.

"Nothing, I just wish I could make things better."

"You can," I tell him as a crazy idea fills my head. His questioning look makes me second guess myself. "Your mind mojo. You can erase it all."

"It's not that easy, Charlie. We...us vampires can't erase memories or emotions, we can only influence, and you should know by personal experience that it doesn't always last forever."

There goes my out, my only way of living a normal life. "It never can be that easy, can it?"

"It can be easier than you're making it." He places his hands on my shoulders and slowly slides them down my arms. He leans in, lowering his head toward me.

"I can't, Maxwell." My hand presses against his

chest, making him keep his distance.

"Why not? You can't keep fighting this, us. Sooner or later it'll drive you crazy and then you'll start doing irrational things."

"You want to know why, why I can't do this," I wave my hand between us, "because it's a death sentence. With this mystery man and his little helper, I'm finally on death row. It feels like I'm living in a concrete cell with no windows, slowly suffocating."

"I'm not death. I might not have a beating heart, but that doesn't mean I don't have feelings. Just because I can't see the sun doesn't mean happiness doesn't fill my day. I'm alive with you. What I am, what you will be one day, is just a different way of living, but it isn't not living."

I don't have time to process what he said or reply before his mouth is upon mine. The little breath I have is taken away. The gentle movement of his lips is everything I need to put my stress at ease. My mouth presses against his without me even knowing it until it's too late.

Maxwell's hand slides up the back of my neck, tangling his fingers in my hair, taking advantage of my accepting body. My limp arms that dangle at my sides finally come to life and instantly grab onto him. One hand grabs a fistful of his shirt as my other hand lays over his neck, some of my fingers curving over his jaw to rest on his cheek. The little amount of breath I have left rushes out as he lifts me off my feet.

My legs wrap around his waist. For the first time I'm taller than him. As our kiss is broken, his face becomes even with my neck. Refusing to keep his mouth off me, he gently kisses my neck. An inhuman growl rumbles in his chest and his fingers harshly dig into my back as he squeezes me tighter. I know he can sense my blood race through my veins.

"Maxwell," I say breathless. He doesn't hear me or he just refuses to stop. I yank on his hair to get his attention. "Maxwell, you're hurting me."

His head follows the pull of my hand. Regret fills his eyes as he finally looks at me. "Charlie, I'm sorry, I didn't—"

"It's fine. I should go gather some clothes," I awkwardly say as he puts me back on the floor.

It doesn't take long for me to gather several pieces of clothes. With them neatly folded in a bag, I head back to Maxwell. I find him leaning against the console table in the entryway. I lift the bag to show him I'm all set.

* * *

Maxwell

Before we get to the hotel Charlie falls asleep. As gently as I can, I gather her in my arms without letting her limbs bob around too much. Her head rolls back over my forearm only to prop itself in the groove of my shoulder. It gets tricky when opening doors, but within minutes I manage to get safely inside my suite. Propping one knee on the mattress, I lay her in the center of the bed. The sound of her heartbeat is calm and steady. With her deep in sleep there's nothing for me to do besides let her rest.

Instead of sitting in here and watching her sleep, I go to the living room. There's nothing to do in here, but it's better than hovering over her. Before I sit down, I gather a small box I have hidden. I fiddle with it between my fingers. She's hell-bent on human traditions and this little box will only connect those human traditions to her future vampire life.

It seems all too soon that the pressure of the rising

sun bears down on me. With Charlie still sleeping, I take this opportunity to dig through her purse. I need to call someone who will help keep an eye on her, someone who has her back as much as I do, if not more.

I scroll through her contacts on her phone until I reach the name I'm looking for. Tapping it into the phone Grace sent me, I click the call button.

"Hello," she answers in her usual perky tone.

"Hello, Morgan, nice to speak with you again."

"Oh, Maxwell. How's everything with Charlie going? I'm rooting for you."

I know her comment has something to do with the reoccurrence of Dave, but I don't want to get into it. "Everything is fine between Charlie and I, but she's a little stressed about someone leaving her hate mail on her doorstep. I think it might be a previous client who's unsatisfied and is threatening her career. Can you keep an eye on her at work? I would be by her every waking moment, but I too have lots of business to conduct."

"How awful. Charlie is the most kind and understanding person I know. I wish I could work half as hard as her. Of course I'll keep an eye on her and pay extra attention to all the customers I come in contact with."

"Perfect. She's supposed to be leaving to help out Juliet today. Could you be so kind as to call me when she leaves the office?"

"No problem, will do. I'll save your number."

"Thank you, Morgan."

"Oh, before you go, I'm supposed to tell you James says hello."

"James?" Not the James I've known for seventy-five years? It's not like I can ask her that to be sure.

"Yeah, my boyfriend, James. I've been talking to him about Charlie and you. That's when he said he knew you. He also mentioned something about seeing you again sometime soon. Maybe he has a double date planned. How fun would that be? It wouldn't be this weekend because we're going on a little trip, but maybe after we come back." She excitedly goes on to tell me.

"A trip to where, may I ask?"

"Austria. Totally blew me away when he offered to take me there, but how can I resist?"

Morgan's dating a vampire and going to the very same place The High Council resides at. Charlie is not going to be happy. "Good to know. I'll talk to you soon." I hang up after I hear her say goodbye.

The more troubling, but yet reassuring outcome of this is that Charlie and Morgan are ultimately in the same situation. If Charlie ever finds out, which won't be by me, she's going to go ballistic. Morgan, her assistant, could be taken away from her, but not by her own departure into the vampire world...by Morgan's.

It doesn't take long for a fully clothed Charlie to exit the room in a manic rush. I keep silent, afraid she'll sense that I'm hiding something.

"Would it kill you to wake me?" she says as she rushes to gather her purse, digging through the contents for her keys.

"I'd rather have you rest. Be careful at work today. I parked the car in the same place."

"Thank you." Her kind eyes briefly stare at me before she bustles out of the door.

Chapter Twenty-Five

Charlie

Five minutes to four o clock my cell phone rings. "Hello?"

"Put your papers away and get those rubber gloves on, because I'm out. Well, not until you pick me up. I'll be waiting for you in my room," Juliet chimes. She sounds like she's back to her old self again and I can't be any happier.

Goodbyes are exchanged and I do what I was told. I gather all the scrambled papers on my desk into a neat pile and head out.

"Leaving already?" Morgan asks me when I come into view. "I love all these different scarves you're always wearing, by the way," she adds as she leans over the front desk.

I adjust the pink plaid scarf tighter around my neck. It's becoming a habit to wear a scarf when leaving the house now. "I love to accessorize. I have to go pick Juliet up at the hospital and then I turn housemaid. Oh how I wish I could stay here for a few more hours and be done for the night. I'll see you tomorrow…right?"

"Yup. I'll be leaving early, though, to get things packed, if that's okay."

"Do what you got to do. Make sure to lock up before you leave and have a good night." I look back one last time before I get too far away and I swear I can see her with her cell phone already up to her ear. I begin to wonder if that's what she does after I leave early or when I'm not present, sit there and talk on the phone. I shrug it off as her calling James to tell him everything is set for her absence at work.

When I reach Juliet's hospital room door, I see her changed out of her gown and fully clothed in yoga pants and a tank top. Seeing her arm in its cast makes dread form in the pit of my stomach. She's an innocent bystander in this chaos and yet she's the only one who looks like she has been fighting in this fight...as of yet. The nurse helps her to her feet and accompanies us to the front of the hospital. At a slow and steady pace, we make our way back to my car. I can't stop myself from joking. "So...you're incredibly lucky that it's summer or you would have a major problem finding clothes."

"Very funny, Charlie, very funny. Soon I'll be the one laughing when I'm sitting on my couch with my feet up watching you clean my house." Her phony laugh causes me to laugh in response.

Juliet examines her cast the whole way to her house. She sings along to the radio until she takes in a sharp breath. I nearly swerve off the road from panic. Juliet clenches the dashboard with her good arm in fear. "Jesus, woman, stay on the road," she yells at me.

"Me...you. You scared the crap out me. What the hell's wrong?" My heart slowly thumps against my chest.

"I just thought of something. I should go over to Chadwick's and have him draw a really awesome picture on my cast."

Chadwick is a friend of Harlow's boyfriend. He's a tattoo artist who happened to give Juliet her first and only tattoo, because she's a crybaby.

"That's all...that's what was so important that happened to scare the crap out of me?" I bicker.

"Uh...yeah."

We erupt in laughter and after a few minutes we arrive at her house with sore cheeks and tender bellies from laughing so hard. I notice the brand new door that Janessa replaced. After a few minutes waiting for Juliet to dig her keys out, I finally get to see the inside. Dropping our purses off in the entryway, I begin to look at the tasks I have ahead of me.

Janessa didn't do much. The floor is littered with wooden scraps and after walking into the kitchen, I see the blood. Juliet made it sound as if it was just a few droplets, but this is anything but. A brown puddle covers a large portion of the kitchen floor.

With a huff, I head to the bathroom to change into something more comfortable. Thank God I decided to throw a pair of shorts into my purse before leaving for work this morning. Without further delay, I get supplies ready and begin to clean. My scarf continually floats over the dried blood, almost touching the dirtiness since I'm forced to scrub the floor on my hands and knees. As carefully as possible without moving it too much from around my neck and not getting any bloodstains on it, I tuck it into my shorts.

After an hour or so of the tedious scrubbing and sweeping, I take a break. The task is taking longer than I expected and as nightfall begins to get closer, I can't help to think what Maxwell is doing. Part of me wants him to show up, but another part of me thinks it's best if he doesn't. By making something to eat for Juliet and myself, I add cook to the ever-growing list of job titles I've been forced to become tonight. We eat chatting about how her students are going to react to seeing her broken arm when she returns to work.

"I would love to sit and relax with you, but I have dishes to do if I want to get home before midnight," I finally say as the only light that illuminates the house comes from her lamps. The sun set over an hour ago and my nerves have been on edge since.

Juliet might have a broken arm, but her legs work just fine. She jumps up from her seat. "What? I got to go to the bathroom. Go on, I don't need your help in there," she jokes.

I start working on the huge pile of dirty dishes waiting for me. Once I hear Juliet prance back to her comfortable seat on the couch, I holler to her. "You know, you really should get a dishwasher." I'm expecting a cocky reply, but the house is silent. "Juliet?" I question the air as I make my way into the living room.

Right there on the couch ignoring me, she intently looks at something in her hands. Taking a few big strides, I pluck the object out of her grip. It's a homemade CD labeled 'Love Mix'. "Where did you get this? Who gave it to you?" I ask, trying to keep the laughter out of my voice.

I actually see her blush and instantly her feet plant themselves on the floor as she straightens her body out. She stares at me, sitting stick straight. "A boy," she slowly replies.

"No shit, a boy, it's labeled 'Love Mix'. What's the boy's name?" My free hand that doesn't hold the CD rests on my hip.

"Nathan, okay?" She bolts to her feet and tries to snatch the CD out of my curious hands, but I'm too fast.

"Juliet, how could you? You lectured me about having a secret boyfriend and I find out you have one of your own." I feel offended.

"He's not my boyfriend." She tries to sound serious and disgusted by my assumption, but I can see through her act.

"I've heard that before. In fact, I've said those exact words. Don't you lie to me, girly, I can see it plastered all over your face. Where's a CD player? We're going to play this bad boy. Do you even know what's on here?"

"No. He gave it to me when he visited me in the hospital, but he forgot to bring me a CD player...so this will be the first time I'm going to be hearing it." She looks at the floor, refusing to make eye contact with me. However, I don't know who's more embarrassed...me or her.

Reluctantly, Juliet instructs me where her portable stereo is while she drops her face in her hands. Within seconds, a familiar tune blares through the speakers. A laugh rumbles in my chest. This is going to be good, I say to myself. The much loved songs turn cheesy once I think about the meaning behind them that this Nathan is sending. I sing along while I scrub dish after dish, making fun of her and her secret boyfriend as much as possible.

Juliet dances in the living room, singing along to every single word while I finish up the dishes. I know I should feel scared or nervous about being alone, well, without Maxwell at night, but I can't help but to sing along and dance to the carefree songs. It's doing its job by keeping my mind off the impending doom that continues to linger above my head.

Out of the blue, the doorbell chimes, almost causing me to drop one of the plates I'm placing in the dish rack. Juliet runs to the door as if she knows exactly who resides behind it. Preparing myself for the worst, I grab a dirty knife. Did I really expect the night to go well? Nonetheless, I hear a familiar voice fill the living room. I quickly place the knife down as I hear his heavy footsteps get closer to the kitchen.

"Charlie, so nice to see you again."

With my back still turned to the guest, I reply, "Dave. What on earth are you doing here?" I try to sound as happy and surprised as possible when truthfully I want to fill the room with my sarcasm of how this whole night is unwanted, including his presence.

"Juliet didn't tell you?" Dave questions me.

"Tell me what?" Now I'm beginning to become more nervous.

"That she invited Nathan and I over." His smile is cocky and sly.

"You know Nathan?"

"Yeah, he's one of my good friends. So…she did tell you about us coming then?"

"No, I had no idea that you or this Nathan were going to show up. The only reason the name Nathan sounds familiar is because I found his love mix and I confronted Juliet about it…she unwillingly informed me. She didn't have a choice in the matter, just like I don't have a choice in the matter now."

"You should be happy, you have a helper now." He picks up a towel and begins to dry the clean dishes. "You know, I helped him pick out some of these songs. When he found out that Juliet was attacked he wanted to do something nice for her."

Nice? I see his efforts as trying to get her into bed, but that's just my opinion. Does he realize that she has a broken arm and will be out of commission for a while? Just then Juliet rushes in with whom other than Nathan.

"Charlie, this is Nathan. The lovely man who's responsible for our entertainment tonight," Juliet informs me. She looks at him with sheer awe and I slightly feel jealous.

"Nice to meet you, Nathan," I say in the kindest manner.

I look over his tall frame and shaggy light brown hair. He's not quite heavy set, but he's not a small guy either.

"I've heard about you from Dave," Nathan tells me.

Oh dear Lord, I can only imagine what Dave has divulged about me to one of his friends. "Only good things, I hope," I say before glaring at Dave.

"Of course." Seconds later he turns to Juliet. "Care to dance?" he asks her. With Juliet nodding in utter excitement, he leads her into the living room. The scrape of her coffee table against the wooden floor lets me know they're making a mini dance floor.

"Why don't you go and dance, Dave? I can finish the dishes." I keep my back to him as I speak, occasionally looking at the window. Just as if I timed it perfectly, I see a blur of something rush past the small window. I would've missed it if I wasn't so intent on keeping my back to Dave. The shadow made the tree line smear together as whatever it was went by incredibly fast.

"Don't be silly, we should all be having fun. Come dance with us, Charlie," he pleads.

"You know what, I think I need some air. I'll be right back." I leave Dave behind with his confusion as I exit the back door.

I stand in the middle of Juliet's backyard, searching every hiding spot I think of without physically going to inspect it. In barely audible whispers I holler for whoever's out here to show their face. I assume it's Maxwell…I hope it's Maxwell. I didn't really think about what I would do if it happens to not be Maxwell. "Maxwell Barnett, you show your face right now," I whisper into the dark. I wait. No response. "Maxwell, this is not funny."

"I don't find it very funny either," Maxwell says as he emerges from a shadow.

"What are you doing here?" I walk out further into the yard to meet him halfway.

"What's he doing here? I thought you were cleaning

her house, not having a party."

"A party? Four people is not a party. And if you'd been here earlier, you would've seen me playing Cinderella. I've been sweeping, down on my hands and knees scrubbing the fucking floor, and now I'm getting wrinkly fingers from doing the dishes. I thought we were past this." What the hell is going on? He's still jealous of Dave?

"Past what? One minute you're pushing me away and the next..."

"Shut up. Do I have to spell it out for you?"

The creak of the back door freezes every muscle in my body. I'm terrified that I'm going to have to explain why Maxwell is in Juliet's backyard, but in the blink of my eyes he's gone.

"Are you talking to yourself?" Dave asks as he stands in the open doorway, allowing the light from inside the house to spill out into the backyard. His shadow blocks the light from blinding me.

"No...maybe...why do you care?" I say, spinning around to face him. Good one, Charlie, continue to act crazy, why don't you.

"I heard you talking about spelling something out?" he argues as he approaches me.

Damn it, Dave. "You caught me, I was talking to myself...there, are you happy now? Time to go back inside." I push him back toward the house.

All I want is to close the door and get this night over with, but Dave stops in the threshold. He stares down at me as if he wants to say something, but no words exit his mouth. A familiar song blares from the living room, forcing me to pay extra hard attention to anything he would say because it's incredibly hard to hear over the loud tune. To make the night worse, Dave spontaneously starts singing along, emphasizing the words. Everything in me is fighting the smile that grows wider without me wanting to.

His hand sticks out, offering to take mine. There's no way to escape this, so I take his hand, which he doesn't let go until we reach the 'dance floor'. I barely have time to look back into the darkened yard, trying to spot Maxwell. Silently, I pray he'll leave and wait for me to arrive home.

Nathan and Juliet dance quite provocatively in the middle of the cleared out living room. Once Juliet notices our arrival, she breaks away from Nathan and drags me over to join them. Grudgingly, I dance to several songs. Dave's grinding body is always nearby, taunting me, but for Juliet's sake I act as happy and nice as possible.

I clap my hands together to get everyone's attention. "Listen up, it's been fun, but I have to go." I give Juliet a hug and wave goodbye to Nathan and Dave before I rush out of her house to my car. I don't feel the slightest twinge of regret because I know Nathan will be keeping her company through the night.

"Charlie, wait up," Dave says, running after me.

So close, I say to myself…so close. My head hits the top of the open car door as I give up altogether. Before I know it, Dave is beside me. "Yes, Dave?" I grumble.

"I need to try something, I need to know." He gently moves a stray strand of hair out of my face; his hand lightly caresses my cheek.

"Need to know what exactly?" A knot forms in my stomach as I back away from his lingering hand. The feel of bile rises in my throat and no matter how far I try to back away I can't. My head and back push up against the car, trapping me in place.

Without answering me and taking me completely

off guard, he grabs ahold of my shoulders and plants a rough kiss on my lips. I feel his tongue lick at my lips that are pursed together, denying him. It seems like forever, but in all reality is just a few seconds before my body reacts to his uncalled for behavior. My palms shove him away, creating a small gap between us. I don't know what came over him to think he can get away with such a thing, but the slap of my hand against his cheek gets the point across that it's not okay.

"What the fuck, Dave?" I holler at him.

He rubs his sore cheek, taking a few seconds to answer my question. "I just thought…"

"Thought what? Obviously, my refusal of anything between us on that cheap shot of a date we had didn't sink into your head," I shout at him.

"I just thought that maybe you still love me, deep down, hiding in there somewhere…I had to try, I had to see if there was a sliver of you that would choose me over that Maxwell. I'll let you get home, because obviously I'm too late in winning you over." He just aimlessly walks away, disappearing in the house.

The whole way home, I debate how I'm going to tell Maxwell what happened unless he witnessed it firsthand. I'm expecting to arrive to my house with all the lights on and Maxwell waiting patiently inside, but it's the complete opposite. My shaking fingers squeeze the keys, causing indentations to form on the pads of my fingers as I make my way to the front door. Unlocking it as quietly as possible, I tiptoe inside.

The complete silence of the pitch black rooms makes my head spin from all the blood rushing to the top of my skull. "Maxwell?" I yell out into my empty house. No answer. I turn on the closest light and see everything in perfect condition and nothing seems to be out of place. I thought he would be here waiting for me, but obviously not.

I stomp my way to my room, angry at my own stupidity. I really screwed things up this time. Midway there, though, I hear something fall in the living room. I know I should be scared, but the idea of Maxwell trying to scare me clouds my judgment.

"Maxwell…this is not funny, so come out right now." I walk back into the living room with my hands balled into fists all ready to strike at him when he pops out from behind some corner. After some time, I learn that Maxwell isn't here and if he is he's playing a hard game.

Leisurely, I walk over to my purse that I left by the door to grab my phone. However, I notice my tall vase that I keep my umbrella in is knocked over. Inadvertently, my eyes scan the front door. I could have sworn I didn't lock it behind me from my mind racing with fear, but now the door is locked, as well as the deadbolt. If Maxwell is in here the joke he's playing is not okay. Refusing to play, I set out to leave. It's unreasonable for me to leave my own house, but a chill runs down my spine, making the atmosphere feel creepy.

I quickly unlock the door and step outside. The fresh air calms me to a point, but annoyance follows close behind. A debate about how I'm going to kill that man plays through my head. Out of the corner of my eye, I see a bright light that illuminates my front yard. My living room light has been turned on. I want to get in my car and drive away, but I left my keys inside like an idiot. Taking a deep breath, I enter the house once again. I was going to yell for Maxwell to knock it off, but a letter that is stuck underneath my purse catches my attention.

Death waits for you.

Same black envelope. Same crisp white paper from the previous note claiming I'm next. I swear it wasn't there when I walked over to my purse just a few moments ago. I turn quickly to dash out of the house, but the whisper of my name makes me freeze up. My mind screams for me to run and like every other time, fear stiffens my joints.

Slowly turning to face the interior of the house, I see the culprit. A tall, slender figure all dressed in black with a ski mask on covering all their features stands in the archway leading to the living room. The glint of my kitchen knife in their hand keeps my full attention. The sound of clicking against my tiled floor as they approach informs me that my mystery guest is a woman.

With my keys in my hand, I dash for the door. My heart races in my chest as I will my legs to run faster, but the sharp yank of my hair slams me to the ground before I can reach the doorknob. I regret not getting that pepper spray, although I wouldn't be able to reach it anyways, deeming it completely useless.

"No Maxwell, what a shame." She leans over me, grabbing ahold of my scarf. Her pulling on the fabric causes it to tighten around my neck as well as lift my head off the ground. She lets go abruptly, which makes the back of my head smack against the floor. Her taunts become more violent as her heeled foot strikes me in the side.

The air that refused to leave my lungs earlier comes rushing out. Rolling over onto my stomach in pain, I try to crawl away. I finally make it to the console table in the entryway to help me stand on my feet. Her laugh mocks me from behind. With a bowl that I put miscellaneous items in tightly in my grip, I wait. The sound of her very high heels gets louder as she comes closer. Giving her no warning, I swing around with the bowl in my hand.

Her anticipation of my move ruins the outcome. She grasps my wrist that holds the bowl in her free hand as I grip her wrist that holds the knife. I refuse to be beaten by a girl, by a human girl nonetheless. I kick her knee forcefully, resulting in her losing her grip for a second from her own pain, which gives me the leverage to twist the knife out of her hand. I don't come away undamaged, though. She fights me tooth and nail, resulting in the blade pointing toward me as I twist out of her grip. In slow motion I watch the knife slice my upper arm, which starts to bleed immediately.

Ignoring the pain and the trail of blood that eventually drips to the floor, I wave the weapon in her direction, taking swings at her body that still hovers within reach. I demand answers in a firm voice. "Who are you? Who's the man with the green eyes?" I know this woman is his little human helper. She knows his plan and I'm willing to do anything to find it out.

"Don't worry so much, Charlie. You'll find out sooner or later who I am, who he is. I'm not supposed to kill you…just play around with you. Your death will be brought on by another, he'll be waiting. See you soon." Just like that, she leaves. The front door hangs open for the cool night air to fill the house from her running away. The breeze feels good against my shaking body. Sweat clogs my pores while my heart tries to slow down.

Where the hell is Maxwell? As fast as my wobbly legs will go, I fetch a towel from the kitchen to soak up the blood from my wound. I look at the gash only once and I know I'm going to need stitches. I couldn't care less about going to the ER when I'm hell-bent on finding Maxwell. I gather my keys from the floor and haul my heavy bag over my good arm. If Maxwell isn't here, he might be at his place...and God help if he is.

* * *

Maxwell

I'm more than ready to barge in there and grab Charlie, demanding that she leaves, but I wait until she exits the house on her own. The presence of Dave makes the little blood I have in my body boil. Hovering in one of the shadows across the street, watching her finally head to her car, relief begins to flood through me. Except when I see Dave chasing after her, I become more than agitated. I listened to him seduce her with a song and now I'm forced to listen to him stumbling over his words.

Balling my hands into fists with anger, I draw that blood out. My vision gets blurry with rage as I see her with her mouth on his. Although, when her sweet mouth starts swearing along with the sound of a slap from her hand across his face there's no doubt that she's just as repulsed as I am by his behavior.

"Maxwell. Maxwell." A soft whisper of my name sounds from behind me.

Being afraid of nothing and no one, I investigate my surroundings. Making my way through a resident's yard, I find myself on a sidewalk around the corner from Juliet's house. A man standing in front of a black vehicle catches my attention. When he instantaneously turns around at my approach, I know he was the one to call my name.

"Hello, Maxwell."

"James. I've heard you were town. What brings you here?"

"I'm here to talk. Why don't we go for a ride? I can accompany you back home."

"I have to go to my bride's house. You've heard of her, Charlie. Considering you're dating her associate, I'm sure you've heard more than you would have liked. More importantly there's a vampire hell-bent on harming her and I can't bear to have her out of my sight. I even enlisted Morgan to help me keep an eye on her during the day."

"You're exactly right. From how much Morgan speaks of this Charlie, it feels as if I know her personally and have also been informed of the secret spy mission you have Morgan doing as well. But I'm afraid I can't let you go to Charlie's house, my friend. This vampire you speak of insists that I take you back to your room alone…now."

Shock and confusion find my expression as I stare at him. "You're working with him? What does any of this have to do with you, James? Or the better question is who is he and what does he want with Charlie?"

"I'm not working with him so to say. He's outside Morgan's apartment as we speak. If you don't come with me and if you interfere with his little plan that he has, then he'll kill Morgan. It's nothing against you or Charlie, but I can't let him hurt her. I'm sure you would do the same if the roles were switched." He opens the door, waving me inside. A flash of his fangs proves he'll attack if he needs to.

Without wanting to start a fight that will no doubt wake all the residents in the neighborhood, I reluctantly enter the car. I can't help but to clench my teeth together as we start to get farther away from Charlie.

"It's not that bad, Maxwell. Charlie will be fine, he assured me of that," he informs me, but the hatred that grows stronger from him saying Charlie's name makes it difficult to listen to him speak. "Morgan would never forgive me if she were to find out I helped in Charlie's death. She looks up to her and I'm grateful that if I decided to take Morgan as my bride that she'll always have Charlie as a friend."

"If he's at Morgan's apartment, then who's at Charlie's house?" I know the answer, but I have to hear it to make it real.

"His soon-to-be bride."

"Who?" I demand.

"I don't know her name. All I know is that someone from your past is going to kill Morgan if I don't keep you away from Charlie. I can't lose her, Maxwell, she's all I have. You at least have Grace if something were to happen to Charlie."

I have Grace...who cares if I have Grace or not. Charlie's my companion, my light in this dark world. Without her it won't matter if I have dozens of people around, because not one of them will stop the pain I will feel if anything happens to her. "From my past?"

"Yeah, no idea who. All I know is that out of all the years I've known you I have never seen him before. This revenge he has for you must go way back."

"You better hope nothing happens to Charlie, James, or I'll be the next one to threaten Morgan." I don't care that I care for Morgan on a small level because Charlie cares for her. She would be a small price in the great list of pain people would pay for Charlie's harm.

"Well, let us hope it doesn't come to that. After this I'm no longer in the mix. I made that clear and I'll make it clear to you as well. I won't help on either side of this fight and I won't tolerate Morgan being threatened either. We're in the same boat here, Maxwell, please understand that I had no choice in this." The pleading in his voice is all I need to know that this is killing him as much as it's killing me.

I refuse to talk to him on the remaining ride to the hotel. I keep telling myself that there had to be a way that he could have prevented this from happening, that I could have prevented this from happening. Thankfully, the ride doesn't last that long. The driver remains in the car as James escorts me to my room. He blocks the door with his phone in his hand.

"Waiting for a call?" I ask.

"Yeah, actually. When his bride leaves the house she's going to call him and then he'll call me. At that time, you're free to go. Just as I'll be free to go to Morgan."

Just about the walk into my suite, I debate whether I should start that fight I should've started outside of Juliet's house. I decide against it. I'm more than willing to put Morgan in danger to save Charlie, but Charlie won't forgive me if I let that happen as well as having no faith in her protecting herself.

The silence in the room makes my ears ring. My leg bounces on the ball of my foot with nervousness that only doubles in size with each second that passes. Putting my head in my hands between my legs, all I can do is wait. I tell myself over and over again that everything is going to be fine, but then I feel it. It's like going head first into a brick wall, as Charlie's fear and pain flood my senses.

At first it's anger then annoyance, but then slowly fear trickles in. That small amount of fear triples within seconds. My breathing hitches and my head throbs, impossible and unneeded actions, but the bond creates them. Some people say it's a warning to prepare yourself for the worst. No matter how awful I feel, I can still sense her fight.

She can only defend herself so much even if it is against a human. This person working with him most likely has been training for this very moment to keep the odds in her favor. And just like that, out of nowhere, searing pain makes me scream out...she's hurt. Then it stops. Her terror fades away only to leave anger and hatred.

James stands on his feet with a pitiful expression on his face. He hopes that he wasn't wrong about anyone hurting Charlie tonight. It seems to be his lucky night, because I can feel the sheer determination and that determination is to come and find me. It seems like eternity, but after a quick glance at the clock, only ten minutes pass before the much anticipated ringing of James' cell phone sounds from inside his cupped hands.

The relay of phone calls last longer than they should have. I begin to have second thoughts that Morgan might not be as safe as James was informed. As best as I can I try to eavesdrop on the conversation, but I can't hear a word the person on the phone says. All I have to go by is the nod and occasional yes from James to know he's pleased with his performance. I stand up straight away after he pockets his phone.

"It's time for you to leave, James. I could have told you a while ago it was safe for you to go, but seeing that my bride was being beaten, I was a little preoccupied. She's on her way, extremely pissed no doubt, but if you don't want to answer to her, which I wouldn't want to if I were in your situation, I would leave now."

A flash of my own fangs makes his hands go shaky. He fumbles with the doorknob before he disappears. He might have played tough guy earlier, but now with no one's life on the line, he knows I mean business. I punch the drywall, creating a large hole in the wall. How in the hell did I allow this to happen? Pacing from one room to the next is all I can do to release some of this bitterness that builds up inside me. The hard pounding coming from the outside of my door is the only thing that relieves my fury.

"Open the damn door, Maxwell." I hear her yell. Her manic fists continue to strike the door.

I open the door, blocking her from entering. "Charlie," I say with liberation.

"Where the hell were you?" she shouts at me. I can't find my words, so she continues in lecturing me. "Really…nothing, not one word to explain yourself with. What's your problem? Just because of this stupid jealously with Dave you let me get attacked." I can see the trouble she is having in finishing her sentence.

"I'm sorry." My eyes instantly go to a bloody rag tied around her arm. "I wanted to help you, believe me, it was killing me." I reach out my arm in efforts to access her wound, but she slaps my hand away.

"Killing you? I was the one getting sliced and diced. Why didn't you come? I thought you said you could sense when I'm in danger. If it was killing you, why didn't you come?" she accuses me on the verge of tears.

"Charlie, all you need to know is that more people's lives are in jeopardy besides your own. He's threatening people to help him do his dirty work. He had…"

"He had who?" I can see her hands ball into fists at my refusal of helpful information.

"James, he had James keep me away."

"James, who the hell is James?" Any sadness from before vanishes.

"You don't know? James is Morgan's boyfriend. Your assistant's life was in danger if James didn't hold up his part."

"Wait…Morgan's boyfriend that she told me she met in church is a vampire?" Confusion distorts her features.

"He most likely implanted that memory to make him seem more appealing to her standards."

"I thought you said you can't do stuff like that."

"We can't get rid of memories, but we can make memories. They still don't last forever unless the donor believes them on a higher level. Morgan obviously is attracted to James and clings to the knowledge that he's a churchgoer. Therefore, there's no need to continue the influence. It would have worked on you, but you're a little more stubborn than most." In all honestly, I have no idea if Morgan knows that James is a vampire or not. She could be hiding James's secret just as Charlie is hiding mine.

"I need to sit down," she mumbles, but before she can reach a chair her legs go out from underneath her. She's lost a large amount of blood and the seriousness of the wound is sending her body into shock.

I untie the towel from her arm to inspect the damage. There's no doubt in my mind that she needs stitches. "We need to get you to a hospital." I lift her up from the chair and carry her to her car. Placing her gently in the passenger seat and locking the seat belt into place, I rush over to the driver's side.

The scent of her blood is nothing I can't handle. However, all that changes when I shut the driver's door. The intoxicating smell attacks my senses. Unwillingly, my fingers grip the steering wheel as I talk myself out of the dark place I refuse to go down. Before when her blood was spilled I had control over my urges, but with the more I take from her the more I want.

Charlie's hand rests on my shoulder. "Maxwell? Maxwell, what's wrong?"

One final squeeze of the steering wheel brings me back to reality. Charlie needs a hospital and a hospital is where we're going to go. "It's nothing important," I reply. With my vampire speed I roll down the window and tear out of the parking spot.

In half of the time it should have taken to get there, I squeal into a spot in the emergency parking area. Making my way around the car to gather her in my arms without drawing attention to myself, we make our way inside. The nurse at the desk covers the disgust on her face from the blood that rolls down both of our arms.

"She needs stitches," I tell the nurse.

"I can walk, Maxwell," Charlie insists, but I have a hard time placing her back on her feet after watching her collapse once already.

Before I decide to put her on her feet, a different nurse who came from behind the closed doors calls her name. Not given a choice, I put her down, although I don't leave her side, and to my joy I'm not asked to wait behind. They bring her into a small room where a doctor greets us immediately.

"Hello…" He looks over some papers in search of her name. "Ms. Preston. I'm Dr. Ridgemount. Tell me about what happened."

"Charlie…call me Charlie. Someone broke into my house and attacked me," she replies with the calmest voice.

"Attacked you?" His suspicious eyes move to look at me. The snap of rubber gloves hitting his wrist echoes within the room.

"I don't know who it was. All I know is that it was a woman and she was waiting for me in my house. She had a mask on, so I really don't know any features."

The doctor removes her makeshift bandage to reveal a slow ooze of blood seeping out of the deep cut. "Well, stitches are needed. I'm going to gather the utensils needed and then we will get you fixed up." He removes his gloves and leaves the room.

There's no time for us to talk to each other before the doctor reenters the room with a tray full of surgical supplies. He puts on a new pair of gloves and positions Charlie so he can do his job. It seems like time is standing still as I watch him remove a needle from a sterile package and insert it into a small glass vial.

"I'm just going to numb the area first." Without waiting for her to reply, he starts to poke the needle inside the gash in several spots.

Charlie sucks in a breath each time the needle pierces her skin. Thankfully it only takes a few seconds and within no time he starts to thread the wound together. The strong-willed, overbearing Charlie unintentionally shows weakness as she refuses to look at the needle. I'm not entirely sure that the numbing solution is even working because every time he punctures her skin she winces with pain.

Mid-stitch the sliding door opens to reveal two uniformed men. "Ms. Preston, we're hoping you can spare a few moments before you leave to tell us what happened," one of the officers says.

It takes Charlie a few seconds to reply due to the pain she's experiencing. However, she nods her head through it with gritted teeth.

"You happen to be friends with the young lady who was attacked a few days ago, correct?"

"Yes, Juliet Anders."

"Does this relate to that in any way?"

"Most likely, except it was a man who attacked her and it was a woman who did this." Her eyes are closed from trying to push back the pain for her to talk without her voice quivering.

"Is there anyone you're aware of who would want to hurt you?"

Charlie bites her bottom lip as the last stitch is pulled through. "No. The answer to all your questions is no. I have no idea and I'm pretty sure you have no idea who attacked my friend, so if you don't mind, I would like to feel my pain without an audience."

"We understand. If there's anything else you would like to add to a statement when you're better, just come on down to the office. Have a good night." Just as fast as they came in, they leave.

"You're all fixed up, Charlie. You can take some pain relievers for any discomfort, but you should heal up without much of a scar. Have a good night, you two." With that said, the doctor waits by the open door for us to follow him out.

We mumble thank you to the nurse behind the desk before exiting the building. With the window still rolled down, we head back to my place. To my joy, Charlie doesn't protest.

Once we arrive back at the hotel, none of us wastes time heading to the bed. She quickly takes off her bloody clothes before covering up. Her voice stops me from leaving. "Maxwell, aren't you going to join me?"

"I was going to take some time to think about—"

Her doe eyes stare at me. "Understood. I just wanted to rest my cut on you like last time, but it's fine."

God, I can't resist her. "It can wait." Slowly, I take off my stained clothes as well before sliding under the blanket. I gently grab her arm and place it over my chest.

"You know...even though you let me get beat up, I forgive you." She pats my chest, but winces from the pain.

"I'll take it." I almost lost her today. I felt like I did lose her and I'll take whatever she says to me when it comes down to it.

She shuffles, trying to find a comfortable spot. Her arm resting on me doesn't move an inch. Right after her eyes shut, in the quietest voice she whispers, "Goodnight, Maxwell. I love you."

"I love you too, Charlie," I whisper back.

Chapter Twenty-Six

Charlie

"I have to go to work. There's no stopping me. I have a party on Saturday and Morgan is leaving on some trip with a vampire, so unless I ask Dave to help me out, I'm stuck going to work." I know all about the threats that wait for me, but I have a business to run...clients to please.

"I can't stop you even though I should be able to. Try not to meet with new clients and stay inside your locked office until I arrive," Maxwell instructs me.

"Can I go now? Morgan is leaving early today for her little outing and I have lots of work to do."

"You have a party this weekend?"

"Yeah, that's what I said. A beach themed party, to be exact, and it happens to be in broad daylight. They even insisted that I show up in swimwear."

"Swimwear? Like a bikini?"

"Maybe. I'll talk to you later about that." I take a few steps away from him, making my way to the door. My hand lingers on the knob as his voice sounds from right behind me.

"Are you forgetting something?" he asks.

My arm grazes his chest as I turn around to face him. A smug smile plays across his mouth. Stretching as high as the tips of my toes allow me, I try to give him a kiss goodbye. It's only when he bends down, closing the gap between us that our lips finally meet. It's nothing more than a small peck because I'm running extremely late.

Not paying much attention, I carelessly round the

corner. Face first I smack into an oncoming body. "I'm so sorry." I immediately start to apologize.

"The fault is partially mine," the woman replies.

"It's quite all right." I flip the hair out of my eyes.

"Ms. Preston? Charlie, right?"

"Yes."

"You don't remember me, do you? Daisy from the Liberty Hotel. You had a party there about a month ago."

After making eye contact with her for the first time, I do recall who she is. The hovering blonde who showed Morgan and I the ballroom for Justice's birthday party. "Oh, yes. Yes, I remember. Nice to see you again, Daisy."

"What brings you to this lovely hotel?" she asks, her interest piqued.

"Meeting with a client before heading into the office. I'm running late. I really should get going."

"I would love to sit down and chat sometime. Your job must be to die for."

I dig out a business card from my purse. "You know where to find me." With that offer laid out on the table and hopes of her never coming around, I head to my car.

I can't make the car ride any shorter due to traffic and when I see Morgan's car in the parking lot nothing but shame fills me. Now to explain myself. My face didn't take a beating in the fight last night, but this warm weather forces me to wear short sleeves. The white bandage that wraps around my upper arm sticks out like a sore thumb.

"Good morning," Morgan sings as I enter the building. Her eyes instantly go to the stark white bandage. "Oh my goodness, what happened to you?" The tips of her fingers graze the thick gauze wrappings.

"Nothing important." I don't want to concern her

and I'm not sure how I would explain the situation either, so I talk about something else. "I'm sorry I'm late. I ran into the most unexpected person. She even is interested in sitting down and talking sometime, which I hope doesn't happen. I mean, I've only seen the woman once and she seems like a snob...kind of."

"Who?"

"Daisy. She's the woman from—"

Morgan speaks over me, "I know where she's from and it wouldn't be the second time I saw her if I were to run into her."

"What's that supposed to mean?"

"I didn't tell you this for a reason, but I've met her before seeing her at the Liberty Hotel."

The tension that fills the room is thick. Her awkward posture and lack of eye contact make what she's about to say even worse. What is she hiding? "Morgan, would you care to explain where else you saw her besides the Liberty Hotel?"

"Here."

"Excuse me, what now? Here?" My chest tightens at the thought of that woman in my business.

"Do you remember when James insisted that we come here and how he brought friends with him?"

How could I forget. "Yes."

"She was one of them. It was her and a man. And he was so dreamy, don't tell James. But he had the most amazing green eyes."

Green eyes. My brain starts connecting crazy dots together. Morgan's boyfriend is a vampire. This green-eyed stranger is a vampire who was seen with Daisy...who just so happened to run into me in the very hotel Maxwell stays at. Coincidence or not. "You wouldn't happen to remember his name?"

"No. Just how he looks. Why do you ask?"

I'm not sure if she can sense the turmoil that's boiling beneath the surface as my brain contemplates my theory. "No reason."

Her concerning words don't offer comfort as they should. "You know you can talk to me about anything. I'd like to think I'm your friend besides just a coworker."

"You are, Morgan. I just have a lot on my mind right now," I say in a half daze before making my way to my office.

As fast as I can, I immerse myself in work without looking at the clock or my phone. Hours go by in pure silence; the only sound in the room is the clicking of my pen. In all honesty, I haven't got a fraction of the amount of work completed than I usually get done. Three light taps knock against my door, forcing me to focus.

"Charlie, can I come in?" Morgan asks.

"Of course," I reply.

She enters the office and immediately sits in one of the chairs in front of my desk. "I'm going to be heading out. You sure you're fine? I know it's none of my business, but Maxwell mentioned something about you receiving hate mail from a prior client. Did they do this to you...did they attack you last night?"

Maxwell told her? I could turn the tables on this conversation and interrogate her, but once again I decide to go the easy way and leave the subject alone. Maxwell knows James, so why wouldn't he ask little things of Morgan. I would ask things of Grace all the time if she were actually here. "It's possible. I can handle it, Morgan, there's no need to worry. All you need to worry about is having fun on your trip."

The clock on my desk stares back at me. Just three more hours until sunset. I can make it three hours...I hope. I walk with her to the front door.

"I'll be back on Monday." She smiles.

Unexpectedly, she gives me a hug. She squeezes me so tightly that I find it hard to breathe. Gritting my teeth through the pain from her arm rubbing against my cut, I pat her on the back as a signal for her to let go.

"Sorry…sorry." She apologizes as her hands brush off the tops of my shoulders.

"Have fun and be prepared to tell me all about it when you get back," I say as happily as I can manage.

"Of course," she agrees before she walks out into the semi empty lot. Double-checking the door before I feel comfortable, I go back to my office. I turn off the front lights, leaving the office building looking closed from the outside. Instead of working on what I'm supposed to be, my mind wanders to Morgan's trip. I wonder if she knows about James being a vampire. Part of me believes she wouldn't care either way.

I shake myself from the idea that Morgan knows all about vampires. I begin to feel sorry for Maxwell. I've been nothing but awful to him. However, he hasn't been the most trusting either. Nonetheless, the past is in the past and there's nothing either of us can do to change that. With my elbows propped up on my desk, I rub at my face.

I don't know how much time passes before my doorknob jiggles. My eyes bolt to the clock. It reads a little past eight. The sun is set so it's quite possible that it's Maxwell, but it also could be an unwanted visitor. The tightening of my chest makes it extremely hard to breathe, but I force each breath harshly, which makes me slightly lightheaded. "Maxwell?" I say in barely a whisper.

The creak of the door fills the room and makes my ears ring. My fingers tightly grip a paperweight on my desk.

"Charlie," Maxwell says as he peeks his head into the room. "Charlie." His hand goes on top of mine, gently prying my fingers off the weight.

I didn't even see him enter the room, but there he is, inches away from my face. "How did you get in here?"

He stands up straight, one hand still on top of mine and the other holds out a key. "You really need to get rid of your spare keys," he replies.

I go to grab it out of his hand, but he pockets it before I can reach it.

"Were you going to hit me with this paperweight?" he asks.

"Yes. It isn't the best of time to just unlock my door and try to barge into my office when there are..." I huff in defeat. "Speaking of lurking strangers, I might have a clue who our 'friend' is."

"And that would be what?"

"I ran into Daisy while I was on my way to work and Morgan confessed that she's seen her before."

"Daisy?"

"She works at the Liberty Hotel. You know, the place of Justice's birthday party that you crashed."

"I've seen her before too. Where did Morgan say she saw her?"

"Where have you seen her? Liberty Hotel?" Please say Liberty Hotel.

"No, I didn't see her that night, but I saw her in the hall outside my door."

"She was outside your door?"

"Not entirely. She was walking down the hall when I was in pursuit of catching the prankster who was buzzing my door. She claimed there were children running about the halls."

"It was her. Morgan saw her that night James

insisted on going to my office. He brought two people with him, Daisy and a man. A man who, Morgan can testify has green eyes."

"You're thinking too much into this, Charlie."

"James is a vampire and the man is a vampire—"

"Charlie, calm down. It's probably just a coincidence. Nothing more. It wouldn't be the first time two vampires were seen together." His hands run down the length of my good arm.

"If you think that's what it is, then that's what it is." Disappointment washes over me. "Can we go now…please?" Sitting here longer than necessary makes my insides turn.

Gently he wraps his arm around my shoulders, walking by my side through the office building out into the parking lot. Maxwell quickly snatches my keys from my hand once I dig them out of my purse. Of course, he goes to sit in the driver's seat. Why is it that he always has to drive? Obeying the unspoken command, I reluctantly sit in the passenger's seat.

"Where do you wish to go?" he asks as his hands grip the steering wheel.

"What? It's a Thursday night. Can't we just go to your place?"

"My place." Maxwell's eyebrows rise in acceptance. He quickly winks at me before flashing me a smile.

"Not what I meant. It's just…ever since the incident," I gently stroke my bandaged arm, "I'm a little weary of home at the moment."

"Of course," he casually replies.

* * *

Maxwell

Sadly, Thursday evening was uneventful. Friday wasn't much better as I sat and thought about what Charlie said yesterday about Morgan meeting the green-eyed stranger and how James could possibly know who he is. I recall the conversation he had with me the night Charlie got attacked. He claimed to not know his name, so why would he invite him along with a snack to Charlie's workplace? Things just don't add up, and with James as well as Morgan in Austria, I won't be able to find anything out for a while.

Today seems like it's headed down the same path.

"Well…are you going to say something instead of just staring at me like that?" Charlie demands.

I could say a lot of things, but I'm having trouble being able to formulate words. I can't help but to gawk at her barely clothed body. She poses in front of me in a black bikini. However, I've never seen anything quite like it before. Four gold eyelets run along her bust and hips, with chain connecting the actual swimsuit to a waistband and choker. Being more modest than her attire, she wears a sheer wrap dress on top.

"You say this is a beach party?"

"Yes, Maxwell, they distinctively told me to wear beach apparel." Besides her posture her voice alerts me of her annoyance.

"And you're going to be there on your own?"

"No. I do have venders who need to come and set up as well. If you're worried, you should be. I know I am, but I have work to do. So let me pretend to be brave for just one day."

Before she leaves me behind, her highly glossed lips press against my slightly chapped ones. Chills erupt across my body as her hand that lingers over my heart scratches down my chest as she steps away from me. All I can do is watch her walk away. Boredom immediately takes over my day within seconds after she leaves. I debate whether to watch pointless TV or go and lie down to stare at the ceiling. I go for option number two.

I place my stiff body in the middle of bed. No matter how much I want to dismiss the truth or ignore the signs, my tired body begs to be heard. It has been years since I felt like this. It has been years since I even had the option to feel like this again. Closing my eyes, I force breaths to come slow yet steady to release some of the tension that's bound to overwhelm me sooner or later.

The sound of my phone ringing jolts me awake. I didn't even realize I fell asleep, but a quick glance at the clock tells me it wasn't that long. Rushing to pick the phone up, I answer it without looking at the number displayed across the screen. "Hello."

"Maxwell."

"Grace, what a pleasant surprise."

"I have been doing some research and I just wanted to tell you I haven't found anything. No one is aware of a vampire out to get Charlie or yourself."

"Looks like your visit is paying off," I say, annoyed. "What are you doing up there anyways?" My curiosity is getting the best of me.

"That's a long story," she hesitantly says.

"I have all day. Charlie's conducting business at the moment." I want to add in a bikini, but I refrain from releasing that information.

The sound of her huffing on the other end causes me to smile. I know from past experiences that this is going to be good. "I was actually looking forward to talking to her. How is she?"

"Grace." My voice is stern as I wish to get the answers I asked for.

"I happen to be a witness." She finally reveals.

"A witness for what?" My patience always seems to be tested.

"I'm a witness in a small trial accusing Emma of contempt."

Emma is Benjamin's second bride. She's the reason Grace turned her back on Benjamin. "Contempt of what exactly?"

"She tried to kill Benjamin. Turns out she doesn't allow any sexual activities with the donors who happen to be their maids. She walked in on a task that was never listed on their agendas."

"Are you testifying for her or against her?" Grace isn't very fond of Emma and the thought that she's helping her is astonishing.

"I'm on her side unfortunately. Only because if the decision is in her favor, Benjamin could get a punishment for his lack of respect toward his bride's wishes. Trust me, if I could refuse, I would."

"Grace!" I hear someone yell her name in the background.

"Listen, I got to go. I should be back home within a week or so." That's all she says before the line goes dead.

I fall onto the bed with the phone still held tightly in my hand. Only how many more hours before Charlie's back? I shut my eyes to calm the panic building in the pit of my stomach. We are no closer to finding out who is after her than we were weeks ago.

"Maxwell? Maxwell!"

A firm hand slaps across my cheek and shocks me awake. A groan escapes my dry mouth, the throbbing ache making my jaw feel very uncomfortable. With my eyes not even open yet, my ears do the seeing for me. The sound of the air whooshing off to my left side tells me that another slap is coming. I catch her arm at the wrist right before it makes impact with my cheek. Her fingertips graze the side of my face.

"Charlie."

"About damn time. You were asleep...at least I think you were asleep. Do vampires sleep? Anyways, I tried to wake you up, but you weren't responding, so I had to result to forceful actions." The sound of worry in her voice makes my chest tighten.

"I'm awake now."

"You don't look too good. I thought vampires don't get sick."

"I'm fine, it will pass."

"What will pass?"

"Nothing for you to worry about. I have been through this before and I can handle it." I don't want to worry her, but I also don't want her to feel.

"Maxwell, spill it. Now." Her stern voice fills the room.

"It's similar to what addicts suffer after they quit an abused substance."

"Withdrawal? You're having withdrawal like a drug addict?"

"Yes, but except my drug is blood."

"What the hell is that supposed to mean? Didn't you have to go like one hundred years without blood? Why are you going through it now? You just had some a few weeks ago."

"I told you I went through this before. I was well fed up until my punishment and it only took a couple of days for the signs of hunger to settle upon me. You can't die from lack of nutrition, but you will feel as if you want to. I went through all those years in agonizing pain until my body adjusted to my circumstances. It's only that once I drank from you my body started to crave again. The first time my body saved it, thinking it would

347

never receive a drop again, but…"

"But what?" Her words are unsteady and I'm not sure what exactly she's scared of.

"But the more I have the more my body responds. I can get through this without offerings." I race from one side of the room to the next, stopping to pick up several heavy pieces of furniture to show my strength that's stronger than any human. "See, I'm fine."

"Don't you show off to me, you need to drink. Now is not the time for your ego to stay intact. Not when my life is on the line."

"I'm glad you think so highly of me. I can take care of you just fine."

"In all honesty, Maxwell, it's what you tracked me down for. Plus, our lives depend on your strength. He's going to be tapping his walking bottle of goodness every day…hell, maybe even more than once a day. I don't want to die and if I have to get bit again to make it through this, then so be it." She moves her hair on the side I previously bit her on. "Same side or would you like a clean slate?" she asks, flashing me the opposite side her of her neck that's untouched…well, healed.

"I can't ask this of you. It's just being greedy." It takes everything I have to peel my eyes away from her slightly tan skin.

"Maxwell, I'm not going to say it again. Stop pretending to be a saint." She pushes me to a sitting position on the edge of the bed.

I don't have time to think before she grabs the back of my head, pushing my mouth against her tender skin. My unnecessary breaths begin to get deeper and heavier in my chest. "I can't bite you where it's so visible again. It's eighty degrees outside and you're stuck wearing a scarf."

"Then where, Maxwell?" I can hear a faint quiver in

her voice.

"There's one other very common place, but you're not going to like it," I say slowly, as if trying to tame the storm that's bound to come my way.

"Not any more than I already don't like this conversation. Where?"

In a blink of condescending eyes, I grasp her around the waist and lay her down on the bed. My hand slides up her bare leg, stopping on her inner thigh, rubbing the spot with my thumb. "Right here, but it'll hurt if I just take a bite. Don't you remember, you have to be—" I whisper in her ear until she pushes me away.

"Shut up." In a fluid movement she grabs ahold of my shirt and forces my mouth on hers.

I kiss her eagerly on her still glossed lips. A smack fills the silent room as we break apart. Hovering over her body, I untie the thin string that keeps her sheer dress together. My fingers tightly grab ahold of her hips, sliding her down to the very edge. Dropping to my knees, I spread her legs farther apart, allowing me access to her inner leg. The pounding of her heartbeat is all I hear. In efforts to calm her more, I reach my hand up, placing it on her stomach.

Unable to resist, I lick the sensitive skin, causing her to shudder in anticipation of my bite. Her hands grip mine and silently I count to three before I pierce through the thin layers of skin. She instantly tries to sit up as she sucks in a deep breath, but for fear of hurting her more I push her back down, trapping her beneath my hand.

"Shit, that hurts. Wasn't ready. Wasn't ready," she yells.

I can't see her face, but from what I already know about her I assume her face is scrunched up as she bites her lower lip.

"Why didn't it hurt like this before?" she screeches.

Her fingernails that dig into my hands disappear only to grab a fistful of my hair.

Biting her without an intimate connection is the reason it hurts so bad. It also brings me back to my murderous past where I just bit people for the hell of it without a care in the world. Charlie's yelps of pain force screams of my past to ring through my eardrums. I don't have the chance to relish the warm liquid that runs down my throat when regret eats at my insides.

Without thinking, my hand glides down her stomach until my fingers rest upon her most intimate spot. I thought she would slap my hand away since I was asking so much of her already, but when her own hands knead against mine, pressing my own fingers harder against her, I know she wants it just as much as I do. Sliding my fingers inside her bikini bottoms, I begin a gentle massage. Her once yelps of pain quickly turn to groans of pleasure.

Feeling satisfied with how much blood I ingested, I release my mouth from her leg. Slowly creeping up the length of her body, I speak slowly. "Charlie, I got enough." It takes every ounce of self-control I have to turn this situation in the opposite direction, in a direction I didn't want to turn away from, but we have things to discuss.

"Good," she agrees, even though her hands are still holding me tightly against her. "Maybe not." Aggressively, she pushes my mouth onto hers.

I can't believe what I'm going to do. "Charlie." My efforts of not taking advantage of her come to a halt as my words stop her needy fingers.

Her hands yank at the hem of my T-shirt before moving to the buckle of my belt. There's no way I can refuse her. In a frantic mess of limbs we each strip away the articles of clothing that separate us. I encircle her waist in one of my arms and carry her up to the top of the bed. My body moves as my mind remains numb with excitement. Her knees feel hot under my palms as I move her legs apart to position myself perfectly center. Red streaks trail down the curve of her thigh.

One deep breath from her is all the hesitation I can take before I slide into her. A sharp intake of breath hisses through Charlie's teeth and the pressure from her fingernails gradually lets up. Trying to tame the exhilaration that rushes through my veins, I grope her mouth with my tongue, occasionally sucking on her bottom lip. I can sense her chest begin to tighten along with her pounding heart. I can only assume that's from the lack of oxygen getting to her lungs. Her heavy pants only make the need to go deeper get greater.

Burying my face in the curve of her neck, I let her try to catch her breath, only for so long, though. The increasing squeeze of her legs that are wrapped around me is my cue that our extracurricular activity is reaching its end. Each thrust gets harder and comes faster. A groan of relief escapes my mouth as I can't hold back any longer. Seconds later, she follows, going completely limp beneath me from exhaustion.

She pulls a corner of the blanket we're lying on to cover herself. "I'm just going to rest."

"I'm just going to go sit in the living room and make a call to Grace."

"Don't take too long."

"I won't." I quietly leave the room as her eyes close.

I wasn't going to call Grace, seeing as I already talked to her. There isn't much she can do for me than she already has. The sound of a group of people talking in the hall breaks the silence that lingers in the suite. Except one body strays behind. Walking up to the door,

I listen to the faint breathing on the other side. An envelope shoved under the door throws me off guard. By time I can take my eyes off the letter the sender is already gone.

Swinging the door open anyways, I catch a glimpse of blonde hair round the corner. Set to go after them, but one thing stops me—Charlie's restless groaning. Mumbles of my name sound from inside the room.

"I'm coming, Charlie," I say before letting the door close.

Chapter Twenty-Seven

Charlie

There used to be a time when the sun's warm rays felt nice against my skin. The days when nightfall brought out death and sunshine held safety…not anymore. The note that Maxwell received as I was sleeping Saturday night still repeats itself in my head.

Tick tock, death awaits.

I'm surprised I make it to work on time today as he lectured me about watching my back all morning. I'll admit it's quite relieving to inhale fresh air since Maxwell refused to let me leave yesterday, best Sunday ever. He kept pacing the length of the suite as he went through plan after plan.

If Morgan wasn't coming back today I'm pretty sure he wouldn't have allowed me to leave again. Most of his plans consisted of me staying locked in his little room, waiting it out. He knows better than I do, it's just a matter of time before they make their move. Before I left, he insisted I carry a weapon. I didn't want to carry a gun and I realize that pepper spray is pointless when it's so easily out of reach. The weight of my handbag makes the image of the old knife Maxwell gave me overpower all other thoughts. The antique wooden handle with a sharpened silver blade is amongst other things shoved in the depths of my purse.

My heart skips several beats when I see Morgan waiting in the parking lot, leaning against her car. A pair of large black sunglasses shade her eyes, but by her stance I know she's annoyed about something. Parking next to her, I get out and immediately strike up a conversation. "Something wrong?"

"Just hot, is all. I tried to get inside, but the spare key is gone."

Now that she mentions it, I can see beads of sweat on her forehead. "Yeah, um, I had to get rid of the key, sorry. I just thought I would be here before you." We start walking to the front of the brick building as we talk.

"All is good. I got to work on my tan a little bit. You never know when that day comes when you wish you were tanner," Morgan adds as I wave her inside the building.

All I can do is nod in acceptance to her comment. A tan is the last thing on my mind right now. "If you need anything, just come on in," I tell her as I hurriedly walk away to the comfort of my office.

She stays away most of the day thankfully, but once it nears our time to leave, she comes in and sits down. I stare at her, eagerly waiting to hear what's going to come out of her mouth. But she just stares at me wide-eyed, waiting for me to address her first. "Yes, Morgan?"

"You didn't ask how my trip went. I know you have a lot on your plate right now, but I just thought you would want to know." She's nervous about something or still excited about what happened on this so-called trip with her vampire boyfriend.

Before, when she was gone, I grew jealous of her acceptance of James with or without knowing he's a vampire. However, now looking at her jittery fingers and bobbing head, I can tell that Morgan and myself are two different people and we each have our own dreams on how life should be. "I would love to hear where you two went this past weekend," I reply.

"We went to Austria. I might have been complaining about the heat earlier, but hell, it's cold up there," she chimes back. Her words continue to flow out and she remains ignorant to my lack of attention toward anything she's saying until a loud snap fills the room, causing her to jump.

The pencil I'm twirling in between my fingers as she speaks breaks in half under pressure at the word Austria. Austria...she went to Austria with James...James the vampire. Instantly, I search for her hands, needing to see if she has committed herself to him in more ways than one. Luckily, her hands rest on the desktop, inches away from mine in efforts to calm me down for some reason. They're completely smooth just like her neck. She makes no attempt to cover her neck or shoulders in this heat like I have been forced to do lately, but then I remember the other place a bite mark could be. She wore some shorts a while ago, but today she's wearing capris that end past her knees. In all honesty, I have no way of knowing.

"Austria you say?" I reply within a few seconds, but I know she sees the concern on my face at the mention of that place.

"Yeah, James has some relatives up there. It's quite beautiful, but too cold for my liking. Have you been there before?"

"No." I shake my head along with verbally replying, but the shake is more to snap myself out of this twilight zone moment I seem to be stuck in. I begin to wonder if she saw Grace, but then again I'm not sure if she even knows who Grace is.

"Well, I can see you're preoccupied with stuff, so I'll leave you to it." With that said, she stands up and turns to exit my office. However, to my dismay, she makes one last stop before she fully walks away. Leaning against the doorframe drumming her thumbs, she refuses to look me in the eyes. "Did you ever find out who's being so cruel to you?"

"Not officially, but I think it's the people James brought with him that night he wanted to come here."

"Holy crap," she says as she figures it out.

"Precisely. I should get back to work." My head drops toward the desktop as I pretend to read the paper laid out before me. However, all the letters are blurry, making me unable to read them.

"Everything will be okay. I'm sure of it."

"Here." I dig into my purse and pull out my key to the office. "I want you to have this considering you seem to be here earlier than me. You shouldn't have to sit out in this heat because I can't make it here on time."

She takes it with a large smile on her face. "Thanks. I'll let you get back to your stuff."

The sound of her retreating footsteps leaves me with my thoughts. I can't seem to get Morgan and James's relationship out of my head. It's further than I expected, but then again it really is none of my business. If she doesn't want to tell me, fine…I'm kind of used to not being told important information. I try to keep my mind on work until the sun starts to set. It's only when Maxwell knocks on my open door that I realize Morgan must be gone already.

"You look like you just found out someone died," he jokes.

"Someone is about to die and it isn't me, it's Morgan. Do you know James took her to Austria…to Austria, Maxwell."

"Charlie, calm down."

"You're right…you're right, I'm just overreacting. There's nothing I can do to change the outcome. Hell, she really doesn't have a choice in the matter."

"Charlie, you know that isn't true. She has a choice just like you have a choice."

Laughter bursts out of my mouth at his words. "A choice, you say I have a choice? You think that choosing to die a week from now or in a couple months is a choice. Let's face the facts; I haven't had a choice since you showed up on my doorstep."

"Is it so bad? Am I that terrible?"

"That's not what I meant." I instantly regret saying the words. "All I'm saying is this isn't the life I had planned out and it's extremely hard to turn my back on what I worked for to live something completely opposite."

"I know that, Charlie. I've heard it multiple times, but I thought we were past this."

Where was this coming from? Deep down I know exactly where it's coming from, though. Seeing Morgan all happy brings out the worst in me. "I guess I'm taking on the stress and fear for both myself and Morgan seeing she's completely oblivious to the impending death that's lurking."

"Morgan is a big girl and she can take care of herself. Everyone is different, Charlie. Some people expect very little out of life or welcome everything that happens with open arms and some…well, don't. I wouldn't want you any other way, even though it would be easier for both of us, but your stubbornness is what makes you so much more attractive." His sly smile makes my heart skip and my breathing hitch, but it doesn't get rid of the dread that hides in my mind.

"Very funny."

"Come on, let's go," he says as he extends his arm. I place myself underneath it so it lies perfectly across my shoulders when he finally lowers it.

We make our way back to his little hotel room without another word said on the topic. In fact, the rest of the night goes in the same direction. I go to sleep after I can't take looking at him sitting at the kitchen table any longer. His head rests upon his hand while he stares at several pieces of paper, not bothering to blink.

Papers I have looked at several times. The letters we received are lost in the mix, multiple pages that consist of plans of action all resulting with various endings, and The Travers Bloodline book. Currently he's reading it for the fifth time in search of some clue he was oblivious to in his life at some point. Who knows and who cares. He knows better than I do that we can't stop this from happening no matter how much preparation we have.

Morning arrives faster than I would like, but it allows me to get away from the despondent Maxwell. "I'm going to work," I holler into the living room toward a frozen Maxwell. He came to bed very late last night and left very early in the morning. When he doesn't respond to me, I just decide to leave. With the door open, I turn back and whisper to his non-attentive ears, "I love you."

The whoosh of my hair stops me before I cross the threshold. "I'm sincerely sorry for ignoring you; I just have a lot on my mind right now. I love you too and be careful. Please call me when you get inside your office." He gives me a gentle kiss before he takes the weight of the door off my hand, allowing me to leave. He waves at my retreating body. I glance back a few times, waving in return as I make my way to the nearest staircase.

"Late again," I mumble to myself as I pull into the semi full parking lot. As usual I park next to Morgan's car. Grabbing my heavy purse, I make my way inside to start my day. My hand blocks the harsh sun's rays that blind me.

Barely getting a few steps away from my car, I bump into a slender frame. Being forced to look at the concrete from the sun, all I can see is skinny legs and black high heeled shoes. "I'm so sorry. It's just so bright out here and I forgot my sunglasses at home." I apologize to the stranger.

"Charlie, it's me, Daisy. I thought I would stop by for that talk."

Of course, my day is starting off just great. "How nice to see you again, Daisy."

"Looks like you're still healing." Her hand grabs my injured arm and gently squeezes it. "I did quite a number on that one, didn't I?"

Wait? What? Did she admit that she cut me, that she attacked me in my house? My heart viciously pounds against my rib cage.

"How about we go for a ride? I have the perfect place in mind."

"I think you should go."

Unwillingly, she forces me up against my car. "Oh, playing brave, are we? He's waiting for you, so I'm not going anywhere unless you're with me unfortunately. Now get in the car and be a good little girl." She fidgets with the hem of her shirt and that's when I see it, the butt of a knife that's shoved in the waistband of her too tight jeans. "Now! In the car. Don't make me use it, Charlie. The love of my life will be very disappointed in me if I do, seeing he wants to be the only one to spill your blood."

She opens the back car door, but the door doesn't open, causing her fingers to slip off, followed by the handle snapping. "Keys," she demands.

I go to dig in my purse, seeing this as a perfect moment to draw my own weapon, but as if she can see right through me, she rips my purse from my hands. It doesn't take her long to find my keys along with the knife.

"Tricky tricky," she says in a nasty tone as she opens the door and shoves me inside.

Once in the confines of the car that shields her actions from speculating eyes that could be watching, she pulls out several zip ties and binds my wrists together. "Don't think about trying anything." In a rush, she slips the knife out of her waistband and throws it on the passenger seat along with my purse. Within seconds, she squeals out of the parking space, driving away.

Only a few minutes go by before she strikes up a conversation. "You know, he's very mad. Maxwell took something of his and he wants payback."

I refuse to say anything in response to a single thing she says. If she wants me to cry and start begging for my life or the complete opposite and show aggression, she's greatly mistaken.

"Not in talkative mood, Charlie? Fine, be that way. We have a bit of a drive, so relax and sit tight." Almost immediately after she says it she turns the radio up. The bass rattles my chest and my ears ring from the loudness, but I close my eyes, breathing deeply, silently wishing for Maxwell to find me…as if he could possibly help. The sun shines brighter as the minutes tick by. I have a feeling that once the real trouble goes down the sun will be at its highest.

A sharp sting radiates on my cheek, followed by a pinch. "Wake up, sleeping beauty," Daisy demands.

Impatiently, she grabs a fistful of my hair, yanking me out of the car when it takes me longer than she approves of to exit the vehicle on my own. Barely standing upright, she shoves me forward. Dust from the loose gravel that covers the ground fills the air due to my skidding feet. Once again trying to block out the sun's rays, I try to get some sort of glance at the building she's leading me into. Aside from being out in the middle of nowhere, all I gather is that it's some abandoned warehouse of sorts. Crows line a metal fence encompassing the large building, giving the impression of death awaiting.

I think about running, because it's just her that I have to overpower. I already did it once…well, kind of and my ego tries to tell me I can do it again. However, when my feet veer off from the straight line I'm walking, a razor-sharp point jabs in between my shoulder blades.

"Don't prolong this," Daisy says, pressing the point of a blade harder against my skin.

I can feel a small spot begin to warm from her drawing blood.

"Ooops." The phony sympathy in her voice just draws anger out of me.

I know I should be scared, but I'm more irritated by the chain of events. I regret not listening to Maxwell and now I'm here. Rubble and garbage line the warehouse floors, along with graffiti that covers the crumbling concrete walls. The lower we go the harder it gets to see. Flickering lights are placed along the walls at intervals, creating shadows that play with my vision, causing me to stumble over my feet.

If I could breathe a sigh of relief I would, but once we enter a concrete room that resembles a cell my breathing is anything but relieving. A man with short brown hair standing by a rickety old table waits for us. Even though I can only see his back, I know exactly who it is.

"Baby, I got her for you." The seductiveness in Daisy's voice makes me gag.

Instantly, Mr. Green Eyes turns around with what is

supposed to be perceived as a pleasant smile, but I see through his façade...I see the monster lurking within gradually coming to the surface to play. "Daisy, love, thank you. Now, you know what to do." He gives her a sloppy kiss, taking the knife out of her hands, the same one she stole out of my purse.

"I'll go fetch him. Be back at sundown." She pouts her lips, trying to look sexy, but once again I see things differently. As she turns around, her fancy nailed hand grabs ahold of my face. My chin is clenched in her palm and the squeezing of my cheeks force my lips to pucker open. Giving my head an abrupt shake, she addresses me. "Don't have too much fun with my man." Then out of nowhere, she heaves me away as if I'm poisonous.

The familiar man who refuses to greet me promptly grabs my zip tied hands. My feet are dragged forward by his harshness. A wall in front of me is the only thing I see. It's completely bare except for a shiny latch that rests a little less than halfway down from the ceiling. Fiercely, I yank my hands out of his grasp and make an effort to bolt out of the room. Fear overrides common sense and when he stands in front of me, blocking the door, I know all I have done is make things worse.

Air rushes out of my lungs as his hand wraps around my throat. The heels of my feet drag along the floor, unable to gain my footing. A flash of black stains my vision from the impact of the wall, which he carelessly slams me into. In my moment of weakness he hauls my arms above my head, securing them in the latch.

"I've been waiting a really long time for this, Charlie," he says as he paces in front of me. "I was going to let you sit and think about the situation you find yourself in, but I'm just too eager to see you bleed." He twirls the knife he got from Daisy in his well-trained hand. He takes slow, cautious steps toward me in efforts to draw the fear out. He doesn't stop until he's a few inches away from my face. "Such a pretty face," he breathily says, bringing the tip of the knife to my cheek.

A scratch is left behind as he drags the blade down the length of my face. I keep my calm composure, not letting him get any satisfaction in my pain, but inside I'm screaming for help. For this to stop even though I know it hasn't even started yet. I would be considered ignorant if I truly believed he would allow this torture session to go by without any screams. I flinch when the knife drops off my chin and digs into my neck. The smile on his face grows wider and more malicious. Chuckles can be heard from deep within his chest.

Without any warning he aggressively slides the knife over my collarbone. It doesn't stop until it reaches the top of my breasts. No matter how calm I want to be, nothing prepares me for the pain that rips through my body. Squinting my eyes closed, I will tears not to come as a high pitched scream breaks free from my mouth.

"The most pleasurable sound in the world, your screams."

I refuse to look at the monster who stands in front of me, so I bring my eyes to the floor. Placed perfectly beneath me is a drain. For some reason I know I was placed here for that very hole in the ground. My eyes catch glimpses of my blood stained shirt as I look down. I can't see the wound, but from the amount of blood that has covered my shirt already it can't look good.

"Oh, you noticed the drain, huh. Well, gradually you'll end up bleeding out and once my dear friend Maxwell comes to see you he won't be able to lick up the puddles. Besides, by the time he comes here all it will take is one killing blow for you to die. He won't be able to save you by the time I'm done with you."

"You're sick," I retort. If only he was closer, I would kick him.

"We have hours before dear Maxwell is going to show up. I have lots to accomplish with you before then. Now, are you going to cry for me, Charlie?"

It all happens so fast. The glint of the blade reflects the light in the room before it comes down on me again, this time across my thigh, leaving a deep gash. Blood pours out, streaming down the length of my leg. Don't cry, don't cry, I chant to myself.

"You see, Charlie, I don't have a quarrel with you, my problem is with Maxwell. Any other woman in the world could be in your situation right now and I would be doing this to them, but since you happen to be my best friend's donor and he chose you to be his bride...here we are." He continues to pace back and forth, flailing his arms around. I catch glimpses of the blood covered knife. Every so often, I see a drop fall to the ground.

He continues, gradually taking several steps in my direction. My hunched body and severely rugged breathing doesn't faze him and his speech. "I feel bad that I have to kill you. From what I was told by Daisy, you're a witty highly motivated individual and from what I can see you seem to be one tough cookie to crack. I could drink you dry, take you on as my own, but there's no fun in that."

"Aren't you going to introduce yourself properly first, Henry?" My words are strained. Hisses come out in between each word as I work through my pain.

His words are slightly difficult to understand due to him laughing. "She's smart too. So you figured out who I am. What gave me away?"

"All I had to do was connect the dots. Maxwell has been obsessed with reading his journal, so I took another look at it. There was this entry I scanned over the first time reading it. You know, for a minute I thought all the transcribers were men, but this entry…the handwriting was too curvy and perfect. It was a woman and she wrote page after page of how attractive Maxwell was. About his friend, Henry, who had gorgeous green eyes. Dots connected. Luckily for you, I just read that little bit before going to sleep last night. Tell me, is Daisy a fine replacement?" It hurts to talk, but I don't have an option.

"Prue will never be replaced." He rushes to me, closing the small gap between us, pointing his finger in my face from his rage. With one deep unnecessary breath, he relaxes. "Daisy knows that. This isn't about me flaunting my newfound glory in Maxwell's face, although it's quite rewarding to know that I have a bride willing to do anything for me while Maxwell has…well, you, stubborn uncooperative Charlie. This is about getting revenge, a bride for a bride. He convinced her to kill herself. He's the reason she's dead and he's the reason you'll be dead soon as well."

I shake my head with a smile on my face at his words. Impending death aside, I can't help but to laugh. His lack of common sense and human emotions brings a smile to my face.

"What's so funny, Charlie? You think laughter will make the pain go away?" Henry spits out.

Honestly, laughing does make the pain go away, but there's no way I'm admitting that. However, that's until he lunges at me, fangs fully exposed. His mouth doesn't quite fall upon my neck as more so the top of my shoulder as his teeth sink into me. A scream rips through my pursed lips.

It seems like eternity before he gets off of me. Once he does, he looks at me dead on and wipes his mouth with his forearm. "You will have no satisfaction in this.

Understood?"

I ignore his threats. "Maxwell didn't convince her to kill herself. I haven't known you for very long, but I know for a fact that he's nothing like you."

"We're both vampires. What makes you so sure lover boy is as innocent as you think he is? You said it yourself, you read the book. He's a killer, Charlie. Back in the day, he wasn't so gentle and caring as he has grown to be now, which just makes my job of breaking him easier."

"You can't convince someone to kill themselves unless they already want to die," I spit out. "Her situation had to be so awful that she wanted to get away from her miserable situation and you, dear Henry, you were her situation. Is it that hard to see how heartless and cruel she thought you were…still are. She's no Daisy, that's for sure. Prue actually had a brain."

"Shut your mouth."

"You think she loves you, but then again you honestly don't know what love is since you loved a person who loathed you. Your precious Daisy just wants to become a monster such as yourself for the eternal youth and beauty. You change her and, mark my words, she'll leave you in a heartbeat, no pun intended."

"Not scared to die, are we, Charlie. Running your mouth will only make it hurt more, it won't make it end faster."

"I guess that's another thing your little Daisy forgot to mention, I talk back. Not used to that, are we, Henry? You're so accustomed to people beckoning your every call. Sorry, not going to happen." I know I'm pushing him further than I should, but I just can't sit back and let him get the best of me.

"No wonder Maxwell is having such a hard time with you. You need to be broken, is all," he barks at me bitterly.

This time I see it coming. The rise of the blade and the path the strike follows. I bite my lip to hold back a shriek, but it's no use. As the now familiar sear of the blade touches me, my screams fill the room. Unwillingly a tear falls from the corner of my eye. I try to examine my fresh wound, but my blurry vision ruins any chance of seeing any detail in the slash that now scars my stomach.

He wipes the tear that escapes my eyes away with his thumb. "Now there's the girl I'm looking for." Waving the knife in my face, he retreats as he begins to lecture me. "I see what you're doing, Charlie. You want to die before Maxwell gets here, because if there's any chance he can save you it means you'll turn into what you despise. Trust me, love, by the time he gets here there will be no saving you. Now I'm going to freshen up and I'll be back a little later. You hang tight and bleed it out." He looks down in disgust at his T-shirt that's speckled with blood. A quick flash of his smile and he disappears behind the metal door, slamming it shut. The bang it creates echoes through the room.

"Fuck!" How the hell am I going to get out of this? I grumble to myself. I yank and twist my arms, trying to jiggle the latch loose, but all I manage to do is make the zip ties bury themselves in my wrists. The feel of warm stickiness trailing down my arms forces me to stop my struggling efforts. I'm stuck until nightfall and then death follows.

* * *

Maxwell

"Slow down, Morgan, take deep steady breaths and tell me again from the beginning, what exactly did you see?" There was a slight rise in Charlie's emotions earlier, but nothing to cause this frenzy that Morgan is in right now.

Her voice is distorted by constant sobs and a steady thump can be heard in the background. I assume it's her palm drumming against the desktop. "I saw her pull in and park next to my car like she always does, but before she could get away from her car her path was blocked by…"

"By who, Morgan?"

"You probably think I'm crazy acting like this just from Charlie talking with some girl and getting into her own car, but…" Her crying gets louder and further away. I realize she dropped the phone.

"Morgan…Morgan. Talk to me, Morgan," I yell into the phone, hoping she hears me.

"She told me she thinks the people after her are the two people James had with him. Daisy. She was the one who blocked her path, she was the one to shove Charlie in the car and drive away. I didn't know what to do, so I called you. Am I overreacting or is Charlie in trouble?"

I'm not sure if Morgan in the fragile state she is in will be able to handle the fact that Charlie is in more trouble than either of us can handle. Not to mention even if I do have a plan there's no way I can put it into action. The sun blocks my rescue. I'm forced to sit here and pray she'll survive until sundown.

"Morgan, we both know the answer to that question. What I need from you is to stay calm and keep things under control there. Conduct her meetings, plan parties as if Charlie is just away on vacation and keep this between just the two us…understand?"

"Okay," she agrees in a raspy voice.

"I'll get Charlie back, all I need is time. Keep your phone by you and wait for my call." I hang up, not wanting to hear her weeping anymore. My eyes jolt to the closest clock; I have about twelve hours before the sun starts to set.

Relying on the connection between us to let me know where she is and if she's in pain or not is all I have. Hours go by with her destination unknown and her angrier than ever. I can't help but to think I should have acted differently this morning, how I should have insisted that she stayed here...but I did nothing and let her walk right out the door.

Sitting on the couch hunched with my head in my hands for who knows how long, it hits me. Searing pain and the sound of Charlie's screams fill my head. It's all an illusion created by the bond and only lasts a few seconds, but it doesn't make it any less real. "It's begun," I say to myself.

I knew it would happen, I knew it would emotionally kill me when it would start, but this is worse than anything I could prepare myself for. I felt awful when James had me trapped here when Charlie was faced with who we now know was Daisy's first encounter, but this is different. Never in my three hundred years have I endured this kind of pain and I never want to again. It lasts less than an hour before silence. I wouldn't call it peace as it's more so recovering in agony.

A fist pounds on the front door. The anxious bangs echo throughout the suite. Unwillingly, I make my way to the door and reluctantly open it to reveal the woman who made this all happen. "Daisy."

"Don't sound so happy to see me. Can I come in? Then again I'm sure you would love to know what I know." She pushes past me and doesn't stop until she's sitting on the couch. She continues to talk all the way there. "You see, I'm here to make sure you don't do anything rash like trying to save dear Charlie when the sun is blazing out. We don't want you dead before you can see your bride die."

"So you're here to babysit me." I refuse to sit in the living area with her, so I reply from the kitchen.

"Not babysit, more like taunt. Henry told me about how charming you can be. Why don't you show me some hospitality? How about a drink, Bloody Charlie, I mean Bloody Mary." The smile on her face is sickening.

It takes everything in me to not snap her neck. Just thinking about it causes my hands to ball into fists.

"Tsk tsk, Maxwell," she replies when she realizes I'm not going to respond to her. "You need me...well, not really, but let's say you do. I'm going to bring you to Charlie all in due time. Let's sit and talk until then, we do have hours to spare."

My top lip curls up in disgust. Her hand pats the couch cushion next to her, indicating that she wants me to sit beside her. I pull out one of the kitchen table's chairs and sit down without saying a word.

"Suit yourself. I was just—"

"I would prefer if you didn't speak."

If looks could kill, I would die from that evil glare she throws in my direction, but her voice is the last thing I want to hear right now. Wave two of Charlie's screams rings through my ears. More than anything I want to thrash out from the pain I'm forced to feel as well as from the rage that continues to multiply. Daisy's mocking laughter taunts me from the living room, keeping my screams caged up inside. Through blurry eyes, I try to read the clock, a little past two in the afternoon.

Daisy abides by my wish of keeping quiet, although her laughter can always be heard when she sees me struggling to contain my composure. She took the will to turn on the TV to keep herself occupied during her stay here. With a glance at the clock, every time Charlie's pain floods through me, I realize that it occurs in intervals…every three hours.

The clicking of Daisy's heels brings me back to my awful reality. I shrink in on myself as she opens the curtains that cover the large window, allowing the orange hue of the setting sun to stream into the rooms. "Sorry, but it's only a matter of an hour or so before we get to go. Are you excited? Because I am."

Devoid of any common sense, I rush over to her, slamming her against a nearby wall, far enough away from the window, so any thought of ripping the curtains open wider are impossible. The feel of her neck underneath my hand as I squeeze without a care, her squirming body and whipping hands that bat at me along with the sound of her raspy breathing excites me. To cause this wretched woman pain gets me one step closer of reaching my revenge on what they have done to my bride.

As I debate whether I should kill her now, her body goes limp from lack of oxygen. "What a shame," I say aloud to myself, releasing my grip on her. Her body falls to the floor in a mangled heap. The pleasure of killing her unconscious body holds no appeal compared to her blue doe eyes staring at me, knowing she's going to die.

With a firm grip on her wrist, I drag her lifeless body to the linen closet located in the entryway. I harshly throw her inside and lock the door for safekeeping. No need to tape her mouth or tie her hands, because being as demented as she is she would most likely get out of them anyways.

It doesn't take long for the orangey sky to turn dark gray. Daisy said she was going to take me to Charlie, but I don't need her, I can find Charlie just fine on my own. When I leave the suite, the ungrateful girl is still unconscious in the closet. I run as fast as I can, remaining out of sight from people who still occupy the roads and sidewalks. Even if they were to spot me, I would appear as nothing more than a blur.

I have no idea how long my journey of reaching Charlie is, but when the filled city streets turn into deserted ones, I know I'm close. Finally, when a rundown manufacturing building comes into view relief washes over me and I waste no time in entering. On my own way here not once pain was inflicted on Charlie, but now her screams echo throughout the empty halls. The ache and thoughts of her screams are nothing compared to hearing them now, in person.

The dim crumbling halls only add worry to my already existent anxiety. A shallow breath is all I can manage before I storm through the metal door that separates Charlie from me. What I see horrifies me, but deep down I expected it. The harsh lighting in the room makes her once tan skin look pale. The stark contrast of bright red that stains her entire body just makes her complexion look whiter. Blood flows freely from several slashes that mark her body.

She dangles from some kind of hook on the wall. The zip ties that bind her wrists are barely visible due from her limp legs being unable to hold her body up, causing the plastic to dig into her skin, allowing blood to camouflage them. Wasting no time, my legs automatically step forward toward her. The slamming of the metal door behind me forces my legs to come to a halt.

"Not so fast, Maxwell," Henry spits out from behind me with his hand still extended, touching the door.

The venomous sound of his voice only makes the

anger I have begin to boil, making it barely containable. "Henry," I state as I turn around to face him, intentionally taking a step backward so I'm closer to Charlie. Before I look up to meet his gaze, he sprints in my direction and slams me to the ground. Power flows from him as he clenches my neck. He made sure he was well fed before today. However, his strength is no match for my fury.

Inches away from my face, he barks at me. "Where is Daisy?"

"Locked up as she should be. This is between you and me, friend." My palms shove against his chest, sending him flying off me. Smashing into the concrete wall, he lands in a semi-squat only to stand up within a few seconds. He shakes crumbs of the wall that broke off from the impact out of his hair and off of his shoulders.

Moans that resemble my name croak out of Charlie's dry mouth. Henry uses my lack of focus to his advantage. In the blink of one's eyes we start to scuffle, except this time I'm ready. At arm's length, with each of our hands on the other's shoulders, we push and shove each other into various obstacles around the room, along with most of the walls in the small cell. Chunks of the ceiling rain down on us from the constant impact of our bodies.

Not to my surprise, Henry gets the upper hand and grabs the back of my neck, forcing me to look at Charlie. From when I first entered the room to now she looks worse. A sheen of sweat lines her face as she tries to hang on the little sliver of life she has left.

Henry heaves me forward. "Look at her," he yells, inches away from my ear. "Watch her die." His intense strength pushing me down makes me struggle to stay on my feet, but I lose my footing on blood that blots the floor. Before I know it, my face is inches away from the red liquid and in a quick second, my cheek touches the cold stickiness only to be pulled back away from it, throwing me to the opposite side of the room. "What a waste, isn't it? Let's be honest with each other, she's going to die, just like you let Prue die."

"Prue hated you, Henry. The sooner you come to terms with that the better it will be on all of us. Take it out on me and leave Charlie out of this." I try to make my voice sound strong, but just lying beneath the surface begging can be heard.

"A bride for a bride, Maxwell, and that's me taking it out on you. You will live in pity for eternity knowing she died because of you. Don't worry, though, I'm proof that another is out there for you. If Prue lived then I would have never met Daisy and if you hurt her—" he retorts.

"Oh, you better believe I hurt that bitch. Tell me one thing, Henry, how did you find me?" A vampire can't track another vampire in any special way other than what the average human would have to result to in finding another human. He had to have some connection in a high place.

"Curious, are we? I only needed to find one person, one person I knew would be by your side. It's quite sad that she still follows you wherever you go. I don't have anybody like her. The only person I have now because of you is Daisy."

"Grace, you tracked down Grace?" My eyebrow perks up in thought. "Who told you where Grace was…Benjamin?"

"Benjamin is under his own scrutiny. If I were to show up asking him about Grace or yourself, he would read my intentions like one of his very many books, not to mention lots of other spying eyes…such as Eugene.

That man would run to you instantly if he knew I was in search of you. He's a very smart and loyal man and sadly one day it'll get him killed. I went on a much more secluded path."

I rack my brain for some kind of connection that Henry had made over the years to any council members, then it comes to me. "Duke."

"Ding ding. Duke being the kind menacing man he is helped me after Prue killed herself. He told me he would help me get my revenge when I was ready. He told me where Grace was and that wherever she was you would be."

If I made it through this The High Council will punish one of their own and Duke will no longer hold eternal life seeing as I won't stop until he sees the sun again.

Henry takes two small steps that are separating him from Charlie as he laughs in my face at how sly he thinks he is. Having not the slightest bit of concern at my presence, he unhooks Charlie's hands from the hardware on the wall that's holding her upright and watches her collapse to the ground. Kneeling next to her, he grasps a fistful of her blood-matted hair jerking her, hanging head upward to look at me.

Her eyes are barely open. Fresh and dry blood trail down her face as well as her neck. She wets her chapped lips with her tongue and faint whimpers seep out of her mouth. Focusing on her floppy body, I don't see Henry draw a knife. It's not until it rests at the nape of her neck that I see the shiny metal in its entirety. He holds the knife I gave Charlie to protect herself with in his steady hand.

Instantly, I hold my empty hands out to him. "Henry...we used to be good friends, we used to do everything together. There has to be some other way to get past this." I try to talk some reason into him, but I know whatever I say doesn't faze him. Therefore, I take slow, cautious steps backward at an angle toward a wooden table that's up against the wall.

"What's done is done." With that said, he raises the blade high in the air before he plunges it into Charlie's chest.

Charlie's eyes go wide with shock and a deep breath is sucked into her dying lungs. A faint groan sounds from her instead of an ear-piercing scream, because she has nothing left in her from being so brutally tortured the previous hours. My fangs extend and finally the monster within comes to the surface. I didn't want kill him, but he leaves me with no other choice. While Henry is gloating from his glory, I dash toward that rickety wooden table, turning it into shards of wood, although I make sure to keep one leg intact.

The noise alerts him, but it's too late. I already stand before him with the makeshift stake in hand. Slivers of wood bury themselves into my hand, but it doesn't hinder my fluid motion. His shirt crinkles in my hand as I grip his shoulder to keep him from moving as I drive the pointed stick into his neck, the same exact way I killed the vampire who made me. Almost straight away his legs give out, leaving him motionless on the ground. Slowly, his skin turns black and flakes away. Within a few hours he'll be nothing but ash.

Rushing to Charlie, I yank the knife out only to see blood pour out at a faster rate. "It's going to be okay, Charlie. You're not going to die on me, just drink." I bite into my own wrist and press it to her mouth.

She tries to wiggle out from under me, but her feeble attempts to push me away don't move me the slightest bit. I know she doesn't want this, but I refuse to let her die, I refuse to let her die like this. I press my bleeding wrist harder against her mouth, making sure she ingests enough of my tainted blood. Like a magician doing his infamous magic trick, the blood that flows out of her multiple wounds starts to slow before it stops altogether. Gradually, all of the slices, especially the one in her chest begin to heal, leaving her stained in her own blood for no noticeable reason.

Her eyes flicker closed before she's fully healed and before I have removed my wrist from her mouth. I carry her unconscious body to her car, leaving her inside. I speed away, leaving everything behind us. Thoughts of a feisty and vindictive Daisy pop into my thoughts on the way back to my living quarters, but I feel like I can take anything and anyone on with the knowledge that Charlie is going to survive and she'll finally be my vampire bride.

I cautiously push open my door with Charlie's limp body in my arms. Shards of wood are scattered across the floor from the closet door being kicked out from the inside. A breeze makes the dark curtains float off the ground. She's gone. There's only one way that she would have been able to get out of that closet and that's if Henry already started the process of turning her. One problem might be gone, but another is definitely on the rise.

Chapter Twenty-Eight

Charlie

As if a bolt of lightning comes down from the sky, I'm jolted awake. Instantly, I observe my surroundings. My heartbeat relaxes just a little as I realize I'm lying in Maxwell's bed. Nonetheless, memories of last night flood my senses. I rip off the blanket and begin slapping parts of my body that should have deep gashes Henry inflicted on me. Except, my once bleeding body is healed and there's no ounce of blood or even scars to prove the events even happened.

"Maxwell," I yell.

He comes walking in, not running…walking. "Charlie, I can explain," he says slowly.

"What the hell did you do, Maxwell?" My voice is uneven from fear. I know the answer, but I don't want to know the answer.

"I had to. I wasn't going to let you die."

My heart feels heavy in my chest, my lungs burn with dread, and my mouth immediately goes dry. "I should've died. You should've let me die. It's unnatural…people don't get second chances in life for a reason."

"Charlie, would you listen to what you're saying? People don't get second chances, but you do and you should be grateful."

"Grateful? I should be grateful for your selfishness." I get out of bed and stalk up to him. I have so much anger, so much regret. I don't know how I feel. All I know is that I'm not ready to be a vampire.

He puts his hands on my shoulders and leads me

back to bed. He even pushes me onto the mattress and covers me up. "I know you didn't want this, but I couldn't let you die at Henry's hand. You deserve better than that and I'm sorry if I believe I can give you better. You just need to rest and come to terms with this. It'll take a while. I know it took me a while to get used to it."

"Where's Henry?" I want to get past the fact that his once best friend tried to kill me...scratch that, he did kill me.

"Dead." Is all he says.

My hand covers my chest to feel the dull thump as it beats against my ribcage from nervousness. "Why do I still have a heartbeat?"

"It takes a while for the transition to be completed."

"How long?" I say in a stern voice.

"Long enough," he says, skirting around the answer to my question, holding my hand in his.

I yank my hand out of his. My voice rises with anger at his words. "Maxwell, don't make me more irritated than I already am. You can count on me knocking you on your ass as soon as I have the strength. Now, how long."

"Three...maybe four days," he reluctantly admits.

"I need to go to work," I say as I whip the blankets back off me. It's the only thing I can think of to make me feel the slightest bit better. Plus, in three, four days I won't necessarily have my work to fall back on anymore.

"No can do—" Maxwell starts to say, placing the blankets back over me.

I cut him off mid-sentence with clenched fists. "What do you mean no can do? Can't I go out into the sun for these last few days of my normal life?"

"You're just as human as before you were stabbed in the chest, but you nearly died. I already—"

"Nearly died? I did die...I'm going to die," I interrupt him again.

He huffs at my lack of respect in not allowing him to finish what he's trying to tell me, but I can't help it. With one deep breath inhaled and slowly exhaled, he continues talking. "I already took the liberty to call Morgan, telling her you won't be coming in today. You might feel fine, but you need more rest." With that said, he leaves the room and shuts the door behind him.

I can tell he's angry with my ungratefulness, but I can't help it. He thinks of my not wanting to be a vampire as an insult, but I just wanted it to be...more romantic maybe. Not so painful and bloody. And now I'm stuck in this room all day, most likely by myself, to face nothing but my own taunting thoughts. I fall back down onto the pillow and stare at the ceiling for what seems like hours. Boredom sets in and my stomach growls with hunger.

"Can I at least have a book or watch a movie? I'm hungry...so hungry," I say into the empty room, hoping that Maxwell will hear my whines.

A few seconds later, he enters with a tray in his hands. He sets it down on the nightstand and I take a look at what he brought me. A book that he must've stolen off one of my bookshelves at home, a few magazines that were at my house as well, and a bowl of what looks to be chicken dumpling soup.

"Soup...you brought me soup. I'm dying, not sick. I won't have the joy of eating anymore and you bring me soup. You could've at least brought me a cheeseburger and chili cheese fries or lasagna." I continue to rattle off all the food I'm going to miss. "Ice cream and strawberries and soda and brats and pizza and popcorn..."

"Okay, I get it. You'll miss food. It'll take some

time, but with plenty of supplement you'll be able to retrain your body to digest."

"Supplement? What the hell is that?"

"Blood. Blood makes us alive."

"Oh." I might be disgusted, but it doesn't stop me from biting into a dumpling. Even though I complained about having soup, it's delicious.

I eat alone since Maxwell leaves the room. He feels guilty and therefore he can't quite look at me. The blame he puts on himself makes me feel awful. It's not his fault and I did express on many different levels that I'm on board with him, with us.

But that doesn't solve my problems. How am I going to inform Morgan of my soon departure? Not to mention how in the world am I going to do handle my business? I could close up shop and move past it or I could leave Morgan in charge.

The thought of leaving my business just brings another obstacle to mind. What about my house? I could renovate it, making it possible for me to live in it once I become allergic to the sun or I could sell it. Then again renovating it seems better than the thought of living in this small hotel room with Maxwell. I decide not to breach the subject with Maxwell just yet. Instead, I'll let him pamper me.

After three chapters read of the book Maxwell left me, my eyelids begin to get heavy and the book slowly starts to fall to my chest. It's not until I feel the slide of the book underneath my still clenched fingers that I realize I fell asleep. I mumble a few incoherent words as I stretch my stiff body.

"Go back to sleep, Charlie." I hear Maxwell whisper inches away from me. He brushes his hand through my hair, moving strands away from my face. Within seconds, I feel the familiar coldness of his body as he crawls into bed.

I unwillingly drift back to sleep. No matter how mad at him I tell myself that I am, I can't deny how comfortable and safe he makes me feel. Just knowing that he's by my side makes facing being a vampire tolerable. I don't know if I could do it without him.

Without the sun shining into the room to alert me morning has arrived, I rely on the clock. With a quick rub of my eyes, I read the bright red numbers that say seven forty-five. It has to be seven forty-five in the morning because I was up past ten last night.

"Rise and shine," I yell, shaking a nonresponsive Maxwell.

"Morning already?" he grumbles.

"Oh please, let's not pretend that you actually asleep. I have to go to work and I just wanted to…well, I don't know why I woke you up exactly."

"You don't have to go to work today. I'm sure Morgan will understand."

"Funny, but I'm not lying in this bed all day again. I have to face the music eventually and figure out my life. I have to tell Morgan something. It has to be a really good believable lie on how I'll be 'missing' during the day, but beyond active at night."

"Maybe you should just tell her. For all you know she knows about vampires because of James," Maxwell says, offering his opinion.

"I don't think so. It'll sound crazy. The conversation will sound something like, oh, Morgan, I'm sorry but I can only come out of the house at night because the sun will kill me. What? You want to know why the sun will kill me…well, you see, Maxwell is a vampire and his once best friend who is also a vampire, you know, green eyes killed me with the help of Daisy on Monday night. Maxwell being too attached saved me by turning me into a monster as well. See, sounds stupid. The only way she's getting the truth is if she tells me about James or about the existence of vampires first," I retort.

"Suit yourself. The truth is the easiest way around things."

"It's the easiest way to get me admitted into the psych ward. And the truth worked out so well for you, didn't it?" I jump out of bed and in a rush get dressed. I ignore Maxwell's protest as I grab my purse and head for the door.

"No kiss goodbye?" he asks, leaning against the kitchen table in his boxers.

"No, I'm still mad at you. I know I should be appreciative I'm not six feet under, but I'm just not used to the fact that my heart is going to stop beating. I need time."

"I understand," he says with his eyes on the floor.

"However, while you sit here all depressed by my lack of compassion, you can think of what I need to do to make my house vampire safe, because I'm not staying here."

"We can always start fresh and move away seeing as this place has left you with such bad memories."

"Move away? To where?"

"My home. It's not far from here, just a few states over."

"My home is here, my life is here."

"Your human life is here. Maybe it would be better to start fresh with your new life."

"I'll think about it after this is all over with." I compromise as I walk out the door, letting it slam behind me.

He has a house? Like actually lives somewhere instead of a hotel room? I never even thought he had a life prior to tracking me down. I never even realized he left everything behind to convince me to become his bride. The least I can do is consider leaving everything I have behind to convince myself that I belong in this new world that waits for me in a few days' time.

Preparing myself for the sun to blind me as I exit the hotel, to my dismay the sky is a cloudy gray. My hopes of seeing the sun before I can't see it again gradually get squashed. The parking lot is mostly empty as I pull into my usual spot. Morgan hasn't arrived yet and thank goodness, because the walk to the front doors brings up nasty memories of Daisy.

My shaking hands show my uneasiness as I sit behind my desk in hope of getting through the day. I look around my office and think about how I'm going to miss it. Not soon after I arrive, Morgan gets here. I can hear her running footsteps coming down the hall.

A breathless Morgan huffs and puffs as she tries to catch her breath in my doorway. Sooner or later she finally speaks. "Charlie, you're back." She might be tired from her run, but not that exhausted because she sprints over to me and engulfs me in a hug, cutting off my airflow.

"Morgan, I'm fine. Really. Not a scratch." I manage to get out of my mouth.

She holds me away at arm's length, inspecting me. "The way Maxwell sounded last night I thought you were dead."

I quirk an eyebrow up at her statement. "Morgan, sit down, I have to tell you something. You see, I'm faced with a very difficult situation that leaves me unable to be here. Either I can close down or if you're willing, I could leave you in charge. You'll still be able to reach me, but I'll be unavailable during certain hours…daytime hours, to be exact." I don't bring up the possibility of leaving the whole city behind. No need to worry her with that until I actually make that decision.

I brace myself for her response. "You don't have to leave, I understand fully. You can come in and work at night and I'll be here during the day. In fact, your situation can give you more business."

"What are you talking about? I'm thankful for your understanding, but you don't know about my situation exactly."

"Charlie, no more lying. I've known about Maxwell for some time now, since you went to Austria with him for your presentation. Why do you think I keep pushing Maxwell on you? I know all about Henry and Daisy and how they tried to kill you. I even know that Maxwell saved you and you're one of them now, but things don't have to change," she pleads.

"One of what now?" I want to play the dumb card and act like I know nothing about what she's talking about, but the things she said were so spot on.

"A vampire, Charlie. James told me everything. I'm in this just as much as you. Well, not as much as you, but you're not alone. Now, instead of leaving, you need to think of new fresh ideas such as parties at midnight and stuff. I'll let you get to work. Glad you're back." With a wink, she leaves my office without anything further to say.

What the fuck just happened? I question myself, shaking my head in disbelief. Morgan has known about Maxwell…vampires altogether for how long? Not as long as me…at least I don't think she has. Yet she's more comfortable with everything more so than I am. That went much easier than I expected. Now, if only this whole transition thing goes just as smoothly.

Turning toward the papers that litter my desk, I put all of my attention on the party that's this Saturday, because for all I know it's going to be the last one I do and it'll be a fun one at that. The ideas that fill my mind for the red carpet themed birthday party makes the time go by faster.

Before I know it, Morgan knocks on the doorframe. "I'm heading out. Are you coming too or are you going to stay for a while longer?" She patiently waits for my reply.

"No, I can leave. I have a lot of preparations to make for the big change." It feels weird and more than awkward talking to Morgan about this whole thing. The idea of being able to talk to someone about it was relieving, but part of me wants to keep it all in, wanting to shoulder the burden myself.

Within several minutes of reassuring Morgan that I'm fine and that I'll see her tomorrow, I finally make my way back to Maxwell. I can only hope he did what I asked of him and has a list of things I can go buy to keep my mind off the inflexible list of things to come. Nothing cures depression like a little shopping.

* * *

Maxwell

Well, she took it better than I thought. She's still not happy with how things turned out, but then again neither am I. It doesn't take much to put a list together of things she needs to vampire proof her house. Since I still have a few hours before Charlie comes home, I call Grace.

"So what's the new word?" Grace bellows into the phone.

"I found out who was after Charlie."

"Do tell."

"Henry."

"Henry as in—" She starts to say, but I interrupt

her.

"Oh yes, our dear friend Henry. Turns out he blamed me for Prue killing herself to get away from him and he…he set out to kill Charlie with the help of his bride, who is now a vampire."

"Charlie's fine, though, right?"

I'm at a loss for words.

"Maxwell? Charlie's okay, right?" Her nervous tone echoes in my head.

"Not exactly."

"She's still not gone, is she?"

"No, she's still walking, talking, and breathing…for now."

A sharp intake of breath sounds over the phone. "She's…one of us now?"

"Yeah. Henry, he did quite a number on her. I either saved her and made her vampire or let her die. I couldn't let her die. And now she's upset with me for not letting her die."

"Typical Charlie." I might not be able to see her, but I know she has a smile on her face. "So what happened to Henry and his bride?"

"His bride, Daisy…not sure, she slipped through my fingers and disappeared. If she's smart, she'll never show her face to Charlie or myself again. As for Henry, he's dead."

"Listen, to make things a little easier, I'll tell Benjamin you need the names and locations of your new donors. It might take a while, meaning she'll already be turned before I'll have the list, but it's the most I can do for now since I'm not there to help her…to help you. Just keep her calm and occupied and the both of you will get through this just fine. She's scared, is all. Do you not remember being scared too? It was a nice chat, but I got to go for this whole trial thing."

I barely have time to say goodbye before she hangs up. I can't believe she's still a part of that trail with Benjamin. How long does it take to convict Emma and be done with it? I know I should be more thoughtful, but I need help with Charlie and I know Grace is the only one who can talk some sense into her.

The rest of the day goes by extremely slow and boring as I wait for Charlie to return. I nearly fall asleep from boredom. Thankfully, the sounds of her huffs can be heard outside the door. Before she pounds on it impatiently, I open it. She barges in and throws her purse on the table before she falls into one of the chairs.

"I take it work didn't go that well," I say, trying to get her to talk through her frustration.

"Oh, it actually went better than I planned only because I didn't have to think of a lie. She confronted me…she called me out and told me how I can continue to work through my 'condition'." She holds up her hands and puts imaginary quotation marks around 'condition'.

I ignore her calling her soon-to-be death as a human and birth as a vampire a condition. "What's the brilliant idea? Because I know it has to be brilliant since it came from a girl who confronted you when she knew that one day soon you could kill her in an instant." I see the look of torment on her face as I say that last part. "I didn't mean that you will, just that you could…if you wanted to." Nothing I say is making this conversation better.

"You're saying I'm going to be a savage? Is that it?" Concern distorts her voice.

By opening my mouth I only made things worse. "No, you'll feel hungry, but nothing more than what a human would feel when they're hungry. Crazed blood lust is a rare occurrence. You'll have plenty of blood already within your body to survive. However, you'll have to make a relationship or I should say friendship with our donors so when you do need to eat they'll be more willing to supply."

"Great...that's just fantastic. Can we talk about something else besides eating people?"

"I completed the list you asked for of items to revamp your house." A smile forms, half cocked on my face at my joke.

"Very funny. Give it here." She holds out her hand, waiting for the piece of paper.

I hand it to her and she starts rattling off all the items. "Really good blinds, dark colored curtains...that's it? I mean, I knew that, but I was expecting more. Maybe tomorrow I'll make a trip to pick the items up and then we can go to my house and put it all up."

"Anything you want. I can let them know at the front desk that I won't be in need of this suite in the matter of a few days. It might also help you change in your own home as well."

I see her exhale harshly as if it took a lot to release after hearing my words. "So now all we can do is wait?" she says, more to herself than to me.

"I wish there was more, but yes...all we can do is wait. At least we won't have to wait long. Only another two or three days."

"I didn't even realize I'm going to miss the party this Sunday. I'll have to call Morgan and set something up, preferably without Dave."

"That would be best. The transition varies, Charlie, you could not change for a week. Grace turned two days after she was turned by Benjamin. As for me, I turned eight days later. Some people think that's because I fought it as long as I could, because like you I didn't want this life. We can't take any chances that you start the change during the day unless you're with Morgan, but that's the last resort. It isn't up for any more debate."

Her voice is a faint whisper as she shows a timid side that I rarely ever see. "What's going to happen to me?"

"What do you mean?"

"Maxwell, don't act stupid with me, I deserve to know. Is it going to hurt?" I can tell she's scared not just by the look on her face, but the sound of her words that she can barely speak.

"We'll wait until the time comes." I refuse to tell her. She has no idea what she's in for and I'm not looking forward to informing her. The change is ultimately your humanity dying and it isn't easy for anyone to experience their life slowly die away, leaving you an empty shell.

Her eyes squint with anger as she bolts up from her chair and stalks over to me. She pokes her finger in my chest as she bluntly says what's on her mind. "Now you listen here, I'm going to die and I think I should know how it's going to happen. You might not want me to know, but I need to prepare myself, I need to be ready in some sort of way, because let's face it, when it happens I'll be anything but ready. It's nothing but a mystery and seems unreal right now. I need to fear it or I'll just be overloaded when it takes place, so please be honest with me. What's going to happen to me?"

I meet her gaze, staring at her for a few seconds before I speak. "It's similar to falling asleep, but you'll be able to feel your heart slow, you'll be able to feel your breathing lessen. Your vision and hearing will fail, leaving you in the dark to gradually slip into slumber just before your heart stops. It doesn't necessarily hurt, it's just…scary." I describe the details about my personal experience as I allow those bad memories to play behind my eyes.

I see dread fill her face, so I take her hands in mine just before a tear escapes her eyes. Engulfing her in a hug, one hand holds her head to my chest as the other rubs her back. "I'll be there when it happens and I'll be there when you wake up. Just think of it like you're going to sleep for the night and you'll wake up in the morning like usual."

Her sobs get louder and I can begin to feel the wetness of her tears on my T-shirt. It's better if she gets it out now and faces the worse that's to come head-on. She can do this...then again she has to.

Just as fast as she broke down, she recovers and pulls out of my grasp. She furiously wipes at the tears that streak her face as if they're acid burning her face. "I'm sorry. I didn't mean to get all crybaby on you."

"You're apologizing for crying? You don't have to say you're sorry for being scared. If it makes it any better, I was beyond terrified and I didn't have anybody to help me through it." Without wanting to, I continue to go down memory lane. "I was locked in an underground cell of sorts almost instantly after I was forced to ingest his blood. I screamed and dug at the dirt walls for days and not one living or not living soul came to check up on me. I refused to die, but once I began to feel my organs start to shut down I welcomed death with the promise of getting revenge...somehow...somewhere...sometime in this never-ending life, I would get revenge."

Her hand goes over her mouth from shock at my horrid past.

"I got past it, though, and years later I met Grace."

"Is that why you killed him, Cornelius?"

"I was never convicted of killing him," I say abruptly, trying to cover my tracks.

"Don't get all I'm innocent with me, I read the book. I'm not pointing fingers, but from what I read he deserved it. I would've done the same," she admits.

I give her an inquiring look. "Are you saying something that I should be paying closer attention to?"

"Don't worry. I'm not going to kill you. I might be angry at all of this, but I know it's not your fault. I'm sorry you had to go through that and I'm sorry for being so—"

"No need to apologize. That was just how a majority of people behaved back then and I'll do whatever I can to make sure my past isn't your future. Now, what do you want to do with the rest of our night? I have something in mind if you can't think of anything," I say, changing the subject with a rise of my eyebrows.

Her laugh fills the room as well as a dull thump as she hits my chest with her palm. "The stores are still open. We could go shopping tonight instead of tomorrow."

"Sounds like a plan." I wrap my arm around her shoulders, walking beside her as she heads to the door. "Maybe pick up some dinner on the way to your place?"

She nods her head in agreement. "Some burgers and fries."

"Whatever you want." The mention of food makes me hungry as well, but her blood is useless to me now since it's infected with vampire blood. Vampires bite other vampires as a sign of intimacy on a much deeper level than vampires biting a human. Therefore, that list of names is just as important to me as it is to Charlie.

Chapter Twenty-Nine

Charlie

All I can remember is the look on Morgan's face when I stopped into work yesterday. She tried her hardest to keep a neutral look. One minute she looked terrified and the next she had a wide smile across her face. Maxwell refused to let me stay any longer than a few hours, but I only made it an hour because I couldn't stand Morgan following me around, ready for me to drop dead.

As if coming to home would be any better. My once bright, airy home now resembles a cave with its dark curtains and blinds. I have to have almost every single light on within the house to be able to walk the halls.

"I'm going to go work on some things. I might not be able to be at the office, but Morgan is still going to need my help." I get up and cross the room in hopes of leaving Maxwell behind, but as soon as I pass the couch, he starts to get up. "You. Stay. I'm going to open the curtains to let the sun blind me one last time...okay?"

"Charlie, if you start the transition while you're in there, I won't be able to get to you. It's best if I come with you or keep the blinds closed." I hear his words, but the look on his face says it all. He feels guilty, and overprotecting me is his solution.

"Well, you can just leave me on the floor until nightfall then."

"It's not that easy. The sun will begin to harm you immediately."

"Well...then it'll just end this before it even starts, which is probably for the better." I regret saying the words as soon as they're spoken, but deep down I can't help but to agree with them. I'm not a pushover and never saw death as an answer for any of my problems, but sadly it's a solution for this situation I'll never be able to get myself out of.

Before I can take one more step, Maxwell is in front of me with his hands harshly gripping my upper arms. The cold look in his eyes reluctantly causes fear to creep into my nerves. His voice is flat and cruel as he lectures me. "If I ever hear you imply or joke about killing yourself again, Charlie, you will never leave my side. I will become the worst person you can imagine from such irresponsible banter. Do you understand me?"

I yank my arms out of his firm grasp. "And what the hell would you do about it exactly…lock me up? I'll be just as strong and conniving as you, there would be no way to trap me against my will," I say just as heartless.

"You won't have all the power you think you're going to have right away. Strength and influencing donors is something that comes with age and practice. It's quite different from your movie vampires. If you want me to speak in your Hollywood terms, newborns are weak. Ending this won't be as easy as you think either. It takes much more than a few seconds in the sun to kill freshly turned vampires, resulting in it being extremely painful. The real world is very different from fantasy, Charlie."

I walk away, refusing to let him scare me. I won't be scared.

"I'll do whatever it takes…I'll always do whatever it takes, Charlie. I love you more than you can imagine and protecting you from harming yourself needs no second thought. You can think of it as cruelty, but I think of it as caring," Maxwell bellows at me as he follows me through the halls that lead to my home office.

"What you really want to say is that you let it happen once and you won't let it happen again," I say as I make it into my office. Hurriedly, I whip the curtains open to stop him from entering. Tears fill my eyes as I stare at his pained expression. I didn't mean to be so...mean, but there's no taking back my actions now. I stare at him in the middle of the sun-filled room.

He places his hands on the doorframe, leaning backward to remain out of the light. "You should want to live, Charlie. If not for me, then for yourself at least."

"If only it were that easy. I don't want to hurt you, Maxwell, I really don't, but I need some time to think...some time to just feel normal before it's taken away."

"Charlie, just close the curtains and we can talk about this." Maxwell tries to coax me out of the room, but it doesn't work.

"There's nothing to talk about. I'm scared, Maxwell, and that's not going to go away." It's not the fact that I'll be a walking corpse for all of eternity or being stuck with him by my side...it's fear, and when I'm scared I push everyone away because I don't want to be perceived as weak. I'm not weak, but this whole thing is making me into someone I'm not sure I want to become and it scares me to death. Aggressively, I wipe away the tears trailing down my cheeks.

"Charlie." He's on the verge of begging.

"I just need to work. It'll get my mind off it. I just need to...work," I say into the room. Before all this happened I lived for work and even though that's going to change very soon, I'm not ready to part with it just yet.

"If you start to feel different or not right, you leave this room immediately," Maxwell says in the hall, finally compromising with me.

"Yes, Master."

"Charlie, I mean it." The seriousness makes my muscles stiffen.

"Yes, Maxwell, I got it," I yell back.

I turn my back to him to sit at my desk. The only sound that fills the room is the tapping of my pen and my thoughts rambling through my head. Think, Charlie, think, I repeat to myself. No matter how hard I try, no brilliant ideas come to mind to allow me to work in the moonlight instead of the sunlight.

Automatically, I begin to rock myself back and forth in my chair with my mind numb, vacant of any thoughts. I stare at my desk, but I don't see anything. Physically shaking myself out of the comatose state I find myself trapped in, I stand up to stretch my limbs. Dragging my feet to the door, I decide that working right now isn't going to happen.

"Charlie, is everything okay?" Maxwell says as soon as I walk out of the room. I catch a glimpse of him sitting on the floor before he stands in my path.

"I'm just tired." I cover a yawn that escapes my mouth.

"It's starting," Maxwell says as he scoops me up in his arms, carrying me away.

I slap him on the shoulder in protest. "Would you put me down? I'm just tired. Haven't you been tired in the middle of the day before? It happens, you know."

"You were sitting on your chair for over an hour, staring at the wall, Charlie. This is not tired, this is how it starts. First, you get fatigued and then you fall asleep, similar to being in a coma, so you..."

"So you can die," I finish for him. I begin the thrash around in his arms. I don't know why, all I know is that I have to move around...I have to fight this.

"Charlie, Charlie, calm down. You need to relax, you need to let sleep take over, otherwise you will feel it all and it's not pleasant."

"All of what?" My voice squeaks with fear.

"We've been through this already. Just trust me when I say you don't want to stay awake through it. I didn't have anybody to walk me through my change and it was excruciating." He places me down on the bed. A quick swipe of his hand across my cheek moves my messy hair away.

"There's no way around this, is there?" For some odd reason I thought maybe if I force myself to stay awake it'll just prolong the inevitable, but I guess not.

"I wish there was, but your time's up. When you wake you'll be different, but the same Charlie everyone loves."

"Well, almost everyone, obviously." Flashes of Henry's evil smile and Daisy's wicked face occupy my thoughts. I close my eyes, refusing to look at him, refusing to see the reflection of my scared self in his brown eyes.

My breathing gets labored and rougher as I force each breath. My lungs burn from the action, but I have to keep breathing. I have to hold on for as long as possible. Maxwell's constant whispers of 'relax' don't stop me from doing whatever I can to remain awake. He said not to, but once again I refuse to listen.

The piercing pain in my stomach and tightening in my chest only make it worse, but when the fast hard thumping of my heart gets weaker my eyes shoot open with terror. I expect to be momentarily blinded by the light from the fixture overhead or see a darkened room with shadowed furniture, but I see…nothing. Pitch-blackness surrounds me. Maxwell's words about the transition sound in my head. First, you'll lose your sight.

"Maxwell. Maxwell," I yell into the vacant room. My arms swing from side to side in efforts of feeling something, anything.

"Charlie." The concern in Maxwell's voice only makes more panic grow, but the feel of his cold hands that clasp around my arms bring some relief.

"I can't see, Maxwell, I can't see anything." My voice is distorted with distress.

"It's okay…it's okay. Things are gradually happening and everything is fine." I feel one of his hands lay over the top of my head. He speaks directly into my ear, but for some reason it sounds as if he's miles away. "You need to let go. Accept it. Accept it and you won't be afraid any longer. I'm right here and I won't leave your side until you wake. Just close your eyes and take one deep breath…"

Obeying his orders, I close my eyes and suck in a deep breath. The pain hitches my breathing, but I make the air enter my dying lungs. My fingers try to scratch at my chest as if the action would get my heart to pump faster again. Nonetheless, Maxwell moves his hands from my arms to my hands to get them to stop.

"…and slowly exhale."

The breath rushes out through my pursed lips. My chest begins to rise to take another breath, but Maxwell stops me. I strain my ears to hear what he has to say.

"One more and after you exhale this time, Charlie, don't take another one. This time just imagine yourself drifting off to sleep. Breathe in…breathe out…and let go." His last words of let go are the last thing I hear before a quiet buzzing fills my head. The pain ceasing my senses fades away, leaving me alone…empty. The touch of Maxwell's hands, which are supposed to be holding mine, vanishes, but I trust him to keep his word of not leaving my side.

I have barely enough time to finish my thought before the small rise in my chest stops, before my heart thumps for the last time, and before my brain can't comprehend words any longer.

* * *

Maxwell

Charlie's stiff fingers curl around mine. I have to pry my hand out of hers in order for me to fetch a chair so I can sit beside her. Keeping my eyes on her lifeless body, my heart breaks as I cross the room to carry the bench to her bedside. I know she's not dead, but seeing her like this is worse than I thought it would be.

I sit on that bench or pace the room for hours in the dark. My anxiousness makes my extremities fidgety in anticipation. All I can think of is how angry she's going to be when she wakes up. Forcing myself to stay seated, I put my head in my hands in disappointment. The blame of this whole unfortunate situation rests on my shoulders. Waiting and patience are not my strong suits, which just makes this even more unbearable.

Vibrations from my phone run down the length of my leg. As quickly as possible I pull it out of my front pocket, allowing the screen to partially light up the room. My voice comes out quiet as if I would wake a sleeping Charlie. "Grace."

"How's Charlie?"

"Oh, you know, just dead for a while."

"Lovely. Well, I have some more not so great news." She stammers over her words as she tries to figure out how to say what she needs to inform me about. "It's about Daisy."

That name causes my hands to ball into fists as well as thoughts of if I ever see that woman again I'll kill her in a blink of one's eye. "What about her, Grace?"

"She showed up today seeking sanctuary along with forgiveness for what her vampire made her do. She graveled at Benjamin's feet saying you would seek revenge for her being one of the conspirators in Charlie's death and that this was the only place where protection would be given to her."

"She did what?" I holler into the phone. My voice echoes throughout Charlie's room.

"She told them about Henry's long thought-out plans of killing Charlie, because of vengeance. She made it sound as if he used her like a pawn in his plan…there might have also been something mentioned that he threatened her life if she didn't kidnap Charlie. She went on to talk about how awful Henry was with numerous feedings and outrageous things he asked her to do. The High Council looks upon her as a victim in this."

"A victim…a victim. She wasn't forced into anything and Charlie almost died because of her." I'm appalled at how she's so effortlessly playing everyone, just like Henry did.

"I've requested a hearing for all to hear what she has to say and there's only one way to get the truth out there and you know what that is."

"Charlie."

"It'll work out perfectly since she thinks Charlie is dead. Eugene will help me get everything to come together."

"Benjamin is not informing her that Charlie is alive?"

"Benjamin is trying to get on my good side, so when I asked him to withhold that information he agreed. Only him, Eugene, and obviously myself know she's a vampire now." Grace sounds quite pleased with herself.

"Duke," I blurt out, almost forgetting the reason Henry found us in the first place. "Tell Eugene to keep an eye on Duke. One of our dear council members helped Henry track us down." I can't stop myself from staring at Charlie's lifeless body, thinking about how she looks quite dead right now all because of Duke.

"What a coincidence. Duke offered to watch over Daisy. He's supposedly helping her get accustomed to being a vampire. Don't worry. She'll get what she deserves, just like Henry got what he deserved."

I didn't hear the last part of what Grace said because I swear I saw Charlie's body twitch. "Grace, I got to go." I hear her question why in attempt to find out what's wrong, but I just hang the phone up and rush back to Charlie's side.

Her fingers are no longer stiff as they now lie loosely over her stomach. Her eyelids flutter just the slightest bit as her lips part. I let out a sigh of relief as she finally starts to wake. Eagerness makes me tangle her fingers with mine as I wait for her to open her eyes. "Charlie...Charlie...love, open your eyes," I whisper.

I know she hears me because she begins to shuffle and stretch her limbs. A groan escapes her mouth as she protests to waking up, but within seconds she bolts upright. Her wide eyes look at me, at her lap, and then back at me. Her mouth drops open in efforts to comprehend what happened.

"Charlie, how do you feel?" I ask.

Without speaking one single word, she yanks her hands out of my grasp and brings them to her chest. "I'm dead," she declares loudly. In a rush she jumps out of bed and begins pacing the room.

"Charlie, you just need to relax, everything is going to be fine. The sun is already down, so we can go out if you want."

"Hollow…I'm hollow," she says as she bangs on her chest some more.

"You're not empty inside, Charlie, just different. You're the same Charlie as before you went to sleep." I try to usher her out of the room, but she stubbornly refuses.

Unexpectedly, she takes two large strides over to the bed and collapses on the mattress. "I might not feel different, but I am. I just have to be, because this isn't normal." She slaps her hands over her face.

"Just calm down, we can get through this," I say as I walk up to her slowly.

"I am calm," she yells back. A disbelieving look crosses my face; she corrects herself in an instant. "Fine…I'll try to calm down." She pulls herself to her feet and stands face to face with me.

Without even thinking, I start to rub the length of her arms. "How about we just stay in and watch some movies? You can call Morgan later and tell her your leave starts now."

Charlie just nods her head in acceptance, keeping to herself. Everything from the way she stands to the fact that she can't look me in the eyes is everything I need to know that she's not comfortable in her new skin. "Come on." I slip her hand into mine and lead her into the living room.

Setting her gently down on the couch, I walk over to where she keeps her stack of DVDs. After rummaging through them twice, I give up. "How about I go to the video store?"

She stares at me unfazed by my words. Her face is expressionless until out of nowhere a laugh breaks through her tight lips, filling the room. She tries to cover her mouth to hide her beautiful smile or to block out some of the noise, but it just gets louder as her smile gets bigger.

"What's so funny exactly?" I ask, amused by her change of attitude.

"Just the fact that we're going to pretend to be normal people and have a movie night." Her laughs get louder. "Except you don't like any of my movies…how sad is that."

"First off, we are normal. We're just two people on this Earth trying to enjoy each other's company. Now, are you going to be accompanying me to the video store or not?"

"I think I'm going to stay here and call Morgan. You can go pick out a suitable movie for us. I'll love to see what you pick out. And make sure it has nothing to do with vampires."

"No vampires, I don't think I'll forget that." Turning back to look at her on my way to the door, I feel like I shouldn't leave her alone, but I can be back from the store within a few minutes. "Are you sure you'll be okay?" I ask with my hand lingering on the doorknob.

"I'm not a child, I can handle being on my own for a few minutes." Her fingers tap her thigh from jitteriness she can't control.

I open the door, trusting her and her judgment. One foot over the threshold and one still inside, I hear Charlie holler for me.

"Maxwell."

Without hesitation, I walk back into the living room. "Yes."

"I'm sorry for being mean, cold, heartless. Where do I stop? I never told you this, but Henry rubbed my unappreciative attitude in my face. He went on how he thought it was amusing that he had a willing exceptional bride and you had…me. I just need to tell you I'm sorry for being rude and for all the hurtful things I said to you."

"Well, Henry didn't have the perfect bride he thought he had. At this moment she's graveling to Benjamin for sanctuary."

"What? She's still alive? Sanctuary where?"

"Daisy was here with me when you were…I could have killed her, but I didn't and she escaped before we got back. She's in Austria, preaching her lies to Benjamin and The High Council as she believes you are dead and I'm out to get her. Grace is requesting that an event be made out of her sudden appearance and that, my love, is where you come in. She thinks The High Council is going to save her, but with your personal testimony she'll be prosecuted to degrees she never knew. As soon as Grace or Eugene inform me of the date, we'll leave to have another pleasant trip to Austria."

Charlie remains mute as she thinks about what I just said.

"How about we just watch something you have here?" I walk over to the cabinet with the movies in it again and pull out one I have the least problem with. I sit as close as possible next to her and wait for the video to start. All Charlie does is curl into my side, resting her head on my chest. We sit here like this for hours, watching nonsense on TV and being completely quiet.

"How come you're still so cold compared to me?" she asks as the movie starts.

"It'll take time for your body temperature to decrease. Within a few days we'll be the same."

"What happens when I get hungry?" she asks yet another question.

"We'll talk about that when I find out who our donors are. Right now you just need to accept what you are and the rest will come. Can you do that for me?"

She nods her head as she looks into my eyes. "I don't know what I would do without you, besides still be alive," she jokes.

"Very funny, Charlie, very funny," I reply with a kiss to the top of her head. A few strands of her hair stick to my face. I can't help but to smile at the fact that now I truly have my vampire bride I've been waiting for.

Krystal Novitzke

About the Author

K.L. Novitzke lives in a small city smack-dab in the middle of the glorious state of Wisconsin with her husband, two boys, and miniature Australian Shepard. She loves everything that goes bump in the night, which sparks her love of paranormal romances.

In her spare time she enjoys crafting, reading all genres, and of course writing! New story ideas and characters continually bounce around in her head, keeping sleep at a distance.

Author contact links:

Facebook Fan Page:
https://www.facebook.com/klnovitzkeauthor/
Twitter: http://twitter.com/kl_novitzke
Website: https://magicbetweenpages.wordpress.com/
Google+:
https://plus.google.com/u/0/100587845487673378459/posts
Goodreads:
https://www.goodreads.com/user/show/13025827-krystal
Wattpad: https://www.wattpad.com/user/KrystalBay
Pinterest: https://www.pinterest.com/blondedaydreams/
Tumblr: http://vampirebrideseries.tumblr.com/

Printed in Great Britain
by Amazon.co.uk, Ltd.,
Marston Gate.